HAVANA NOIR

HAVANA NOIR

EDITED BY ACHY OBEJAS

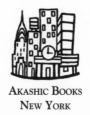

AKASHIC BOOKS
NEW YORK

This collection is comprised of works of fiction. All names, characters, places, and incidents are the product of the authors' imaginations. Any resemblance to real events or persons, living or dead, is entirely coincidental.

Published by Akashic Books
©2007 Akashic Books

Series concept by Tim McLoughlin and Johnny Temple
Havana map by Sohrab Habibion
Editorial assistance by Sarah Frank

ISBN-13: 978-1-933354-38-5
Library of Congress Control Number: 2007926097

"Abikú" by Yohamna Depestre first appeared, in Spanish, in *D-21* (Pinos Nuevos/Letras Cubanas, Havana, Cuba, 2004); "Nowhere Man" by Miguel Mejides first appeared, in Spanish, in *Las Ciudades Imperiales* (Editorial Letras Cubanas, Havana, 2006); "The Last Passenger" by Ena Lucía Portela first appeared, in Spanish, in *Crítica*, No. 119, January–February 2007, the cultural magazine of the Universidad Autónoma in Puebla, Mexico; "Staring at the Sun" by Leonardo Padura first appeared, in Spanish, in *La Puerta de Alcalá y Otras Cacerías* (Ediciones Callejón, Olalla, Spain, 1997).

First printing

Akashic Books
PO Box 1456
New York, NY 10009
info@akashicbooks.com
www.akashicbooks.com

ALSO IN THE AKASHIC NOIR SERIES:

Baltimore Noir, edited by Laura Lippman

Bronx Noir, edited by S.J. Rozan

Brooklyn Noir, edited by Tim McLoughlin

Brooklyn Noir 2: The Classics, edited by Tim McLoughlin

Chicago Noir, edited by Neal Pollack

D.C. Noir, edited by George Pelecanos

Detroit Noir, edited by E.J. Olsen & John C. Hocking

Dublin Noir (Ireland), edited by Ken Bruen

London Noir (England), edited by Cathi Unsworth

Los Angeles Noir, edited by Denise Hamilton

Manhattan Noir, edited by Lawrence Block

Miami Noir, edited by Les Standiford

New Orleans Noir, edited by Julie Smith

San Francisco Noir, edited by Peter Maravelis

Twin Cities Noir, edited by Julie Schaper & Steven Horwitz

Wall Street Noir, edited by Peter Spiegelman

FORTHCOMING:

Brooklyn Noir 3, edited by Tim McLoughlin & Thomas Adcock

D.C. Noir 2: The Classics, edited by George Pelecanos

Delhi Noir (India), edited by Hirsh Sawhney

Istanbul Noir (Turkey), edited by Mustafa Ziyalan & Amy Spangler

Lagos Noir (Nigeria), edited by Chris Abani

Las Vegas Noir, edited by Jarret Keene & Todd James Pierce

Paris Noir (France), edited by Aurélien Masson

Queens Noir, edited by Robert Knightly

Rome Noir (Italy), edited by Chiara Stangalino & Maxim Jakubowski

San Francisco Noir 2: The Classics, edited by Peter Maravelis

Toronto Noir (Canada), edited by Janine Armin & Nathaniel G. Moore

HAVANA ●

CUBA

GULF OF MEXICO

Malecón

Vedado

Flores
Siboney

Jaimanitas

Ayestarán

El Cerro

Marianao

Santos Suárez

Vibora

HAVANA

STRAITS OF FLORIDA

BAHÍA DE LA HABANA

Alamar →

Cojímar

Casablanca

Centro
Habana

Chinatown

Old Havana

Regla

Lawton

For Eva, for so much patience

Many thanks on this project to Arturo Arango, Haydeé Arango, Tania Bruguera, Kalisha Buckhanon, Norberto Codina, Arnaldo Correa, David Driscoll, Esther Figueroa, Ambrosio Fornet, Gisela González López, Casey Ishitani, Elise Johnson, Caridad López del Pozo, Bayo Ojikutu, Oscar Luis Rodríguez Ramos, Patrick Reichard, Juan Manuel Salvat, Lawrence Schimel, and the inimitable Yoss.

I am especially grateful to Sarah Frank, whose assistance was invaluable throughout the project, and to Johnny Temple, for the opportunity and the faith.

Yo no quito nada	*I don't take anything away*
yo no pongo nada	*I don't add a thing*
Yo no invento	*I don't make stuff up*
Solo cuento lo que veo	*I just tell it like it is*

EL CURI, "SOLO CUENTO LO QUE VEO"

TABLE OF CONTENTS

15   *Introduction*

PART I: SLEEPLESS IN HAVANA

21   **MIGUEL MEJIDES**   Old Havana
Nowhere Man

52   **ENA LUCÍA PORTELA**   Vedado
The Last Passenger

86   **MYLENE FERNÁNDEZ PINTADO**   Malecón
The Scene

96   **LEONARDO PADURA**   Marianao
Staring at the Sun

PART II: ESCAPE TO NOWHERE

113   **CAROLINA GARCÍA-AGUILERA**   Flores
The Dinner

144   **PABLO MEDINA**   Jaimanitas
Johnny Ventura's Seventh Try

155   **ALEX ABELLA**   Siboney
Shanghai

179   **MOISÉS ASÍS**   Ayestarán
Murder at 503 La Rosa

190   **ARTURO ARANGO**   El Cerro
Murder, According to My Mother-in-Law

PART III: SUDDEN RAGE

215   **MARIELA VARONA ROQUE**   Santos Suárez
The Orchid

220   **MICHEL ENCINOSA FÚ**   Vibora
What for, This Burden

239   **YOSS**   Lawton
The Red Bridge

264   **LEA ASCHKENAS**   Centro Habana
La Coca-Cola del Olvido

PART IV: DROWNING IN SILENCE

283   **ACHY OBEJAS**   Chinatown
Zenzizenzic

321   **MABEL CUESTA**   Regla
Virgins of Regla

328   **ARNALDO CORREA**   Casablanca
Olúo

339   **OSCAR F. ORTÍZ**   Cojímar
Settling of Scores

353   **YOHAMNA DEPESTRE**   Alamar
Abikú

356   **About the Contributors**

INTRODUCTION
A Feral Heart

To most outsiders, Havana is a tropical wreckage of sin, sex, and noise, a parallel world familiar but exotic—and embargoed enough to serve as a release valve for whatever pulse has been repressed or denied.

Long before the Cuban Revolution in 1959 and the United States' economic blockade (in place since 1962), Havana was the destination of choice for foreigners who wanted to indulge in what was otherwise forbidden to them: mojitos and ménages, miscegenation and revolution. A photo taken in Havana has always authenticated its subject as a rebel and renegade.

Havana has frequently existed only as myth: a garden of delights, a vortex of tarantism, but also—perversely—the capital site of a social experiment in which humans somehow deny the worst of our natures. In this novel narrative, Cuba is mystical: without hatred, ism-free, brave and pure, a stranger to greed and murder.

But Havana—not the tourist's pleasure dome or the Marxist dream-state, but the Havana where Cubans actually live—is a city of ironic and often agonizing contradiction. Its name means "site of the waters" in the original indigenous tongue, yet there are no beaches. It's legendary for its defiance, but penury and propaganda have made sycophants of many of its citizens before both local authority and foreign opportunity. Its poverty is crushing, but the ingenuity of its people makes it appear resilient and bountiful.

In the real Havana—the aphotic Havana that never appears in the postcards, tourist guides, or testimonies of either the political left or right—the concept of sin has been banished by the urgency of need. And need inevitably turns the human heart feral. In this Havana, crime and violence, though officially vanquished by revolutionary decree, are wistfully quotidian and vicious.

In the stories of *Havana Noir*, current and former residents of the city—some internationally known, like Leonardo Padura, others undiscovered and startling, like Yohamna Depestre—relate tales of ambiguous moralities, misologistic brutality, collective cruelty, and the damage inured by self-preservation at all costs.

The noir, it seems, may be particularly apt for Havana: Descriptive rather than prescriptive, noirs explore the symptoms of an ailing society but rarely suggest remedies. They are frequently *contestaire* in their unblinking portraits but unnervingly apolitical. Their protagonists are alienated and at risk, caught in ethical quandaries outside of their control, and driven to the very edge.

Perhaps surprisingly, these stories—though fresh and original—have precedent in Cuban literature. And I don't just mean Padura's morally conflicted detective fiction of the '90s, nor the recent novels of Daniel Chavarría and Arnaldo Correa (who's included here with "Olúo").

Crime stories, especially those with detective protagonists, try to find order, to right things; noirs wearily revel in the vacuum of values, give in to conflict not as a puzzle to be solved but as a cul-de-sac. Noirs explore and expose but refuse to solve.

As such, the stories in this volume may have more in common with the nihilistic prose of Carlos Montenegro's 1938 novel *Hombres Sin Mujer* (*Men Without Women*), Lino Novás Calvo's

1942 psych-thriller *La Noche de Ramón Yendía* (*Ramón Yendía's Night*), or even Virgilio Piñera's hellish 1943 poem about national identity, "La Isla en Peso" ("Island Burden")—all secured within the canon of mainstream Cuban literature—than with what might pass as normative crime fiction, or even the usual noir.

Actually, when a master like Alejo Carpentier produces a suspense story like 1956's *El Acoso* (*The Chase*), and Eliseo Diego opens his 1946 book of blasters, *Divertimentos*, with a wicked murder story like "Las Hermanas" ("The Sisters"), it's clear that noir is so bold a streak in Cuban literature that it barely contrasts enough with the mainstream to be recognized as such. And did Reinaldo Arenas ever write anything in which the protagonist—nearly always an alter-ego—wasn't vehemently alienated and at risk?

In all of *Havana Noir*, there's only one detective—Alex Abella's pre-revolutionary Jason Blue—and he's not even Cuban.

Instead, there are the merciless and doomed young men and women of Michel Encinosa Fú's "What for, This Burden," and Yoss's street toughs, trapped by mediocrity and hopelessness on "The Red Bridge." These are the children of the Revolution—both the writers and their characters—wandering aimlessly in a post-revolutionary world, a place with no past or future or blame to assign.

Even Padura goes from ambivalent to eerily bleak. "Staring at the Sun" features an irremediable and forceful confrontation instead of the peaceful arrests and conclusions familiar to fans of his Mario Conde novels.

These, however, don't come close to the chilling amorality of Depestre's "Abikú" or Mariela Varona Roque's "The Orchid."

In the meantime, Cuban-born but U.S.-raised, Carolina García-Aguilera marinates "The Dinner" in a macabre nostalgia that stubbornly underscores what was lost for so many, on and off the island, after the Revolution. Moisés Asís, who left Cuba as an adult, walks an uncertain tightrope in "Murder at 503 La Rosa" and grieves for the greatest loss of all—that of the soul.

Ena Lucía Portela's "The Last Passenger," with its deliciously caustic and unreliable narrator, lifts the veil of life in the best and most beautiful country in the world, where there is no crime and no crime report but a constant battle against imperialism and the enemy and . . . can she trust what she sees and hears on TV, in the courtroom, on the phone, or at the open-air bar across the street from Colón Cemetery? "The truth is, I don't know what the hell to believe," says her protagonist, whose mission seems to be to witness.

There are other stories here by writers young and old, established and emerging, male and female, on and off the island, of clear and of dubious sexualities, black and white, and—because it's Cuba—everything in between.

We begin with Miguel Mejides's marvelous "Nowhere Man," which takes place in a beautiful, sinister, and very real Havana. It's the story of a life, many lives perhaps, in which the possibility of finding happiness is experienced as moments in time to be treasured later, only as memories in the dark, when the final sentence has been pronounced.

Achy Obejas
Havana, Cuba
March 2007

PART I

SLEEPLESS IN HAVANA

NOWHERE MAN

BY MIGUEL MEJIDES

Old Havana

To the memory of my father

There are people who need to go against the grain but I'm not going against anything. Perhaps everything stems from the great handicap which life has given me: I'm cross-eyed. Ever since I've been able to reason, since the first time I was able to contemplate my image in a mirror and saw my own eyes, I told myself I was a man meant for silence, for meditation, a man made to work at smiling, fated to take long walks through the city I choose for my solitude.

My mother, thank God, always knew about the shadow of the silent songbird that surrounded me. Likewise, she understood my decision to leave my hometown to go to Havana and find work. I've never been able to forget her, bidding me farewell at the train station with her linen handkerchief waving between the smoke and her saintly smile, which never left her, not even in death.

Even though it's rained a lot these years, until very recently I could still give myself the pleasure of contemplating Havana through the same lens as when I first glimpsed it in January 1990. Back then, Havana still retained that halo of light and mystery. My bus came in on the old central highway, continued past Virgen del Camino, and straight through the disastrous streets of Luyanó. At the end of my journey, I was awed by the statue of Martí in the Plaza de la Revolución and the sparkling Ferris wheel in the amusement park in front of the bus terminal.

I'll never forget the taxi that took me to Infanta 234; it was a mandarin-colored De Soto, with the coat-of-arms from an ancient Spanish province affixed with the number 13. The driver was a little old man with an Andalusian accent and a multicolored hat.

"That's the place." I remember the stains on his teeth that flashed when he talked. As I paid him, he betrayed a certain anxiety about my eyes. "Buddy, buy yourself some dark glasses," he told me.

My Aunt Buza welcomed me half-solicitous and a bit taken aback too. She looked at me just like the taxi driver and talked about spells that could cure whatever was wrong with my eyes. Her husband greeted me gruffly and asked me if I knew how to drive. When I said no, he began talking about modern times, how a man of this century must learn how to handle machinery. Later, he coached me about the interview I had scheduled for the following morning.

"Say only what's necessary, don't blow your nose, and lie: Say that you know how to drive."

To this day I have no idea what any of that had to do with the job for which I was interviewing. That night they set me up in a tiny room adjacent to the kitchen whose only charm was a large window looking out at Havana. Everything was so different from my hometown. I was struck by the city's traffic, by the sea on the horizon which at night I could only imagine, and by Radio Progreso's building right in front of me, from which flowed the station's love stories that made my mother sigh. I was in Havana, I told myself, and now I would never leave its flame—which could easily become either pleasure or hell.

But because I was still in a grieving phase—I don't know if I'll ever really get over it—the interview was a disaster. At 8 o'clock in the morning, we planted ourselves in front of the manager's door at the Hotel Nacional. I was so nervous that I told my aunt's husband I needed to go to the bathroom. He pointed the way, and I found myself in front of a mirror. I noted that I'd never been more cross-eyed. I was afraid my pupils would fall out of their sockets and drop into the bathroom sink.

When I came back, they were already waiting for me. We went into the manager's office. He was a man in his thirties, with a mole on his nose. He said something about Greek beauty, or Greek ideals of beauty, and that hotels were like the palaces of kings.

"You have to understand, Jerónimo," he said abruptly.

"Maybe with dark glasses no one will be able to tell," my aunt's husband said.

"But he won't be able to use them at night, and a hotel is a living organism," the man declared. "If there's a single alien cell, its beauty is spoiled."

On the way back, I remembered what the taxi driver had said. I needed to buy myself a pair of dark glasses. My mother had managed to convince her sister to have Jerónimo get me a job interview at the Hotel Nacional, where he'd worked since his youth. But the one thing my mother had not mentioned was my eyes. She had sent photos of me in profile, as if I were the most beautiful boy in the world. Now my eyes were going to force me back to my hometown, they were going to force me to grow old in that part of the world where only a tiny cemetery marks the turn to the single road that connects to Camagüey.

"Stay a week if you like, then buy a ticket back," suggested my Aunt Buza.

"There aren't any opportunities there," I said.

"In small towns, people get used to oddities like yours more easily," she declared.

That same day, in the afternoon, I went out and bought a pair of cheap glasses. I decided to walk all over Havana with my new face.

At 7 the next morning I was already on the street. First, I explored all of El Cerro, then Marianao; by the time I began to stroll by Carlos III, it had been more than a week. I didn't spend much. I didn't turn the lamp on at night, I rarely flushed in the bathroom. In the morning I only drank coffee, and when I returned late at night, I ate whatever was left for me on the stove. I had the firm hope of finding work and staying in Havana. But everywhere I went, I was told there were no openings and everyone looked at me funny.

After a month, my aunt's patience was finally exhausted. I still remember the night I arrived and found nothing to eat for me. Where there had always been a pot, there was just a note telling me they'd bought me a ticket on the next morning's train. That's when I knew I was truly alone in Havana.

Without asking questions, I took my suitcase and left. I headed for Prado Boulevard and made myself comfortable on a marble bench in front of the Hotel Sevilla. The laurel trees made a fine roof over my abandoned self. I put the suitcase near my feet and crossed my arms under my neck and settled in to sleep.

I was just drifting off when I heard voices coming from the roots of the laurel trees. It was a debate about the previous Christmas, about curses that had befallen the city.

"Who's there?" I asked.

I thought about the kinds of dreams hunger provokes. Yet that endless conversation had a strangely calming effect on me. The voices seemed to be coming from a megaphone. Now and again, they were drowned out by a droning laugh.

"Eh! . . . What are you? Fish? Angels? What?" I pleaded.

I threw myself down at one of the laurel trees and put my ear to its roots, where I could now hear a jazz band, Glenn Miller and his "String of Pearls." I stayed there a long time, my face resting on the ground. Finally, I heard a bizarre dialogue.

"That hive of humanity that lives up there, that Havana that is enslaved by the light, will one day build a monument to our catechistic work, a monument to our galleys which sail the earth's furrows, a monument to our warehouses chock-full of salt and coffee, cured meat and garlic, brimming with commerce and customer service, filled with the soundtrack of the world's life."

It was at that moment that I heard the scraping sound of my suitcase being lifted from the park bench on the Prado. I saw two people fleeing with it into the night through the street next to the Sevilla. Laughter rose from the bowels of the earth, and I uttered one of those words reserved for when you're miserable. My voice was completely drowned out by the sound of the jazz band.

I didn't sleep that night. I spent it running up and down the Prado and Central Park. A lot of people think that if you're cross-eyed, you see objects differently. But I saw the city as it really was. Even though I'd only seen it for about one month, I could, in an instant, sense danger. There was no light in the public areas. All I could make out was the marquee of the Hotel Inglaterra. The García Lorca Theater seemed like a sylph's castle. The Payret movie house sign featured Catherine Deneuve. The capitol building was the city's ultimate reflection. Central Park looked like it does anytime people go out to find the latest gossip. Black guys in colorful shirts looked like they were AWOL from a carnival. Women wearing dresses made by pious seamstresses on Monte Street strolled through the shadows. Sodomites tattooed trees with men's hearts, and other creatures of the night lost their money on the Chinese lottery.

I was walking through the forbidden city. My hunger chased after the smells, my guts doing somersaults.

A mulatto made me an offer from his selection of sweets: "C'mon, big man, buy a little piece of rum cake."

"Pain and fate," I muttered like a fool.

I was thinking about what I'd just said, that phrase that I'd always heard coming from my mother when talking about human travails. Havana was so different from my hometown, the sounds of the night so alien. My hometown didn't have the nightlife that now spread before me, only a few early commuters taking the train to Camagüey. The great city was like a shop window on display for those who were denied the light of day, creatures who lived in caves in the tenements, in shacks where the daughters' beauty was discovered too soon by the fathers, shacks where the sky was never seen, where the sun was a curse on the law of switchblades and blood, the law of an Old Havana made for carriages and slaves, for light from bitter firewood, a city still getting used to the workings of the modern era.

In the farthest corner of the park, there was a newsstand with little or no sign of life, a newsstand with an old man selling and buying old magazines: Nat King Cole singing at the Tropicana, Che Guevara with his visionary gaze, Camilo Cienfuegos astride his huge mount, the 1962 missile crisis, Khrushchev with a black showgirl on his arm . . . People bought the magazines that were the biographies of their souls. And me, I was running from those experiences, from the photos that weren't of me, and yet were all about me. I wandered aimlessly by the doorways of the tobacco factories, still hearing the echo of the fluttering of leaves from Pinar del Río, the specter of the binnacles whose treasures were Romeo y Julietas, Partagás, Montecristos.

I searched for the Prado again via the sleepy routes of the buildings in ruins, and then, once there, just killed time until it was morning and I had to take my train back to the pastoral world of the provinces, back to my mother, back to the habit of pissing every night at 10 and going to bed, beaten down by obedience and pretense.

I was now standing right in front of the marble bench from which my suitcase had been stolen, the laurel trees placid in the absence of Glenn Miller.

"Get your peanut brittle right here!" chanted a dwarf at the corner of the Hotel Sevilla. He repeated his mantra like a suicide: "Hey, kid, peanut brittle!"

I wanted to tell him I didn't have one red cent, that I felt like the biggest loser and nothing could save me, except maybe the train, which would take me far away from Havana.

Then the dwarf crossed the street and stood right in front of me, grinning, wearing a corduroy cap, giant shoes, and muslin pants.

"Here," he said, extending a piece of peanut brittle my way. "It's on the house. C'mon, c'mon, take it."

I looked at him and he looked at me.

"Who do you sell to at night?" I asked him.

"No one. Nighttime's just fun."

He left, intoning his chant.

Everyone here's nuts, I said to myself, and looked out at the abandoned streets, where the only sound was a distant voice coming from the upper floors of the Sevilla, a woman's voice wailing because of the loneliness that boleros provoke, then this was followed by quieter words of comfort, coming, I think, from another woman.

I woke when a crow's shit splattered next to me. The sun was coming up and the crow seemed polished with tar. Sparrows flew from their hiding places to initiate anonymous battles in the laurel trees. I checked my pockets and realized I still had the train ticket, the ticket that would spirit me away from all hope.

I started to make my way to the train station when I saw the Prado had come alive. People hurried from one side of the boulevard to the other aimlessly, lining up at bus stops to board nonexistent buses. On my way to the trains, there wasn't a single restaurant open, not the slightest aroma of coffee. As day broke, the city was a mere geographical point, with no odors, only a fresh breeze that blew in from the sea; that was probably the only smell: the morning sea, awakening.

"God exists," a fifty-something woman said as she passed me near the station.

"So does the devil," I replied, not giving her another thought.

I was soon showing my ticket to the security guard at the door of the station lobby, then standing in line for the window where they would verify that the ticket was mine. I took out my ID, my stamped photo, which showed my crossed eyes. The woman looked at me, then at the photo, checking my ID number as if it were the number of some domesticated animal, my height in inches, the nervous tic on my mouth, my travel permit.

"The train will leave early for the first time in fifty-two years," the woman said ecstatically. "Go to platform three, coach fifty-two, seat eighty-one. If you're traveling with food, it may be confiscated; no animals are allowed; the traveler's responsibilities include . . ."

I stopped listening and made my way to the entrance to platform three, where they asked for my ticket again and insisted on seeing my ID. This time it was a short, fat man with a graying mustache. Finally, with a little push, he let me through and I ran down the platform, always terrified that I'll be late for everything. Where was coach fifty-two? All were there but that one. I started screaming. A crowd of about thirty gathered around me. The locomotive whistled its final warning.

"Coach fifty-two!" I demanded.

The fat man came up to me and explained that because of an unforgivable error, they had not hooked up coach fifty-two. Later, with an asthmatic voice, he told us our fares would be refunded and we could leave the next morning. I drew up to my full height and demanded to see the supervisor, anybody, to claim coach fifty-two. Pulling on his mustache, the man muttered something about the effects of the imperialistic blockade, the need to have a conscience and a spirit of sacrifice.

"Travel tomorrow, folks."

I decided not to go on. Nobody was paying attention to me anyway. I went back to the cashier and the same woman who'd boasted about an early departure now gave me a refund for my ticket. It barely totaled twenty pesos. At that moment, I reached a decision. I would not leave Havana. Maybe my destiny rested among the two million souls who lived facing the Gulf. If I died trying to make a go of it, nothing of value would be lost. Who would care about a cross-eyed guy? Who would cry for a cross-eyed guy? My mother would be the only one who suffered, but she'd get over it. It would be like when my father died. Days of grieving, days of mourning, and then Christian comfort.

I left the station, headed nowhere in particular. Since I've always been a dreamer, I convinced myself someone would take pity on me. But in the meantime, where would I go? Hunger kept tapping at my stomach. I thought that with my twenty pesos I might be able to buy one of those fish fritters they sell down by Puerto Avenue. I only had to go down a few winding alleyways and I'd soon be there. But as I was about to set off, I saw the same dwarf who'd given me the peanut brittle that morning, and he was now standing on top of a manhole cover sticking out of the street like a metal helmet. He recognized me and waved his corduroy cap. I went up to greet him, but he was muttering under his breath. He was saying something about young people, that it was impossible to recruit them these days, that the chosen few would be fewer each time, that the Grail would have to import creatures from another planet.

"What are you talking about?" I asked.

"Nothing," he said, "just an old dwarf's crazy ramblings."

Then he gave me another piece of peanut brittle. I was grateful, but my hunger was calling for more. Nonetheless, I ate it with the same frantic appetite as before, and he asked me where I was headed. I told him what had happened and shared my determination to stay in Havana.

He immediately asked me, "Do you dare work for a dwarf?"

"Just tell me what to do and I'll start right now," I answered.

"I'm going to take a chance with you," he said.

I was about to tell him I was a good man when he suddenly leaned down and removed the manhole cover, reached in, and—I don't know how, through what act of magic—retrieved a package.

He looked both ways then spoke, pronouncing each word

very carefully. "Someone I trust has to deliver this package to Aramburu 111. I can't move from this corner, maybe you'll understand someday. I trust you can complete this task; your future depends on it."

He paused, took off his cap, scratched his head, and talked about the forces that govern the underground, about the palaces King Solomon had built after his death under the cities.

"Take it or leave it," he said.

I grabbed the package and felt it rattle like an old treasure chest.

"Sausages! Inoffensive sausages!" the dwarf chanted, overcome by a strange giddiness. "Be very careful. At the first sign of trouble, just toss the package at the feet of the police; they won't follow you then."

That's how the dwarf pushed me into my first black market venture, which I completed nicely. Of course, my nerves were on edge the whole time I moved along the streets. Whenever I saw a cop, I got ready to toss the damn sausages at his feet. But I arrived on Aramburu Street without any problems, rang the doorbell on number 111, and was received by an old couple. They grilled me about a password I didn't know. I explained that it was my first day on the job. They said that whenever I visited them, I had to say, "Pontius Pilate!" Then they led me to the living room and opened the package. It held about thirty cans of frankfurters.

"Here," the old woman said. I saw two twenty-dollar bills and two singles.

I headed back to the train station but there was no trace of the dwarf. One of the taxi drivers said he'd seen him getting into a blue car. I didn't know what to do with the money. It was past noon and I wanted to sit down to a real meal, to sit at a table and stuff myself, like I hadn't done since I'd left my hometown. With that in mind—more daydream than reality—I went back to Puerto Avenue, not via the Old Havana shortcuts but through Central Park and the Prado, which at that hour was burning with a heat that scorched every corner.

Once on Puerto Avenue, after some haggling with a woman in a colonial doorway, I was able to buy a fritter and a tamarind soda from an illegal vendor. From there I went window shopping at the tourist places around the cathedral and became enchanted by the lighters with little scenes of Havana on them, and by the pens which showed naked rumba dancers in oily seas when you shook them, and by the racks of fashion magazines from all over the world. I toured the Bodeguita del Medio and scrawled my name into the graffiti on the bathroom wall. Then I went back to Central Park and saw the Catherine Deneuve movie at the Payret.

When I got out, sunset was coming on, and I moved down to the docks again. With the little money that was left, I ordered a double rum at the Dos Hermanos Tavern. From the bar, I could see the ferries to Regla and Casablanca, their passengers coming and going. There was a lot of serious drinking going on in the bar. The stevedores drank bottles of that hellish rum as if it was water, the bartender shouted out orders in a lingo I couldn't understand, and the women that came in and out resembled characters from a Japanese comic book, their tight dresses like badly rolled cigarettes.

"Take off those glasses," one them said to me provocatively. She was a mulatta with Chinese blood who was supposedly about thirty-five years old, not at all unattractive, although tourists no longer looked her way; she was forgotten in the game of international flags of love. She'd put on weight and her hips were square.

"I'm cross-eyed," I told her bravely. I lowered my glasses

and she looked at my eyes, scrutinized them, and said that cross-eyed guys brought her luck.

She touched my head with an exorcist's flair meant to transmit that luck, then turned around and shouted something like, "This guy's cross-eyed!"

Two other women came and touched my head. The gentle bartender refilled my glass of rum. A black stevedore came up to me and told me about a blind virgin on an altar in a church near the outskirts of the village of Guanabacoa. "In the wilderness, right on the edge of the jungle, there's a chapel with a virgin that's said to be from Toledo who cures anything that's wrong with the eyes," he said.

The black guy left and the Chinese mulatta said he was a bullshitter. She ordered a drink and made the bartender fill my glass again.

"Does the virgin exist?" I asked.

"God only knows," she said.

To make a long story short, I got the drunkest I've ever been in my life. At 10 o'clock, I left that hole in the wall with those wasted women and other port dwellers, arm in arm, everybody touching my head. Surrounded by so much alcohol, my only concern was those forty-two dollars that, if the dwarf never showed up again, would be my only salvation.

In that state, we strolled down Puerto Avenue, leaving behind the customs office and the old stock market. The Chinese mulatta shamelessly licked my eyes like a windshield wiper, then stuck her tongue in my ears, between my teeth; her tongue and my tongue parried . . . that mulatta's tongue and that deadly alcohol. Right at the Point, with Morro Castle and its lighthouse before us, she stuck her hand in my pants, shaking me like a bottle of elixir; I practically overflowed in front of all of Havana.

"C'mon, fill me with your suds," she begged me.

But her voice worked against her and made me bolt. I don't know what lonely thoughts or fear caused me to dash toward the Prado and leave the mulatta behind, down to the Malecón, that barrier between the ocean and the city's captive souls. I only paused when I got to the Hotel Sevilla. I took refuge in its doorway, next to the dwarf in the corduroy cap and his card table display of peanut brittle.

Right away, he saw the strange trance that had overcome me and said, "Hey kid, kid . . ."

But I was jabbering about the virgin who cures sick eyes, that virgin in Guanabacoa, the virgin from Toledo. Demanding to know if she existed, I kept moaning, "Hey, dwarf . . . that's it, dwarf . . . c'mere, dwarf . . ."

Then he offered me the third peanut brittle in less than a day and I began to eat. "Did they pay you?" he asked.

I dug around in my pockets and I gave him his forty-two dollars. He took the bills, held them up to the moonlight, checked them closely, and handed me two dollars.

"Your pay . . . hee, hee, hee . . . your first pay as a man."

I started to vomit and splattered the dwarf's muslin pants; all life was draining from me, and in the midst of all that, he said, "They call me Pascualito, now don't drink anymore—it's not allowed in our business."

I made my way to the bench that had been my first refuge when my Aunt Buza threw me out of the house, and I leaned on one of the laurel trees. I could hear the dwarf shouting at me from the Sevilla, saying we'd meet tomorrow at the station, and to be there. I spewed another bilious black stew between the roots of the laurel trees and detected a conversation coming from beneath the earth, and somebody shouting a song of praise to vegetables and grains. Glenn Miller and his impetuous music filled my head's every nook and cranny. I finally lay down on that marble park bench, thinking about the crow's shit that would surely awaken me at daybreak.

The next day, I found the dwarf at the station and he told he was expecting my approval at any moment. "The Grail meets at dawn to okay the permits," he said very seriously.

We passed the time talking about my future. Pascualito insisted that I needed to get better clothes "and lose that air about you of peasant with nowhere to go."

Someone under the manhole cover said something, which I guessed was the okay. Pascualito patted me on the back and bragged about his good eye with people. "I'm never wrong," he said.

He gave me a ticket I was supposed to take to a woman named Carmen Rosa at the Hotel Inglaterra, who would supply me with new clothes. Then he gave me a letter of introduction so I could get a room in a crumbling building that had once been a hotel and a Packard dealership in the '40s.

"You'll live like a Christian there," he said. "I'll come by tonight and we'll have a long talk about your future."

This was the most radical change that had ever occurred in my life. I got some clothes at the store in the Inglaterra and then went to the Packard, where I was received by a very sad woman wearing a lace blouse with a monogram. She told me I'd share the room with Jeremías Batista. "He's an absolute nut case," she warned me. Also, the city housing authority was not responsible for lost articles and visits from women were strictly prohibited. "Here's your key," she said.

The room was nothing to write home about. It had two beds, a pair of nightstands, a tall armoire, a bathroom with a very big tub that stood on steel claws, and a towel rack which represented—or so they told me—the imploring arms of the goddess Minerva. The fact that the walls were cracked and the rain and noise came in from the busy street terrified me. But could I really ask for more? It had only been two days since I'd slept in the park and, I thought, today I had clean clothes, a bed, and I could even bathe. Happiness, I knew, was never complete. Water had to be hauled from six floors below. But it was better than the park, it was better than the crow that shit at daybreak.

"Five lights for Pontius Pilate," Pascualito called from outside the door at 7 that evening.

As soon as I opened it, he shouted a heartfelt, "Hallelujah!" He praised my good taste in clothes and told me I had to work in the morning. He brought out a map of Havana and unfurled it over one of the beds. Cheerfully, he explained that the city was divided into business districts along the sewer lines, where there were manholes. He made marks at 23rd and 12th, the Falla Bonet mausoleum at Colón Cemetery, the corner of the Hotel Sevilla, the Esquina de Tejas, the taxi stand at the train station, the Virgen del Camino, the League Against Blindness, Rumba Palace in Playa, 70th Street in Miramar, the capitol building . . . then leaned back and said he was pleased I'd been approved as a messenger for the Congregation. He informed me that I'd been investigated, and that they knew everything about my mother, my Aunt Buza and her husband, my years in school, and that everything suggested I was trustworthy.

"From now on, you're one of us," he asserted. "You'll be paid punctually, with bonuses for extra effort. You'll rule the city and its needs; you'll have Havana at your feet because you'll become the link between the promises of the underground and the humans above."

"And who are you?" I asked.

"Oh, don't worry about that," he said evasively. "Tomorrow you'll begin your routes under the supervision of Jeremías Batista. Your password is, *Five lights for Pontius Pilate.* Every time you knock on a door or address yourself to me, you'll say, *Five lights for Pontius Pilate!*"

I walked him to the door; we shook hands and he said, "The virgin who cures eyes does exist. Someday I'll take you to her sanctuary in Guanabacoa."

At 8 o'clock I went to the hotel dining room. The food was awful but I ate it gratefully. I thought about going to the movies, the América over on Galiano. But I soon reconsidered and thought it best to get some sleep. The city had given me a warmer welcome than I'd foreseen. It's true that my new profession was illegal, but who can live off decency? I was a humble supplier of merchandise on whom God would take pity.

In the room I met Jeremías Batista. He was in his underwear, muttering, clipping his toenails. I introduced myself and he said he knew who I was. Then he tried to clear up a few things.

"All that glitters isn't gold. I can't say more than that, you'll learn the lesson yourself. I carry out my orders without fail. Tomorrow we'll initiate a meat delivery. In terms of our life as roommates, I'll tell you up front that I like to bring women up here at night. When that happens, you can go for a walk. I don't like farts. I don't like snoring or people with long nails. One other thing: You're going to have to get to know this fucking city inside and out or you won't be any good to the business. I'm going to give you your wake-up call at 3 in the morning."

He did indeed get me up at that hour and we quickly headed for the Virgen del Camino. We took our positions with barely a word between us. When it was almost dawn, a truck full of cows showed up. Jeremías Batista chatted up the driver and suddenly Pascualito popped up out of a manhole with a half dozen dwarves in tow. Shouting the whole time, Pascualito ordered them to open the trucks. They poked the cows, which began jumping into the emptiness of the manholes. After a while, all that was left was the irrefutable smell of animal fear on the pavement.

"It's as if there's a sacrificial altar down there to which we have to make offerings," Jeremías said.

We then committed ourselves to our messenger duties. That's how it was every Friday, which was slaughter day. Saturdays and Wednesdays we distributed canned goods. Sundays we barely worked and Mondays we started off with orders for clothes. Tuesdays were for miscellaneous items, and we might just as easily load up an elephant as a bag of needles. Thursdays was medical day and medicine would pour out of the Falla Bonet mausoleum in Colón Cemetery to be distributed all over Havana. We pulled in a ton of money and soon Jeremías showed me how to work this to my advantage. We bought and sold in fistfuls of dollars. To this we added the rich bonuses that Pascualito handed out on the corner of the Sevilla.

I decided to buy myself some things; I got a Walkman, some cowboy boots, flower print shirts, and a new pair of glasses. I started sending my mother a monthly remittance; it seemed like this could go on forever. Late at night, I'd go dancing at the discotheques, where I met my first love, a little mulatta who was a real babe. Jeremías let me have the room and I discovered what it was like to make love.

Eventually, however, I started to lose some of my enthusiasm. Around that time, Pascualito finally took me to the sanctuary in Guanabacoa and I got to see the virgin. She was very pretty, surrounded by flowers. I asked for her blessing half-heartedly. After all, how could a blind virgin cure a cross-eyed guy? Pascualito argued that the artist who drew her had been drunk and hadn't completed her eyes, that in fact she was the Virgin of Toledo, who, discovering herself in this condition, had decided to perform miracles.

I have to say a few words about Jeremías. He was a fox when it came to the ladies. There wasn't a woman along the Prado who Jeremías hadn't taken to bed. He seduced Chinese girls, mulattas, well-dressed black women, and white married women. He dressed in a flashy, streetsy style: flannel hat, riotously loud pants, and two-toned shoes that he couldn't be seen without. That gruff character he'd been when we first met turned out to be pure show. I'll always remember him as a good person who taught me the profile of a changing city as its buildings fell to ruins. "Behold Havana," he'd say, "a morning like any other morning. It changes its skin, it's both man and woman, it's the god Changó's city sacrificed at mid-century . . ."

With little Pascualito I kept up a family-like dialogue. He never expressed an opinion about the world of waste water. Only by letting things unfold naturally did I come to know and understand his secrets. He never once discussed changes in the Congregation's hierarchy, nor the Supreme Chief's ups and downs. I also found out that dwarves could not be buried underground, that they'd eliminated the possibility of having cemeteries below, and that to this end they'd taken over part of a cemetery in Guanabacoa which had been abandoned in the '60s by Jews fleeing to New York. That's where I had quite an adventure after Pascualito ordered us to make a grave.

"You and Jeremías will dig the final resting place for a brother who's died," he said.

I've always been scared stiff of cemeteries. We went in terrified, with Jeremías muttering angrily. The cemetery was on a small hill, full of ceiba trees and rounded by a crumbling wall. The graves of the Jews were lost among the fallen leaves and only patches of the Hebrew lettering could be seen on the tombstones. In the back, next to the wall, we found the small mounds under which the dwarves were buried. We began to dig and by noon we had a pretty decent hole.

When Pascualito showed up alongside the wall, he offered us swallows of a potion made from roots and said he was going to give the go-ahead to start the funeral. He immediately asked us to leave, saying that the ceremony was only for denizens of the underground. We took our time collecting our tools and that way we managed to catch a glimpse of the entrance of the Grail's court, with a huge chalice up front held by a dwarf boy. For the first and only time I also saw the Supreme Chief.

"Art among arts, guidance and splendor, sovereign of the sun!" proclaimed the boy.

The Supreme Chief was fat, pot-bellied, and bare-chested, with a navel as big as a tomato. That's about all I got to see before Pascualito shooed us away.

A week later, I was promoted to work in a special service delivering household goods. Tulle, flowers, and good champagne—the underground was ready to offer it all. That's how Rosendo Gil came into my life. He'd set up a laundromat in his house on Muralla Street at the request of the dwarves. There was a sign at the entrance that read: *Lightning Laundry: washing and ironing in a flash.*

Rosendo would give me a list of deliveries every morning. I don't think, to this day, that I've ever worked as hard. I was always loaded down with lace dresses on the buses, traveling all the way to Miramar and Nuevo Vedado. I saw so many pretty girls completely untouched by bad times! But what I didn't like about those grand mansions with gardens and dogs was that the people there always looked at me as if I was a criminal. To fuck with them, I stopped wearing my glasses. Whenever I went to ring one of those bells *à la* "Avon calling," I'd make myself even more cross-eyed.

That's how things were going for me in Havana, although I was growing a little disconnected from Jeremías. We continued to share the room at the Packard, but our different work schedules made it so we hardly ever saw each other anymore.

That is, that's how it was going until an angel came along—or just bad luck. I remember it was a Wednesday, during my second Christmas season in Havana. It was December 25 and a delivery was slated for Masón and San Miguel streets, headquarters of TV Cubana; I was to ask for Reinita Príncipe. So off I went, and I asked for her when I arrived and they brought her to me right away. She was the actor who played the servant on the latest hit telenovela. I'd taken off my glasses and my crossed eyes had gotten worse and I wanted nothing more in that moment than for my eyes to be uniform, straight. The woman told me that we'd have to wait, that Lucecita was taping. "She's my daughter, you know, Lucecita," she clarified. "I want her to try on the outfit, then we'll figure out the bill."

Later she invited me to the studio and I saw a TV show for the first time. They were taping *Snow White*. Lucecita had the starring role. I'd never seen a girl like that. I've never again seen such beautiful eyes. Reclining on a rock, she seemed the picture of happiness, radiant. It was the scene in which the prince saves her, when he arrives and kisses her and Snow White comes back to life. Then the dwarves danced and ran around the studio, and the end of the story made me cry.

"This is the guy who brought the ball gown," Lucecita's mother said as she introduced me. I held the box with the dress out to her, she smiled at me and happily went to try it on. I waited in limbo, just staring at the cameras that captured dreams.

"Doesn't she look lovely!" Reinita Príncipe exclaimed when her daughter returned. The dwarves fawned over her, petting the tulle. The entire studio admired her.

"Let's go home," her mother urged.

Right now, I don't know, I couldn't honestly say if Lucecita was pushed on me or if I fell for her all on my own. We were at the entrance to their apartment—that first day they didn't invite me in—around the corner from Masón and San Miguel, right next door to the Napoleonic Museum facing the university, when Reinita Príncipe, with her best servant's voice from the telenovelas, told me she only had half the money. She told me TV was a living hell, that they weren't making any real shows, and that beauty was dying. Given the situation, I certainly wasn't going to let her down. I was a businessman, I had no way of knowing if everything that went on in Havana was just the dwarves' doings. Logic indicated that if they'd gotten as far as TV, they could be anywhere. Nonetheless, this woman inspired me to trust her. That's why I said what I said.

"I can extend credit, but only for a few days."

"So I can keep it!" Lucecita rejoiced.

From that moment on—and that's why I believe life can change with a single word from a woman—I became Lucecita's biggest admirer. There wasn't an afternoon I couldn't be found in the studio. I managed to get myself a special pass so that I could always sit in the very first row to watch the shows.

"Is it love?" she asked me.

But it really hurt when they didn't invite me to her birthday party. That night I wandered around the university walls and gazed up at the festive goings-on at Lucecita's; I couldn't work up the nerve to go in. I remember that I headed to the Napoleonic Museum instead and paused in front of the bed that once belonged to the Great Corsican. I became enchanted with Josephine's portrait, and I had a strong urge to steal it, so that I'd finally have a lover. Yet imagination is one thing and real life is another.

"Put the squeeze on the mother," Rosendo Gil, who'd now become my confidante, advised me. "Either she pays or she gives you her daughter." Then he laughed salaciously.

So that's how I approached Reinita Príncipe. I told her my bosses were demanding payment and if I didn't come up with it, they'd retaliate. She got very serious and talked about some money she was owed and that she'd been cast in a starring role. I turned a deaf ear to her and told her about a terrible tribe of thieves who would lie in wait at night. She promised to pay the debt that same week. Later, after a complete transformation, she scolded me for not attending the birthday party. I looked at her with such disdain that she changed the subject and invited me to have coffee at her house.

"That way you'll meet my husband," she said.

Theirs was a typical Havana apartment that had seen better days: furniture that needed upholstering, crumbling walls, broken windows. Reinita tiptoed in and said, "Nicanor José . . ." But we only heard a loud cough.

Reinita told me to follow her and we went into an office, a room where we found a sixty-something man smoking a cigar. Behind him, there was a wall covered with photographs, posters, certificates, and a map of Havana. The biggest photo had a caption in German and featured a crane placing a concrete block in the middle of a street. The man was barefoot and wore a sweater which fell over his wool pants. He saw that I was interested in the photo and told me that it was the unyielding Berlin Wall.

"It was the wall that saved us," he said. Then he showed me his certificates, describing them like in a newsreel. "Ah, this one, this one's from the KGB, a year-long course in Moscow! And this other one, from the second-rate Czech intelligence agency! And that one, from the very disciplined German police force!" He coughed and spit out the window, then pointed to the map of Havana. "Do you see those circles? Do you? Those are the exits from the sewers, the manholes. I was the first to discover the plague, the first to declare that the city was being overrun by Jews, those same Jews who fled from their Havana synagogues just as the Berlin Wall was being built. They've gone underground, where they've turned into vermin who suck the blood of the people!"

From then on I became a regular visitor. It was from Reinita Príncipe that I learned her husband had been an officer who'd traveled the world taking courses in espionage and counter-espionage, and that he'd been forced into retirement after he threw a tantrum at a meeting of generals and insisted there were dwarves in the Havana sewers.

"Then the wall fell," Reinita explained, "and he never got well again. He lives cursing Vaclav Havel, who he met in Prague."

Lucecita didn't like that I visited every day, much less the manner I had about me. I always showed up loaded down with canned sausages. Her mother pushed her to be polite but she was determined to sour my existence. At the dinner table—because in a month's time I was having dinner there regularly—she'd roll her eyes back and make nasty comments about people who try to buy love. And all the while I was drooling for her, praising her more and more, blowing all of my savings. But she never gave me a break. She egged her father on to declare war against me. The old man began his campaign by threatening to go to his old comrades so that I'd be arrested as an agent of the synagogues.

"Make yourself scarce," my friend Jeremías counseled.

That's what I did, and what a terrible loneliness came over me! I didn't have any desire to get back at her by being with some girl who sold love. I started to hate Havana. In the afternoons, I would go to Dos Hermanos and get drunk. The same stevedores were there, and the Chinese mulatta who had once made me come by the light of Morro Castle. They all touched my head.

It wasn't until a month later that my life took another turn. One Sunday afternoon, I ran into Pascualito at the entrance to the Packard. He told me he'd been waiting for me for a while. Discreetly, we made our way to an Andalusian bar on the Prado. We ordered two anisettes and then, in a low voice, he talked about the Great Grail, the Supreme Chief, and the problems they were having underground picking up TV transmissions. He asked if I was still hanging around the studios on Masón and San Miguel. When I told him about my romantic travails, he insisted I go back and dedicate myself to spying.

"You will be very well paid," he said.

"But why me?" I asked. "There are all those dwarf acrobats there, the ones who work with Snow White. Surely you can contact one of them."

"They're artists, and the Grail doesn't trust artists," Pascualito answered.

I returned to Masón and San Miguel to try and regain Reinita Príncipe's favor. She was very accepting, and thanks to her I became friends with producers, scenic artists, and video technicians. In just two weeks, I was able to lift some blueprints and a list of security guards. Reinita Príncipe turned a blind eye, banking on my promise that I would not make her pay her debt. Lucecita also made a radical change. She began to flirt with me and urged me to visit her at home again. I didn't get as worked up this time, but there's no doubt I did let myself fall for this unrequited love again.

When I visited one evening, I came loaded down with provisions. They locked the old man in his room, Reinita lit some incense, and we all got drunk. Lucecita drank too much and started toasting the swallows that flew alone at dawn above the water—that's how inspired she was. At midnight on the dot, we uncorked a bottle of champagne and Reinita pushed me into the girl's room. Lucecita kept talking to the swallows and I was so scared that I started stammering, as if I'd been smoking weed. She begged me to never take off my glasses.

"They make you beautiful," she said. And so I lay down next to her, barely touching her. "It'll be our secret that we embrace only with our spirits," she said conspiratorially.

That dawn, in a spectacular robbery that left Havana completely in awe, the studio at Masón and San Miguel was taken apart piece by piece. Reinita told me that they'd found the night guard fast asleep and that there would be a no-holds-barred investigation. The city would be dredged up like a minefield.

"There's so much hate," she said.

Nobody gave me a second thought. They even interviewed the studio janitors, but no one thought to ask me squat. It was as if I didn't exist.

"I'm invisible," I told Lucecita.

"Thank your lucky stars," she said. "Maybe precisely because of that I'll love you someday."

Pascualito met me at Rosendo Gil's house and told me that the Great Grail sent its congratulations. He added that the Supreme Chief would give me a medal, and that I could ask for whatever I wanted. I didn't know what to say. It was actually Pascualito who suggested the idea of the restaurant.

"What do I have to do?" I asked.

"Nothing, just live and look out for the Grail's share."

It was easy to convince Lucecita to let us build the restaurant at her house. We worked hard during those days. From the sewers came tables, tablecloths, the goods for the meals, everything. The only condition I laid down was that my friend Jeremías would be the sole supplier for the new business. He just radiated happiness. Reinita Príncipe reacted the same way, and I've often wondered if he had conquered that poor and faded star's heart.

And as it turned out, Lucecita did grow to love me. I don't know if her love came from pity or because we were making so much money, but one night she told me to stop acting like a fool. I made love to her like never before, so that daybreak found us still in bed, and after that, at least for a little while, I became the hardest working man in the city.

My restaurant was always full, open twenty-four hours and decorated with posters from our heroic period. There's nothing a foreigner likes more than somebody else's heroism. They went crazy staring at the posters of a worker's fist held high, or that one in which the gears of a machine smash the bureaucracy. Lucecita's father got in on the act too. The tourists would go into his room and hear the tales of his travels to KGB headquarters and that afternoon when he saw Vaclav Havel under the falling snow in Prague. The old man would tell his life story with pride, wearing his old military uniform and showing the map of Havana which he used to repeat his conspiracy theory. He never tried to charge a fee. Nonetheless, Reinita always left a dollar on a silver ashtray to try and inspire the tourists.

It was during this time that my mother died. I had her frozen and brought from my hometown to Havana, where I buried her in one of the niches in the Falla Bonet mausoleum, between bags of aspirins and cough syrup. My mother could never have imagined her eternal sleep on Carrara marble.

A few days later, Lucecita and I got married in a church. It was a sumptuous wedding and I wore a new black suit and turquoise tie. Five months later, Pascual Jeremías was born.

You're a winner! my mother had written to me in a letter shortly before her death. That's how I felt too, proud, so much that I'd forgotten I was cross-eyed, I'd forgotten my suffering, I'd forgotten the injustices. I'd begun to look at life as an endless spending spree. There was no one taking care of my heart, no one to give me a wake-up call.

Soon, however, laziness was catching up with me. Little by little, Lucecita had been taking over the reins of the business. She knew exactly how to fix the day's receipts, and with great care she'd divvy the Grail's share, the money for the inspectors, money for bribes to keep everything quiet, and, of course, money for us.

"With the extra money, we'll be rich," Lucecita told me one night.

"What if they find us out?" I asked fearfully.

"How will they find out?" she replied, as she kissed my waist and took my glasses off for the first time. "Are *you* going to talk? Am *I* going to talk? Is *Jeremías* going to talk . . . ?"

I know, of course, that life's adventure is filled with big

risks. But our good fortune went out with the old man; it was flushed right down the toilet. We did everything we could so that he wouldn't talk. But the old man put off his antagonism toward the dwarves long enough to send them messages. He saved every jar of mayonnaise, every bottle of mustard, every container we threw away, and he sent them down with every flush of the toilet, each one stuffed with a letter that told about our various transgressions.

The first warning came the Monday that Jeremías disappeared. I tried in vain to find him. I went to the Packard, searched his room, then checked out every corner of the Prado where he made his conquests. Nobody had seen him since Friday. I visited Pascualito at his spot in front of the train station. I tried to hug him but he held back. He talked about a moon so cruel that it poisons men's hearts. He told me about how certain waters can wash shame away.

"Something strange is going on," I told Lucecita when I got home.

"Jeremías is in love and Pascualito is a neurotic dwarf," she responded, trying to calm me down.

"Dark times are coming," I said.

"No, our son won't be subject to the same struggles as you and me."

"Dark times are coming," I repeated.

And I was right. At dawn, we were attacked by a horde of dwarves. Within minutes they'd taken everything. A big-breasted female dwarf snatched Pascual Jeremías from his crib. Then they took Lucecita and Reinita Príncipe. They took the old man too, wrapped in his map of Havana. I was left without the strength or will to act.

That's when Pascualito came in and repeated what he'd said about the cruel moon and signaled for me to pick him up. I kissed him on the cheek, and I don't remember anything after that.

I woke up in a shed made of ice deep in a cave. My body shivered. My good friend Jeremías approached me. And, my God! He was now a despicable dwarf! Jeremías had short legs, an old double-breasted coat over his tiny body, and his ears were mangled. He was wearing flannel boots instead of two-toned shoes, and he seemed so resigned that I was terrified.

"I don't exist anymore," he said, helping me up.

My scream chilled the cave even more. I too was a dwarf! I too was a dwarf with lips twisted in confusion, a dwarf without eyelashes.

"You'll get used to it," he said like a priest, and then he talked about Christ's commandments, about punishment and absolution. He said Pontius Pilate was our wasteland's patron saint.

"How long will we be like this?" I sobbed.

"Forever," was his reply.

Today there was a slaughter. The slaughterhouse is next to this freezer and from dawn through the rest of the live long day, the cows' mooing has been tormenting me. I wonder if cows think about life and death. But those are subtleties that don't really matter. My tragedy is double: I no longer breathe Havana's air and I'm despised. The dwarves—I still talk as if I'm not one of them—have a unique standard of beauty. They love their short bodies and the familial shine in their eyes.

I have to do the worst jobs: carry boxes, cut out cow livers, cremate their bones, and slice off bull's tongues.

"The Big Show's about to begin," Jeremías tells me. He's still my good friend.

I'll finish up these notes right now and sit myself in front of the TV—it's the only entertainment allowed—where I'll be face to face with Lucecita. It's a show produced just for underground TV. They'll introduce her as the World Famous Vedette. She'll play up her underappreciated sensuality. When I see her, I'll forget all about the real woman, the lover I so desired, and merely ask myself if my Pascual Jeremías was able to save himself like his mother.

Jeremías yells at me that the show is starting. I'd give anything to stop hearing Glenn Miller, that same melody that always comes over the loudspeakers! I want to have wings and fly, to escape with my son as if he were a sacred feline and climb the mountain that's Havana, and be a man. My Lucecita sings the show's theme song and I travel through space and light, to the dream on the screen, and love her.

Translation by Achy Obejas

THE LAST PASSENGER

BY ENA LUCÍA PORTELA

Vedado

It's well known that the guy never confessed. But neither
did he ever deny the charges that were leveled against
him. The night he was arrested, he said, "Fuck you, dick-
heads, I shit on the whore who birthed all of you motherfuck-
ers!" Or something like that. And after that initial statement,
he never uttered anything vaguely coherent again. Once he
was at the police station at Zapata and F streets, between
the braying and the shrieking, he got obsessed with a certain
clattering caused by the vermin whose little feet galloped up
his spine—*plick! plack! plick! plack!*—and dicked with him
all night—*the bastards!*—not letting him sleep, driving him
crazy—*hee! hee! hee!*—crazy, just fucking wacko . . . All of a
sudden, he'd howl frenetically, roll his eyes back, and hit himself on his temples with his fists; he'd even foam at the mouth.
It was quite the spectacle!

According to what I've been told, there was no human
way to get him off that. They interrogated him without rest
for hours and hours, for whole days. They showed him photographs of his victims, exactly how he'd left them (if the
facts I have are true, those photos are even more hair-raising
than the ones of the Tate-LaBianca murders), they smeared
the photos under his nostrils, they threatened to crack his
head open like a pumpkin and even gave him a few good
slaps—and nothing. The guy never responded. Maybe he

was making up the stuff about the galloping vermin so as to avoid responsibility for his actions, maybe it wasn't so much that he was pretending, or that he was bald-face lying, but that . . . heck, who knows! The forensic psychiatrist concluded there was nothing insane about him, that the guy was fine in the head—more precisely, that he was perfectly capable of distinguishing right from wrong when he did what he did.

Yet they never called him to testify during the trial. The psychiatrist testified, of course. But not the guy. I remember him sitting on the front bench on the left side of the courtroom, immobile, wearing a brownish-gray suit, still handcuffed, quieter than an oyster at the bottom of the ocean. Had he seen me? I don't know. I don't think we ever made eye contact. He seemed dazed, lost in thought, far away, as if the proceedings in Criminal Court #7 of the Provincial Court of the City of Havana had nothing to do with him. Had they sedated him so he wouldn't make a scene in public? Hmm. Maybe. Because in the end it wasn't really necessary that this guy tell about each one of his exploits in any kind of detail. There were eyewitnesses, a preponderance of evidence, and the results of a DNA test, which, from what I'm told, is infallible. Everything was very dramatic, as the relatives of the victims were in attendance. There were screams, sobs, one or two people fainted. As was to be expected, the prosecutor finished his argument vehemently demanding the death penalty. Later, I heard that this particular prosecutor was affectionately nicknamed "Pool o' Blood" (although I must recognize that, at least in this case, the accused could also be called this). The defense attorney, for his part, limited himself to asking for clemency.

That's when I raced home. I was dying to throw up and, though it may sound strange, to laugh as well. I had never witnessed a trial before and I hope, in what's left of my life, that I never will again, because in American movies—and in the TV series *Law & Order*—I find them fascinating, but in real life, not so much. I don't know if a legal system with twelve jurors is more efficient than this one, where the verdict is determined by three professional judges, but it's certainly more pleasant. Two days after the trial, it was announced publicly that the Provincial Court judges had found the accused guilty on all counts and had sentenced him to death by firing squad. The sentence was upheld later by the Supreme Court.

A few months have passed since then. No one talks about it much out on the streets anymore, and I think it's been awhile since the newspapers have published anything. Now the guy's on death row. It's probable that they'll never execute him, because of all the fuss around human rights. As far as I know, after the international hullabaloo because of those fast-track executions back in the spring of 2003, they haven't executed any other civilians.

Me, I just go on with my same routine, like always. I sleep, or at least I try, almost all day long, and then come alive at night. To sleep, I drink chamomile or valerian root tea, or I take diazepam, trifluoperazine, chlordiazepoxide, haloperidol, or some other pharmaceutical. The important thing is to sleep. Although there are days when nothing works and all I want to do is bang my head against the wall or throw myself out the window. I live alone in an apartment with a view of the sea, on the ninth floor of the Naroca building on Paseo Avenue, around the corner from Línea Street, in Vedado. Little vermin with galloping feet don't come this high. Nothing gets up here; nothing stays for long up here either, not even a mosquito. It's just that I suffer from insomnia. Why? Ufff, I have no idea! I'm thirty-three years old, I have twenty-five thousand cucos deposited at the Banco Financiero, pretty legs, and I'm white (well, to be frank, I just pass for white in this country, in fact I'm Jewish), divorced, a smoker, Sagittarius, I like film noir and noir stories, black clothes, Johnnie Walker Black, darkness, Rachmaninov, and Russell Crowe's brutish face. I loathe Caribbean summers (so humid and muggy), salsa orchestras, rum, radical feminism, encounters with many kinds of people, Ayn Rand's aesthetics, and being called "privileged." It's been a long time since I stopped asking myself the why of things.

These days, I've been seriously considering the possibility of visiting the convict. Do they allow visitors on death row? Who knows! In any case, I don't think I'll go. They'll want to know who I am, what my relationship is with the guy, etc., and I couldn't explain without getting in trouble. I can just see it: "I'm the enchanting unknown woman who the asshole psychopath would call in the middle of the night to talk to about his ups and downs, fears, successes, frustrations, and plans for the future." Sounds easy, doesn't it?

As I said, I'm not going. No way! Deep down, I'm grateful that the asshole psychopath didn't tell the police about me (and didn't write my number down anywhere). I confess that I'm surprised by so much discretion on his part. I always assumed he was a bit of a wuss, a hack, someone who wouldn't be able to take the slightest pressure and would give it all up right away, not stop talking until he'd spilled everything. As soon as they nabbed him, I thought all was lost. I assumed they could come for me at any minute and accuse me of harboring a fugitive, or complicity, or instigation, or God knows what craziness. Those were hellish days, nights of furious anxiety. But no. False alarm. The son of a bitch didn't turn me in. Hmm. How weird. Even today, I can't explain it. Well, the truth is that there are a lot of things about this nefarious situation which I can't explain.

Sometimes I have no choice but to be out during the day—as much as I hate that. I'll need to go to the bank to get money, since everything here has to be paid in cash, or to sign for the wire transfers sent from Europe. I also need to pay the electric bill, the phone, the water, buy groceries for the week (never forgetting the pharmaceuticals nor the whiskey), return the videos, rent new videos, take a little stroll by my dentist's office, go to the hairdresser at the Cohíba or the boutique at La Maison, or deal with the process of taking a trip abroad, which involves a head-on crash with the world's most grotesque bureaucracy, among other needs. I hate to walk in the sun around other people. It's true that my neighborhood is pretty safe compared to the disaster of Centro Habana, for example, or Alamar, or El Hueco in Marianao, where tourists don't go even by accident. But Vedado also has its black holes, of course, tucked away behind the pleasant façades. Perhaps it's my own problem, but I frequently think the streets stink. They stink of misery, of desperation, of violence. Basically, the streets are bad. If it were up to me, I'd never go out.

I can't stop thinking about the guy, about the incredible surprise I got the first time I saw him. It was at the Provincial Court, during the trial. Until that moment, I'd only heard his voice on the phone. A low voice, beautiful, boyish, although it had something metallic about it, and sometimes even squeaky, especially when he had fits of hysteria or threatened me by describing how pretty I'd look once he'd gutted me—*swish! swish!*—with his lethal blade (that's actually how the fool expressed himself), or when he screamed about how females, those degenerates, those shitty whores, weren't worth a hill of beans, and I—the most disgusting of all!—was guilty of who knows what.

At those times, I'd hold the phone away from my ear, lean back in my chair, and light a cigarette. Sometimes I'd get up. I'd leave him there, talking to himself, without hanging up or letting him know. I'd go to the kitchen, pour myself a whiskey on the rocks, and return to the bedroom at my leisure. When I got back on the phone, he'd be going at it at the top of his lungs, threatening to strangle me with my own intestines, but not before tearing out my liver and eating it, among other lovely things. In the midst of his fits, he never noticed my absences. Or who knows—maybe he just didn't want to let on. He was egocentrism itself. I'd happily get comfortable again in my chair, or on the bed among the big pillows, with my whiskey on the rocks and my cigarettes. I'd listen to plans for my future murder, which would be quite atrocious, while contemplating the Havana night. Then he'd finally calm his nerves, or surrender to exhaustion, or ejaculate. He was always the one who would say goodbye, until the next one, hope you have horrifying nightmares, etc. He'd hang up indignant, absolutely furious, telling me that I was a piece of shit, a goddamn cactus, a frigid neurotic, an insensitive bitch, a monster! And he just couldn't talk to me anymore. Those farewells were never avatars of anything even vaguely healthy. Generally, the next day, or a few days after that, the mangled cadaver of some girl would be found in some tenement slum, or in a ditch, or in the bathroom at the bus terminal, or in a dumpster, or floating down the Almendares River. Not much time would pass before he'd call again, to brag about his latest prank.

Even as he gave the impression of being an inveterate narcissist, the fact is he never described himself physically. Not seriously anyway. One night, I asked him what he looked like, only to see what he'd come up with, because I never thought he'd be honest about it. (People who describe themselves physically on the phone, or on the Internet, generally don't tell you what they look like but what they'd like to look like.) Then the guy quite delightedly swore that he was basically green, that he had three fluorescent yellow eyes, two reddish antennae, and a few exquisitely violet dots.

"Oh, and a twelve-inch cock," he added, with great pride. "You want some . . . ?"

"Hey, stop that. I've told you, I can't right now. But don't worry, Daddy, I'll let you know. And watch that flying saucer so they don't steal it, okay? The streets are nasty these days."

"The flying . . . ? Ha! Ha! Very funny! I *looooove* it when you try to be sly, foxy, all-powerful! Trying that with me . . . Ha! Ha! As if I didn't know you!"

"That's right, I love you too." I blew him a kiss. "You're my favorite martian."

"Really? Then tell me what you're wearing right now. Tell me! I need to know before I go out to . . . well, you know. C'mon, whore, tell me!"

"What I'm wearing . . . hmm. Quite the little question. Let's see . . ."

I imagined him younger than me. Not an adolescent, but almost. Let's say, some young thing in his twenties terrified of growing old. Somebody who's, say, a miserable twenty-three but gets totally offended if you miscalculate and suggest twenty-four. Of course, when I asked him how old he was—and, let it be said, I did so with the utmost care—he told me I was a crone—ha! ha!—and old enough to be his great grandmother. That's how he was, a vile clown. He hardly ever answered anything seriously, maybe out of self-importance, or to come off like a tough guy, or to compensate for the utter dismay he felt because I wasn't afraid of him.

I imagined he was white. Not white in that apocryphal fashion in which so many Cubans are white, but really white, from the roots, with all European ancestors. Immaculately white, maybe blond or red-haired. I also imagined him college-educated, or at least well-read and well-traveled, with a comfortable economic situation (not like me, because I struggle and work, but something of a fortunate son. Everybody knows what I mean: nomenclature, upper class, elite. In other words, the truly privileged in this country—those people who manage mixed enterprises, hotels, and franchise stores, who have Swiss bank accounts and spend their vacations in the Bahamas), and the look of every mother's son, the face of an angel, and a pianist's hands, very clean, a bit shy, elegant, with impeccable table manners, a genuine gold Rolex on his wrist, without a police record—except, perhaps, a little fine for speeding like a madman—a loner, nocturnal, bored, and a habitual user of cocaine and hardcore porn.

I said *I imagined him*, but that's not very exact. Back in the days when we talked freely on the telephone, before they arrested him, I didn't imagine anything. No, that's how I *knew* things were, no more, no less, and there was no way they could be any different. I didn't need him to explicitly confirm anything for me to be certain of it all, regardless of prior promises in the service of truth. I mean, his way of speaking, his allusions, even the slightly faggy way he pronounced certain words, the insults and the threats, as if he were trying to be the wicked wise guy or the neighborhood tough guy, the big spender, street expert, and supreme connoisseur of women of the night—*everything* about him seemed to indicate unequivocally that I was right.

He never told me his name. When I asked him during one of those telephonic chitchats, he assured me in his unique style that his name was Ted Bundy. Ha! Ha! He also said I needed to become a police inspector, since I obviously enjoyed interrogating sinister suspects. I didn't pursue it. What for? I never pressured him about anything. It's possible I may even have laughed a bit. The big shots in this country, in order to distinguish themselves even more from the average joe—so they confide when they're in trusted company, or when they think they are—never give their kids extravagant names like Yoandrys, Plastidio, Inkajurel, or Amón Ra. No way! So the sinister suspect had to be named Fernando, Ernesto, Camilo, Rafael, or something like that. And just like he didn't tell me his name, he didn't ask for mine. He didn't need it. He always called me "you," just "you." That's not counting the expletives, of course.

A little before his arrest, a photo of him ran in *Granma* and other newspapers. Well, not of *him*. The guy in the photo wasn't him, it couldn't have been him. The press release that went with it warned the citizens of Havana to remain vigilant, ready for combat. And to collaborate by providing any pertinent information that might help the biggest manhunt ever to catch the most dangerous criminal our country had known in these last few years of revolutionary struggle against crime and blah blah blah. Very grandiose, that little press release. So much so that I almost called them at one of those numbers they give to let them know they were after the wrong guy, and that if they persisted on that path, the biggest manhunt ever would be a miserable flop. In fact, I did call. One, two, three times. But I could never get through. The lines were always busy. Apparently, there were a lot of people wanting to call in with pertinent information. I recovered my senses after a while—thank God!—and I stopped calling.

Soon word got out that the image wasn't an actual photo but a police sketch created on a computer according to a description by a witness, his latest victim, who, by some miracle, had managed to escape into the thicket around the Prince's Castle. Ah, well, that explained the mistake, I told myself. The poor girl had been, quite understandably, a nervous wreck, and had lost her sense of reality. That's why she hadn't described the real assailant but rather some demonic being sprung from her imagination or from popular mythology, like the Man With the Backpack, the Fat Guy, the Rascal on the Run, or whatever; nobody who actually exists. That explanation struck me even then as a little convoluted, a bit of a stretch, but it gave me a certain relief, I don't know why.

I was waiting for the guy to call me so I could hear his version of what had happened on the night of the unfortunate incident by the Prince's Castle. Curiosity coursed through my veins. Although, I admit, I was also looking forward to the malevolent fun of mocking him. As far as I knew, until that incident, none of his "meatballs," as the stupid pig called his victims, had gotten away before.

"You're losing your touch, baby," I was going to whisper in a cold, cruel tone. "Ha! Ha! You're on a slippery slope, going straight down. You're practically finished. Why, you can't even take the dog out for a walk on a leash! Don't you see that at the end of the day, no matter what you do, the babes are going to beat you? Don't you see, you fool, that we're better than you? Oh, Ted Bundy, you have no idea how much I pity you. You know, if I were you, I'd retire. Don't get mad, man, but with your utter lack of street smarts and that microscopic little dick, you're not going anywhere. You know what I think? You should get yourself a husband, that's what! A really brutish macho, with a real twelve-inch super dick who fucks you up the ass the way you deserve and makes you see stars and . . ."

I was really quite inspired. I spent various nights waiting for his call, very excited, smoking cigarette after cigarette, with all my lights off and my gaze turned on the sky above Havana—one of the darkest in the world—as I went through my burlesque speech in my head, making it even more hurt-ful, sadistic, and devastating. I really wanted to fuck with this guy, to offend him, humiliate him, and chew him up and out. I confess that there are times when I have very violent impulses toward others, but I contain myself. I am, after all, a civilized person. But when life's crazy turns bring me in contact with someone who doesn't repress those impulses in himself . . . well, then the walls crumble, there's no point to being civi-lized, and we willingly go deeper into that wild and tenuous territory where everything is up for grabs. And when I say ev-erything, I mean exactly that: *everything*. So I was really sharp-ening my claws, ready to dig them where they would most hurt my nocturnal interlocutor as soon as I got my chance. Ah, but woman proposes and God disposes! That bastard son of a bitch never called again. And because I had no way of getting ahold of him, I was left on my own. What a drag.

A week after the police sketch was published, news of the dangerous criminal's arrest came with much fanfare, followed by effusive praise for the wisdom, heroism, and selfless work of the National Revolutionary Police, the party, the govern-ment, the community organizations, and, more generally, the people of the capital, who had remained firm in their resolve, without allowing themselves to be distracted by the enemy, blah blah blah . . .

As incredible as it may sound, I didn't tie any of these things together. For me, it was clear—clear as day—that the scarecrow in the photo didn't exist. For me, if they'd caught anybody, it could only be the real him, the psychopath with the lethal blade, the bastard who so reveled in his telephonic chitchats with me, and who had, unexpectedly, stopped calling. And, as I said, that's when I panicked. I freaked out. It's not that I had done anything terrible, nor that I felt responsible for the guy's deeds. No way! Looking coldly at the facts, what could I be accused of? Of accepting calls from a serial killer at nearly midnight all summer long? Of having heard on numerous occasions the detailed plans for a crime from its perpetrator? Of never having run to turn him in? Well, I suppose that is also a crime, a very serious one. Of course, I could swear and swear again until the end of days that I never believed a word uttered on the phone by that guy, that I always believed those florid and malicious narratives pouring into my little ear were never more than nocturnal jokes, just jokes. Jokes in supremely bad taste, of course. Cruel, stupid, macabre jokes, but no more than that. Regardless of whether the police inspector believed me or not, it would be difficult, if not impossible, to prove the contrary. But I was terrified just the same. Just thinking about it, my hairs stand on end.

The last thing I wanted in this life was to raise the police's suspicions, to be investigated, to have them sticking their noses in my personal business. I didn't want them to know I don't work for the state, that I don't belong to my block's Committee for Defense of the Revolution or to any other community organization, that I barely deal with the people in my neighborhood, that the people in my building think I'm weird, that I frequently cheat on my taxes, that my parents live in Israel, that I have an illegal Internet connection, that my brother is gay and lives in New York, that I sometimes do drugs to go to sleep, that my ex-husband is a former political prisoner and now lives in Miami, that I have a nine-millimeter Beretta (which is extremely illegal in this country) stashed in the top drawer of my night table . . . Basically, I had an abundance of reasons to be scared of the National Revolutionary Police noticing my existence. My anguish was such that, for the first few days after the guy's arrest, I was utterly paralyzed. I didn't even try to get rid of the gun. In the end, that turned out to be a good thing, since no one ever came to arrest me, or to attempt to search my apartment, or even to ask me anything about the case, nothing.

To be frank, I have no idea why I went to the trial. At that point, I was pretty serene, completely—or pretty much—recovered from my fright. I wanted to take a look at the guy, even if it was from a distance. What for? Well, maybe just to see the incontrovertible proof that I was right (and not the stupid *Granma* and the other little newspapers) in terms of what the guy looked like, and then leave the whole terrible story at that. Or who knows—maybe deep down I just wanted to add a little more suspense and drama to my life, since by going I ran the risk that the guy would recognize me and let slip—in public!—all that had been carefully withheld until then. But I wasn't really sure that he could identify me. I never knew how the devil he'd hit on me, whether by just dialing numbers randomly, or from a phone book stolen from a mutual friend, or by following some numeric or cabalistic criteria, or via some other mysterious formula that I couldn't decipher. It's probably unnecessary to state that the guy never bothered to explain any of this to me. He assured me I'd caught his eye—those were his words—a million times, at the movie theater on La Rampa, at Coppelia, at the cafeteria on the first floor of the Focsa building, on the seawall at the Malecón, in an open-air bar across the street from Colón Cemetery . . . In other words, all places where any Havana resident has been at least once in her life, so that mentioning them didn't mean anything. One night, I told him I had splendid tits, that I'm a size thirty-eight, and he thought that was great. In fact, he really got into that detail. He *loooooved* it, as he liked to say. Too bad it wasn't true! I do have a good ass, but tits, no way. The sad truth is that I'm a size thirty-two, and that's stretching it. Of course, none of this means anything either. Maybe the guy was just going along with me exactly like I went along with him about his twelve inches.

Just in case, though, I decided to alter my appearance a bit before going to the trial. I straightened my hair and dyed it brown. I dropped a black beret on my head and wore a long leather coat, all the way down to my ankles, and donned a pair of dark glasses with smoky lenses. And to make myself look interesting, I applied a vivid red lipstick. Dressed like a character out of *The Matrix* (or whatever the hell), I took a taxi to Old Havana and showed up fifteen minutes before the start of the trial at the Provincial Court.

Ufff, they almost didn't let me in! Outside the building, on Teniente Rey Street, there was an unusual crowd of people, and there was a lot of pushing, kicking, punching, yelling, and a ferocious stink of human flesh in the air. My God! No doubt I'm a warrior, though. I refused to budge. I had to practically break an arm to push my way through the tumult, get in the actual building, and, finally—a little worse for wear with my hair out of place, sweating, and with the beret crumpled into one of the coat's inside pockets—I arrived at Criminal Court #7. I was in luck: I managed to get a magnificent seat, not too far from the bench where they'd soon sit the most famous criminal of the decade.

When I saw him, just a few meters from me, first face to face and then in profile, I couldn't believe my eyes. No, no, no. No way! It wasn't possible. I remember I took my glasses off so I could see him better. Mother of God, what was that? I rubbed my eyes and looked again. Jesus Christ! I couldn't get over it. I elbowed a man sitting to my right and asked him if that was really the guy, the one in the brownish-gray suit, if he was the accused, the one who had allegedly committed a dozen or more murders. And it turned out that, in fact, it was him. Wow! The way he looked had nothing—I mean *nothing*—to do with what I'd thought he'd look like based on our phone calls. He was identical to the police sketch! Everybody knows now: a light-skinned mulatto, with very light naps, a flat nose, and very big round eyes, like a frog's, and a total thug look. He appeared to be in his fifties, although he was probably younger and life had just treated him badly. It was easy to see he was a lowlife from a million miles away. He looked less like a laborer than an outcast, a ratty vagabond or beggar, maybe an alcoholic or pot smoker, hungry, brutish, a dumpster diver, totally awkward in a suit . . . And then . . . his name! That was the worst of all, at least for me. They referred to him as citizen Policarpo Meneses Landaeta, alias "The Beast from Macagua 8." Oh! I don't know what hurt more, Policarpo or the Beast! Of course, on this island we can't hope that a rapist will be called Peter Kürten, alias "The Düsseldorf Vampire." You can't ask for pears from an elm tree. Which is not to say that Policarpo, topped off with the Beast (not to mention that Macagua thing, whatever that was, followed by its enigmatic little number), wasn't taking things just a bit too far.

No one else in that courtroom seemed the least bit perplexed. All around me, people were making faces: of disgust, of anger, of fear, of satisfaction, of justice served and morbid curiosity. But none of surprise. I suppose that for most Cubans, it must be a relief that a murderer should reflect back what they think a killer should look like. That is, that he should be black, ugly, on the older side, badly dressed, and look like a dork. And the fierce Beast of Macagua 8 certainly fit the bill. He was practically typecast! Only I couldn't imagine him saying that he *loooooved* anything; or that the night before he'd had a stupendous Cabernet Sauvignon from a particularly good year; or that, now that psychoanalysis was no longer in vogue, men could fall in love with their mothers again without fear of being called fags; or that he was basically green, with antennae and all the rest; or that he was a much better poet than Jim Morrison, that blockhead; or that this or that film by Pasolini struck him as too eschatological—that it was impossible to get to the good part, the part with the torture, without your stomach turning and a strong desire to slap the director and run him over—ha! ha!—with a flaming Ferrari Testarossa . . . among other things. Truth be told, I simply couldn't connect these and other comments he'd made in the dead of night with the mute ghost in front of me now. In the end, I told myself, though I pride myself on knowing human nature, that I'm just another superficial person, filled with prejudices, and very depressed. I looked disapprovingly on the malevolent Policarpo, sighed, and went out to smoke a cigarette. But I didn't stay out of the courtroom long, and I was right to come back, I believe, because that trial held many other surprises for me.

Of all the witnesses, the one who made the greatest impact was, without a doubt, the victim who had gotten away from the guy near the Prince's Castle. Right now, I can't remember her name, only her story, which stunned me. She was a Chinese mulatta, more or less my age, with straight hair and light eyes, pretty actually, but who could never pass for white, not here or in Hong Kong. And that in itself struck me as odd, because he'd often bragged that he'd never "burned oil" in his whole life. In other words, he didn't like black women or mulattas, nothing at all coming from Africa. He was no jackoff perverted peasant, he said, to have to go fuck animals. Certainly that was somewhat offensive or, as they say now, "politically incorrect," but it was also good news for so many young Cuban women. I can't say what other women might think, but as far as I'm concerned, I wouldn't be in the least bit insulted if a killer didn't find me attractive enough to be his victim. And I'm absolutely sure the guy wasn't kidding about this. The revulsion that laced his voice every time we touched on Afro-Caribbean topics was so deep, so visceral, that I could practically smell it over the phone line. Later, when I saw the relatives of the other victims, I noted that they must have been white. Hmm. What the devil made him change the menu at the last minute? Ufff, who knows! Of course, in the end none of this mattered one bit, I thought. By contrast, I have indeed "burned oil," and the difference—what they say is the difference—is in fact nil, just idle talk, myths. But that was nothing. The most astonishing aspect of all this was still to come.

She—the one who got away—was a nurse who worked at Calixto García General Hospital. The night of the incident she was working the graveyard shift, but at about 2:15 in the morning, her grandmother called to say that her young son was having a hellish asthma attack. She left immediately through the large door on Avenue of the Presidents, which is only used by Calixto staff. As might be expected, there wasn't a soul out . . . or so it seemed to her. She didn't pause to contemplate the scene but ran over to Carlos III Street, to see if she could find a ride to Lawton.

But she didn't get very far. She'd barely rounded the monument to José M. Gómez when some lunatic popped out of nowhere, grabbed her from behind, and put a knife to her throat, threatening to cut her if she uttered a single word.

At that moment, all she could sense was an odor, like a dead rat—so she said—coming from the criminal, his breath reeking of alcohol, rotten, as if that revolting swine had more cavities than teeth in his mouth. And, at least as far as she could see, there wasn't a single cop anywhere—not even a casual transient!—no one to ask for help. So she didn't resist.

Without quite letting go, the ruffian eased his hold on her and removed the knife from her throat. He was bigger, stronger than her. He put an arm around her shoulders and, as if they were on a romantic evening stroll through Vedado, he forced her to cross Avenue of the Presidents.

"Giddy up, whore," he whispered in her ear. "Giddy up or I'll make mince meat out of you—and don't look at me!"

The nurse was so terrified, she peed her pants. But as soon as they stepped onto the sidewalk on the other side of the street, the Prince's Castle side, in a moment of sheer valor or temerity, she swiftly turned toward the criminal. And that's when, under one of those bluish spots from the mercury bulbs of the street lights, she saw his face. An absolutely horrifying face, she said, that she'd never, ever forget.

Furious, the guy punched her so hard in the stomach that she tumbled to the ground.

"You fucked up now, whore!" he hissed, kneeling next to her. "Who the fuck told you you could look at me, huh? Now you really fucked up! Cuz I'm a freak, absolutely fucking freaky . . . !" And he threatened her again with the knife. "See? Freaky! Hee, hee, hee!"

He pulled her by the hair, practically lifting her off the ground, and dragged her to the thicket around the Prince's

Castle. He raped her there, in the shadows. Understandably, the victim didn't offer many details during that part of her testimony, only the most necessary in order to clearly establish the case. I mean, I put myself in her place and the truth is that I can't imagine having to talk about all of this in front of an audience. By the end, he had her flat on the ground, on her back. Although she felt a very acute pain, as if her insides were being burned by hydrochloric acid, she explained, she didn't lose consciousness for a single moment. All she thought about was surviving. She lifted a rock from the ground and held it in her right hand without the guy ever noticing. A few minutes passed, though it seemed like years to the nurse. When the maniac finally ejaculated, she took advantage of his momentary weakness to smash him with the rock, as hard as she could, right on the head. *Bam!* She left him groggy.

She quickly pushed him off, got up as fast as she could, and, in spite of her own dizziness, the nausea, and that piercing pain she felt in her lower abdomen, she took off running toward the avenue. She ran faster than she thought humanly possible, all the while screaming for help . . . Groggy and everything, the bastard ran after her. But there's ample evidence that it's difficult to get anywhere when your pants are down by your knees. So the lunatic from Macagua 8 was only able to take a step or two, then he let loose a horrific howl, got tangled up . . . and fell flat on the ground.

That turned out to be his Waterloo. The nurse went straight back to Calixto and avoided doing what any inexperienced girl would have done. She did not take off all her clothes and throw them into an incinerator, nor did she swallow a paracetamol or piroxicam or any other powerful analgesic, nor did she set herself under a long shower—thereby destroying all material evidence of a crime which could in the future serve to indict the delinquent, praying to all the saints that she not be pregnant, that she not have contracted AIDS or any venereal disease. Those are the kinds of things that free all sorts of bastards. But not this time. To the asshole's dismay, this nurse had some street sense. Without any drama, she went directly to the emergency room and explained everything to the doctor.

After that, everything flowed according to the law. First, there was a call to the police. Then there was a medical exam to confirm that in fact there had been a rape and to collect, among other evidence, semen, for future DNA comparison. By dawn, they had created the police sketch and had faxed it to the newsrooms at *Granma* and the other papers. This last tactic of going to the press is not a typical part of the process in cases such as this. The official media here—in other words, *the* media—usually just focus on letting us know that we live in the best and most democratic of all possible countries, that the imperialist enemy jealously tries to make us look like cowards because we were almost champions in the World Baseball Classic, that there will be sunshine and heat this afternoon with some scattered rains and lightning storms, while we will continue to do heroic battle against the mosquitoes which perpetuate the dengue epidemic, and that it's those treacherous Jews who are the real bad guys in the Middle East. It's always the same, exactly the same. And there's no crime report, of course. Whoever said there was any crime in Cuba the Beautiful? Had to be an imperialist, no question about it. Oh, I don't think there's ever been more boring media!

This, however, was an exceptional case. The rumors on the street about the malevolent psychopath and his perverse activities had far exceeded the limit of what could be an acceptable urban legend. Horribly mutilated corpses kept showing up at the morgue at a dizzying rate, while the police just ran in circles, disoriented, without a single lead, without any ideas of any kind, without anything to go on in order to even begin a manhunt. The assassin had them cornered and was making them look like fools. It had gotten rather shameless, insolent, and disrespectful. It was simply intolerable in our Socialist nation! So much that, finally, for once, they crawled for help to the media.

And the gambit paid off. A retired old man who knew by sight a certain ne'er-do-well nicknamed the Beast, and who, to top it off, had just seen him acting rather suspiciously, hiding behind a flamboyan tree in John Lennon Park no less (how shameless could he get?), rushed to offer the location of the suspect's usual hangout. And so various squad cars, with sirens going full blast, ran full speed to arrest him. It turned out that this Beast guy, so lacking in inhibitions, was not lacking a police record. He was trapped. He had already been arrested in the past for disorderly conduct when he threw glasses and bottles against the wall in some dead-end bar; for stealing a chicken (live, tied by the feet), a sack of taro, and a bunch of plantains at the farmer's market at 19th and A streets; for pickpocketing among the citizenry; for groping the female citizens' asses on the "camello" bus headed toward San Agustín; for being a peeping tom in the ladies' room in the Department of Arts and Letters at the University of Havana; and for snatching a purse from a New Zealand tourist.

As if all this weren't enough, it turned out the jerk was an immigrant from the provinces, what we call a "Palestinian," without legal residency in Havana. More than once he'd been hauled back to his birthplace at Macagua 8, out there somewhere in the wilderness around the Sierra Maestra, in the hope that the authorities that way would deal with him. But the crafty bastard always found his way back to the capital, and once here, committed new crimes. In court, he liked to rationalize his acts with a single argument that never sounded anything but frivolous, which was that he was absolutely crazy. Of course, that never did him any good, and certainly not in this case. A few hours after his last arrest, the nurse didn't so much as pause when she fingered him in the line-up at the Zapata and E streets station. A little later, she identified him again with the same aplomb, this time before the judges at the Provincial Court.

Honestly, I don't think that woman was lying, much less that she'd lost contact with reality because of nerves, which is what I thought at first, before I saw her and heard her. No way. Nothing like that. On the one hand, she seemed like a very solid woman, essentially reasonable, adult, capable of dealing with difficult circumstances without losing her head. On the other, what possible motives could she have to incriminate a poor innocent man who would have never otherwise said a word to her? Bribery? Boredom? A bet? A desire for notoriety? Pure and simple malevolence? Who knows . . . The fact is that I've gone over her story more times than I care to count, looking at it from different angles, and I have to admit that, to this day, I haven't found any contradictions or holes. Basically, the nurse's simple and direct testimony strikes me as real from A to Z. Plus, she has all that material evidence to back her up. The DNA positively identified citizen Policarpo. So then, there's no doubt that the guy threatened her with a knife, insulted her, kidnapped her, hit her, raped her, and, if she hadn't had her wits about her, would have probably killed her too. Everything seemed to fit beautifully, right? Hmm. Well, no. There's a problem. And what a problem! Something which—to my surprise—no one talked about during the trial.

It turns out that during this, his last act, the guy changed what we could call his modus operandi. What I'm saying is, he completely renovated his tactics, his style, his methods, his entire strategy for nocturnal hunting. And I'm not talking about variations on a theme, but rather a radical metamorphosis. It's as if the guy, from one minute to the next, had decided to transform himself into a person wholly different from the one he'd always been. For starters, the guy did not hang out at night on the streets of Vedado on foot, but in a car. Probably not in a Ferrari Testarossa, since that was obviously over the top. His flying saucer, as he referred to it in our phone conversations, was probably more sober, more discrete, say, a black Mercedes, a classic model, elegant but not too showy, or something like that. And also, he did not throw himself on his victims in the middle of the street, nor did he capture them by grabbing them from behind or threatening them with a knife at their throats. No sir. It's true that he had a knife, the lethal blade, but he only unsheathed it when he was going to dip it in blood. In his own way, he had excellent manners. Without ever leaving his car, he would invite girls to climb in, one at a time, with the promise that he would take them wherever they wanted. They almost always accepted, of course, and even said thanks. There are serious transportation problems in Havana. An offer like that, so generous and seemingly without ulterior motive, is not so easily dismissed. The poor girls didn't stop getting in the fateful flying saucer even after the rumor on the street about a serial killer who was out there decimating the young female population had reached its point of climax, which, if you think about it, shouldn't be all that strange. C'mon, who was going to suspect a young white man, well-off, well-dressed, and charming—what we'd call a gentleman? And, if by chance, some girl actually refused to climb into the nefarious flying saucer, he never insisted too much, he didn't chase her no matter how good she looked. He just took his music somewhere else, to find a less suspicious prey, or he would call me from his cell phone to tell me about his tribulations.

"Hey, whore, who the fuck were you talking to at this hour? It's past 3 in the morning! I'm like a fool here, calling and calling, and all the time it's busy, busy, busy . . . What were you thinking? What the fuck were you thinking, eh? I've been calling for an eternity!"

"Oh yeah? Well, take it easy, Mr. Fool. Slow down, you sound like a cranky old woman in line for potatoes. I was on the Internet."

"Internet? Shit! What the fuck were you doing? Looking at porn?"

"Yes, of course, looking at porn. Oh, Ted Bundy, it's so easy to see that money just falls from the sky for you! But that's not the case with me, you know? Not with me. I have to earn my money, because I'm working class. I was working. How do you like that little word? *Work-ing.*"

"Oh, don't flatter yourself. What working class? You mean *whoring* class? Ha! Ha! What you have to do—now, listen to my advice—is get yourself a damn cell phone and pull yourself out of this underdevelopment."

"A cell phone? Me with a cell phone? No way. Too expensive."

"My God, what a tightwad! If I don't say so myself . . . you've got to be a Jew!"

"Hey, hey! What is that, man? Don't start in on stereotypes at this hour of the night. Fine, I may well be a Jew. That's okay. I accept that. Hey, in the end, nobody's perfect . . . But you, my dear, are much worse than me. You're a Nazi."

"Nazi? This here . . . ? Ha! Ha! That's a good one, little whore! I like that one. I really like that one. I *looooove* it! Ha! Ha!"

"You *looooove* it, eh? Hmm. I knew you would. You're a piece of work."

"Tell me about it. I'm a helluva guy. Always have been and always will be!"

"Kiss, kiss—kisses for you! But hey, big guy, now that you've called, tell me, lay it on the line, tell me everything. What are you waiting for? Tell your momma a delicious, dark, spine-tingling story . . . I'm all ears. C'mon, how'd you do tonight?"

"Fucked up! Ufff! I haven't gotten a thing. Can you believe that, slut? Nothing. There was a meatball standing at the corner of 23rd and Paseo, next to the traffic light. I think she was looking for a ride . . . but I'm not sure. She didn't want to get in the goddamn flying saucer—she just refused! You know what that imbecile told me? To mind my own business! Did you hear me, you ugly thing? Yes, just like that. That's what she said. To mind my own business. As if I—me!—as if I could give three shits about anything in her retarded life . . . What a bitch! That's what she is. That's it exactly: an ungrateful bitch. You understand?"

"No, my love. I can't understand how anyone would dare treat you in such a vulgar way. You're right, as always. That girl on 23rd and Paseo is nothing but an ungrateful bitch. You do her a favor just by noticing her, which she surely doesn't deserve, and look at how she repays you . . . Daddy, there's no respect, no one has any moral values anymore. Our whole culture is in crisis. Do you know why? Because of globalization and neoliberalism."

"Oh, well said. A better world is possible! Ha! Ha! But

you know, you sarcastic bitch, these things would never happen if you were with me, at least now and then . . . Not because I can't do it alone, of course—don't ever think that, okay, bitch?—I don't need you one twit! But the girls, if they saw a couple instead of just a guy . . . well, you know, they'd feel safer. Don't you think? Oh yes! They'd all fall in the trap! Each and every one of them! Ha! Ha! C'mon, Momma, c'mon, don't be so hard on me . . . C'mon, what's the big deal with helping me out, huh? Look, just tell me whenever you want me to come by in the flying saucer and I'll—"

"Please, stop that, for God's sake. Don't you get tired of that, baby? I've already told you a million times *yes*, I think it's an genius idea; I'm going to go out with you one of these nights and do whatever you want . . . when I'm done with my work. What language do I need to use for you understand? Don't be so immature, man."

"Work, work, work! What an obsession! You're going to burn out, Momma. Believe me, I'm serious. You're going to go nuts if you continue like that. Absolutely nuts. Because that's no way to live, working away in your cave like that. And anyway . . . what is your work?"

"Nothing important. Forget it. I've already told you: As soon as I'm done with this, we'll go out together, we'll go hunt bunnies. Do you think I don't want to go? Of course I want to go. Hmm. Very much. Ted Bundy, you have no idea how much fun we're going to have!"

"Bunnies? Mmm. I get hard just hearing you say it . . . So when the fuck do we get together?"

"Well, I don't know . . . exactly. But I'll let you know, don't worry. Soon."

Besides the business with the car, there were other discrepancies between the nurse's story and the guy's previous mischief. In the past, he'd never cared if anyone saw his face. He didn't kill his victims to keep them from reporting the kidnapping, rape, and torture. He killed them *because*—because of hate, because of boredom, because of some atavistic blood thirst, or because of revenge, or because of power, or because whatever. The fact is, he always went out to kill. What the hell did he care if the passengers in his flying saucer got a good look at him? There was even the possibility that he actually wanted them to see him as he went about his infernal exploits, that he actually showed himself on purpose, as if he were saying, "This is me, yes, me, you piece of shit, so what? In the end—ha! ha!—there's nothing you can do anyway," or something along those lines.

For his part, he never said he was crazy during our conversations. To the contrary, he considered himself quite sane, and more lucid than most. He was capable of distinguishing between good and evil as well as I could, or as well as anyone, except that he preferred evil deliberately, just because he had the blessed balls to commit it—that's how he said it—and he bragged about it without the slightest inhibition. According to his philosophy, there are two kinds of people in the world: the strong and the weak. The former (among whom he, of course, included himself) have every right, by virtue of their very strength, to destroy the latter whenever and however they choose. And if the written law didn't sanction this, well, too bad; those laws were hypocritical and unjust and there was no reason to respect them. In any case, he was above any law. Why? *Because.* That's why.

I remember I asked him one night what he considered the ideal parameters to catalog anyone as strong or weak. He said that I belonged to the weak group, of course, because I was female, but that, for the moment, he would spare my life because he got such a kick—oh, yes, such a kick! ha! ha!—out of my aimless arrogance, the utter lack of originality in my philosophical ideas (I fear I have never in my life generated even one solitary idea that could be considered philosophical, but, hey, why argue?), and my delusions of grandeur. Mine— that's right, *mine*. Hmm. Honestly.

"Listen to me, you idiot," he continued in his condescending tone, "and let's see if you wake up. To *not* squash a cockroach like you with my foot every now and then is also within the power of the strong. This power thing really has its swing, I swear. Yes, because this way there's a . . . a . . . how to explain it? Oh, I know—there's a certain sense of . . . refinement. You know what I mean?"

"Oh, well, thank God," I sighed in relief. "I'm so grateful for your refinement."

"I don't want gratitude, whore. As far as I'm concerned, you can shove it up your ass. And drop the sarcasm, okay? I've never liked sarcastic people!"

"Of course, of course. Me neither. Sarcastic people? Ufff!"

As if all this wasn't enough to make me uneasy, there were other discrepancies between the guy's usual behavior and the fateful encounter with the nurse. He was an absolute fanatic when it came to hygiene, one of those guys for whom a daily bath is an impossible-to-postpone religious ritual, and dirt, any kind of dirt anywhere on the body, is a horrible blasphemy, a mortal sin. So it seems to me unlikely that he'd smell like a dead rat, or that his breath would reek. He was also a supreme hypochondriac. He lived in fear of all sorts of viruses, bacteria, molds, parasites, and other infamous microorganisms with scientific names in Latin. I think he even dreamed of hordes of bugs attacking him. Whenever he got going about contagious diseases, he was impossible to stop. His fear of contagion bordered on pathological. That's why he always used a condom during his nighttime adventures, sometimes two condoms, one on top of the other, so as not to have a mortal accident; he also wore latex gloves. The only thing left to do to reduce direct contact between himself and his victim was to wear one of those old diving masks, a diving suit, or a cosmonaut's helmet. Perhaps it's reasonable to ask how a lone rapist went about putting on all those artifacts (the condoms, the gloves) without the prisoner of the moment taking advantage of the distraction to escape. Hmm. Good question. The thing is, his methods have always been considerably more sophisticated than his last assault, which, when compared with the previous ones, was really pretty sloppy.

See, every time he got a girl—grateful and glad—to get in his car, the guy would take off. He would talk to her gently about some banality as he drove: their respective Zodiac signs (he was a Leo, or so he pretended), our shitty climate which gets shittier every year—although I suppose it can be very pleasant if you get around in an air-conditioned flying saucer—or a recent novel by Paulo Coelho, or some film by Almodóvar, President Chávez's idiotic face, the most recent reggaeton hit's grotesque lyrics, etc. The fact that his future victim thought she was safe gave this maniac untold pleasure. The asshole laughed to himself. Sometimes he'd even, ever so naturally, bring up the rumors about a serial killer who was loose out there somewhere. Of course, he didn't believe such crap, he'd say, it was pure fiction put out by the Revolution's internal enemies, mercenaries in service to the empire, out to terrify the people, disrupt order, and bring down Socialism's achievements. After tossing out this tidbit, or something like it (he had talent for this sort of thing), he'd look over at the girl, smile, and assure her that, in any case, she was in no danger, since he was there to defend her, much like Don Quixote with his Dulcinea. And they'd go on driving happily through the Havana night. Until he braked abruptly in some dark and deserted alleyway. Fast as lightning, before the girl had a chance to recover from the surprise, he'd hit her on the head with a blackjack, knocking her cold. When she came to, she'd be someplace else, in a garage whose address I never found out, her hands and feet bound to a cot, and her life now pure hell.

So is there any similarity between this and the nurse's story? Can anybody change their patterns of behavior—that is, their character, their personality—so, so much from one minute to the next? Well, in theory, yes. When it comes to human beings, I think that everything, or almost everything, is possible. In other words, anyone can give us a real surprise at any given time. But in practice, this is very unlikely, and even more unlikely when dealing with a serial killer. In general, they act in a very compulsive manner, which is why it's possible to profile them, and from that, to determine within a certain margin of error their future actions.

In spite of everything, while I was there at Criminal Court #7 of the Provincial Court of the City of Havana, after the nurse's testimony, I still waited anxiously to hear, or better yet, I *needed* to hear, that they'd also found the DNA from citizen Policarpo Meneses Landaeta, alias "The Beast of Macagua 8," on the bodies of the other victims. And if not on all of them (the condoms and the latex gloves could make it difficult, if not impossible, to collect the genetic material), in at least one. But nobody talked about that. The forensic pathologist barely mentioned this, as if it were a mere detail. The prosecutor didn't ask him about it either, which, in my opinion, meant his case against the Beast as a serial killer lost some of its weight, which is a kind way of saying it fell apart. The defense attorney could have easily used this to his advantage. He should have. But he didn't. Why? Was he some sort of fool? Hmm. Who knows. From what I could tell, nobody in that courtroom was interested in bringing it up. Not even the judges, who never asked the forensic pathologist a single question. A hell of an omission in a trial in which you could practically smell the death sentence! I just wanted to get up and scream a stream of profanities. It's not that I'm a great admirer of citizen Policarpo, that's not it. I just think that everyone who's been accused of a crime deserves the fairest possible treatment. Everyone. Even that light-skinned Negro with half a cell in his brain, if that. But I controlled myself. After all, who cares what I think? I left, totally dismayed.

I continue to be dismayed. Perhaps not as much as two months ago, when I shot out of the headquarters of the Provincial Court with my head a haze, or full of shit, which is more or less the same thing, and I was almost run over by a motorcycle while crossing Teniente Rey. Now I look both ways before risking my life to cross any street. But it's not as if I have any peace of mind. No way. If only. Yesterday, during the day for God's sake, I downed three meprobamates in a row and . . . nothing. I didn't manage one wink of sleep! Isn't this the kind of thing that makes you want to hang yourself? And the worst part is that I can't stop thinking about the guy and his many facets that do not go together . . . I fear that's not going to help me sleep but I can't help myself.

There are times when I think that something terrible happened during that trial, something as sordid as the killings themselves, something that I don't dare put into words . . . although deep down, I'm not sure. That I know of, there haven't been any more crimes like those in Havana. Other crimes, yes. Like those, no. Of course, if I really think about it, that doesn't prove much. It could just be coincidence. Maybe *somebody* went abroad, just for the season, with Daddy's help. Or maybe he's still here, lying low in his luxurious trench, waiting, like the great son of a bitch that he is, until they shoot someone in his place, to then reappear, with new vigor, to re-start his nighttime doings. Or maybe he's experienced some sort of traffic accident and might be, for example, dead, or comatose, with a leg in a cast, or his head cracked, or with any other variable that would make it impossible for him to drive. The more I think about it, the more possibilities I consider. It's more maddening than a Rubik's Cube. There are times when I scold myself, when I tell myself there was no conspiracy, that the trial was utterly transparent, that all this is nothing more than my own paranoia, that I've read too many books and I've seen too many film noirs, etc. The truth is, I don't know what the hell to believe. There are times that I feel my head is just overflowing, that it's blowing up like Cantoya's balloon, and later exploding in a million pieces . . . Ufff! Horrible. If I go on like this, I'm the one who's going to wind up in a coma. If only he would call me . . .

That's it. The telephone. That's the first word that comes to mind whenever I think of the convict. It's clear that I won't go visit him. If he's waiting to see me, which I doubt, then he should wait sitting down. I don't want any trouble. But maybe we could talk on the phone. Is there a phone on death row? I suppose there must be one, though there's none listed in the directory. I've looked, and there's nothing. A state secret. Perhaps I could find the number through some less orthodox route (c'mon, I wasn't kidding when I said I was a warrior), and then call later, from a public phone far from the Naroca, so that I won't be identified by those who are always spying, should they decide to trace the call. That little trick might work. But it still wouldn't be citizen Policarpo who answers the phone. How could I get them to put him on? Hmm. I have no idea. I'm going to have to think about it with calm. I only need a half a minute with him, maybe less. Just enough time to see if I recognize his voice . . . or not. Whichever way it went, it would be a huge relief for me. What bothers me most about all this is the uncertainty, the doubt, the suspicion . . . But how in the devil can I access him or, more precisely, his voice? How? How? How? There was a period of time when I was brilliant and could come up with all kinds of schemes to get my way in all sorts of complicated situations. But now I think I'm getting kind of dumb because of the insomnia, since I can't come up with a thing.

I don't have anything to do tonight. The work I had—that part was true—I finished at the end of last month and sent it off. I've gone back to dying my hair ash-blond, which is my natural color. So I settle languidly into the couch in my studio, with just one light on, a couple of big pillows under my head, a whiskey on the rocks, a cigarette, and the phone close at hand. Meanwhile, Horowitz plays Rachmaninov very softly, as if caressing my ears.

After forty-eight hours straight without sleep, I can't think about anything. I go off on tangents, just letting the ideas flow however they wish. London. I'm supposed to go to London, next month at the latest. But I'm not exactly dying to do the paperwork. My Israeli passport is valid everywhere in the world, I think, except here. To get through security at the airport here, I have to use my Cuban passport, which means asking for an exit permit, something I find irritating. It makes me feel like a prisoner, though I know at this point in my life I should be used to these things. Although, in service to the truth, that's not the only reason I'm reluctant to begin the process of traveling. Deep down, I don't want to fly to London, or anywhere else, because I still hold out hope that the guy will call. If my suspicions turn out to be true, if he's alive and well and loose in Havana, he will call me. Oh yes. He can't *not* call me. It's an essential part of his routine, we could even say its culmination. His thing is kidnapping, raping, killing . . . and then telling me all about it. If he calls, I'm going to go out with him. It'll have to be quick, right away, before there's another scattering of corpses and the whole city goes up in arms and something comes between us, whether it's the police or an inopportune jerk like the Beast of Macagua 8. Yes, I'm going to dive into the black of night for once. It's decided. Well, it's *always* been decided. From that first call, when he described from A to Z what he was going to do to his victim that night, and I later realized he had in fact done it to the T, well, he proved he was no joker calling just to talk stupidities. That's when I smelled blood. And I went on alert, just lying in wait. There's no point in fooling myself: I'm a predator too. Except that I'm not turned on by bunnies, I'm not turned on by easy prey. No sir. What gets me hot is always difficult, always requires ingenuity, courage, and patience; it's challenges. That's why I'm going to fire a shot right into my dear Ted Bundy's neck. I'll be his last passenger. Later, who knows . . . maybe I'll finally get some sleep.

Translation by Achy Obejas

THE SCENE

BY MYLENE FERNÁNDEZ PINTADO

Malecón

I was sitting on the terrace when the electricity went out over the part of the city that I can see from here. Just then I heard my mother calling me. She is very ill. She'll die soon. I've got a calendar in the kitchen where I've circled two dates. One is my mother's death. The other is the last day to move out of this building. I should have inverted the order, because we have to leave the building tomorrow and my mother has two weeks to live.

When my mother was first diagnosed, everyone who cares about her advised me to leave her at the hospital in the care of doctors and nurses in case of an emergency. A few volunteered to sit with her. These were the same people who insisted that I don't love her, that I'm selfish and don't know anything about sacrifice. They thought I couldn't hear them, that I'd fallen asleep in the rocking chair I brought into my mother's room so I can watch her while she rests, and to be near when she needs me.

When the building was in working order, we had a woman who came to take care of the house and a nurse who gave my mother her shots. But now they can't climb so many stairs. Now I give my mother her shots and do all the grocery shopping. I've told my mother that these people don't come anymore because we can't afford to pay them. I don't want to tell her that the building barely exists anymore.

There's no one here but us now. And since they turned off the electricity, no one comes to visit. We live on the fourteenth floor and the elevator doesn't work anymore. Nor the motor that pumps water. But none of that is important. All the water tanks on the roof are full. And there are a lot of them, so there's water all day long and there will be water long after we don't need it anymore. It's true that the refrigerator doesn't work, but I buy my mother's drinking water already chilled at the market. I buy her food there too. She only eats ham-and-cheese croissants and ice cream. Or *ate*. Lately, she barely touches food; she makes a pained gesture and abandons the plate between the sheets.

I found out about the city's plans for our building when I was asked to a meeting at the Office of Architecture and Urbanism near our home. It was on the twentieth floor on Malecón Avenue, with a view of the sea. The hallway walls were full of photos of our neighborhood in Vedado. Sometimes I think Vedado is so scattered and rife with transients that it's difficult to think of it as one neighborhood, but rather many. People like to come here, to go to Coppelia dressed in their Sunday best and spend the entire day in line, to stroll La Rampa on the sidewalks still carved with things by Lam and Mariano. They go to the movies and sit along the Malecón.

The same exact photos were on the office wall too. There was one of the seawall on the Malecón. The most curious thing was that there was no one on the seawall in the photo. Not a single fisherman or couples kissing, not one kid playing. There were no brave suicides portrayed, depressed poets, drunks, street musicians, or hustlers. It must have been one of those scenes they can create now on computers. Just erase all the people with a touch of a button.

The other photos were busier. People strolling on La Rampa, cars on Paseo and Avenue of the Presidents. Coppelia without lines, with satisfied customers eating different flavors of ice cream.

Since the man I was meeting took his time, I looked at the photos and then at the city from the balcony next to the office. There are little homemade structures all over the rooftops, mansions turned into barracks, houses that can barely stand. The rooftops have become dovecots. There are fields of laundry lines; residue of homeless people; plants that grow between the tiles on the eaves; dogs that can't be kept inside anymore so that instead of guarding homes, they've turned into lookouts who scan the horizon. Sun-drenched treetops, humid and green; church steeples. Little gray streets, a few cobblestone, which intersect, sometimes timidly, as if hiding from the multitudes. And then the sea, always lying in wait, and the Malecón which keeps us safe. It's a wall of lamentation, the entrance to and from the country of Never Again, a fixture on postcards and calendars. Therapy for my mother.

Every time my mother could gather her strength to get up, she'd ask me to take her out on the terrace. With the very first remittance sent by my brother from San Francisco—once he realized that experiencing the spectacle of my mother in the process of dying would affect his biorhythm and would keep him from his successful life as a designer—I bought a lounge chair, a down pillow, and a thin mattress pad, and she began to spend her hours sitting out there. I brought her books. But later I realized she preferred chatting. Still later, it became clear that what she wanted more than anything was to gaze at the part of the city that was ours. One day she said, in a whisper, that she'd never had much time to look at the sky and that the clouds passed much too quickly.

On those afternoons, she discovered a million things. She heard the sound of the bells from San Juan of Letrán and the songs from the day care center nearby; the whistle of the scissors sharpener; the riot of pigeon wings on the roof across from us. And then, as soon as the sun started buzzing on the water, I'd take her back to her room.

We talked about the buildings around us and what they might be like inside. We would describe those we'd actually visited and later make ambitious plans about how we would renovate them without tearing down the original structures.

I had time to think about all this until the man I was meeting came and asked me into his office. Almost giddy as he spoke, he explained that our building would be going through a major renovation, and that the current tenants would be given new housing according to their needs. I explained that we needed to stay. I told him about the situation with my mother and that I wasn't sure we could move her.

The man understood that my situation was delicate. But so was his. He had plans to complete, deadlines and tasks, expenses that had been given the okay in order to procure resources. Everything was architecturally and financially aligned. Emptying the building was just the first task. But he could give me an extension. I smiled—sometimes I can be truly charming—and thanked him. As we were saying goodbye, I felt that he wanted to say something, maybe just the usual good wishes for recuperation, but he seemed to think better of it and kept quiet.

That same day, I met with the doctor; I was ready to have my mother at home until the day she died. I explained about the therapeutic qualities of the terrace, how she delighted in the architectural view, the sea, and the dawn. I told him I'd been born in that neighborhood, in that house, and that my mother felt in her element there. I said nothing about the plans to empty out the building.

The doctor was glad to hear our home was fresh and high up, with sun and light, air and space. He was also glad it had such a good view of the water and said that Vedado reminded him of Manhattan. I nodded so he'd feel comfortable and I got his approval. He told me that if I made sure we had the proper conditions, I could keep her there until she died.

I then quickly talked to him about my brother and his help. The doctor asked if my brother had any plans to visit my mother. I lied, saying that his papers were still not in order and that he suffered a lot because he couldn't come.

A few weeks after that, my neighbors began moving out of the building, many coming by for a last goodbye. But my mother didn't pay much attention to them. The morphine and phenobarbital left her with just a few lucid moments, and I took advantage of them to bring her out on the terrace, where we would continue "renovating" Vedado. Everyone asked when we were leaving. Everybody was very concerned about the work on the building and how soon even the most minimal of services would be unavailable. I calmed them down, saying that everything was ready, that I'd made the pertinent arrangements with the hospital to comfortably transport my mother using a powerful anesthetic the minute the psychologist determined it was appropriate.

After they all left, there came a happy time, having a sixteen-story building all to ourselves, knowing that no neighbor would stop me in the hallways to ask me the same things: how she was this morning, how much morphine she was taking, if she was eating, when my brother was coming, and, poor woman, what bad luck . . . I never gave an honest answer: My mother woke up radiant every day, spent hours entertained with her 2000-piece jigsaw puzzles (her collection of puzzles, all famous portraits, was well known), and the morphine was just so she'd sleep quietly. The stampede out of the building spared me the obligation of lying to them all, though I'd never felt the slightest bit guilty about it.

The best part was the sensation that came over me when I arrived home after getting morphine, or juice, or phenobarbital, the syringes, or something for her cravings. I walked 17th Street in the shade of the laurel trees and came in the entrance without worrying about the manager, vendors, or people looking to trade housing, knowing that I had exclusive rights to the place. There was no one murmuring behind the doors that my brother was a jerk who thought money could solve everything, or that I have a heart of steel and what I really wanted was for my mother to finally die. The theories vary on this last hypothesis.

The simplest one is that I'll finally be able to go live with my brother. The truth is that we were always very close; the two of us would play house, and cowboys, and later we both ended up studying art and architecture. He adored the houses designed by Le Corbusier and I was taken by the Impressionists. Now he's in San Francisco, sending money so I don't need to do anything other than care for our mother until she dies.

Another theory, which requires more neighborly shrewdness but is actually expired, is related to the Sorbonne professor who used to visit me because he was interested in the Cuban movie posters I had once researched. He would come by frequently, long after he'd viewed the entire national poster collection, finished his thesis, and curated his exhibit. Then the real goal of his visits became sleeping together as much as possible, to which I had no objections. Just around the time my mother got sick, he invited me to Paris to give a series of presentations on how the French posters of 1968 had influenced Cuba. Though I wrote out my script at first, I ultimately answered that I could not travel because of my mother's illness. And I apologized, as though my mother's death were a mere inconvenience disrupting his magnum plans. He has never written again.

For those neighbors who don't sign on to either of those two theories, there's a more general option, which doesn't really pin anything concrete on me. According to this one, I want to be free so I can do whatever I want, like sleep with lots of men and women; drink until I fall on my ass; smoke marijuana and take pills and watch a lot of porno films on giant screens with quadraphonic sound. In other words, to manifest this dark side which my ex-neighbors insist on having seen in me since I was a little girl. They're convinced that my mother not having left for paradise yet is the only reason I haven't descended into hell.

Now that we're without them—they're far away, furnishing other homes and surely missing Vedado and its excellent bus routes (on which no buses actually pass) and its movie theaters (always without air-conditioning in the summer) and Coppelia (with its serpentine lines) and the Malecón (which is the only real populated part of Vedado, because it's free)—my mother and I are quite content.

She doesn't know that the neighbors have moved out and so she innocently enjoys the magical breeze that has blown away the radio and its shrill music, the hammering at 6 in the morning, dogs barking all through the night, fights between parents and children, brothers and sisters, husbands and wives.

A little after the neighbors left, our phone was disconnected. I thought God was on my side. In any case, I'd had it off the hook for most of the last few weeks. That was how I had avoided giving a health report every five minutes to the curious; the worst part was hearing their comforting words and the sense that, behind them, there was such relief that it was my mother and not theirs who was about to ride with Charon.

When they cut the gas, I started using the two-burner hotplate we kept for emergencies. My mother was eating less every day. So when we finally lost our electricity too, there wasn't much to worry about.

I fired the nurse, who cried a bit as she showed me how to give my mother her shots, regulate the oxygen pump, take her blood pressure, and raise the Fowler bed to the right height so my mother could get up. I also learned to smile when I wanted to cry and to convince myself that she was going to die anyway.

We have been very happy here, my mother and I, absolute rulers of this beautiful building in ruins, I thought as I left the terrace to answer my mother's call on the last night in my neighborhood. When I went back, the city was black. I imagined that the tourists on the cruise ship—the only line of lights on the water—must have a very interesting view. What must it be like to face a city completely in the dark?

When my mother called me—thank God the building's empty or the neighbors' noises would have never let me hear her, especially now that her voice is not much more than a whisper—she said she was very tired. But it wasn't exactly a complaint, more of a statement of fact. My mother, who had never been the kind of Catholic who sat in church pews or wore chains with little crucifixes, had had a priest visit just a few days before.

I had tried to make sure the priest was as young as possible, so he could make it up all fourteen flights. I found one who did all his rounds on a bike, so that the elevator not working didn't strike him as a great obstacle. Nonetheless, he was exhausted when he arrived and needed some time to get himself together out on the terrace, looking at the sea and the nearby buildings. He said it gave him a great deal of peace. I told him about my mother, how much she enjoyed it too, and that I'd found a way for her to have pleasant days out on those few square meters. I didn't tell the priest that we only had a few days before we had to move out of the building.

They spent four hours chatting. I spent the time sitting back on my mother's lounge chair, with her pad and her pillow, trying to see our view of the city through her eyes. I imagined her opening her eyes in the hospital or in some other house. And then I closed my own eyes firmly to shut out this image.

After the priest's visit, my mother slept for forty-eight hours straight. I think the absence of telephone, electricity, and neighbors helped. I don't think it rained, or that the north wind blew, that humid breeze that smudges the windows and gives Vedado an air of impatience and cosmopolitanism. I think that after this dialogue with God, my mother began preparing herself to die.

Now, with tonight's deadline approaching, I hear her say in a weary voice that she's very tired. It's midnight and she doesn't even have the strength to stir in bed. Anyway, there's nothing to see outside. Nor inside either. I'm going to find the battery-powered lamp in the kitchen so I can look at the calendar, the one that reminds me that we must leave the building tomorrow and that my mother still has two weeks of life.

I come back with the lamp and she's fallen asleep, complaining through her dreams. What must it be like to never get relief, even from sedatives? Or to close your eyes and not open them again? Or to spend your last days in a strange place?

I start to fix the syringe. I do it very slowly, and it's not because I'm clumsy; I've actually gotten quite agile with this business of giving shots. I review all the decisions I've made in the last few days. After my mother passes, I will not go to San Francisco; there's nothing for me there. It's possible my presence would disrupt my brother's biorhythm and inhibit his successful life as a designer.

Nor will I go to Paris to look for the poster man. A person who's incapable of writing two lines to ask about my sick mother is not anyone I can trust. In any case, I've got my presentation written. It doesn't matter to me if it gets published. It felt good to write it. It was like old times, as if my brother and mother were out on the terrace with me, with our toy soldiers, dolls, or jigsaw puzzles, depending on the day.

Now I hold the syringe in my right hand. I make sure the needle can spit out the first few drops, which indicate all is well, and I make my way to the bedroom. I don't need the lamp. I've gotten to know my mother's body well in these dark but blissful days. I should move out of the building tomorrow. With my free hand, I go to the calendar and mark off my mother's dying day. And then I go to her.

Translation by Achy Obejas

STARING AT THE SUN

BY LEONARDO PADURA

Marianao

I t's been two hours I've been staring at the sun. I like to look at the sun. I can look at the sun for an hour straight, without blinking, without tears.

I'm still staring at the sun, leaning against the wall at the corner, listening to the old women as they come out of the bakery, complaining about how shitty the bread is but eating it anyway cuz they're dying of hunger. On this corner, you can smell the smoke from the buses as they pass by on the avenue, the stink from the many dogs who think they've found something in that awful piece of bread, the bitter stench of desperation, like in that shitty song my mother likes. It's a disgusting corner and I think I like it even more for that very reason; I spend huge chunks of time here, waiting for something to come along, just staring at the sun. I'm singing a little bit of that song and don't notice when Alexis comes up.

"Hey, man, what's going on?" he asks.

"Nothing. You?"

"Hanging."

"Cool," I say, looking at Alexis. I suppose Alexis is my best friend. We've known each other from before we even went to school, from when his father and mine worked together at the Ministry. Later, they fucked over Alexis's dad, but not too much, cuz he had good friends. They didn't even take

his car, although they did relieve him of his gun. That, yeah.

"Let's go get a liter," he says.

"Who's got some?"

"Richard El Cao."

"C'mon," I say, and I forget about the sun and the bitter vapors . . . Fuck, it's actually the bitter taste of desperation. Same shit.

El Cao always has liquor. Sometimes it's good. Sometimes he also has pills. He gets them easily: He steals a script from his mother, who works as an administrator at a hospital, and he signs her name, and then they give him the best pills at the pharmacy. Easy, right? But there are no pills today. We took the last ones yesterday, with four liters of liquor. Yesterday was fucked up.

Now we're drinking, not talking. It's always like this: At first, you hardly talk. It's as if your brain goes dead for a while. Later, we talk a bit, especially if we pop some pills. Alexis and El Cao talk the most.

After we've been drinking awhile, Alexis says, "There's a fight today."

"At El Hueco?" El Cao asks.

Alexis nods.

"I don't have any money," El Cao says.

"Me neither," I say.

"I do," Alexis says, and since he's been drinking, he tells the whole story of how he got the cash: There were about twenty liters of oil, the good cooking kind, in the trunk of his father's car, and he stole three. He sold them, so he has money. Three hundred pesos.

"Let's go," says El Cao.

"Let me finish," says Alexis.

We drink a little more. This liquor's pretty good. When we finish drinking, that's when we leave.

When we arrive, the fight hasn't started yet. We're told today it's Yoyo's stanford against Carlitín's boxer. I like the stanford. His name is Verdugo and he's won like twenty fights. He almost always kills the other dog. The boxer is also somewhat famous: His name is Sombra and they say once he clamps down, he doesn't let go. There are already twelve people here, waiting. There are two black guys, with their gold teeth and Santería necklaces around their necks. They must be Carlitín's friends. He's always hanging out with black guys like that. He has business dealings with them, and sometimes he pulls jobs with them too.

The betting begins. Alexis puts his three hundred pesos on Verdugo. I tell him to set aside fifty, for another liter in case he loses. But he says no, that there's still plenty of cooking oil in his father's car and Verdugo's gonna win.

They set the dogs. And everybody's screaming. Myself included. They let them loose. Verdugo sinks his teeth into Sombra's shoulder, drawing blood on the very first bite. It's practically black, this blood. Drops of this practically black blood swirl around Verdugo's mouth and drop on the ground. Then the screaming intensifies. Sombra starts to turn and gets ahold of Verdugo's paw. He's gonna tear it off. Verdugo's gonna leap right over him and Sombra's unaware. Then Verdugo hits his neck. Carlitín and Yoyo jump in to separate them but Verdugo won't let go, and neither will Sombra. They jam sticks in their mouths to control them. Sombra lets go first but comes around the side; Verdugo still won't let go. Yoyo finally pries his mouth open and Sombra drops: Two streams of blood pour from his neck, even blacker and thicker. The

boxer's dead. Everybody's still shouting and the losers start to pay up. Carlitín kicks his dead dog. Alexis gets his winnings, two hundred pesos, and tells one of the black guys to pay the hundred they bet. The black guy says the fight was bullshit. Alexis says he doesn't give a shit about that, what matters is his hundred. The black guy says he's not paying shit. Alexis says he can stick it up his ass. The black guy pulls a piece and sticks it in Alexis's face.

"What you say, you little white shit?" the black guy asks, then hits his jaw with the gun's butt.

Alexis doesn't say anything. The other black guy has a knife in his hands and is looking around at everybody else. The two black guys laugh. Nobody moves. Should I do something, given that Alexis is my friend? I make my move.

"Let it be, bro," I yell at the black guy. "Alexis, forget the cash."

"Fine, big guy, you win," Alexis says, and the black guy pushes him and laughs. The other black guy joins him. They leave without turning their backs. I like black guys less and less all the time. I swear to God that's true.

Alexis talks even less than usual. And he drinks more. Between him, me, El Cao, and Yovanoti—that's what we call Ihosvani now—we've downed two liters and a third's almost gone. There's one more. Here, on El Cao's roof, there's no fear: We're encircled by a Peerless fence and, even if we get drunk, no one can fall off. Then somebody calls El Cao from the street corner.

"Richard, Richard!" a woman shouts. Or two women.

It's two: Niurka and Betty. El Cao tells them to come up. They come up. They already know the black guys hit Alexis, cuz the whole neighborhood knows. They're thirsty so we start the fourth liter.

"Either of you got anything?" I ask, but they play dumb. These two love to play dumb. "Don't play dumb," I tell them.

"I've got two parkisonil left," Betty says, so I ask her for them. They're two little white pills. I think I wanna have one. But I give them to Alexis, who swallows them with a gulp of liquor.

"Stop thinking about those black guys," I say.

"I'm gonna get them back," Alexis says, then lays down on the ground, closes his eyes, shakes a little, and starts to fly. That little parkisonil is a rocket when it's fueled by liquor.

It's nighttime and, since there's no sun, I stare at the moon. I don't like it as much, but it's better than nothing. Betty is still sucking me off, and though I'm hard and the head is red hot, I don't feel like coming. Sometimes it's like that: It just feels swollen. Alexis is still sleeping on the floor while El Cao is sticking it up Niurka's ass and Yovanoti rests. I think he's singing, softly. I have the seventh bottle from our ordeal in my hand and I take another swallow. Suddenly, I don't wanna be sucked off and I take it out of Betty's mouth.

"Get on all fours," I say, and I start to fuck her up the ass, and I think about movies in which men are sticking it up the ass of some woman. But nothing happens anyway; I'm not gonna come tonight.

"Here, my man," I say to Yovanoti, and he comes over and Betty sucks him.

I start to look at the moon again, take another swallow, and fall asleep.

When I open my eyes, I see the sun. I'm alone on the roof.

I don't know why there are days I like to come to church. Not to pray or to think about God, cuz I never learned to pray and I was spared the whole speech about God and the saints and the angels. I just like to come. My parents don't care anymore if I come, cuz it's not seen as a bad thing anymore. A few years ago it was really bad, and they didn't like it when I came here. You don't believe in squat, they said to me. Don't you know that could get us in trouble? What the hell do you think you'll find in church anyway? they asked. I just shrugged: I didn't know then and I don't know now. Well, I do know one thing: I like it cuz I feel calm. But I don't pray or think about God. I just look at him, nailed up there.

This car runs really well. El Kakín spends the whole day cleaning it, tuning it up, putting little things on it. Whenever El Kakín's father's abroad, he gets the car all day. Sometimes he lets us know. *Everybody, go to the beach*, and then we all go to the beach. Like today. Alexis is still pissed off about what happened with the black guys. He doesn't even wanna get in the water. He just drinks rum and every now and then mutters, Fuck those black guys. Me, El Kakín, Yovanoti, and El Cao all get in the water. The water's wonderful today. We get out and drink a little rum, and then I go back in the water and shit and the turd follows me around. But we go back in. Then we go back out, drink more rum, and Vivi and Annia show up. Since we've been drinking so much, we talk for a while. Annia says she's leaving for La Yuma[1], her and her entire family. Some people from a church—Jehovah's Witnesses—got them the visas. They go to that church once a week. They sing, they pray a lot, and everybody thinks they really believe in all that, now that they don't smoke, or drink, or curse, or harbor ill will

[1]*Cuban slang for the U.S.*

in their hearts, as Annia says. But my brother's always losing his temper, she says later. Well, it doesn't really matter that they don't believe in Jehovah, since what they want is to get to La Yuma, just like a bunch of other people I know. Not me, though. They say there's everything over there, but you have to work like a dog. El Cao says he doesn't wanna go either; he does fine with moonshine and pills no matter where he's at. El Kakín wants to go: He wants his own car, with five-speed transmission, four-wheel drive, eight cylinders, diesel motor, hydraulic suspension, cruise control. He knows that car like he already owns it. Alexis says he wants to go too: He says you kill a black guy over there and they give you a thousand dollars. He's obsessed with black guys.

But the one who likes La Yuma most is Yovanoti. He's always talking about it, about how well everybody lives over there, about his brother who owns the racing track in Miami, and that other cousin who, just two months after arriving, was already sending his mother a hundred dollars a month, and about his ex–brother-in-law who has a restaurant, I think, in New Jersey. He says if he ever gets there, he'll give up alcohol and pills and marijuana, even cigarettes, so he can earn a lot of money. Then he takes another chug of rum. And he talks some more.

Since I haven't taken any pills in two days, I'm gonna have fun now. Vivi has a very narrow little ass. At first, you don't think you can get it in, but she opens up good, tickles herself with her finger, and then takes a deep breath and says, "Put it in me." And then you just push a little and it goes in all the way. The downside is that I wanna go a little longer before coming but I come really fast, and then I can't get it back up. El Cao always gets it up: He's come twice in Vivi and once in Annia. I don't know how El Cao can come so much. He hardly ever eats. Alexis didn't wanna do anything. He wants a pill. It looks like he jerked off and drank some rum so he wouldn't get bored.

"Look," Alexis says, and he shows me a strip of pills.

"Where'd you get that, man?" El Cao asks, dazed.

"I stole them from my grandmother."

El Cao cracks up. "Man, what if something happens to the old lady?"

"She can die, for all I care," Alexis says, and he takes two with a chug of liquor.

He gives me two and hands two over to Richard El Cao and two for Yovanoti and he keeps two more for himself.

The good thing about pills is that you really don't have to keep drinking. They multiply what you already have in your belly, I think, by, like, ten. They're also good cuz if you're not drunk, then you wanna talk, fuck, listen to music. Well, for a while at least. Alexis starts talking.

"I need you to lend me your old man's piece," he says to me.

El Cao cracks up again. "You're gonna kill those black guys over one hundred shitty pesos?"

"Yeah, one hundred shitty pesos and cuz they're mothafuckas, those shit fuckin' black faggots. I need the gun," he says.

"You're crazy, Alexis," I say.

"Fuck crazy. You gonna lend it to me or not?"

"Trouble, man."

"No trouble. Bring it tonight and in three hours I'll have it back to him."

"You don't even know where those black guys live."

"I'll find out—where they live, where they drink their beer, where they bet on cockfights, where they play the lottery, where they smoke pot, where they steal hens. They're two dead black guys. Just lend me the fucking gun. Look," he says, and he sticks his hand in his pocket and pulls out six bullets. He takes another chug of the rum with the last two pills.

"You're crazy, Alexis," I say, but I don't think he hears me.

Yovanoti got a movie and we're gonna watch it in his room on the VCR. First, there are two blondes. It looks like they just got home from work, cuz they're carrying purses and that sort of thing. But they start undressing each other right away and they get a really good lezzie thing going. Just when they're getting hot, a mulatta comes in, pushes them apart, and joins them. The mulatta has a red pussy which is practically hairless and must weigh about ten pounds. The two blondes lick the mulatta all over, until one of them pulls out a dildo and straps it on. She sticks it in the mulatta until she comes. While all that's going on, El Cao is the first to take out his dick and start jerking off. Then me. Then Alexis. Then Yovanoti. Then the other blonde in the movie, so she's not left with nothing to do, starts jerking off too. The worst part of all this is how it smells like jism in the bedroom now. I keep thinking about the mulatta's pussy. Just for a while. Cuz now another movie has started and El Cao has brought out a bottle of liquor.

I wake up during the night. I think I'm still in Yovanoti's room. Alexis is still sleeping, on the bed now. Vanessa is naked and sleeping too. El Cao and Yovanoti are gone. Vanessa, the blonde, is between Alexis and me. That seems odd cuz Vanessa never fucks us, much less without protection. She says we're savages, that we're all gonna die from AIDS and that we leave bruises and what she wants is a Yuma to give her dollars and let her live in Paris. I don't know what her deal is with Paris. But that's Vanessa, and the truth is she's hot. She's got a little lock of blond hair on her fat pussy and two tits that are even hotter. All of a sudden, I get a hard-on. I touch Vanessa but she doesn't even flinch. I stick a finger inside her and realize her crack is all slippery. It seems to be jism. I rub my finger on my dick, to get it wet. Then I shove it in her. She remains the same. How'd she get like this? I keep on fucking her until I get bored and then I pull out. I suck her tits for a while. She laughs, asleep, and I stick it back in her and this time I come. But not much.

I look out the window and see that it's raining. I hadn't noticed. I don't know what time it is. It must be very late cuz there's no one on the corner and I'm a little hungry. There are some burned papers on the floor. Of course, we must have smoked some pot. But I don't remember. There's a liter bottle with three fingers of rum left. I drink it to calm my hunger then lay back down. But beforehand, I suck Vanessa's tits again for a little while, thinking the whole time about the mulatta's pussy.

Since El Kakín hasn't shown up, we take off for the coast, where the water's just fine. The drag here are the rocks on the bottom. One time, I almost cracked my head open. Of course, I dove in drunk. You can still see the scar: They gave me sixteen stitches, and since I was so drunk, the anesthesia didn't take. Better to forget about all that. I drink some more rum and listen to El Cao, who just yaks on like a fucking parrot.

"So I go up to the Yuma and say, *Míster, guat yu guan?*

Girls, rum, tobacco, marijuana? And the guy's a little scared.
Since he was blond and pink, he got red. *Nosing, nosing,* he
tells me, and I say, *No problem, mister, yo tengo lo que yu guan.*
And the guy, *Nosing, nosing,* but by then Yovanoti was right
behind him and I just landed one, and Yova got one in behind
his ear, and I grabbed his backpack and kicked him in the balls
so hard, I think one came out his ear . . . I swear! So we took
off and when I turned around about a block later, there's the
guy still shaking on the ground, so we slowed down a little.
We went through the backpack and trashed all the crap, until
we found his wallet and realized the sucker was German. And
you know how much money he had? Ten miserable dollars.
Yovanoti had to hold me back, cuz I just wanted to go back
and give him two more kicks. What the fuck is that, all the
way from Germany with only ten dollars on him? That's what
we used to buy these liters . . ."

We laugh, a lot. And we drink more rum.

Then Yovanoti says, "Let us drink to the solidarity between
the German and Cuban peoples!" And we drink some more.

Alexis doesn't drink this time. He says, "So you gonna get
me your father's piece?"

"You're still tripping on that?"

"Are you gonna get it for me or not?"

"Fuck, Alexis, you know he doesn't let it out of his sight,
not even when he's taking a crap."

"He sleeps with it?"

"Of course not."

"Then . . ."

Alexis laughs when he sees the gun. It's a Makarov and it's so
clean, it looks new. I hand it to him and he just stares at it. He
really does like pieces like that. Not me.

El Cao and Yovanoti also look it over. "That's a nice one," they say.

Alexis takes out the clip and empties it. He puts in his own bullets, one by one.

"Tomorrow, the whole world should pay me tribute," he says. "There are gonna be two fewer black guys. Let's go," he says, and we leave.

But first we take a couple swallows of rum. Or three.

"I'm sure they're there," Alexis says, and he shows us the house. "That's where they go to drink beer."

And so we wait at the corner. No one speaks. While we wait, I look at the moon. Tonight, it's round and very bright. This corner's shitty, I like mine better. It smells of piss here. Yovanoti is smoking cigarette after cigarette. Richard El Cao is sitting on the ground; he's singing, softly. Alexis just stares at the house.

"That's where those mothafuckas are," he finally says.

The two black guys come out and head for the other corner. We go after them, unhurried. We turn the corner and see them make like they're looking into this one house. They're probably gonna pull something there. All black guys are the same. Well, almost all. My father says not all black guys are thieves but that all thieves are black. And he says black people have five senses, just like whites. Except that they have two for music and three for stealing. He should know, since he's a cop. That's why he laughs so hard when he tells these jokes and when he talks about the black guys they've arrested. When they're in jail, he says, those black guys aren't so tough.

We continue along the sidewalk and when we get near the black guys, they feign indifference and light cigarettes. Even though there's so much moonlight, they don't seem to recognize us. As soon as we're in front of them, we jump them and Alexis shows the piece. The black guy who held the knife sees it first. What a black rat he is. He takes off and that costs him his life: Alexis lets fly some lead and the guy falls to the ground. He starts thrashing, like a rabid dog, and Yovanoti and I kick him and yell at him, Black faggot, you got scared, huh, you black faggot. We do that until he shivers really weird and gets stiff, with his tongue hanging out. The other black guy's just standing there, frozen, seeing how his buddy's dead as a doornail. Alexis stands in front of him.

"Now you're gonna pay me my hundred pesos, aren't you?" he says, and hits him on the nose with the piece.

"Fuck, white boy, no need to be this way," the guy says, and shoves his hand in his pocket.

"Careful!" screams El Cao, and Alexis doesn't think: He shoots him right in the head. The black guy's head explodes and rolls back. Even I get splattered with his blood. It's practically black, like the dog's, although it's got little white dots. Then the black guy falls and Alexis leans down to talk to him, though I don't think the guy can hear him anymore.

"See what happens to tough little black guys like you and your buddy?" He takes the guy's hand out of his pocket. The black guy doesn't have a gun today, just a roll of bills: more than five hundred.

Since everybody on the block's already looking and screaming, we start running. That's when everything gets fucked up: Two cops appear on the corner and Alexis doesn't even give it a thought. He never gives anything a thought. And with the aim he's got. He shoots and downs one, and the other one flees. We run off and no one else comes after us.

If you kill two black delinquents, you get in trouble. But if you kill a cop, then things go from bad to the very worst. We know this, which is why we all agree when El Cao speaks up.

"Let's steal a boat from the river and head for La Yuma, cuz this is really bad now; this is what happens when you hang out with punks like this," he says, taking the gun from Alexis. When Alexis starts to say something, El Cao interrupts him: "Shut up or I'll shut you up."

It's been two hours now I've been staring at the sun. I like looking at the sun. I can look at the sun without dropping my lids, with my pupils intact, and without tears. It's been two hours since the boat ran out of fuel and more than four that we've been without water. It's been at least an hour since Alexis slipped off the side, when he went to drink some sea water and never came back. Yovanoti says a shark probably got him. Then he starts to cry and babble, "I'm glad, I'm glad," and to spit in the water. I don't like that. I think Alexis was my best friend.

I've never worried so much about time passing. Richard El Cao says it'll be dark in two hours, and that this is good. I don't know if it's so good. The best thing would be to be on the corner, listening to the bitching of the old women, singing a little, and staring at the sun. Without water, without food, without rum in the middle of the ocean, yeah, there's nothing better . . . It stinks of vomit and shit. If an American coast guard doesn't show up, we're fucked. And if one does show up, we're even more fucked. I ask myself, What the fuck am I doing on this boat? I wanna throw myself in the water like Alexis, but I control myself.

It's nighttime and I fall asleep.

The sun's fucked up, intense. My head hurts a little. I'm really sleepy. It's been awhile since Yovanoti has said anything about what he's gonna do when he gets to La Yuma. He's thrown up so much he doesn't have anything left to throw up. He's just oozing green spit. El Cao says we should think about good things, we shouldn't think about how thirsty we are. That's hard to do. I think about sucking Vanessa the blonde's tits and then I think about being in church and then about the corner. Later, still, I think about the mulatta's pussy, the one from the movie. And, to be honest, I do feel better, I even get a hard-on.

When El Cao speaks up again, he says, "Now it's night-time again."

Yovanoti starts to cry and El Cao slaps him twice. So that he'll calm down. Then Yovanoti throws up a little more. There's not much moon tonight and I can't see anything; I don't stare at anything either.

When I wake up, I see the sun and I see the helicopter. It doesn't look like the Cuban police. From way up there, with a bullhorn, they shout down something in English. When I look around the boat, I see only El Cao, just lying there, fainted, I think. Yovanoti is nowhere to be seen. To think he was the one who most wanted to go live in Miami. Tough luck. I really need a chug of rum right about now. I splash some water in El Cao's face and he wakes up, but he stays down.

"We're saved," I tell him, but I'm very sleepy again. I open my eyes real wide and look up at the sun, just as if I were back on my corner, and I sing a little of that song about the bitter smell of desperation.

Translation by Achy Obejas

PART II

ESCAPE TO NOWHERE

THE DINNER

BY Carolina García-Aguilera

Flores

Señor Luis, I walked all over Havana, I promise, I went everywhere, all over—but nothing!" Eladio Martínez was close to tears as he stood wringing his hands on a rag of a handkerchief that was once beautiful, beautiful linen. "I couldn't find any!"

Eladio reached out for the railing around the terrace, balanced himself, and then slowly raised his feet—first one, then the other. He wanted his employer to see that the soles of his shoes had eroded almost completely, so much so that the paper he'd lined them with was also worn through in places, and the balls and heels of his feet were walking directly on the ground.

"Just like the other times, Señor Luis, nothing!"

"Thank you, Eladio, I know you tried your best—it's not your fault. As always, I appreciate all your work." Luis Rodríguez-López looked down at the shoes and shook his head in sorrow. Lifting his head then, as if it were heavy, he gave Eladio a wan smile. "I'm so sorry about your shoes. I'll see what can be done; maybe get you a new pair to replace those."

Even if Luis had been able to afford to purchase a new pair of shoes, it would be highly unlikely he would find them, as footwear was either in very short supply or priced out of reach in present day Cuba. Life in the Special Period was brutal, a never-ending struggle for survival. Both men knew that Eladio's loss in trying to accomplish what Luis had asked of him was permanent.

Eladio raised his right hand, and then slowly, as discreetly as possible, dabbed his forehead with his handkerchief. Even in such extreme heat, gentlemen did not show sweat. But in the steaming air—and wiping with a bit of fabric worn to a fragile lace—fresh sweat continued to pour down his face.

"I would appreciate that, Señor Luis," Eladio replied, though he knew there was no chance that the señor would be able to fulfill his promise. "New shoes would be nice." They had both been living such a duplicitous life, pretending all was as before for so long.

Luis nodded. "You look so very hot and tired. Please, go inside the house and drink some water, and rest."

"Thank you, Señor Luis, I will." Eladio bowed—the habit was ingrained. "Before I go inside, is there anything I may do for you?"

"No, Eladio, I don't need anything right now, thank you very much. I think I'll stay out here a bit longer myself. But you go now, before the heat and your exertion make you ill."

Eladio had worked for the Rodríguez-López family for more than forty years, but the relationship between the two old men was more like friends, especially as he had not been paid for the last thirty years. Still, a sense of rank remained, and manifested itself in their formality with each other.

At this point in their lives—they were both seventy years old, their sunset years—Eladio and Luis were so similar in appearance that one could easily have been mistaken for the other. They had both once been over six feet tall but they had each lost a few inches with age. And, as was the case with most ordinary Cubans—because they never had enough to eat—they were both quite thin, and their clothes hung loose on their slight frames.

Ever since 1959, when Fidel Castro's revolutionary army swept into Havana, life in Cuba had been difficult for both of them. For the past three years, since the collapse of the Soviet Union, life had become almost unbearable. The Soviet government had kept Cuba afloat with fuel, food, and supplies for decades; its demise left the people of the island to cope as best they could. Power shortages and blackouts occurred daily, worsening the situation. The Cuban government was no longer able to feed its citizens—the most basic needs were unmet—and as a result, Cubans had to fend for themselves and scrounge for food.

Castro tried to rally his compatriots by proclaiming, "Socialism or death!" but both were a hard sell. Rather than choose Socialism, a number of Cubans had hurled themselves onto rafts and taken their chances on the high seas, risking drowning or sharks, rather than continuing to struggle at near-starvation.

But Luis and Eladio had managed to escape some of the ravages of time and privation, though: The eyes of both men still sparkled with intelligence.

On this exceptionally hot July afternoon in 1992, Luis had spent most of the afternoon outside, sitting in his favorite wicker rocking chair on the terrace of his family's house, fanning himself, trying to escape the oppressive heat. For the past three hours he had been awaiting Eladio's arrival, wanting to hear his report. He knew what the other man was going to tell him, but the truth was he had nothing else to do.

The Rodríguez-López house, which was located in the Flores section of the city, had once been beautiful and majestic. Unfortunately, it had fallen into such disrepair that it was difficult to imagine what it had once been. To those few individuals who still visited, the sad state of the house and its grounds brought to mind an aging but still beautiful woman: She had good bones and erect carriage, and one wanted desperately to do something, anything, to help her regain at least part of her once famous beauty. Whatever paint was still on the walls was so faded that it was impossible to tell what its original color had been. The deadly combination of neglect, mold, and mildew had caused chunks of plaster to fall from the walls and ceilings with terrible consequences. The few treasures—items of only personal value, mainly Luis's photo album—were kept wrapped in layers of old newspaper. Even in such dismal circumstances, there was the hope that the house wasn't too far gone to be restored to her former life.

Although Eladio dusted and swept several times daily, his efforts made no noticeable difference, as there was always a white layer of fine dust everywhere. He kept on, with as much fresh energy and vigor as his seventy-year-old body would allow.

With the passing years, the physical deterioration of the house was such that gaping holes would appear all over, creating bizarre, puzzling patterns in the walls and the floors, as if whoever had built it had run out of materials to finish the job. There was nothing Eladio could do about that either, except to watch it happen.

And it wasn't just internal damage that had caused so much destruction. In earlier times, only hard, sustained rains could cause the ceiling to leak; but because the structure had been so weakened, lately even the lightest rain would cause damage, adding to the slow wrecking of the structure.

The large garden surrounding the house was now a clutter

of broken fountains, toppled stone statues, overgrown bushes, and fallen trees sunk in the tangle of weeds. Throughout the years, so much debris had dropped into the swimming pool, filling it to the rim, that sometimes the residents of the home forgot it had ever existed. For them, the state of the house and garden was heartbreaking, and it was difficult to believe that the property had been featured in magazines as being one of the most beautiful of pre-revolutionary Havana.

Although the house was very large, only three individuals—Luis Rodríguez-López, his wife María Eugenia, and Eladio Martínez, their servant—had lived there for more than forty years. It hadn't always been that way, however. All three could still clearly recall the days prior to the Revolution, when the house had been filled with noises from the kitchen, with the clacking of ladies' shoe heels against the marble floors—the times when it had not been unusual to have thirty or forty family members come over for Sunday lunch, after the noon mass at Santa Rita. The house, built in the Napoleonic style, had been in the Rodríguez-López family for more than one hundred years, and if the current owner had his way, would continue to be so for the next hundred.

The fact that Luis believed so strongly that the house should remain in his family was the primary reason he had refused to go into exile with his family when they had all left Cuba in the early '60s. For him, the house was much more than just a structure; it represented a way of life that he refused to let go of—for Luis, to leave the home would mean forfeiting his family's history.

As the Castro government would immediately confiscate—without any form of compensation, of course—the homes of any Cubans who fled the country, Luis knew the only way to keep the house in Rodríguez-López hands was to stay and

118 // Havana Noir

protect it. Even so, remaining in the home was no surefire guarantee that the three of them wouldn't be evicted, or be forced to open the house for others to move in with them. He'd heard stories of that happening to other families, and each case had made him more determined than ever to avoid those scenarios.

Staying was better, Luis believed, than just walking out. As if losing their properties were not enough, those owners who left Cuba were forced by law to hand over the keys to the government upon their departure. Fearing that one day he would need the knowledge, Luis had become increasingly obsessed with the laws that governed all aspects of Cuban property rights under the Castro regime. Since he, María Eugenia, and even Eladio lived in the house for more than three years, supposedly they could not be evicted. Eladio, by virtue of having lived there so long, had the same rights (in other countries, those were referred to as squatters' rights) as the actual owners of the property. In truth, as long as the three continued living there, they could feel reasonably secure—or as secure as anyone could be under the present regime—that they wouldn't find themselves out on the street, homeless, especially since they were all over sixty-five years old, the cutoff age for eviction. Yet knowing how mercurial and arbitrary the Cuban government could be, Luis worried nonetheless.

He knew he could make some extra money by renting out some of the bedrooms—an illegal but commonly practiced activity of the cash-strapped residents of Havana, especially those who lived in or near tourist areas. Luis feared, however, that this might jeopardize his ownership of the home. Suppose whoever he rented to would not move out after three years and became another owner? Also, the idea of strangers living in a house that had been the home of eight generations of the Rodríguez-López family was truly distasteful to him. Special Period or not, he knew his ancestors would turn in their graves if he were to do that.

María Eugenia hadn't originally been as attached to the house as her husband. It hadn't been her family's home, and she had only lived there, in the old times, for a few months as a bride. Still, she had married Luis for life, and if "life" meant staying in Communist Cuba with him and saying goodbye to her family and friends, then that's what she would do. She knew that nowadays her husband mostly lived in the past—even while looking forward to the future, for the day when the nightmare that was Castro's Cuba and this wretched Special Period would end and a more civilized, refined life would return.

As the Rodríguez-López family had not been blessed with children, the couple was on their own, except for Eladio's assistance. Eladio had never married—he had gone to work for the family as a young man, rising from junior assistant in the kitchen to chief butler, his position when Castro came into power—and so he too had no children, at least none that he was aware of. Like his employers, he was on his own.

Of course, all three had numerous friends and relatives, but most had long ago left and gone into exile in different countries. Visitors to the house were few. The only ones who still came around were Luis's three oldest friends: Roberto Cruz, Ricardo Mendoza, and Eduardo Menocal, all of whom, for various reasons, had chosen to remain in Havana.

In pre-Castro Cuba, members of certain upper-class families had been friends for generations, and their offspring were expected to continue the tradition, even if they loathed each other. The difference in the case of Luis, Roberto, Ricardo, and Eduardo was that they genuinely liked each other.

From kindergarten through high school, they had been classmates at Belén, a Catholic school for boys in Havana—ironically, the same one Castro had attended. And because they had been outstanding students, they'd gone on to Ivy League universities in the United States: Luis and Eduardo to Harvard, Roberto to Yale, and Ricardo to Princeton. Since the colleges were all located in the northeast, relatively near New York City, it hadn't been difficult for them to get together frequently. They were as close as brothers, and had been ushers at each other's weddings and, on occasion, gone into business together.

They would often discuss their friendship while lounging on one of their boats, after having tossed aside their on-land seriousness and consumed many beers. They had decided somewhere along the way that the strong bond they enjoyed could be attributed to their mutual love of the ocean. As Cuba was surrounded by the beautiful waters of the Caribbean, it was not surprising that children—those of the upper class, at any rate—learned how to swim almost as soon as they began to walk. The four friends dabbled in almost every sport that related to the ocean, but their two favorites were fishing and crew.

This choice was no surprise to anyone who knew them, since they each had a strong competitive streak. The four of them rowed so well as a team that when they trained and entered competitions—even as schoolboys they crewed against grown men—they invariably won. The more they won, the more they enjoyed rowing. They tried to stay in the best shape possible, training after school and on weekends.

For practical reasons, they couldn't keep up that schedule—though they wanted to—during the four years they were away at college, but they still fit in rowing during vacations. Being overly serious—apart from their water adventures—none of the four had much of a social life, so they used that free time to dedicate themselves as much as possible to the sport.

For members of the Havana Rowing Club, their sports club, there was no higher achievement than the coveted gold medal given to the team that won the regatta which, in the Olympic spirit, was held every four years. The friends knew that if they were to win the medal, they would be looked at differently: Instead of bookworms, they would be recognized as athletes, as jocks. Because they were as ambitious as they were talented, the friends set their sights on winning the race, which would be in August 1950.

It took a lot of early morning hours of rowing practice, but not only did they win the medal, they did it in a shell—a boat—they had built themselves. In the years prior to the race, they'd endured the comments of others who made fun of them and their boat. But confident that one day they would prove their detractors wrong, they persevered—and they were vindicated one cloudless morning when, at the age of twenty-three, they were awarded the medal.

They won not only because they were superb athletes but because they had faith in each other, and in their boat. That day, in the summer of 1950, when they came in first, was, and remained, the most important day of their long lives. They would never admit it to anyone else, but having won that race meant more to them than anything else—wives, children, family, professional successes. It had been a perfect day in an increasingly imperfect world.

Whenever they'd gotten together in the forty-two years since the race, Ricardo, Roberto, Eduardo, and Luis would relive that one glorious morning when they had defied all odds and set out in *La Milagrosa*—the boat they had lovingly, patiently, and reverently built with their own hands—and passed the finish line far ahead of those who'd laughed. That day, they had celebrated their victory by throwing a huge party at the Rodríguez-López house, feasting on seafood heaped on enormous platters: lobster, shrimp, Moro crabs—all of which they had caught themselves the day before. For, in addition to being outstanding rowers, the friends were exceptional fishermen.

Through the years, as often as time permitted, they would meet—early on weekend mornings, just as dawn was breaking—at the marina where their boats were docked, and jump onto whichever vessel was next in their rotation, and motor out to different diving spots. They would drop anchor and jump off the boat, emerging only when they were holding a lobster, or a crab, or a net full of shrimp.

Sometimes they wouldn't wait to get back to land to eat their catch—usually the hapless lobsters were first choice. They would break out the bottles of rum, and then, properly lubricated, they would drop the live creatures into a big pot of boiling water they had prepared earlier. After eating the fresh lobster meat out on the rolling sea, they would return to Havana by 11 o'clock in the morning—happy, laughing, sunburned, and slightly drunk.

The race, with the celebratory meal that had followed it, was the one memory that had allowed them to survive all that they'd had to for the past half-century. The friends considered that day to be such an important milestone in their lives that each year for the forty-two years since they'd commemorated the occasion—come hell or high water—by getting together and eating the same exact meal: lobster, shrimp, and crabs. Afterwards, they would take out the album in which they'd chronicled their adventures, and look again and again at the photographs.

As time passed, and life in Cuba became ever so much more difficult, those once-a-year gatherings became the centerpiece of their lives. Their importance could never be overstated—in the hardest times, it gave them each a reason for living.

The items chosen for the menu now were the same they had always fished for in pre-Castro Cuba. That had been a happy time, a carefree time, a time of plenty, when the waters around their beloved island had not been overfished to produce a bounty—denied to its citizens—reserved for tourists. Eating the seafood was a luxury that transported them back to that time when they'd actually looked forward to a future. Castro may have taken everything else away from them, but he could not take away the memory of that glorious day.

At their yearly dinner, the old friends would take out their identical sets of photos—which Luis's mother had given them—and examine each one, discussing the circumstances under which it had been taken, recalling every detail as clear as if it had just happened. Years ago they would disagree about some of the details, but they had long since arrived at a composite memory that satisfied them well. Instead of being four old men sitting in the dark in a decayed house crumbling around them, their too-loose clothing hanging on their skinny frames, they were the triumphant young men in the pictures, holding a trophy high over their heads, their boat clearly visible in the background.

As the years passed and their situation became worse—their health was deteriorating, food was scarce—putting on such a dinner became more and more difficult, not just physically, but emotionally as well. Although the subject was not discussed, it was apparent that soon not all of them would be around for the following year's meal. As each get-together might be the last one for any of the four, the dinner took on even greater significance.

One of the only legal means of acquiring food under the system instituted in 1962 was through government-issued ration cards. But acquiring seafood—absent on the ration card—was close to impossible. With the celebration held annually, each man's time to serve the meal came around every four years. For the host, making sure the dinner was as perfect as conditions would allow took on an almost supernatural charge: the sense that their future, the future of their families and their homes, was at stake.

For each one of them, bringing the meal to the table was what pride and manhood required. How else could they tolerate their situations and live with themselves?

The year before, when it was Ricardo's turn, he had served white flakes of meat picked from the poorest sort of fish scraps, with barely a bite of lobster. The quantity was so meager that there had only been a few spoonfuls of food on each plate. His guests, of course, had left bits of food on their plates—even though they had been close to famished—insisting they were so full that they could not possibly eat another bite. The Special Period was consuming them slowly, and not just physically.

Since women were not allowed at the dinners, María Eugenia had to rely on Luis's descriptions of what transpired on those special nights. For the first few dinners, the ones that took place in pre-Castro Cuba, the wives were miffed—after all, they were friends as well—but as the years passed and the items for the meal became scarcer and scarcer, they recognized it was best for all concerned that they not insist. And it wasn't just the difficulty of acquiring food that stopped their asking; it was also sad to see their husbands drunk, reliving their glorious youth while looking at photos of themselves when they were handsome and vigorous. The women, sometimes more practical than their husbands, preferred to avoid inflicting unnecessary pain on themselves—and that was a luxury they did not often have.

After the dinner the previous year at Ricardo's house—as always, on August 10, the anniversary of the race—Luis told his wife that the host said he'd had trouble assembling all the seafood for the meal: Hell, for the first time in forty years there'd been just one tiny lobster served. María Eugenia became alarmed and made a few discreet inquiries as to what, exactly, Ricardo had had to do to acquire even the meager meal he'd served his friends. She was told that Ricardo had been forced to sell his beloved portrait of the great Cuban patriot, José Martí—a painting that had been in his family for generations—to get the money for the meal. This news had so upset her that she locked herself in her room and cried copiously, an indulgence she thought she had given up years ago. If María Eugenia had ever needed proof of how much the dinners meant to her husband and his friends, this sad event provided it.

This year it was Luis's turn to host the meal. For months, he had agonized about how and where he was going to find the seafood. Time was running out. With one week remaining before the dinner, the only item that Luis had been able to procure was rice. He wasn't too worried about the eggs for the flan, as he had a neighbor who raised hens and sold eggs on the black market, so he could probably buy some from her.

As a longtime veteran of the ration system, Luis hadn't

been surprised that neither he nor María Eugenia nor Eladio had been successful in finding the other necessary items—scarcity was the norm and not the exception in the Special Period.

He had once heard that an American economist calculated that a ration book's monthly allotment would last—that is, if all of the items were available, an event that was a rarity—between a week and ten days. This same economist had compared a citizen of Havana's pre–Special Period monthly beef allotment, a half pound of meat, to a McDonald's Big Mac. Now, three years after the Special Period had begun, even that meager amount seemed an overabundance. Few in Havana had tasted meat in three years—at least not from the ration book.

When the Rodríguez-López family had needed anything, they would sell some of their belongings: jewelry, furniture, silver, clothes, etc. After forty years of doing that, they were out of things to sell, and had so few possessions left that they often worried how they could live out their lives.

Their old friends who were parents—those few who had chosen to stay in Cuba—were better off, as they had children who looked out for them. The fortunate ones were those who had sons and daughters outside Cuba to send them money—cash—which made all the difference. Roberto, Ricardo, and Eduardo were among these fortunate few, which was why—although they'd had difficulty giving the yearly party—they were still able to procure through the black market enough to make a minimal meal. But now, even they had trouble paying for seafood, as it was nearly impossible to find—and the fines for getting it illegally were exorbitant.

Luis had too much pride to let his friends know of his difficulty. Four years earlier, when it had been his turn to host, he'd been forced to sell his gold wedding ring—the last of his jewelry. The Patek Philippe watch that had belonged to his grandfather had been sold years before that. María Eugenia still had her wedding ring, but they had vowed that would only be sold if they were truly starving.

As the months passed and the date for the dinner approached, Luis supposed that he could either serve a different main course or cancel the dinner altogether. But being able to serve his lifelong friends the exact same meal they had been eating for the past forty-two years had become as important to him as breathing. And he did not want to be like Ricardo, who didn't have enough food for his guests. It was all or nothing for Luis.

María Eugenia and Eladio watched helplessly as Luis descended into a deep depression. Nothing they said or did could pull him out of it. The situation had become so dire that now even María Eugenia, who seldom left the house, had ventured out and visited a couple of long lost friends and acquaintances to see if they might know of any source of seafood, even remnants of the cheapest of bottom fish. No one knew where to look, which couldn't have been surprising to her, as everyone was in the same situation.

María Eugenia still had her gold wedding ring, but because of the pact that she and Luis had made, she could not sell it (though being a realist, she knew that day was not far off). Although it would have saddened her to part with it—she had sold her diamond engagement ring years before—she was so worried about Luis that she would have sold the gold band in a heartbeat. As the time for the dinner grew closer, María Eugenia repeatedly offered to do exactly that, but Luis would not even contemplate it. For him, selling the ring would be admitting there was no hope left, none at all. Castro would have essentially stolen the symbol of his marriage, and this was unacceptable to him.

Eladio scrambled to see what he could do to help his employer, and he too came up empty. Unlike the couple, he had no valuables to sell, but throughout the years he had made a bit of extra money here and there by working at odd jobs—running errands, fixing appliances, repairing old machines, so he had been able to contribute a small amount of cash to his keep. But now, because not even his considerable skills and ingenuity could keep forty-year-old machines running, even that little money had dried up.

However gifted a mechanic and handyman, his real skill was making a palatable meal out of the scarce and low-quality government-issue foodstuff available. With herbs he grew in the garden he lovingly cultivated in the rear of the Rodríguez-López property, he was somehow able to turn even the tasteless three-quarters of a pound of soy blend that was each individual's monthly allotment into a succulent roast.

Although he had never received any formal training as a chef, he instinctively knew how to bring out the best in everything he was given to work with. Over the years, he'd developed such confidence in his abilities that he was able to successfully transform certain foods—items that conjured up repellent images in most people's minds (chicken feet, fish cheeks, etc.)—into meals that people would not only eat, but which actually tasted delicious. Sadly, in spite of all his abilities, Eladio was not able to come up with the most important ingredient: seafood for the dinner.

In spite of not having received a salary in more than three decades of working full-time as butler, maid, handyman, and family cook, Eladio considered himself fortunate to have a roof over his head. He knew that he was considered a member of the family, so his fate was their fate.

And although life had been difficult for all three, by combining their resources they had managed. They had never really undergone the worst privations of the Special Period. Until now, that is—since this dinner was upsetting a very fragile equilibrium, bringing Luis close to a physical and mental breakdown.

The important day was now less than forty-eight hours away, and what should have been a happy occasion had turned into a dreaded event. It was obvious to María Eugenia and Eladio that Luis had totally forgotten the original reason for the dinner, and was instead fixated on what food he was going to serve his guests.

Early that morning, after eating what passed for breakfast—at this point, not even Eladio's culinary inventions could hide the fact that they were always hungry—Luis told Eladio that he wanted to speak with him privately, away from María Eugenia's hearing. They decided the best place for such a conversation would be at the back of the property, near Eladio's herb garden. María Eugenia would not question them going there. It was part of their daily ritual.

As he followed Luis, Eladio was taken aback at how thin and fragile-looking his employer had become. How was it that he hadn't noticed the change in Luis's appearance earlier? Had it occurred so slowly that it was difficult to see, or had it come over him quickly as a result of his preoccupation with the dinner? Eladio, saddened by what he was seeing, could not tell.

Making their way across the property was difficult, as Eladio had not had the strength lately to tend the grounds. After long minutes of carefully stepping in the overgrown tangle that was once flowers and shrubs, they reached the area beside the herb garden. Luis immediately headed for the wrought iron bench and sat down.

Luis was flushed, Eladio noticed, and breathing hard from all the exertion. Alarmed and not quite knowing what to do, Eladio stood a respectful distance from Luis while he waited for his employer's command—much as he would have done in pre-Castro Cuba. Although he did not look directly at Luis—his eyes were pointed at the ground—he still had enough peripheral vision to see Luis reach into his sweat-soaked shirt, presumably to take out one of the few handkerchiefs he had left to mop the sweat from his face. But much to Eladio's surprise, Luis instead took out three photographs. Luis slowly studied each of the them, smiling at the images of himself and his three friends, laughing, sunburned, drunk, sitting on the stern of one of their fishing boats, eating from the enormous platter of seafood in front of them.

"Eladio, how long have you been with our family?" Luis asked abruptly, peering up. "Around forty years by my calculations, right?"

"Forty-one, Señor Luis. Forty-one last March," Eladio replied, a bit warily. As far back as he could remember, neither Señor Luis nor Señora María Eugenia had ever brought up the length of his employment. A terrible thought occurred to him. Was he about to get fired? Where would he go? What would he do? Now it was Eladio's turn to begin to breathe hard.

"Yes, I'm sure you're correct." Luis leaned back, resting his body against the bench, and closed his eyes. He sat motionless for so long that Eladio began to think he had fallen asleep. Suddenly, he opened his eyes and sat up. "Eladio, I've lived a long, long life—some of it good, some of it not so good. Now I'm close to the end of it."

"Oh no, Señor Luis, don't talk like that!" Eladio had never before heard his employer discuss his mortality. "You have many, many more happy years ahead with Señora María Eugenia. Things will get better, señor, they will improve. This Special Period is only temporary."

"Well, I'm not so sure about that, Eladio, that's why I asked you to come out here, to have this talk with me." Luis turned to look at him with a stern expression on his face. "I need your help with something—it's a big favor."

"Of course, Señor Luis, ask anything you want of me. As always, I am at your service." Eladio struggled to speak in a normal tone of voice.

Luis waited for a few moments before speaking again. "You know how important the dinner—the dinner with my friends—is to me." Eladio nodded. "Well, this favor I am going to ask of you has to do with that."

During those years, Eladio had come to both love and hate the dinners. He loved them because they gave Luis something to look forward to. For weeks before the event, Se-ñor Luis would discuss with great animation how wonderful it was that he would be getting together with his oldest and best friends, what a blessing it was that, although they were old, they were in reasonably good health and could still recall "the good old days" when they were young and had their lives ahead of them.

For weeks before that night, Eladio would watch as his employer took out the photo albums and pored over the pictures, searching each one for details he especially cherished—an expression in the eyes of Ricardo, the way the salt spray made Roberto's hair coarse like a scrub brush. He studied them as a detective might examine a crime scene. Luis would always dwell longest on the same three photographs, the ones of him and his friends on his fishing boat, eating the seafood they had caught.

Eladio hated the dinner for the exact opposite reason that he loved them: the get-together with the childhood friends would remind Luis of the sadness, the hollowness, the despair of the lives they had led for the past forty years. The photographs were taken when Luis and his friends were in their early twenties, at the beginning of their lives. It was when looking at the photos in the season of each year's dinner that Luis felt it most strongly: that all hope was gone, and suffering and indignities, hunger and old age were the only things ahead of them. None of their ambitions had been realized, and none were going to be. Their lives had been wasted. Now all they had to look forward to was more suffering.

This dinner was so much more than just a meal. Eladio was willing to do just about anything to make it as successful as it could be.

"Señor Luis, I am happy to go back out again to try to find the seafood." Relieved to hear that the request from Señor Luis was nothing more serious than that, Eladio spoke quickly.

"No, Eladio, I'm not asking you to go look for any more lobster, crab, or shrimp. You've looked, María Eugenia has looked, I've looked." Luis shook his head slowly. "There's none to be found anywhere, we know that." Luis stood up and took a few steps forward, until he was only a foot away from Eladio. "No, Eladio, the favor I am going to ask of you is much more serious, more important." Luis put his hand on Eladio's shoulder.

Eladio felt his body turn ice cold, and he began to shiver almost uncontrollably. Eladio could not recall a single time

when his employer had touched him in all of their years together. "What is it, Señor Luis?"

"Eladio, I am going to ask that you do something for me
that I have no right to ask of you, but I am going to ask it anyway, because I think you understand why I have no choice."
His grip on Eladio's shoulder became so tight that it was starting to hurt. "If I cannot serve my guests a proper dinner, I cannot continue living. The shame will be such that my life will
be over. For me, admitting that when it came to be my turn
to host the dinner, I could not deliver what was expected of
me—this is something I cannot contemplate. I can live with
the humiliation of life as it is now—but shame is something I
cannot accept, will never accept. I will not be the first one of
my friends to fail to properly host the dinner when it was my
turn. I cannot!" Luis took his eyes off Eladio and looked away
into the distance. "The Rodríguez-López family is a proud
one—150 years ago, we fought for our freedom against the
Spaniards, the bastards, and we paid dearly for that stand. So
many young men died—but it was the only honorable choice
we could make."

Eladio, of course, had heard the stories for years. "Señor Luis, what is this big favor you want to ask of me?" Even
though he was fearful of the answer, he felt he had no choice
but to ask.

"Eladio, as you know, I've been giving the situation a lot of
thought, and I've come to the conclusion that I've exhausted
all my options. There is no seafood in all of Havana—in Cuba,
for that matter—for my meal. And with the celebration only
two days away, we're unlikely to find any."

Eladio shook his head. "Señor Luis, no, don't give up, I
can try again. We can all try—you, Señora María Eugenia,
me."

Luis smiled. "No, Eladio, you're wrong. The only way I can get through this predicament—the only way I can free myself from my obligation—is by dying."

"No, Señor Luis, no!" Eladio was horrified. "No! What you serve at the dinner is not what matters. The important thing is that you get together with your friends. They want to be with you. You can serve something else, anything! They don't care what they eat. Or cancel the meal."

"You're wrong again, Eladio," Luis said. "This dinner *is* that important. It is the reminder of what I once was! Not to do it and do it well would negate everything that my life was. I can't control the events around me, but this—this is the one thing I can control." Luis took a deep breath and let go of Eladio's shoulder. "No, Eladio, this dinner—doing it right—is more important than what remains of my life."

"Señor Luis, please, I don't mean to be disrespectful, but you are not thinking clearly," Eladio ventured. "The other señores, they will understand—everyone understands—life is so difficult now for everyone. Your friends, they just want to be with you."

"That may be so, Eladio, but it's not the way I think." Luis spoke in a calm, measured voice. "I know what has to be done. The only way to resolve this situation with honor is for the dinner to be canceled because of my death."

"Your death? No, there has to be another way." Eladio was close to tears. "Señor Luis, with all respect, I don't think you're well. I'm going to fetch Señora María Eugenia."

With unexpected strength, Luis grabbed Eladio and pulled him close. "No, you are not going to do that—she cannot be involved."

"Señor Luis, please let me go and get the señora." Now in tears, Eladio was pleading with his employer. "You are sick. She can help you."

"Eladio, listen, you have to do this for me. I've watched you, I've seen how you've killed chickens, pigeons, that suckling pig we had for Christmas years ago. You twist their necks—you do it quickly and without the animals feeling pain. It's fast and painless."

"You want me to kill you? Señor Luis, are you crazy?"

The two men stood by the wall in the garden facing each other for what seemed like hours. Each was desperate—Luis needed Eladio to follow his final orders, and Eladio, who for the last four-plus decades had always done as his employer asked, for the first time ever, would be defying him.

It was Luis who broke the silence. He knew his window of opportunity was closing fast, and he had to convince Eladio to do his bidding, otherwise his plan would not work. "Eladio, it's the only way, trust me. I know that I am asking a lot of you—it's not right, and it's not fair. If there were another way, I would not ask this of you. But I'm seventy years old, I've lived a full life, and this is the way I want it to end—with honor, without shame, not a failure because I could not deliver the meal to my friends. But to do it, I need your help."

"No, Señor Luis, I cannot do it." Eladio looked down at the ground. "I understand what you're saying, but it doesn't matter. I still cannot grant you your request. I cannot. It's not right. No meal is worth your life."

By then, it was close to midmorning and the August sun beat down on them, making the air sizzle with tropical heat. Luis decided that the only way to get Eladio to do as he asked was to act in an authoritative manner. Decades of following orders would take over, he was sure of that.

"This is what you are doing to do. Right now, right here, you are going to twist my neck—the way you do the animals. Quick and painless. I've already been to see Father Antonio, and I've confessed my sins to him and asked for his blessing. Of course, I didn't tell him what I was going to do—he wouldn't allow it. The Catholic Church condemns suicide—I couldn't be buried in consecrated ground, which would kill the señora. So my confession omitted this one matter. Afterward, I stayed in the church and prayed for forgiveness, and prayed for you, what I'm asking you to do."

Eladio stood speechless. All that was sinking into his brain was that he was supposed to kill Señor Luis—in this moment, to put his hands around that neck and head. It was too much for a simple man to understand.

Luis continued outlining his plan. "After you kill me, you will go to see the señora and tell her that we were out in the garden getting some herbs for the dinner, and that I collapsed, I fell down on the ground, but I did not want you to leave me to run to get help. I dropped dead—you think it's a stroke; maybe the heat brought it on, maybe the stress about the dinner, but my last words were for her not to notify the authorities of my death, so they would not take the house or move strangers here to live with you. Everything has to stay the way it is, for the future, when, God hopes, this madness will stop. She knows how important this house is to me—so she'll agree to that. Tell her also that I asked you to bury me in the back, by the wall, so that no one knows I'm gone."

"Señor, no, please! Please, I beg you, don't talk like that!" Eladio put his hands over his ears so he would not have to hear what Luis was saying. Luis, ignoring him, started laughing, not in his normal way, but manic laughter—the sound frightened Eladio even more.

"Listen to me, Eladio. So that all is not lost, you can use my body for fertilizer. You're always looking for compost for your garden—at least I can help you out some." Luis smiled at his own feeble joke. Then, seeing the stricken look on Eladio's face, he shook his head slowly, raised his arms, and reached over, removing his employee's hands from his ears. "Eladio, whether you help me or not, I will still take my life. I promise you that." He took a step closer. "You know that we Cubans have the highest suicide rate in the Americas, don't you?"

Eladio's eyes grew so large that for a moment it looked like they might pop out of his face.

"Yes, well, that's true," Luis said, laughing bitterly, "it's the one thing we can do correctly: kill ourselves. But you wouldn't want to see me add to that statistic, would you, Eladio—make that number grow by one? You don't want to see if I can kill myself correctly, do you? And if I botch it and end up with bigger problems than I have now?" Luis got a cunning look in his eyes, an expression that Eladio had seen on a couple of previous unpleasant occasions, which meant that his employer was going to use an argument he knew would win. "And after I kill myself, how would you explain a suicide to the señora? How do you think she would feel if she knew I killed myself?"

"No! No! Señor Luis!" Eladio was babbling in an almost incoherent manner. Sweat was pouring down him, dripping off his body in such copious amounts that soon he would be completely dehydrated.

Luis continued giving instructions, so that there would be no mistakes, no unforeseen eventualities. "Tell her I asked you to contact my friends to cancel the dinner—that's important, you cannot forget that part." Then Luis added, smiling, almost as an afterthought, "Tell the señora also that I love her—those were my last words."

"Señor Luis, please, don't make me do that, please."

At this moment, Luis knew that Eladio would do as he asked. And Eladio knew Luis well enough to be certain that if he, Eladio, did not do as ordered, his employer would do as he threatened and find another way to end his life. But Señor Luis was clumsy with tools and his method wouldn't be as quick or as painless as what Eladio could deliver.

With much reluctance, Eladio crossed himself several times and prepared himself to carry out his employer's wishes. He kissed Señor Luis on both cheeks, then knelt on the ground, head bowed, and asked for Luis's blessing.

At his advanced age, Luis Rodríguez-López was so frail and thin that twisting his neck was as easily and quickly accomplished as with the chickens, maybe even easier. Blinking back the tears that were flowing down his cheeks, Eladio looked at his employer lying at his feet and realized for the first time: He had really loved the man.

As Eladio stared at the body of the man who had meant so much to him, he could feel in his own heart the reason that Luis had asked him to end his life—not just because he could not serve his friends a proper meal, but because he had become tired of living. Luis had felt it was his time to leave this earth, and he had wanted to do it on his own terms. He needed to be able to control something, and the end of his life was the only thing left. And Eladio was the only person he trusted to do the job properly.

After taking the photographs from Luis's hands, Eladio carefully laid the body down on the garden bench, arranging his employer's features in such a way as to make him look as comfortable and peaceful as possible. He wanted María Eugenia to see her husband in the best way, so she would be assured he did not suffer in his last moments. He waited until he felt composed enough to get her and then, with one look back at Señor Luis, headed up to the house.

"Señora María Eugenia!" Eladio called out as he ran toward the house. "Señora María Eugenia!" No response. He called her name again. Now he was frightened, his heart beating so fast he thought it would explode inside his chest.

Eladio went into the main quarters of the house and looked everywhere, to no avail. The house was deserted. He went room to room again, this time searching more carefully. The only thing he noticed amiss was that the photo album was nowhere to be found. Had Luis taken it? He'd had only the three photographs with him in the garden. Where was the album?

Not knowing what to do, he went back outside to the terrace and sat in Luis's rocking chair. He did it as a reflex, an impulse: It was suddenly the right thing, to take this seat. He remained where he sat, in the chair that belonged to Señor Luis, for the better part of the day, with terrible thoughts coursing through his brain about what he had just done, and fears of what horrible fate could have befallen María Eugenia. Making matters much worse was the fact that the day was exceptionally hot, and knowing how heat affected corpses, he kept having visions of what was happening to Luis's body.

Rocking in the chair, he felt he was going mad from worry when, finally, he heard the familiar sound of the front gate. He jumped from the chair, ran over to the entrance of the house, and almost wept with joy when he saw María Eugenia slowly making her way up the path. He saw she was carrying the photo album.

"Eladio, hola!" María Eugenia cheerfully waved to him. "I'm home!"

It had been a long time since Eladio had seen María Eugenia in such good spirits. "Hola, señora," Eladio replied. "I was worried about you, you left without letting us know you were going—you've been gone all day." He knew it was not his place to scold his employer's wife but he'd been so concerned about her that he was past caring about behaving in a proper way. This day had devastated him.

"I know, I know, I'm sorry, Eladio, but I had to run an errand. I needed to do something that I did not want Luis to know about, and I didn't want to have to tell him a lie. So I slipped out of the house. I'm sure he'll be happy when he sees what I've done."

María Eugenia stepped closer to Eladio and took one of his hands in hers. She looked so happy, with her eyes sparkling and a huge smile on her face. "You know how worried Luis has been that he can't find the seafood to serve his friends?" she whispered in his ear, as if telling him a secret, and waved the photo album.

Eladio thought he was going to pass out. It took all the self-control he could muster not to fall to the ground. How could he say to her that her husband was dead? Oh God! He wished it was him lying on the bench in the garden, not Señor Luis!

"Yes, Señora María Eugenia," he replied. How was he going to tell her? He couldn't bring out the words; this was worse than what he'd already done. It was starting to get dark and Señor Luis had been lying outside on the garden terrace for close to ten hours.

"Well, I wasn't supposed to do it," she said, "but knowing how important it was for Luis to make this dinner perfect, I sold my wedding ring! We were saving it for a time when we had nothing at all to eat. But I knew that this crisis was, for Luis, even worse than starvation. You want to know what I did with the money I got for the ring? It was worth more than I had thought—it was white gold, Eladio, not just regular gold. Luis never told me it was white gold!"

María Eugenia held out the photo album and began turning the pages. "You see, Eladio, I've been thinking about the dinner, and all that seafood—the lobsters, the crabs, the shrimp—and how there is nothing to be found in Havana." She began to laugh triumphantly. It was so strange to hear the señora laugh that all Eladio could do was watch her helplessly. He should have told her immediately, the moment he saw her. It was a mistake to wait. "Well," she said, "I thought and thought about where Luis was going to get the seafood for the dinner. He would never consider serving anything else, he's stubborn, we both know that, no?" She leaned over to Eladio and—looking around, as if to make sure she was not being overheard—whispered, "You know Ricardo had to sell his family's painting of José Martí to pay for last year's dinner?"

"Yes, señora, I heard that," Eladio muttered. "Very sad."

"Well, we don't have anything like that—only my ring— so I had an idea." María Eugenia opened up the photo album and looked up at him. "You know, there are three pictures missing—maybe Luis took them—I have to ask him about that when I see him."

Eladio jumped back as if the pictures he had slipped in his pocket earlier that day were burning a hole. "Yes, señora, I know those pictures," he mumbled.

María Eugenia looked so happy, so pleased with herself, that now Eladio felt suicidal. For a fleeting moment he wondered if it was possible to wring his own neck.

"I decided," she said, "that since Luis and his three friends were great fishermen, why couldn't they fish for the seafood for the dinner themselves? I know it's against the law for Cubans to fish for lobster, crab, and shrimp—but, Eladio, they know the waters around the coast of Havana like they know the backs of their hands. After all, that's where they used to fish!

They would be too smart to get caught!" María Eugenia was so thrilled with her solution to the dilemma of what to serve for the dinner that she was beside herself with joy. "Don't you see, Eladio? Fishing for the meal is the perfect answer! They would feel young, happy, and resourceful! They could drink the rum you make—just like in the photos!"

"But, Señora María Eugenia, what about your ring? You said you sold it for the dinner. I don't understand."

"Oh, Eladio, you're right—I'm sorry—I forgot to tell you the most important thing!" María Eugenia seemed years younger as she almost sprinted away. "I sold the ring and bought a small boat with the money—I went to the pier by the old Yacht Club, you remember, where the señores used to row? Luis told me there were old boats for sale there. I traded the ring for one of the boats, not a very big or fancy one, but it won't sink—I made sure of that. It needs some work, but it'll do!" María Eugenia placed the photo album on a table and began to walk away, the smile on her face making her look like the young girl Luis had married forty years before. "It's the Special Period, you know, Eladio, everyone wants and needs something—everything anyone has is for sale—so it wasn't very difficult to buy. And now all our problems are solved! The dinner—with seafood—will take place . . . I'm going to find Luis and tell him not to worry anymore." She turned to Eladio. "Where is he?"

He couldn't answer. He only could shake his head as she walked past.

He didn't follow. Instead, he took his seat again in Luis's chair, knotting and unknotting his hands. She would find his body. It was better that way, because if he spoke, she would know he was lying.

But there was one more thing he would do for his employer of more than forty years. He would push out to sea in the little boat, dive for crab and lobsters, haul a net for shrimp until he had found all he needed and more. Then he would serve that dinner, and he would make it a feast. The three friends would eat his catch and drink his rum—they would drink and grieve—and they would toast the eternal honor of Señor Luis.

JOHNNY VENTURA'S SEVENTH TRY

BY PABLO MEDINA

Jaimanitas

for Gerardo Alfonso Piquera

On September 23, 1995, Johnny Ventura settled into the bow of the *Ana María*, a fifteen-foot launch he built expressly for the voyage, and took his last look at the city of Havana, illuminated dimly by the first rays of dawn. It was Johnny's seventh attempt at crossing the Straits of Florida, and having consulted a babalao in Arroyo Arenas, he was certain that the *Ana María* would land him in La Yuma, if not in Miami, then somewhere along the Florida Keys, where he could claim his right to political asylum. He had spent six months in jail after his previous attempt when the raft he'd put together in the back room of his mother's house had fallen apart in rough water three miles from shore and he and his two companions had been forced to swim back, landing on the Malecón just as a patrulla drove by. If he failed again, he was certain the authorities would make him rot in jail. That is why he had been extra careful, consulting the babalao (not that he believed in any of that Santería nonsense) and paying a hefty amount, in fulas, for a Russian outboard motor that sputtered and smoked the two times he started it but otherwise ran beautifully.

Despite the care he took in building the boat from plans left behind by his grandfather, Alepo Rodríguez, the great shark fisherman who had been swallowed by the waves off Jaimanitas in 1952, and despite the babalao's blessing, Johnny had already acquired a reputation as a salao, a fellow forever mired in the salt of bad luck. Crossing the Florida Straits was serious business. If the storms and sharks didn't get you, the Guarda Costas would and they'd put you in the same jail cell with a gang of pathological pederasts. The several friends he approached who were as desperate to leave the island as he refused to join him. The most circumspect simply kept the secret of Johnny's voyage to themselves. At least two, however, spread the news around the neighborhood, and when Cacha Manguera, the head of the neighborhood Committee for Defense of the Revolution, heard that El Salao was at it again, she gave a big, raucous laugh and didn't bother reporting Johnny to the higher-ups or paying a visit to his mother to ask the usual impertinent questions. Only Obdulio Martínez, the dim-witted son of a garbage collector who lived down the street, agreed to accompany him.

Johnny ignored the neighbors' comments, the sly half-smiles as he walked by, the occasional shout, "Bacalao Salao," coming from one of the balconies overhead, and went about his business with the aplomb of a seasoned old sailor. Mornings he waited in the rationing line to get whatever food he and his mother were entitled to—split peas one day, dried mackerel the next. On a good day they might have some eggs, cheese, or a half pound of rice. Afternoons he'd go to his aunt's house in Lawton to meet up with the pork man. Black market vendors required dollars, however, and if he didn't have any, he'd simply head in the direction of the Malecón and walk along the seawall, looking at the ocean as it stretched all the way to the horizon and beyond where the Promised Land lay. Everyone was leaving the island. Why couldn't he? He was home by

6 usually, when his mother served him rice and beans or, on bad days, which came all too often lately, watery split pea soup. After 8 o'clock, when his mother went to sleep, he'd leave the house again and walk through the streets of Havana, never taking the same route twice in a row, to the old garage where his Uncle Berto hid his 1956 Chrysler Imperial, waiting for the day when the nightmare of the Revolution was finally over and he could drive it proudly down the street like the old-fashioned capitalist he fancied himself to be. The garage was about thirty feet deep and the Chrysler was all the way in the rear, up on blocks and quietly rusting away. In the front, unbeknownst to anyone but Obdulio the dimwit, Johnny would work through the night building the *Ana María*, a boat so sturdy nothing but the most extreme act of God would sink it, and even then, Johnny would think while taking a cigarette break, the Old Man would have a real struggle on his hands.

And so, building the *Ana María* made Johnny a creature of the night. Often he could hear, or thought he could hear, a faint but comforting susurrus settling over the city after midnight. Off in the distance a dog barked or a radio played; outside the garage two lovers spoke.

"My love, did you bring the banana?"

"Yes, darling. It's ready for you."

Johnny listened to them while Obdulio slept in the backseat of the Chrysler and salivated, whether from lust or old hunger he didn't know. All conversations in Cuba somehow devolved into matters of food.

"Give it to me, papi."

Johnny dropped the hammer he was holding against a metal bucket and made a loud noise.

Obdulio woke with a start. "Qué pasó?" he said, sitting up and looking through the rear window.

"Nada. Go back to sleep," Johnny answered, and kept on working until his eyes closed involuntarily and he dreamed of Miami Beach nightclubs and gorgeous tanned women with large, shapely breasts.

Johnny, it must be said, had a wife, but she was one of those women who consider sex an unpleasant marital duty to be performed twice monthly without abandon or fanfare, like getting an injection. In the three years they had been married, Johnny's wife had grown dull and morose, feeling betrayed that Johnny had not made good on his promise to get her pregnant. She was subject to fits of resentment that took the form of burning Johnny's coffee so that it became undrinkable, or salting his food to such a degree that he had to spit it out. When she finally went to live with her sister in Cotorro, Johnny was overjoyed. In fact, he celebrated that night by drinking a bottle of rum and running the Russian motor until it whined and rattled like it wanted to die.

"A Mayami me voy, a Mayami me voy," Johnny chanted, dancing round Obdulio, who hooted and leaped like an African warrior about to wrestle a lion.

In six months the *Ana María* was finished and it was such an exemplary visage of a seagoing vessel that Johnny entertained the thought of selling her for a thousand dollars and staying in Havana until the son of a bitch Fidel died. With a thousand dollars he could fix up his uncle's Chrysler. With a thousand dollars he could approach that girl with the long legs and jet-black hair who lived on the corner of Manrique and Lagunas streets and call up to her, "Come on, sugar, let's take a drive around the city." With a thousand dollars he'd be a big man in this godforsaken city.

But those thoughts stayed with him only two nights. *By God*, he said to himself on the third night, *I'll make it to La*

Yuma or die. With a renewed sense of purpose he went off to Jaimanitas, a little fishing village in the outskirts of Havana, to observe what time the patrullas passed by; he did so for two weeks, hiding behind a stand of sea grape, swatting at mosquitoes, and recording the times in an old notebook.

Rather than tell his mother directly, he decided he would leave a letter for her stating that he was sorry but he had no option and reassuring her that he would send for her as soon as he was settled. She still loved El Comandante as she had loved Johnny's father, who abused her and disappeared for weeks at a time, showing up to take her money and beat her up again. "Fidel is the most wonderful man in the world," she would say, raising her eyes to the ceiling as people sometimes do when contemplating Jesus. After reading the letter, his mother would cry for a day, then go downstairs to gossip with the neighborhood ladies and forget about her son. At least this is what he told himself.

In preparation for the voyage he had been gathering provisions any way he could, buying some, borrowing others, and, when he had no choice, stealing the rest. In the forward compartment of the *Ana María* he stored ten liters of water, several bags of stale bread, a block of farmer's cheese, and seven cans of Russian meat. Carefully balanced along the sides of the boat he placed a flashlight (stolen), two oars he had borrowed from his uncle, a fishing line with several hooks and sinkers that Obdulio's father had given them, a knife that had seen better days (taken from his mother's kitchen), a compass and an ancient sextant, both stolen from the Naval Museum in La Cabaña, and sixty liters of gasoline that had cost him several hundred dollars. Also on the boat, well hidden from view for now, was a small American flag he hoped to wave once he got within view of La Yuma. In a frivolous moment he decided to take the leather backseat of the Chrysler, cracked and brittle with age, and glue it down on the deck of the boat with marine epoxy so that Obdulio could sleep comfortably on the way across.

At midnight of the appointed day, Johnny and Obdulio waited for Obdulio's father, Manolo, to arrive with the garbage truck he had commandeered to transport the *Ana María* to the little cove in Jaimanitas. At 12:30 Johnny grew worried; at 1 o'clock he was desperate. At 1:15 Obdulio's father finally showed up, not in the twenty-five-footer with a canvas cover he had promised, but in a small Moscovitch pickup with a six-foot bed. Johnny's heart sank to a level it had never known before. He sat on the front fender of the Chrysler and felt tears welling in his eyes, but he contained them.

"Manolo," Johnny said to Obdulio's father, "how are we going to load a fifteen-foot boat on that cockroach?"

"Don't worry, asere," Obdulio's father said. "We'll do it. I brought enough rope so we can tie it securely on top. No problem."

Obdulio's father was determined to have his son in the United States so he could send remittances home.

"What are people going to think when they see a Moscovitch with a boat twice its size tied on top?"

"Nothing, asere," said Manolo. "Because there isn't anybody out at this time of night. You think this is Nueva York?"

"I thought you were going to bring a big truck," Johnny said.

"Asere, what happened is somebody else took it for the night. But don't worry so much. This is going to work, you'll see."

It took the three of them an hour to load and tie the *Ana María* onto the Moscovitch. Johnny thought for sure the shock absorbers would give way but he was wrong. The pickup merely lurched and groaned and finally settled nicely six inches from the ground. The *Ana María* lay upside down, its prow extending six feet beyond the cab and blocking all but a six-inch band of windshield. Manolo reassured Johnny that he could drive the streets of Havana with his eyes closed. Given that the government shut down the city's electric power at night, that was pretty much what they'd have to do: drive in the dark with the headlights turned off.

"One pothole and there goes the front axle," Johnny said.

Manolo once again tried to calm him, then reached under the driver's seat and pulled out a bottle of chispa de tren that he passed to Johnny. Johnny took a swig and gave it back to Manolo.

"That's for the trip," Manolo said, pushing the bottle away. "Make sure you make an offering to Yemayá before you push off."

They drove in silence and darkness without hitting a single pothole and reached the turnoff at 2:45 a.m., with plenty of time to ship out by 3:27, when Johnny had determined no patrullas passed by. As Manolo negotiated the sandy road that led to the cove, the Moscovitch waddled and almost tipped over a couple of times, then hit a rut where the wheels spun themselves into the sand and lost traction.

Manolo smacked the steering wheel with the palm of his hand. Johnny cursed God and all the angels, and both left the cab simultaneously, walking around the truck to gauge how deeply the tires were embedded in the sand. Manolo dug around the two front tires while Johnny stood by the passenger door and looked at Obdulio, who was sleeping soundly inside. What he wouldn't give to sleep like that! He had already resigned himself to going back to the garage to wait for another day, when Manolo stood upright and proclaimed that they would have to take the boat off the Moscovitch. He would let some air out of the tires and that would do the trick. "Easy," Manolo said. *Easy*, Johnny thought, momentarily feeling sorry for himself. Nothing had ever been easy for him.

Suddenly he sensed someone next to him, and when he looked to his right he saw a round bristly face peering up at him. Johnny's blood turned cold, the back of his neck tensed up.

"Señor, what's the problem?" The man was being overly formal given the circumstances.

"Nada," answered Johnny, too nervous to say anything else.

The man looked at the truck's wheels sunk halfway in the sand, then back up at Johnny.

"It looks like something to me."

Manolo came over and asked the man what he was doing there at such an hour.

"The same thing you're doing, trying to get off this shitty island."

He led them on a path through a stand of sea grape to the water where a boat, or what passed for a boat, was waiting to shove off. The man called to two others who were helping some women and their children board, and between the five of them—Obdulio remained blissfully asleep—they were able to unload the *Ana María* and drag it across the sand to the water's edge. The three men were impressed by Johnny's launch and wanted to tie it to their ramshackle vessel, an old wooden boat with no motor but a sail made out of two bed sheets sewn together. Four empty oil barrels, fastened on either side, kept the boat from sinking. Johnny said no. "We have women and children with us," one of them complained.

152 // HAVANA NOIR

Johnny had heard of men fighting over provisions out in the open sea and pushing the weaker ones overboard. Besides, the *Ana María* could move faster without dragging the boat. He said that he and Obdulio were going it alone. One of the men made a threatening move in Johnny's direction but Manolo intervened, thanking them for their help and offering the men four liters of water and a few cans of Russian meat for their efforts. Two of the men finally went back to their boat. The guy who had first approached them remained behind.

"Who do you think you are?" he said to Johnny. "This is a Socialist country."

Johnny waited until the other vessel was well out to sea and out of his sight before pushing the *Ana María* into the water. She bobbed a few times; then her prow settled squarely against the waves. She was a good boat, he thought with no small amount of pride. After feeling the bottom with his hands to check for leaks and finding it dry as bone, he helped Obdulio on board.

Johnny shoved off and took their leave of Manolo, who stood on the sand with his shoulders hunched and his large hands dangling helplessly at his sides. Johnny heard him crying and assured him that his son would soon be sending a thousand dollars home every month. Manolo's weeping grew more pronounced, then stopped altogether. Obdulio waved at the darkness and sat on the leather car seat, giddy with anticipation.

Once the *Ana María* was in deep enough, Johnny lowered the Russian outboard into the water, opened the throttle, and gave a pull on the starter rope. The motor sputtered and died. Johnny yanked several times, each time harder than the last, until he was out of breath. *Stupid Russians! They can't even build a good motor. No wonder the Soviet Union fell apart.*

Then he heard a dim voice through the gloom, "Ta hogao. It's flooded. Let it rest."

At first he thought it was Manolo; then he realized it was Obdulio's voice, which was like his father's but younger and rougher. Johnny found the bottle of chispa de tren wedged under the seat and spilled some on the water as an offering, then took a drink. He offered the bottle to Obdulio, who refused, saying, "Eso eh' el diablo." Now he sounded less like his father and more like Bola de Nieve, the singer.

After listening to the water lap the sides of the boat for what seemed an eternity, Johnny tried again. The motor coughed and started, releasing a burst of burnt oil smoke that smelled like the perfume of his dreams.

"Hold on, Obdulio," he said, and revved the engine as high as it would go. The *Ana María* lurched, gained speed, and was soon skimming the flat sea like a flying fish.

It was about two miles out that Johnny turned and looked back at Havana. From this distance the city was nestled in a soft gray light that made it float over the sea, over the land, over all material things. It was the most beautiful sight he had ever seen. Havana was the world to him, heaven and hell and purgatory combined, and he understood that he was leaving his world behind for good; yet even as he was reaching this realization, he started turning the boat around until it was pointing back to shore. Obdulio sat calmly at first, like a prince enjoying a ride on his private launch, but slowly became aware of what Johnny was doing.

"No, no," he said. "Coño, no!"

Johnny woke from his reverie and headed back north. When he reached the approximate spot of the first turning, he remembered his mother whom he had abandoned. This time he slowed the boat down and made a broader arc, and when the city came into view, Obdulio said, "I want to go to La Yuma." His childish voice cracked with plaintiveness. Johnny kept turning until the boat completed a full circle. This time he thought of the girl on the balcony with the pearly skin and beautiful black hair. How could he abandon those delights? Now Obdulio was screaming and it sounded to Johnny like a high-speed circular saw cutting through a dry log. He turned again.

The *Ana María* circled seven times. Every time Johnny thought of someone or something he was leaving, he pointed her back in the direction of Havana, then hearing Obdulio's scream over the sound of the motor, he would turn the boat northward. As he was about to circle yet one more time, the sun appeared over the eastern horizon, red and massive, spreading its rays until the sea, the city, and the sky grew indistinct and became suspended in a blaze so pure and ubiquitous it was directionless. Johnny screamed louder than Obdulio, louder than the Russian motor, and passed the turning point, weeping for what he had left behind and hurtling faster than his longing toward the new.

SHANGHAI

BY ALEX ABELLA

Siboney

1959

The Chinaman lurched violently to the left, the impact of the slug blasting open his blue silk robe, drenched by the gush of blood out his side. Dropping his knife, he felt his ribs, his features distorted into a mask of incomprehension, as though it was inconceivable that he, of all people, should be on the receiving end of my smoking .45.

He stumbled backwards, bumping against the rickety wall, arms flailing, knocking down the porcelain vase with the tulips, the long clay opium pipe, the little smiling Buddha. The framed scroll with the hand-painted tigers fell on his lap as he eased down to the floor, his eyes wide in the knowledge of swift death.

It was only then that I heard the girl screaming. Dressed in the pasties and g-string of her chosen profession, Miss Raquel La Pasión's full mocha breasts were aquiver with the emotion closest to lust, terror. She pointed at the dying Chink and let out a loud string of Spanish curses as she cowered behind the shirtless tow-haired boy. Tall and lanky, with the soft features of the country club set, the boy held a .38 in his trembling hands. He fired, the bullet smashing into a fruit bowl. I jumped over the settee, grabbed the gun out of his limp hands, and then I slapped the girl, hard.

"Cállate!"

She whimpered, hid behind the boy.

"David Souther?" I asked, as I slipped his gun into my jacket pocket. The show tunes from the theater above had stopped, the clatter of footsteps on the stage booming in the stillness.

He turned to me slowly, his eyes still hazy from the drug. "Who the fuck are you?" he drawled.

"Jason Blue. I'm a private detective. Your dad sent me to get you out of Havana. Let's go!"

"Hey, fuck you, man. My old man can't tell me—"

Drug fiends are like dogs, either you pull rank right away or they run away with you. I took my .45 and whipped him one across his baby face, then jammed the gun in his skinny ribs.

"You do what I say or I'll break every fucking bone in your body. Put your shirt on *now*!"

The boy blinked twice, wiped away the trickle of blood from his nose with the back of his hand, and slipped on a soiled striped shirt.

"And Raquel?" he said, jerking his chin at the girl. "I'm not leaving without her."

I hesitated for a moment, debating how much fight the kid still had in him, then grabbed the lacy dress from the Chinese canopy bed and threw it at the heaving hussy.

"C'mon."

The opium den was at the far end of a warren of rooms under the Shanghai Theater in Havana's Chinatown. I held my gun out in front, finger on the trigger, and quickly glanced down the corridor, barely lit by a yellow light dangling from the cobwebbed ceiling. No one around.

Coming down I had looked into all the other cubicles. All

were empty except for the very last one, where I had found David Covenant Souther IV, of Woodside, Princeton, and Pacific Heights, heir to the Souther Chemical and Mellenkamp Frozen Food fortunes, wrapped up with a colored bimbo and a pipe of dope, staring at an enraged Chink intent on loping off the boy's privileged, aquiline, and so very American proboscis.

"What are we waiting for?" asked the boy now. He stood right behind me, his breath a sour mix of rotting teeth and sweet opium perfume.

"The main chance, sonny."

I counted four doors on either side of the hallway. At the far end, thirty feet away, an old wooden circular staircase led up to backstage. From there it was another long forty feet to the double exit doors—forty feet past dressing rooms with showgirls, bathrooms with drunken patrons, and offices with goons and gunmen, before finally getting out of the building and down the alley to my rental DeSoto. A friendly Cuban dishwasher had snuck me in through the side, but I couldn't count on his generosity anymore—he was probably still knocked out in the closet where I'd sapped him. The hundred-dollar bill in his pocket would buy a lot of ice for his headache.

"When I say go, you run right behind me, you understand? Don't stop no matter what."

I translated for the bimbo, who nodded vigorously. At least she had the good sense to recognize that the big Chink's death could not be good for her business. Besides, she had her ticket out of the Shanghai life right in front of her, the wobbly befuddled kid who for once was using his brain—and arriving at all the wrong conclusions.

"Hey, man, dig, this is too much."

"What?"

"Hey, you just, you just shot that cat, man. Maybe we

should call the police. Yeah, let's call the American consul, man, he'll get us out of this. This is Cuba, man. The dollar is almighty here. I'm an American, I want my consul, man. I mean, I didn't shoot him, that's your problem." The kid sank down to the floor, crossing his arms and legs. "I'm not moving, man, I'm sitting down for my rights."

"Excuse me?" I said.

"Yeah, man, I demand to see—"

"Aw, shit."

This time I broke his nose. I gave him my handkerchief, told him to hold his head up and press down to stop the bleeding.

"If I have to bring you back in a full body cast, that's what I'm going to do, David. Get off the fucking floor."

The kid stretched out his long legs and got up, holding onto the girl for support.

"You'll pay for this, Blue."

"Get in line. Now, at the count of three. One, two . . ."

We rushed down the corridor and up the staircase, the girl pushing the boy up behind me, calling him estúpido, cobarde, and a thousand other endearments.

At the landing, I thought I was home free—I could see the exit doors open to the alley—and then I saw shards of brick fly in front of me and heard the loud report of the gun in the hallway.

"Down! Down!" I shouted at the boy and girl as I rolled away, taking cover behind a Chinese sarcophagus prop. I fired back at another Chinaman in a white suit. The shooter hid behind a piano when I returned fire, then stood up with a shotgun, blasting away at the quickly splintering casket in front of me. *Where is everybody?* I kept thinking, even as I told myself this was not what I had in mind when I took on the job.

* * *

You understand, pulling crybabies out of jams is one thing. I don't mind doing that so much; in fact, probably about half of my business in San Francisco consists of clean-up work. Make sure the pictures disappear, make sure the witness doesn't remember, make sure the society columnist is well-greased, make sure the police blotter gets misplaced, make sure the recording wire nails somebody else. It's what society detectives do, and in five years solo I've carved out quite a little practice for myself. Not quite orthodox detective work, but then, I don't do divorces or children—I got two of each and they're not experiences I particularly want to relive. However, I'm not in the market to be somebody's carnival sitting duck either, particularly in a foreign country undergoing a revolution.

The call from the kid's father was not that surprising. I had just brought a couple of society chickees back from New York, where they had deluded themselves into thinking they were beatniks in love with a Commie juvenile delinquent. This little feat had drawn the attention of a host of Peninsula and City families, who were also struggling with the weird choices made by their money-addled offspring.

My office is on Market Street, down from Lotta's Fountain and across from the old Souther Chemical Building. *"The progress of mankind is measured by the advancement of science,"* reads the company's credo, etched in ten-foot letters on the limestone front. Pretty classy for an outfit founded by an alcoholic French chemist who made his fortune by accidentally mixing up the tailing samples of an abandoned silver mine in Reno with those of a played-out hole in Virginia City, leading a disillusioned miner to kill himself and the chemist to file a claim for the dead miner's bonanza.

When Lorraine, my secretary, handed me a slip that old

man Pierre Souther wanted to meet me in his executive dining room at 4 o'clock sharp, I knew it wouldn't be for old sherry and stale walnuts. In any event, he was almost done eating when I came to discuss the job.

He waved me to a cushy leather chair in the vast room at the far end of his penthouse. Milky sunlight eased through the stained glass window behind him, illuminating the company's coat of arms, a chemist raising a test tube next to a knight on a white steed killing a dragon, while an empty cross bearing the sign *Lux* floated above them both.

"Are you hungry?" He gestured at a steaming bowl of creamed spinach. "It's about the only food I can hold down. We get it from the little old ladies at Searle's. Best in town."

"No, thank you, the only green I like is the kind I fold and put in my pocket."

"So I hear." He blew on his spoon, slurped the soup. Rail thin, with deep-set gray eyes, Souther seemed like a defrocked priest, eating seminary food to remind himself of his transgressions. "That divorce cost you a bundle, didn't it?" he said.

"The house, the ranch, and the Cord, if you want to know. I was hoping you'd help me make it up."

"Maybe I can," he said. He pushed aside the half-full bowl, lit a filterless cigarette, and dropped the match in the soup. He blew out a cloud of smoke. Then: "You love your children, Mr. Blue?" He gazed at me with cold curiosity.

"Is that a trick question, Mr. Souther?" I replied. "Because if it is, nothing I say will please you."

"I just want the truth."

"That's all I'm going to give you, and this is it: Sometimes I love them more than life itself; sometimes I could wring their little necks and jump for joy. But it's always a real emotion, there's nothing fake about my feelings for them. Don't ask me about their mother."

"Do you miss them?"

The twenty questions game was over. I got up, picked up my briefcase. "Since you obviously had me investigated, I don't need to tell you that I see them twice a week and every other Sunday and it's never long enough. Whoever it was you had on me should have told you I don't like to waste time—mine or anybody else's."

"Sit down, Mr. Blue. There's twenty thousand dollars in this for you. Half now, half on delivery."

"Delivery of what?"

"My son. My only son. He left for Cuba six months ago for some revolution nonsense and now he's refusing to come back. I want to see him before I go."

"Even if he doesn't?"

"Love knows no bounds, Mr. Blue. I was fifty when I had him. His mother died when he was little and I didn't know what to do with him. I sent him away to boarding school. He's always hated me for that. I can take his hatred. I just can't take his absence."

He put out the cigarette on a large crystal ashtray bearing the inscription, *Lux et Veritas*.

"Bring him back, Mr. Blue. He's the only one I want."

The object of old Souther's affection now raised his head from the floor of the Chinese theater. Who knows what half-assed vision of valor was going through his head at that moment, but he decided to make a run for it. Grabbing hold of his girl by the hand, he bolted for the door at the same time that the Chinaman came out from behind his piano. I aimed, but the bullet that dropped the shooter wasn't mine. He fell forward on his chin, the impact shattering his jaw, a couple of teeth tumbling out of his mouth like liar's bones on the worn wooden floor. I doubt he felt anything given the gory hole the rifle bullet had opened in his back.

Presently four college student types in short-sleeved shirts bearing armbands with the letters *26-7* came in from the hall, pointing their hunting rifles at us. I threw my gun down right away. The oldest in the group, a skinny redhead Cesar Romero look-alike, waved at his cohorts to put their weapons down—but he kept his tommy gun aimed squarely at my chest all the same.

"Turistas!" I shouted, hoping they'd buy it. "Muchos problemas de policía."

Cesar Romero laughed.

"No shit, Jack, everybody's got a problem with coppers down here," he said in a thick Bronx accent. "What are you fishing for?"

Obviously, the stupid Yankee bit wasn't going to get me far with this gent. I figured I'd take my chances.

"The kid and his girl. I gotta get 'em outta here."

"How come?"

"I'm a private dick. His old man paid me to get him back to San Francisco, in California. El viejo se está muriendo."

Cesar looked hard at me, trying to decide if I was telling the truth. I was sweating, hoping he'd buy my song and dance.

Finally: "You picked a fucking fine time to get him out. You know what just happened?"

I shook my head no, even though I had a fairly good idea of why the crowds outside were shouting, "Viva Fidel!" full blast when twenty-four hours before just whispering "Castro" was enough to get you thrown in the slammer.

"Batista left at midnight. He hightailed it out of here with his buddies and ten million in cash."

I gestured to put my hands down, take out a cigarette. He nodded, eased down the barrel of his gun.

"Congratulations," I said, as two of Cesar's minions brought Souther junior and his doll, kicking and heaving, back into the hall. "I assume you were no fan."

"Are you kidding? Son of a bitch had my brother killed in one of his prison cells. Cut his balls off."

"Sorry to hear that," I said, lighting my thirtieth Chesterfield of the day. "No offense, but what business do you have with a Chink theater?"

Cesar's expression changed to hurt pride and I wondered for a moment if I'd overstepped the bounds of Castilian etiquette—the kid's skin was whiter than mine, after all. I was also gauging how fast I could wrest the gun out of his hand and clear our way to the car. Fortunately, something somewhere in his troubled Cuban psyche kicked in and he let a sly smile out.

"We just thought we'd come see the girls. Verdad, muchachos, venimos por las jebas?"

Lots of embarrassed grinning and jostling here. Then Cesar was all business again. Damn mercurial Cubans.

"We're also here to close down the place. This is un antro de vicio y prostitución, a, a . . ." Suddenly his perfect English went south on him.

"A *den of vice and iniquity* is the usual phrase back home."

"Sorry, it's been five years since I left Bronx Science."

"Hey, man, you speak English!" shouted David at Cesar, "I demand to see the American consul. I'm an American citizen!"

Cesar looked at him with awe, then back at me. "Jesus, where did you get this monkey?"

I shrugged.

"I said I am an American citizen and I—"

In a lightning swift motion, Cesar lifted his tommy gun and fired over David's head, missing him by scant inches.

"The next time is right between the eyes, comemierda!"

David grew deadly still, his eyes bulged, and this time he nodded quietly. I had to grin.

"Just get them out of here," said Cesar. "Guys like him never learn, they think being American makes them better than anybody else."

"I understand. May I?" I gestured at my gun on the floor. "I have a feeling I might need it."

He nodded. "You might. Everything's closed down. You got a car?"

I bent down, picked up my .45. "Around the corner."

"Make sure you got gas. Things are going to be pretty hairy the next few days, until Fidel comes down from the hills. Now beat it."

"I didn't catch your name." I offered my hand.

He shook it, warmly. "Rolando Cubela. And you?"

"Jason Blue."

"Well, Mister Private Detective Jason Blue, if I'm ever in California, I will give you a call. But you and your friends better fly the coop now."

The crowds were all going at it as we drove through Chinatown up to the house in Siboney. An angry mob had surrounded the police station on Zanja, down the street from the theater. I caught sight of one lone officer still in his blue uniform thrown down the steps, kicked, and beaten with shoes, sticks, and brooms. All the stoplights had been shot out of commission, traffic piling up as pedestrians and cars swarmed the streets. Fireworks—Roman candles, rockets, firecrackers—

exploded in Chinatown, celebrating a new year like no other. Bands of teenagers in convertibles leaned on car horns, waving giant flags with the black and red of Castro's party, and the lone star Cuban flag, singing the national anthem and some other military song about libertad. Every so often I would also catch the strains of the "Internationale," accompanied by riffs of machine-gun fire. On every street, men and women were attacking parking meters with the ferocity they wished they could have shown to Batista's henchmen. Swinging sledgehammers, they struck until they beheaded the meters, coins spilling like so much blood on the ground, which people would scoop up in a little triumphant dance. I suppose a little craziness is to be expected when a dictator meets his end.

In the backseat, David had passed out on top of Raquel. She hugged him to her abundant chest like a mother while she worriedly looked out the window, taking in the chaos all around.

"Mister," she said in Spanish, "are you sure you'll be able to get us out of here with no trouble?"

"I don't know about the trouble, but we have a boat waiting for us. In a few hours, at the muelle."

"No aeropuerto?"

"Sure to be closed," I said, still in Spanish. I know it sounds funny, but at that moment I wished that I spoke better Spanish. Now that I had gotten a good look at her in the rearview mirror, I realized what a magnificent specimen of femalehood she was. I wanted to comfort her in all the ways a man can for a woman, but all I could do was say it would be okay and drive on.

We parked at the corner of 180th Street between 15th and 17th in Siboney without incident. The hubbub was now worlds away, back around the capitol building, shining ghastly white with the floodlights turned on, as people streamed in and out, taking files, artwork, boxes of papers. I had never been in a revolution before, but in Korea I had seen how, when authority suddenly vanishes, it's every man for himself. I figured with the usual snafus there wouldn't be a single port or customs officer on duty to stop us.

Raquel helped me carry David inside. We laid him on the bed of the coach house I'd rented from a Canadian I'd met at the Bodeguita del Medio the night I got into town. The coach house—clearly the servant's quarters—was behind a two-bedroom white house of fairly recent construction, modest by neighborhood standards. She lay down with him and I went to the kitchen to make myself some coffee. It was going to be a long night. I had told the captain of the boat to meet me at the dock at 7 in the morning with a full tank and food for the trip to Key West. It was now close to 3 and the efforts of a whole week of searching for David were finally beginning to take their toll.

I had eaten all my meals out since coming into town, so I had no idea what the Canadian's kitchen contained. I strolled across the grass to the empty house. There was a fence around the property and bushes taller than me. I walked in through the terrace to the kitchen and opened up a few cupboards, uncovering crackers, a jar of pickled herring, and a bag with a log of dried meat called *pemmican* that smelled suspiciously of old socks. Finally, in the refrigerator, behind two bottles of Big Rock Ale, I found a can of finely ground coffee. However, hard as I looked, I could not find a percolator anywhere in the place.

"Te puedo servir?" asked Raquel from the kitchen door. She'd apparently followed me over.

She leaned her head on the doorframe, her wide doe eyes slightly closed from fatigue and sleeplessness. It wasn't her eyes I was looking at, but her full figure, like a Maidenform bra ad, barely covered by the flimsy crocheted lace dress she'd thrown on at the Shanghai.

"I have coffee but no coffee maker," I said in Spanish.

"It's right there," she said, entering the kitchen. She slid next to me, her jasmine perfume as intoxicating as Tennessee moonshine. She grabbed hold of a metal conical object with a lid. She opened it, took out a piece of cloth shaped like a windsock, then turned, displaying it like a model at a fancy department store.

"This is how we do it in Cuba," she said, dumping the dried coffee grounds in the garbage and rinsing the cloth under the faucet. She bent down, picked up a small pot, put it under the faucet to fill.

I came in close behind her, pressed myself against her back, breathing in the smell of her body, her perfume, her excitement. She didn't move away, she just extended her arm to place the pot on the stovetop.

"You see, we have to wait until the water boils and then we put in the coffee."

She turned to face me, her head cocked sideways. "Maybe you have a light?"

I dug in my pocket, pulled out a box of waxy matches, and lit one. She took my hand, guided it to the burner under the pot, then turned to me again, still holding my hand in hers. The match was burning down to my fingertips but I didn't care. She brought it to her lips and blew it out.

"Pobrecito," she said. "You burned yourself." She kissed my fingertips then stuck them in her mouth, softly suckling them.

I took my fingers out of her mouth and put my tongue in there instead. She suckled that too and soon we were down on the kitchen floor, her dress over her head, her arms held together as though by a lacy rope as her full breasts with her big brown nipples bumped against my chest while I entered her, and soon we were both riding a wave of light that filled the room until it burst like a balloon and we were back on a grimy tile floor in Havana waiting for the boat to get us to a better place.

I lit a cigarette while she went to the bathroom down the hall, the overhead water tank of the toilet clanging like a fire bell when she yanked the chain. She came back into the kitchen, put the coffee in the boiling pot, and was soon serving me the inky sweet concoction Cubans call a *cafecito*. She sat at the table, knees together like a schoolgirl, unsure of my reaction. I said nothing and simply stared. I was waiting for her request and it didn't take long in arriving. No free lunch in this world, my daddy always said.

Raquel looked toward the coach house where David was still passed out on the bed. "He sleeps a lot when he takes the drugs," she said in Spanish. "He's always trying to run away from himself."

"Y tú?" I asked her. "What about you? What are you running away from?"

She gazed back at me, weighing her response, then took a cigarette out of my pack without asking. I would have slapped her hand but sometimes you have to be tolerant to get where you want to go. I even lit the cigarette for her.

"Me, I am running away from Camagüey. From my old man's hut, the son of a bitch, from this fucking crazy country."

"Is that why you're with the kid?"

She cracked a hard smile. "A little American boy comes

in looking for easy love and revolution? Sure. You understand. You know what they call us? Las putas del Chino." She stopped to make sure I understood. The Chinaman's whores. I nodded.

"I hate fucking Chinamen. They smell of rotten fish. But that's what I had to do, until David came around."

All of a sudden she dropped her cigarette, grabbed her stomach, put her hand to her mouth. "Ay Dios mío!" she said, rushing to the bathroom, barely making it in time to upchuck something green and brown and vile. I blew concentric rings of smoke watching her from the door as she flushed, rinsed her beautiful mouth, straightened out her flimsy clothes. She saw my reflection in the mirror and she knew her game was up.

"What month?" I asked her.

She stared back, put on some ruby red lipstick. "Cuatro."

"It hardly shows," I said.

"It's a good thing, otherwise I . . ." She turned to me, her doe eyes pleading with a mixture of fear and pride. "You're not going to tell him, are you?"

I shook my head. "No. But I'm curious: What would you do if I wasn't here?"

"I don't know. But eventually, I guess I would have told him."

"Do you love him?"

She shrugged, came up to me, kissed me lightly on the lips. "What is to love?"

I saw my own reflection in a mirror above the stove—my crooked nose, the scar on my forehead, the wide-set blue eyes that were the only thing my father left me.

"Sí," I repeated, "what is to love?"

We didn't say much after that. There wasn't much to be said. We understood each other. She wanted out and so did I.

The boy in his opium-induced dream in the bed was our ticket and we had to baby him. She did it her way, I did it mine.

Raquel returned to lie with David for a while as I waited for the sun to come up. I went out to the terrace and sat on an ornate iron bench, staring out at the sky, at the lights revolving madly above the fence and thick fortress of trees. The noise was far away now and dew was alighting, a low gray mist that seemed like a sponge wanting to wipe the whole town clean of the past, of the wrongs that had been done, of the hearts that had been broken. Or maybe it was just wiping it clean for the next round, I pondered, as I thought I heard a cry for help followed by a yelp of pain followed by the echo of a shot or two followed by silence.

The sky was a riot of mauve, purple, and red, the sun rising like an orange ball over Marina Barlovento when I walked down to the docks. The streets were eerily empty, but Siboney—in spite of its concentration of diplomats and foreigners—had woken up as fiercely revolutionary as before it had been cravenly Batistiano. The banners of Castro's 26 of July Movement hung from windows, while above doors a few sycophants had already put up signs announcing, *Fidel, esta es tu casa.* Fidel, this house is yours.

The prospect of a five-hundred-dollar payout had been enough to rouse the old black capitán from his house in nearby Jaimanitas, enough to make him venture out, load the supplies, and chug-chug his creaking boat out to the pier.

"Viva Fidel!" I said as I stepped on the *Buena Vista*, a trawler that had last seen a varnish job when it was a rum-runner's boat docking in the rushes of Cedar Key. It had absolutely nothing in common with the sleek yachts parked at Barlovento.

"Sssh! You want to get shot at?" said Anselmo in his low, slurring speech. "There's a lot of Batistianos here desperate to get out. No se habla de la soga en casa del ahorcado." *Don't mention rope in the home of the hanged.* "Look, there goes Ventura's boat!"

He pointed at a gleaming Chris-Craft churning its way through the gray waters, carrying on board the once feared head of Batista's secret police.

"Sic transit," I muttered.

"Qué?"

"May lightning strike him . . . You will be ready for us?"

"Sure, chico. Just make certain to return within the hour. Fidel's people and the boys from the Directorio are already taking over City Hall. I'm sure they will be here soon and who knows how long before they let people out again. They are out for blood today, compadre."

I turned the shower on in the coach house, dousing the still sleeping David. The water came out brown at first, but by the time it had cleared David was up and on his knees, gasping for air. I turned off the faucet, threw him a towel.

"Let's go, sleeping beauty. Time's a wasting."

Looking like a wet retriever, David took a few bumbling steps out of the tub, then heaved into the toilet.

I stepped outside and waited until he came out and drank the coffee Raquel had brought in for him from the main house. He looked around, taking stock of the place, obviously not remembering how he had gotten there. He smiled at me, still silent, then nodded in greeting. I nodded back and was lighting a cigarette when he dove for the window. I managed to grab him by the waistband.

"What the fuck is wrong with you anyhow?" I said, heaving him back inside and slapping him around a couple of times. He sat on the floor, Raquel hugging him.

"I told you, I'm not going back to San Francisco," he replied, rubbing his face where I'd landed my punch.

"Are you crazy? You want to stay here and do what? Do you know what just happened last night?"

"What?"

"Listen up, you idiot. Batista just left."

I turned on the old shortwave radio by the window. The plummy voice of the BBC announcer cut through the moist air: *"Here is the news. The President of Cuba, Fulgencio Batista, has fled the country, his government in ruins, in the face of a relentless advance by the rebel army led by a thirty-two-year-old lawyer, Fidel Castro. Thousands of Cubans took to the streets in celebration this morning as word spread of Batista's departure for the Dominican Republic in the early hours of this day. There are reports of looting in Havana. Hundreds of slot machines from casinos have been dragged into the street and smashed. One casino has been looted. President Batista handed over power to a military junta before he left. They ordered a cease-fire and appealed to the rebel forces of Dr. Castro for cooperation. Dr. Castro, however, announced this morning on rebel radio that operations would continue. 'The triumph of the Revolution must be complete,' he said."*

I turned off the radio. "Now do you get it? If we don't leave now, we're going to be stuck here for weeks until they get this mess straightened out. I promised your dad I would get you back to the city. Once you're there you can do whatever you want. You can get on the next plane and come back to join all your revolutionary amigos, for all I care. Although I have a feeling they won't wanna have a junkie yanqui on their side just now."

"Papi, listen to the man," said Raquel. "Please."

"So either you come willingly or I'm going to have to do it the hard way," I added.

David rubbed his face with his hands as though in deep concentration—or disgust. "All right, all right, you win. Let's go."

"Oh, papi, you are so good!" said Raquel, hugging him to her chest. I looked away, opened the front door.

"Vamos."

At Marina Barlovento, Esteban was jumping around the trawler as though the deck was on fire. He waved his raggedy porkpie hat at me when he saw me trooping down with David and Raquel.

"C'mon, c'mon, chico, they're here already!" he said, hurrying to cast off the dock lines.

"Who?"

"The muchachos from the Directorio, they're trying to stop people from leaving. Look at those guys over there."

He waved his hat at a group of men with rifles and machine guns boarding a large yacht three piers away. "They're checking all the papers, they say nobody can leave without authorization. Por suerte, the harbor master is not here, so once we're out in the water . . . Coño, what the hell is wrong?" The engine stopped its chug-chugging, coughed, then died. "Carajo!" cursed Esteban as he opened the engine cover by the stern and peered into the well. He cranked the engine, which let out a wet, sloshing sound.

"What was he saying?" asked David.

"Fidel's people are trying to stop all the Batista people from leaving; they're checking papers and whatnot . . . What's wrong with the engine, Esteban?"

The captain shook his head in desperation, slamming the motor with his hat. "Jodida mierda, coño," he cursed, "this piece of shit just flooded. I can smell it."

He raced over to the controls by the wheel, turned off the choke, then returned to the engine well, opening the throttle. He cranked the engine, which sputtered but refused to turn over.

"We've gotta go, tell him we've gotta go right now," urged David.

"I know, I know, what's *your* sudden hurry?" I asked.

"Jesus, are those them, those guys?" He pointed at a group of four men approaching the pier, led by a skinny redhead who looked familiar. *That couldn't be him*, I thought.

"Yeah, I suppose, what's the problem? Aren't you in good with these guys?"

"I gotta go, I gotta go," said David, terrified. He moved as though to jump in the water but I grabbed him, wrestled him down, pinning his shoulders with my knees.

"Jesus, will you fucking settle down?"

"You don't get it, do you? I didn't come here to help Fidel's people; I came here to bring weapons to Batista!"

"What?"

"Yeah, you moron. The State Department froze all arms shipments to Cuba last fall. Through a friend of mine I got ahold of some old surplus rifles and brought them down here. The Directorio people found out and they've been looking for me for the last week. What the hell did you think I was doing hiding out at the Shanghai?"

"But before—"

"I was whacked out of my mind, idiot. I couldn't tell my ass from a hole in the ground. But now I know what's coming and I don't want it!"

I let go of him and sat down on the deck, thinking fast. Then: "Hurry down below. I'll handle this."

David scurried away on all fours, slamming the door to the cabin behind him. I got up, whispered quickly to Raquel, and walked out to the dock, just in time to be greeted by my now old friend Cubela.

"Nice day for a cruise, Mr. Blue," said Cubela, while his four minions craned their heads, looking around the boat. Soon their eyes were fixed on Raquel, who walked out to the bow, where she proceeded to strip off her dress and sunbathe in her underwear.

"That's exactly what I was thinking, Rolando."

"You know, strangely enough, after we parted, I received information from my compañeros that the gentleman you are escorting back home is wanted by our people."

Out on the bow of the boat Raquel turned and displayed her best assets to the gunmen, who walked up to her and began a no doubt learned conversation on buoyancy, Archimedes, and fluids displacement.

"Really? I didn't know Dr. Castro was so concerned about drug fiends."

"Well, Dr. Castro is concerned about the welfare of all people. But he is particularly interested in arms smugglers who help Batista's torturers."

Now even Cubela himself sneaked a look at Raquel, distracted by her charms. As though constrained by ecdysiast duty, she stood and removed her top.

Esteban glanced up from the engine well, gave me a furtive thumbs-up. I nodded. He cranked the engine, which awoke with a roar.

Cubela turned his head back to look at Esteban, but at that very instant I grabbed the machine gun out of his hand and threw my left arm around his neck in a stranglehold. Placing the barrel of his gun on his shoulder next to his neck, I fired a warning shot over the heads of his men. Cubela squealed from the noise in his eardrum and the burning hot barrel against his skin.

"Tell your men to throw their weapons in the water, now!"

A moment passed, a gull flew by, and I wondered, *Is this all there is?* Cubela nodded, gave the order. The men cast their rifles into the bay, the weapons bobbing in the water for a few seconds before starting their descent into the blue-gray depths.

"Now tell them to move back up to the pier. Slowly."

"You know we will find you," warned Cubela as the men passed by us, hissing with contempt.

"I'll be waiting. But first, you and I are going to walk to the boat very slowly and you are going to board with me. Understood?"

"Perfectly."

We took small steps to the boat, then, with the barrel of the tommy gun still to his neck, we stepped onto the splintered deck of the *Buena Vista*.

"Cast off, Esteban."

"Yes sir, Mr. Blue."

The boat shuddered and trimmed in, still powerful even after forty years of service. The pier quickly receded as we headed out for the open water.

"What are you going to do with me?" asked Cubela.

"I haven't decided yet," I said, letting go of him to hold onto the gunwale momentarily as we bumped into a wave.

"Well, I have!" said David, who had come out from the cabin upon realizing we were heading out. Without warning, he pushed Cubela off the stern into the water. David stood on the transom, waving his fist at the bobbing head of the revolutionary. "Go get fucked, you damn Commie!"

I glanced back at the pier and saw that another group of Directorio people had come down from the dock. One of them raised a rifle.

"Get down! Get down, you fucking idiot!" I shouted, just before the sharpshooter fired and the bullet tore through David's windpipe, slamming him to the deck.

"No, no! Dios mío, no!" cried Raquel, who threw herself on the boy with the voracity of the lonely and the dispossessed. I bent down, took a cold look. I'd seen a lot of people like him in Inchon, when the Chinese attacked our positions and the guys fell like flies. There was nothing anyone could do to stop him from dying, he was choking on his own blood.

"What should we do, mister?" asked Esteban, looking worriedly down at the boy.

"Keep going. He's beyond saving." I knelt down next to him. "I'm sorry," I whispered. He grabbed at my hands, gurgling hoarsely, wanting to let me know one last thing, one final message. I put my ear to his mouth as he said his last word, then he seized up and died.

I let Raquel cry over his body for hours until she grew tired and worried and I reminded her she was carrying his child, and that seemed to comfort her some. I told her I'd make sure she would get her share of the old man's money, and I laid her down to sleep in the galley. Esteban and I cleaned the deck as best we could and then placed the body on ice down below.

It wasn't until the sun was setting out by the Tortugas, just about an hour from Key West, that Esteban put the boat on cruise, popped open a Polar. I took a swig, the bitterness in my mouth making the beer taste almost sweet.

"So what did he tell you, mister? What did he say at the end?"

I lit another Chesterfield, watched in silence the deep blue of the Gulf begin to meld with the green waters of the shallows by the Keys. Esteban was still looking at me, waiting.

"He said *Shanghai*," I answered, tossing out my cigarette.

"Shanghai? What does that mean?" asked Esteban.

I contemplated that for a moment, then I thought I should say, *It's the city of dreams, it's the city of sex and drugs and revolution and pleasure never ending*, but I realized that wouldn't do, so I answered the only way I knew how: "Yo qué sé."

What do I know.

MURDER AT 503 LA ROSA

BY Moisés Asís

Ayestarán

W*hat am I going to do?* That's what I keep asking myself over and over as they lead me through the airport.

"We have a problem, sir," the secretary at the law school had said. "You can't take the state's graduating exam because we found you have penal antecedents, a police record. It's been more than twenty years, so you can ask that they be erased and then you can take the state exam," he added in a conciliatory tone.

Of course I knew this; that police record had made a pariah out of me, without the right to study the career of my choice, without the right to seek a better job, or to have any kind of social acceptance. For more than twenty years I'd been walking around socially and politically castrated, and I'd been hoping that the University of Havana would never find out about my past if I just denied it.

"There was a mistake and it's been rectified," the legal adviser to the Ministry of Justice said this time, months later. "When you were tried and sentenced, you were a minor and so you should have never had an adult police record."

You're telling me this now, after decades of ostracism, you fucking legal adviser to the ministry?

But it's never too late to start again. So I graduated from

law school and decided not to practice, since the profession doesn't actually allow the defense of those accused of ideological crimes such as thinking aloud. I can't even defend myself. Under what law, and with what proceedings? I think back and I regret that I was so dismissive of that court-appointed lawyer who didn't bother to mount a defense for me back when I was seventeen years old. Where could he be now? Has he been imprisoned for thinking without hypocrisy, has he deported himself, has he allowed himself to be debased?

After two or three hours of pedaling my bicycle, sweating my guts out, I can't find my way home: Night has come too soon, and the stars are on vacation as it rains nonstop on this new moon. For those without direction or hope, there are no sadder nights than those that are moonless. And it won't matter how much I plead, the moon will not so much as peek.

The last time that I couldn't distinguish day from night was when I'd just turned seventeen and was locked up in a police cell during two weeks of questioning. The cell was windowless and it was impossible to tell the difference between dawn and the most intense noon hour. They wanted to reeducate me so that I would not only confuse day for night but so that I'd learn that good and evil were relative concepts.

I was frequently dragged from that nine-by-six cell that I shared with three other inmates and asked about my terrible crime: wanting to leave my country. Days before, the overloaded boat in which I'd hoped to row hundreds of miles had gone down near a fishing dock; we'd barely even started out on that moonless night. Nobody knew anything and there was no evidence, but a word from the political police was enough to label it a Crime Against the Integrity and Stability of the Nation. A military tribunal passed judgment on this civilian, a minor, with a court-appointed lawyer who stayed quiet, trembling, while the political police's prosecutor presented a fantastic story that steered clear of the truth. Of the four-year sentence I was given, I only served one, in labor camps where there were also moonless nights.

The police are not very efficient, or they're really so preoccupied with trying to deal with the miserable problems in their own homes, which they have in common with every other Cuban, that they really don't care about doing a good job of investigating crime. They never bothered to find out how Victor, my fourth-floor neighbor at 503 La Rosa Street, died. The octogenarian passed away three days after being hospitalized. Nobody bothered to find out how he'd hit himself so many times against the wall. But all the neighbors heard him, in the silence of the blackout, and Juana the mulatta, sixty years his junior, violently shaking him.

Victor and Juana had married four years before for the exclusive benefit of the young domestic servant, who would soon inherit the apartment and a juicy widow's pension. Now Juana and the three kids she had while married to Victor could finally enjoy a better life. Victor had been resigned to those kids, black babies who arrived one after the other without a smidgeon of their presumed father's Caucasian DNA.

Everything might have been more believable if on the night of the wall-banging and Victor's subsequent hospitalization, their door hadn't been furiously kicked in by Francisco, Juana's nocturnal lover, who arrived and couldn't understand why she wouldn't let him in.

Each night, Francisco, a thieving dipsomaniac from the neighborhood, would fornicate with Juana while Victor slept a few steps away. As soon as Juana became a widow, Francisco installed himself in the apartment and continued with the only things he knew how to do in his life: stealing and drinking.

They'd met at the bar adjacent to our building, at the corner of La Rosa and Ayestarán, a sad little place where lost souls would fill their bladders with alcohol only to empty them later in the neighborhood's recesses. It was a little after the man moved in that my life became more miserable, and I decided that killing him could be rationalized as an act of justice for the greater good of society.

I should be used to these interminable blackouts, omnipresent since my early childhood. If sunlight is a gift from God that has accompanied us always and will be with us forever, electric light is also an intangible miracle that doesn't depend on us but on a group of men who tell us day in and day out that we must save what they squander, who make the blackouts coincide with the hours in which the radio and TV broadcasts from the United States to the Cuban people are most intense. Or worse, the blackouts drag on when I need to write or study or when friends come over. The drunken thieves from the adjacent bar take advantage of the darkness to make off with what they can. It seems to me that the blackouts are a punishing reality that haunts us daily, from infancy to our deaths.

"We're going to let you go," says the bureaucrat who has just given me the approval to leave Cuba. "We're going to let you go because your soul is no longer in this country, you don't think or feel like us. You haven't matured enough to forget the idealism of your youth. You have not taken advantage of all the opportunities we've given you."

I am left dumbfounded, trying to figure out what these opportunities were that I didn't learn from or appreciate. But in this moment of joy, I mentally thank him instead, for not torturing me with a long delay in approving the leave for my family and myself.

The dark of the blackouts pursues me while I work, during dinner, trying to read or attempting sleep under the heat's caress, hauling buckets spilling water up and down the stairs, waiting in interminable lines to buy something to eat, as I make love, or during a funeral, healing or teaching others, trying to heal myself or trying to learn. I should be used to this since it's been the same thing since childhood, when the city of Havana began to lean on crutches.

I live in what could be called the clitoris of the Ayestarán neighborhood, which was built in the mid-twentieth century between the old colonial district of El Cerro and elegant Nuevo Vedado. My apartment is in a part of the neighborhood that looks like a giant vulva right in the middle of Havana; it's south, at the perineum of the intersection of Ayestarán Road and Rancho Boyeros Avenue. To the north, both avenues stretch for various blocks like thighs inserted in the city's hips, crossed on the west by 20 de Mayo Avenue, parallel to La Rosa, and headquarters to the National Library, the Ministry of the Armed Forces, the Ministry of the Economy, and other public buildings.

The worst part of pedaling incessantly in the dark isn't the actual darkness or not being able to perceive the difference between the street and the sky, the asphalt or the pit. It's not the fact that you see the same thing whether you raise or lower your eyes, whether you look ahead or to the side. The worst isn't even having to go slow enough so that you can jump off when the bike's wheels slide into the ditches, invisible because of the water. Nor is it getting lost, but rather losing your life, if this can be called a life.

For some time now there have been rumors about events which the mass media obscures: dozens of adolescents and adults have been killed while riding their bikes on the darkened streets. Following the bikers, the murderers hide behind the giant ocuje trees then bash them with baseball bats, or they trip the bikers by stretching a nylon cord from one side of the street to the other, which they then pull quickly and violently around their necks, before the bats deform their craniums. Life is the price of a bounty that is nothing but a pair of used shoes and a cheap, obsolete bike. And, of course, the police don't investigate; they can't be bothered with the everyday.

The domestic battles between Juana and Francisco began a little after they started living together. They always ended with vociferous screaming and Francisco getting kicked out. Apparently, he didn't steal enough to support the young widow and her three children. Soon, the lightbulbs from the building's common areas began to disappear, and more than once the motor that pumped water up to the higher floors vanished.

We all suspected Francisco, and I wanted to punish the crook who had me carrying dozens of buckets of water up the stairs every night: Francisco would leave the building and find a bottle of rum in the same hiding place where he always hoarded his alcohol; Francisco would be unable to resist taking a mouthful of rum, and a little later he'd be vomiting, having convulsions, his extremities stiffening involuntarily, then he'd finish off with a respiratory collapse and cardiac arrest. Sodium monofluoracetate, also known as Compound 1080, dissolves in water, is colorless, tasteless, and without odor. Francisco's fate was sealed.

I am going around and around the puddles and I can't seem

to find my home. If only there was a star to guide me! In the distance I see a very bright building, the Palace of the Revolution. Now I can orient myself; I'm going in the wrong direction so I turn right, go straight. I soon feel like I'm falling off a precipice, there's no asphalt anymore but an enormous emptiness, and my bike and I smash against the rocks below. Can anyone see me or hear me from here?

Once, during Yom Kippur, I felt the same way. I had begun my fast well before what was religiously necessary. It was unavoidable. I walked and walked toward the synagogue, dead tired, hallucinating, not from the incipient fast but because my body could no longer tell the difference between one day and the next. I saw the synagogue filled with well-dressed people and I imagined, as in a dream, that I was a dybbuk who sexually possessed a beautiful young woman I'd never seen before. What terrible thoughts for the Day of Atonement! I was enraptured by the hazzan's voice flying high with the most impressive of melodies and words: *Kol Nidre . . . ve'esare . . . vecherame . . . vekoname . . .*

The melody abruptly stopped when someone sat down next to me. That's when I opened my eyes and saw that the synagogue was actually almost empty, only seven people attending the service, there was no hazzan, there was not then and there never would be a Kol Nidre, that young woman and hundreds more had been living abroad for years and who knew if they were even dead or alive.

If this pit is anywhere near where I live, I should be able to hear Quimbolo, my nearest neighbor. Quimbolo is the only Cuban who is allowed the privilege of screaming improprieties against our absolute Big Brother without anybody ever thinking of locking him up for the rest of his life. Quimbolo's real name is Everardo and he's mentally retarded.

He wanders down the street in utter filth and repeats the rich and profane lexicon that drunks have taught him. I've never heard anybody scream *Pinga!* so stridently, so forcefully and sonorously. *Pinnnnnnnnnnnnnnnnnnnnnnnnga*, drawing out that *N* until the middle of oblivion. I remember hearing that word many times in the dark and at dawn like a war cry. For years, there wasn't a child born within three blocks in any direction who learned to talk by first saying *Papá* or *Mamá*, but rather by repeating Quimbolo's word.

One day Quimbolo was diagnosed with diabetes, I'd forgotten. His ulcerous legs got dirty and he died, amputated and septicemic, depriving the neighborhood of its most obscene crier.

"It looks like he had a heart attack! Run and call an ambulance or a doctor!"

"There are no doctors at the polyclinic?"

"The man is dead!"

People scream around Francisco's body. Now he'll never again steal the lightbulbs from my building or the motor to pump water. There will no more thefts in the building. One thief less.

I'm not afraid to come out of the pit in the middle of the street. This huge trench must be the hole at the corner of Ayestarán and Lombillo, in front of the dilapidated pharmacy, with its empty shelves. So I'm only a block from home. I crawl up the rocks until I believe I've reached the surface. I paw at the loose stones around me that should indicate wet asphalt. There's no sign of a bus or car that might illuminate me and possibly hit me; bikes pass in the distance. I crawl and carry my broken bike with me, its wheels destroyed. Now there are only three more flights to go up in the dark . . . a few more steps . . . a breather, twelve more steps . . . another pause. I take care not to hit what remains of the bike against my neighbors' doors. This stairway is such torture! I place the key at the same height as my navel, and this makes it easier to find the lock.

It was much harder to find the key to graduating from law school. It had been an incredible sacrifice to study at dawn, after each blackout, beating back sleep with abundant quantities of bitter tea.

From my balcony, the buildings and the street and the sky around me all seem beautiful, black like a great ocean of ink. That's also how I see my future, and that of my family. Why not try and find a bit of light, even if it's not so early in life?

In the months that followed, the streets remained littered with craters, ever darker, covered with trash, reeking. People walked by aimlessly, their eyes blank, resting in line after line, going from frustration to frustration.

Cats and dogs almost reached the point of extinction as adolescents discovered their flesh was edible, and the only ones seen on the streets were the most famished, abandoned pets dragging along their torn tufts of skin.

A girl faints next to me on the bus, a woman drops to the sidewalk one morning as I'm looking out my balcony. I'm told about an elderly woman who committed suicide because she couldn't take the cries of her little grandson begging for another piece of bread, even as the radio broadcasts announced that ours is the best fed nation on earth, with the lowest infant mortality and the highest life expectancy. My friends and acquaintances are dying so quickly, at early ages.

"We're so lucky to live in this country," my young daughter says to me as she watches the haunting images from the rest of the world on our TV.

But I can't believe it when I see two neighbors dive into a dumpster to scavenge through the fermenting garbage that had been feasted on by a myriad flies. Why is it that this country's fertile soil is so sterile? Why don't women want to give birth and why don't young people want to live? What makes people support so euphorically that which they in fact hate? Why do they work against themselves? Why do they seem to experience such joy as they dig hopeless tombs for their grandchildren?

Sodium monofluoracetate is infallible. Its chemical formula is CH_2F-$COON$ and I've read that it takes less than a tenth of a teaspoon to kill a degenerate like Francisco.

But what if the police perform an autopsy? They probably won't, though; there aren't many doctors left in this country now that the majority has been contracted out to Venezuela and other places. And those left are overwhelmed with work, so they're more likely to determine it was a sudden cardiac arrest and not expend limited resources on an autopsy.

I've read that this poison interrupts the Krebs cycle, that it alters the citric acid in the body. The poison turns into fluorcitrate, creates a citric concentration in the veins, and deprives the cells of energy. Cellular death is slow and painful.

The cops aren't going to waste time over whether some guy like Francisco died from a cardiac arrest or a few drops of sodium monofluoracetate. The cops have highly qualified experts and forensic doctors working with them who can find traces of the poison lingering in the liver, the brain, the kidneys, hair. But what if the morgue technician removed Francisco's liver and viscera and sold them on the black market as beef liver, beef viscera? Did other families die—children too—poisoned by Compound 1080 residue in meat?

* * *

The police officer who asks for my documents, for my passport, has a threatening expression. Behind me, the giant automatic glass door is closing forever.

The glittering lights blind me. It's been a long time since I've seen so much artificial illumination. The airport's hallways seem so beautiful, even though they have nothing by way of decoration other than their cleanliness and tang. I walk. I go very fast so that the doors won't close anew. I run to the escalators, then run again until I reach the counter where there's a man with a quizzical but apathetic expression.

"Your documents are in order but you cannot be completely admitted to the United States until you prove that your soul came with you; your body has arrived but you've left your soul in Cuba," the immigration official at Miami International Airport says coolly. "What are you going to do?"

What am I going to do? What am I going to do? I ask myself over and over as I leave the airport. I'll start over, that's what. I'll transform my hopes into a new soul until I can recover the lost soul that they tell me here I left in Havana, and which in Havana they say I brought here.

Somebody else can take care of the thief at 503 La Rosa Street. I could never get my hands on even two drops of sodium monofluoracetate, and I could never actually kill another human being. Perhaps they would have never found me out, but I'm glad that crook Francisco lives on and can still hope to change. I will, from here, far from Cuba, try to reconstruct my soul from its own sense of hope, which is only possible where there's light.

MURDER, ACCORDING TO MY MOTHER-IN-LAW

BY ARTURO ARANGO

El Cerro

for Achy, guilty

Her name was Lucrecia, they called her Pupy, and my mother-in-law couldn't stand her from the moment we met because it was rumored all over the neighborhood that what she liked most were black men. Whenever her name came up, my mother-in-law would make a face and say, "That pig."

Arguing with my mother-in-law is one of my favorite pastimes.

As far as we knew, the black men that popular opinion attributed to Pupy came down to just one: Guillermo, the father of her younger children, a strapping, smiling man who had once been a police officer, and with whom Pupy lived a few blocks from our house.

"He is a great guy," I'd tell my mother-in-law.

"He's better than her," she'd concur. "But she's still a pig."

Pupy's oldest boy, whose father we had never met, had blue eyes and lived with his grandparents, right across the street from our house.

I was at the stadium the night "it all happened," as my mother-in-law says, always reluctant to actually let out of her mouth words such as *cancer*, or *murder*, believing that by not pronouncing them, she can keep these misfortunes from herself and her family.

To live in Havana and say "the stadium" means only one thing: the Latinoamericano, an ancient structure that's been renovated over and over, and which, in extreme cases, can hold up to 150,000 people. At my age, I prefer the comfort of the rocking chair and the TV, with coffee in hand during the breaks, and the bed nearby for when a game gets boring. But during each playoff series, I keep a ritual of going at least once to that place which is both circus and temple, to become part of the spectacle that takes place in the bleachers.

The championship was being decided and the same two rivals were facing off as always: the most arrogant of teams, the one that can't stand to not make it to the postseason, the one that's so worshipped, protected, spoiled—and whose name will never come out of my mouth and I will refer to only as Las Ratas—and Santiago de Cuba, in which I always place my hopes, and always support.

Luis Lorente had been calling me since Friday night to remind me that Santiago would not be back again to play at the Latino after this because Las Ratas had very little chance of reaching even the quarterfinals that year. The stadium might be closed until November, at which time the next tournament would begin.

Saturday morning, I returned his call: I'd go by his house an hour before the game. After talking to Luis, I agreed to another duty I found considerably less pleasant: I took my mother-in-law grocery shopping.

Markets make me weary, and my mother-in-law says the same things week after week when she gets back in the car with a handful of scrawny scallions and a pale pumpkin. It's true that prices keep going up and that she's the one who cooks for the whole family, but living through those Saturday excursions—watching her make faces when she squeezes the avocados or cabbage, or the anxious way she pulls the wrinkled bills from her wallet, without any certainty about what she's actually handing the cashier—it's like sinking in an endless swamp.

There were a few other things she wanted to buy (cooking oil, a can of pimientos for Sunday's chicken and rice), and so on the way home I took a detour to the Villa Panamericana. Coming down the main avenue, I looked over at what used to be called Plaza de las Banderas (a string of empty flag posts pretends to justify the name) and saw some of the players from my team who were staying at a nearby hotel in that fairly new and somewhat pretentious neighborhood. I thought that if Luis Lorente had been there, I might have gone over to talk to them. But it's not especially easy for me to approach people I don't know (or, more precisely, people who don't know me).

I let my mother-in-law go into the store by herself and asked her to come get me when she was done at the place on the corner, a small glass square, like everything in the Villa, where they sold beer by the liter. There were two people waiting to be served. I did my duty and asked who was the last in line: The mulatto who turned to respond struck me as familiar. He looked back, searching for the table where some folks were waiting for him, and I recognized his features from TV: Orestes Kindelán. I felt my shyness challenged. It was like being next to Babe Ruth, or Pelé, or Michael Jordan. I asked how his team (my team) was doing for the final (though his answer was never in doubt).

"Good," he said. "We've just started training."

I should have said something else but my mind was too

slow. Until that moment, I had supposed that training was a daily routine for all the players. As my glass was being filled, I said something like, "Good luck," and followed him with my gaze. In his huge hands, he was carrying six glasses spilling foam. There was a table waiting for him on the terrace: two other ballplayers and two women. One of them was Pupy. Next to her was the only white guy who played on the team: tall, reedy, big-nosed. He was a pitcher nicknamed El Torpedo because of his lightning fastball, and he was slated to play that night.

It bothered me that he was drinking beer. Hours later at the Latino, I'd be following each one of his pitches breathlessly while his own breath would still have an alcohol residue. The game, it's true, really wasn't that important to Santiago, but to beat Las Ratas at the Latino was a matter of honor.

I told my mother-in-law that I'd seen Pupy with the ballplayers, next to a white guy. This time, my mother-in-law defended her, but in her own unique way: Guillermo, Pupy's husband, had been inside the store arguing about the price of some product. Perhaps the sixth glass of beer had been meant for him.

My mother-in-law actually placed more significance on the presence of the other woman, Olivia, who was also with the ballplayers. She lived two doors down from Pupy's parents but we didn't know they knew each other beyond the natural comings and goings of the neighborhood.

The one who liked Olivia was my wife. When we first met her, she was studying for a degree in geography, which she received with honors. But no sooner had she begun her professional career than she went to work at the Villa Panamericana's hotel. My wife considered that career change practically an act of treason.

At the hotel, Olivia was in charge of public relations, and according to what my mother-in-law related once I'd told her I'd seen the woman at the table with the ballplayer, she was so good at her job that people in the neighborhood were beginning to feel sorry for her husband. While Pupy was all vulgarity and cockiness, Olivia, whose father was a journalist with a weekly radio program, pretended to be an elegantly plain woman. (I once made the mistake of commenting in front of my wife a bit too enthusiastically about Olivia's undeniable poise, her graceful walk, the way she moves; my wife has never forgotten the words I used, comparing her to a gazelle . . .)

However, Javier, Olivia's husband, was untouchable as far as my mother-in-law was concerned: Shortly after we moved to the neighborhood, my son, who must have been three or four years old, fell, hit his head, and was left dazed, pale, and barely conscious. My mother-in-law was alone in the house. She went out in desperation and practically ran into Javier, who did not hesitate for an instant and pulled his old Pontiac from the garage to drive my son to the hospital.

"I see things as they are," my mother-in-law said on the way home from shopping, "and if one's a slut, the other one must be too."

When I went by Luis's house to pick him up, he was already outside, waiting impatiently on the sidewalk. Next to him was a tall, thin man, dark with green eyes. Luis introduced him as Azúcar, a friend from the neighborhood, a Ratas fan, and asked if he could come with us to the Latino. The deed was done but it had its upside. Azúcar had two principal occupations: He played basketball (although the gray hairs dotting his clean scalp indicated he was close to my age) and he sold auto parts. "Whatever you need, bro, you know . . ." His occupations were manifested in a narrow half-block corridor on 23rd Street between B and C, where there's a state-owned store that deals in auto and motorcycle parts. On the sidewalk right in front, on the corner of B, there's a basketball court.

The two of them had bought a bottle of rum which, as was required, had been poured into various plastic receptacles so as not to be discovered by the stadium ushers. I told them I'd seen El Torpedo drinking beer.

"Well, Artur," responded Luis, "what do you want him to do?"

Azúcar's comment made me sorry I'd accepted his company for the day: "Those hicks are always drunk. I don't know how they manage to win."

Like us, thousands of people had also thought it might be the penultimate game of the season, and when we went in we actually had a hard time finding three good seats. Perhaps the Latino's greatest charm is its cosmopolitanism, the way the city's demographics are reproduced in the stands. If you sit behind first base, you can be sure that those around you will be fans of the visiting team. The rest of the stadium (the gardens, the third base line, behind the plate) will be jammed with spectators, with small clusters of opponents, but these will be isolated, overwhelmed by the local joy.

It had been a year and a half since Luis and I had set foot in the stadium and we were surprised to see that about half the seats in our area behind the plate (the best, because of their excellent view of the playing field) were empty, and police officers stood in the aisles to close off access.

"They're for foreigners," explained Azúcar.

"What a waste," said Luis, seeing, even as a voice called out "Play ball!" to begin the game, that nearly a hundred seats remained empty.

Azúcar kept eyeing that area. I thought he was looking out for the opportunity to switch seats to that more neutral territory, some distance from the scandalous crowd around us cheering for the boys from Santiago. But just as the first inning was ending, a throng of tourists showed up, the majority dressed as if on safari, or as if we'd gone back a century or so and were attending one of those games that marked Cuba's *belle époque*: straw hats, felt hats, baggy white linen pants, huge fans, colored handkerchiefs around the necks, and, as if to indicate contemporary times just a bit, a beret here and there.

The blue that characterizes Las Ratas (and the New York Yankees, their supposed equals) shone brightly on the head of a woman who I thought I recognized. Was that Olivia? It was impossible to tell, the lighting in the stands was tenuous and a brim covered her forehead; my neighbor wore her hair long so I assumed it had to be tucked into the hat. But there was a way of moving when she came down the stairs, just like a gazelle, which certainly resembled hers. If Olivia was at the Latino, if those tourists were guests at the hotel, just like the players from Santiago, then her presence next to Kindelán and El Torpedo made more sense than Pupy's: Pupy, and not Olivia, was the stranger, the upstart. Was one as much of a slut as the other? I figured I'd ask my mother-in-law over breakfast the next day.

But I forgot about Olivia pretty quickly: Suddenly, it was as if the entire stadium had entered another dimension, as if we'd been completely covered by a veil of silence. The arm with which El Torpedo was pitching seemed to belong to God. Inning after inning, the zeros were adding up on the electric scoreboard. In the fifth, Orestes Kindelán hit a high one, and the ball fell among fans way up in the highest stands of the central gardens. Among us, there was much applause, hats in the air, and high-fives. After Orestes Kindelán was congratulated by his teammates and the scoreboard reflected the run, the only (and miraculous) score by Santiago, the silence returned, even deeper now.

Luis taunted Azúcar, who wasn't spared from the muteness that had fallen over the spectators. Whoever might be strolling by outside the Latino could never have imagined that there were forty thousand people in there, their hearts in their throats, entranced. What mattered now wasn't the score, but the spectacle offered by El Torpedo, his super fastball doing arabesques, lines breaking on the inside, on the outside, balls that dropped in flight as if fleeing from the batter, who was left dumbfounded, looking ridiculous on the third strike and forced to make that walk to the bench behind third base with his head down, the bat landing uselessly on the red sand.

In the seventh inning (they call it the lucky inning, because that's when pitchers start getting tired or the batters start figuring out pitches that had defied them before), El Torpedo opened with a walk, the only one of the game. The guy on first was a fast runner and, on the pitch, he sprinted toward second. In the meantime, the batter hit into the infield, where the defender had abandoned his position, and the play ended with men on third and first, with no outs. About two-thirds of the stadium awoke from its stupor. The other third debated the play. The batter had been right-handed, so the infield players should have never left their posts. Just one run ahead, the team on the field could screw up one of the best games of El Torpedo's year.

I looked at the clock: It was just 10 o'clock at night. I thought about the pitcher's fatigue, about the beers from this afternoon.

"This is getting good," said Luis, who only really cares about the stakes and the beauty of the game, not about any one team.

"I'll be right back," said Azúcar, and then we saw him in the aisles behind home plate.

A gasp (of surprise? admiration? reproach?) went through the stands when El Torpedo decided to release the next pitch facing home, and not from the side, as the unwritten rules of baseball demand. The man on first took off immediately, stealing second. The next batter was a power hitter ("This guy could do some damage," said Luis, not to me, but to a little guy devouring a pizza next to him) and I thought the pitcher was going to go for an intentional walk. But the three consecutive outs that El Torpedo managed were humiliating for Las Ratas and their fans: a silly fly ball to first base, a strikeout, a ground ball caught with his own hands, each one cheered on by the five or six thousand spectators around us (I was on my feet, clapping wildly for each of those outs).

Later, after the danger had passed, it wasn't El Torpedo's pitches that caught our attention, but his composure, the dignity with which he took the pitcher's mound, serene, smiling. Azúcar returned to his seat at the beginning of the eighth inning.

"My condolences," Luis said, and Azúcar told him to go to hell. Chewing on his cigar, eyeing his friend sideways, Luis was having as great a time as me, and he made fun of my earlier apprehensions. "I told you, Artur, those guys drink beer the way you and I drink water."

My greatest happiness occurred on the way out of the stadium, when I heard Las Ratas fans praising El Torpedo.

"He's a genius," Luis declared.

"He's a motherfucker," Azúcar responded.

It was a great game, though it lacked any real significance for either team. Sometimes glory is wasted. I remember it now for other reasons.

At dawn the next day, it was my mother-in-law who first opened the front door. I was in the kitchen preparing coffee. She called me to come look: Two squad cars were parked in front of Pupy's parents' house and various cops and neighbors were standing on the porch, their faces worried. My mother-in-law crossed the street. I remained at the front door, waiting for her. I saw her put her hands on her head, then hug and kiss Pupy's sister and go into the house. When she came back, she looked like she'd been crying: Pupy had been found murdered in the women's bathroom at the Latino. Guillermo was a suspect.

All day, news kept coming in waves that were often contradictory: The body had been found during the eighth inning and not at the end of the game; no, it was found during the ninth; actually, it was two hours before the lights were turned off at the stadium; she'd been strangled; she was stabbed; it'd been a devastating poison; the body was stuffed in a closet; it was left in the parking lot; it was found sitting in the bleachers and she looked like she'd fallen asleep; they'd found her because Guillermo had called the police; Guillermo had left the Latino without the slightest concern about his missing wife ("Were they actually married?" my mother-in-law asked, astonished).

Shortly after lunch, we saw the new widower arrive. I asked my mother-in-law to go back and get more information (she could always take some fresh coffee over, since the flow of visitors had not ceased all day long). But she was embarrassed. She thought I wasn't dealing with Pupy's death the way I should. She mentioned the newly motherless children, the pain her parents must be experiencing.

They released the body that night (that's how they said it in cop speak, and that's how the neighbors repeated it: Her possessions had been retained, examined, and now they were free—to satisfy the rituals of death? So as to actually have peace in death?) and though my mother-in-law insisted we go to the funeral home right away, I refused to go until the next day. The burial was slated for 3 in the afternoon and there would be plenty of time to offer condolences.

There wasn't room for one more soul at the funeral home. There were two squad cars outside (the cops inside sweating through their heavy gray shirts, were they her husband's old colleagues? Or were they still investigating the murder?). As soon as we went in, my mother-in-law made her way, as expected, to the viewing room where she found Pupy's parents, children, and sister. She distributed kisses and approached the casket, peering at Pupy's face, which I imagined pale and dark around the eyes (as if she hadn't gotten sleep in the morgue). She strolled among the other neighbors huddled throughout the funeral home. I did not see her greet the widower, who was talking nonstop, surrounded by about a dozen people.

The haze in the funeral home caused by the smokers drove me outside, far from all the chattering, where I engaged in monosyllabic exchanges with acquaintances who went in and out. My mother-in-law came out now and then to share what she was hearing inside: It looked like it was true about the closet and the knifing, though the stab count varied between one and five (the theories about strangulation and poisoning, which had struck me as crazy, had disappeared). The issue of the time also appeared to be resolved: A little before 10, Pupy had left her seat to go to the bathroom. The game had ended at 10:40 and Guillermo didn't think it was particularly strange at first that his wife hadn't come back before the game's last out. On nights like that, with the stadium full, the lines in the women's bathrooms were long, interrupted now and again by employees in charge of flushing the toilets by forcing buckets of water into them.

I approached the chorus surrounding the widower: He was ashen, and he kept pausing to explain more than tell about the moment when he arrived at the women's bathroom and found an employee closing the door. The woman had assured him that there was no one inside except an older woman, whose description didn't fit the person Guillermo said he was looking for. He thought maybe Pupy had gone to the bathroom on the other side of the Latino (those near where we had been sitting), and he went around, avoiding the employees who'd started to put up gates and burglar bars, only to find that bathroom empty as well. He climbed the stairs to the stands, looked over to the area behind third base: There was no one there except the cleaning crew, which was sweeping. He went out to the streets, moving from one entrance to the other.

"I was just walking from here to there and there to here," he said. Somebody from the chorus asked what he'd been thinking during his search. "You know, Pupy was kind of nutty," he answered, "and since I'd moved from where we'd been sitting to go look for her, it occurred to me that maybe she'd gone ahead to the bus stop."

According to the police, what made Guillermo a suspect was that he'd been found at home, fast asleep, when Pupy's body was discovered in the closet in the third base women's bathroom, surrounded by buckets and mops.

"They just don't know how it happened," the widower tried to explain. "How was I supposed to know she was dead?"

According to Guillermo's own telling, the two of them had drunk an entire bottle of Patricruzado at the stadium just before the seventh inning. Azúcar, Luis, and I had finished off our rum in the ninth, with the last out.

"I was beat when I got home, I threw myself in bed, and I was dead to the world," Guillermo said. The cops came knocking on the door around 2 in the morning. A stadium worker had found the body when she went looking for the acid to pour into the toilets after the general cleaning.

The mourners demanded that Guillermo enlighten them about possible motives, that he name suspects, that he repeat every word uttered by the police.

"You all knew Pupy," he said, "and there was stuff, but she always tried to get along with everybody. As far as I'm concerned, they just got her mixed up with somebody else."

I asked him if she'd left her seat before or after the seventh inning.

"During the walk," he responded.

It was almost 11 o'clock in the morning. Sunday's game started at 2 and the players from my team might still be hanging out in the hotel lobby. I asked my mother-in-law to wait for me. When I parked next to the Plaza de las Banderas, I saw the players' bus leaving. A few foreigners waved goodbye from the sidewalk with a certain familiarity. I identified a few picture hats, a cap with a Marlins logo.

At five till 2, I entered the Latino. The stadium felt like a different place. The sun washed out the colors in the stands, the worn field sparkled, and a few kids ran in the aisles. The silence came not from awe but from abandonment. I found

the place where the tourists had been seated the night before. Nobody was watching the access door now. I sat down
in the very middle of the section by myself. The applause and
whistles after good plays sounded like the echoes of a small
town stadium. The players were closer, and more visibly tired;
the uniforms dirty; the bats scarred. I left before the game
had even reached its midway point. Las Ratas were ahead but
nobody seemed to care, not even me.

A few weeks later, the radiator in my car began to leak; days
later, it had become a stream that lined the walk from my
garage. When it got to be a hose watering the garden, I remembered Azúcar.

I found him on the basketball court in a bad mood: His
team had just lost and the players were arguing about whose
fault it was. He told me there were no radiators to be found,
and then gave me an obscure address on the banks of the
Almendares River where I could get a box of balloons and
the sealant to repair the damage myself. The postseason had
already begun and Santiago had destroyed its first rival in only
three games. I told Azúcar that I was sure El Torpedo would
take us through to the championship.

"That guy throws rocks," he said. "That night was different, but anybody can have a game like that." Then he laid out
El Torpedo's career statistics, which were, in fact, mediocre.

I mentioned that a neighbor of mine had been killed at
the Latino.

"You're neighbors with the late Pupy?" he asked. "Well,
you *were* neighbors." He grinned. "Hell, you still *are*—you
didn't move." He stood there thinking. "Fuck, how would you
say that?"

"I was neighbors with the late Pupy."

He repeated it. "You were neighbors . . ." He wasn't sure I was right.

"I guess she had to pay," I said.

"She was out of her league," he responded.

"How much did you lose?" I dared to ask.

He looked at me uncertainly. "Forget about that."

Two months later, Pupy's death was still in the shadows. Guillermo was brought in once or twice and Pupy's mother told my mother-in-law that something had happened with the woman who cleaned the bathrooms. It was also being said that a woman's wig and high heels had been found that night abandoned in the stands.

"Did they make him try on the shoes?" I asked her, trying to imagine that robust black guy in high heels and crowned by a brilliant blond wig. Were we now playing some kind of Cinderella game in reverse, with the police going door to door to see which of the men who had been at the Latino that night could fit into the shoes worn by the killer transvestite? My mother-in-law suggested I be more respectful.

The championship was about to end, my team looked invincible, and I invited Luis and Charo, his wife, for lunch at my house to watch the decisive game, being broadcast from Santiago. As my friends rang the bell, Pupy's father, bent over an old cane that looked like a stick of wood, passed by on his morning walk from one corner to another.

"Poor man," Luis said after I told him who it was.

I lit the coals and brought out the plate of chops marinated in sour orange, salt, and garlic.

I tried to make sure Pupy didn't get dropped from the conversation. I reminded Luis of El Torpedo's exploits. The chops, now resting over a slow fire, began to drip on the burning coals and release a smell of burning fat. I suggested to Luis that we make a game out of guessing Pupy's killer.

He laughed. "Artur, you're such a kidder . . ."

My mother-in-law brought out a tray of pork rinds, "so you have something with which to fill your mouths." I asked her to join us. She preferred showing off her flowering rhododendrons to Charo, as well as the lilies that would dry up if the rains didn't come soon.

I got a piece of paper and drew a few lines that could be the field and others that attempted to define the stands. Underneath, I made a mark suggesting a timeline. At the beginning I wrote in *twelve noon*.

Luis asked me if that was when I'd called him. "I don't remember a thing, Artur."

I knew I'd gotten his interest. On the timeline, I started scribbling in words to define actions: the moment I saw Pupy with El Torpedo, when we arrived at the Latino . . . And on the diagram of the stadium, I marked the hours in which these events occurred: A little before 10, Pupy gets up to go to the bathroom; minutes later, second base gets stolen from under El Torpedo and he allows a hit; then Azúcar leaves our side.

As soon as I wrote *Azúcar*, I could see Luis's eyes getting worried.

"No, Artur, not Azúcar."

I calmed him. I explained that his neighbor being a fan of Las Ratas did not, in my opinion, make him a killer. But later I did raise the topic more soberly: If in fact Azúcar had gotten up from his seat with the purpose of murdering Pupy, fate was sweeping by us (I only said "us" to implicate Luis) with such force that, in a way perhaps we didn't yet understand, we might also be guilty.

Luis shot up, his hands in the air as if asking for a time out, and made his way to the pork rinds. He grabbed a fistful (some were hard, or "past their prime," according to my mother-in-law). "Let's see, let's see," he said. "So Azúcar didn't kill her?"

"Correct." I needed him not to feel compelled to defend his friend.

"Well, then, go on."

But Azúcar could certainly be useful: Why did he get up from his seat just as Las Ratas were threatening in the seventh inning?

Luis demurred—how could he possibly know?

I was as clear as I could be: Azúcar had gotten up to make a bet.

Luis narrowed his eyes, now two little lines on his face.

I told him about the conversation I'd had with his buddy when I went looking for the radiator.

Luis pulled a cigar from his pocket and asked me for a light. The flame on the stove was better than the burning coals on the grill.

"You want me to tell you the truth?" he asked on his way back from the kitchen, a little bit of malice in his voice. "That night, Azúcar lost a bundle."

I liked the phrase, and it sounded natural in Luis's voice: "a bundle."

I called over to my mother-in-law and my wife, who was prepping the salad. "I've got it," I said euphorically.

My mother-in-law told me to lower my voice: Behind the patio fence bobbed the heads of some of our neighbors. She always assumed their ears were on alert, spying on our conversations.

I explained the diagram and the timeline. On another sheet of paper, I scribbled my logic:

a) Someone whose identity we'd yet to discover contracted Pupy to seduce El Torpedo and somehow convince him to lose the game;

b) El Torpedo went to bed with Pupy ("Pupy slept with El Torpedo," my wife clarified) and agreed to drop the game. We can assume that the sex alone was not enough to convince him (Pupy was no longer young and, according to my wife and mother-in-law, had never been pretty). The pitcher was probably also offered a substantial amount of money.

c) At the end of the sixth inning, Santiago was ahead by one run and El Torpedo seemed invincible. It would have been easy to get a bunch of neophytes to bet on them.

d) Pupy went to complete the second half of her assignment—to promote big bets against Las Ratas.

e) The walk, the stolen second, the hit all made it look like El Torpedo was doing his part.

f) Azúcar got up to go bet a bundle in favor of Las Ratas—that is, against the popular current.

g) El Torpedo reacted. We could attribute it to his pride, perhaps because of something said by a teammate, or maybe an insult hurled from the bleachers, or perhaps he simply realized he was having an exceptional night and he wasn't prepared to throw it away.

h) When he decided to stand facing the batter to pitch, with men on first and third, El Torpedo defied those who were trying to buy him. The dimwits figured he was just shamelessly screwing up. The more alert understood he was laughing at them.

i) When El Torpedo managed to dominate Las Ratas without allowing the tying run, Pupy's fate was sealed.

I repeated Azúcar's words: "She was out of her league."

"So who do you think killed her?" my mother-in-law asked. Her look wasn't curiosity so I was prepared to have her contradict me.

The chops were just about ready, the game was about to start, and there were still two outstanding questions. Or three. And a clarification.

"Do you know why Azúcar isn't a suspect?"

Luis shook his head.

"Because he got up before Las Ratas became a threat, and because he came back too quickly."

My wife said it was all absurd and went to deal with the lettuce and tomatoes.

"Who's an easy touch for a lot of money on a bet? Who would bet against Las Ratas at the Latino?"

I've always admired how keen Charo can be, and her response was what I expected: "No Habanero would dare it, and people from Santiago never have enough money."

So who was in position to lure the foreigners, for whom betting was probably not illegal, to the stadium? Who, in fact, was in a position to make the bets that, in the language of the profession, could be called part of the "tourist package"?

My wife brought the salad. "Olivia," she said.

"Oh, please, be quiet," my mother-in-law admonished, immediately surveying the top of the fence for listeners.

"The one whose father's on the radio?" asked Luis.

Trying to imagine the actual killing seemed futile to me, but my audience demanded it. The women's bathroom, where the stadium security guards have little access, could easily be a betting spot.

Olivia might well have been with her guests in the stands,

explaining the doings on the field. "The one who's going up to bat next is the loud one from the restaurant," she might have said, and the tourists would have looked at the guy under mercury lights, hardly believing he was the same man who had slept in a chair in the hotel lobby.

Did Olivia kill with her own hands or merely order the hit? My mother-in-law, for the second time, said she didn't want to hear anymore. I couldn't imagine Olivia going into those flooded bathrooms, which you could smell from far away. At the third out of the seventh inning, there would have been plenty of resentment to go around.

"Olivia probably didn't even have to have her killed," Charo proposed.

I declined to accept the idea. How much money did those people lose who'd trusted in Pupy, in El Torpedo? Who had thought up the operation?

So that it wouldn't be Olivia's cadaver that showed up in the hallway at the Latino, or in one of the dark little streets around it, Pupy had to die.

"Thank God they didn't kill El Torpedo."

"Too risky," I said.

"Yes, here we're all equal, but some are more equal than others," added Charo.

My wife came to tell us that they were singing the national anthem in the stadium in Santiago. "Are you finished wasting time yet?" she asked.

"This has given me a headache," Luis said.

"That's because you let him get to you."

But Luis and Charo agreed that my conclusions were irrefutable.

"If it's so easy to solve the murder, why haven't the police been able to do it?" my wife asked.

"Because they're idiots," explained Charo.

"I don't think they'd play around with a murder." My wife had lost her sense of humor. "It's a good thing you never wanted to be a policeman."

According to her, the detectives had to know everything we'd come up with, and more. In fact, we didn't really know much about that world of gambling and revenge. For what I was saying to be true, wouldn't Olivia have had to pay something to someone? Where would she get that kind of cash? Was Javier, her husband, unaware of her dealings, or was he in on it too?

My wife might very well have been right, but in cases like this, I know she can get insufferable, and it becomes impossible for me not to argue against her.

"She's a murderer," I said conclusively.

Luis took his plate to the living room and I went ahead to tell my mother-in-law she could serve.

"She's always up in the clouds," my mother-in-law said, as she gave the black beans a final touch by pouring just a smidgen of olive oil and vinegar on top. "And you don't even know what I know!"

I tried to get her to at least drop a hint: Had the police interviewed Olivia?

"Are you crazy?" When my mother-in-law decides to bite her tongue, she's as silent as a tomb. Anyway, El Torpedo was on the pitcher's mound and Luis was screaming for me to come watch.

I went to bed early and in a foul mood: El Torpedo was spanked and the championship had slipped through our hands. By the fifth inning, the game was a mess and we had abandoned the TV. Out on the terrace, which was still haunted by the smell of the grilled chops, Luis and I silently finished off the two bottles of rum that were left. I fell asleep out there, without noticing when our friends went home. The world was still in balance inside my head when I dropped into bed. I shut my eyes. Then the world made a sudden turn. I opened my eyes and tried to focus until the ceiling above me almost righted itself.

"You know you screwed up," my wife said.

I pleaded with her not to move the bed; I assured her I was feeling better. But she was talking about Olivia. The ceiling was now just about flat again and parallel with the floor.

"If she finds out what you were saying about her, she could make trouble for you, and you won't have an easy time of it."

The ceiling was once more intent on oscillating, on coming closer then retreating. I got up and had a glass of ice water. Dawn found me in a chair in the living room.

Some days after those pork chops had been served and devoured, I was sitting on the porch reading. My mother-in-law was in the garden admiring some gardenias that were beginning to sprout. Olivia and her husband walked by on the street and greeted us. Their arms were full and their exhaustion was obvious. My mother-in-law didn't even lift her eyes from the gardenias' pale, fragile stems.

"Has their car broken down?" I asked my mother-in-law.

Olivia and her husband stopped to talk with Pupy's parents.

My mother-in-law watched the scene, then shook the dirt off her shoes. "They had to sell the car," she said. "It's a miracle they didn't kill her too." As she walked by me, she muttered, "Degenerate."

Translation by Achy Obejas

PART III

Sudden Rage

THE ORCHID

BY **Mariela Varona Roque**

Santos Suárez

The man takes the orchid down from the balcony wall. He breathes, as always; his breaths seem like sighs. He considers the poor orchid, tied unjustly to this fake branch, and he imagines the size, number, and thickness of the petals if, instead of this fourth-floor apartment, he had a house with a yard. The yard would be filled with ancient trees, worthy of this orchid.

The excited, almost hysterical voices of his wife and a neighbor come to him from the kitchen. Oh my God, only seven years old, and Marta had told him to come straight up here, that Alfonso was going to babysit him, but Alfonso says that when the boy didn't show up, he went down to his house to get him and found the house locked; that's when he figured Marta must have decided to leave him with his grandmother . . . Alfonso? Just imagine, he's been struck dumb by this terrible thing, like me, that boy was like a son, or a grandson, to us, you know that. I imagine the police will want to question us now . . .

The man has taken the orchid to the bathroom. He poses it delicately on the rim of the pan in the shower stall and pours water from a bucket, filling the pan to the exact brim so that it is perfectly balanced. The voices can still be heard in the bathroom, though they're deadened by the thickness of two concrete walls. Yes, of course, she's under psychiatric care, they have her on pills. She came home at 2 in the morning, and since her son has stayed here so many nights before, she didn't want to wake him up at that hour, believing the whole time, poor thing, that her little angel was fast asleep, when by then he was . . .

The orchid has two withered petals the man tries to remove from the stem. One falls into his hand but the other still has some sap and refuses to fall. The fleshy, bright texture of the petals remind him of animal skin rather than plant leaves. The man sits on the toilet lid, sighing constantly, and he takes the little jug that his wife has used for the last twenty years to wash herself and dips it in the bucket. He surprises himself when he tries to remember the last time his wife washed herself before going to bed.

It's her voice he hears, rising in tone, becoming more dramatic. Whoever did it should be castrated, should be left to bleed until his mouth overflows with ants . . . He was an innocent creature who couldn't defend himself. It must have been a mentally ill person, one of those drunks who spend all day on the corner, over there at San Benigno and Zapotes, with their bottles in hand. One of them is an ex-convict, he has tattoos. You can see it in his face that he's capable of all kinds of savagery. It was probably him—he saw the boy walking all by himself and sweet-talked him; kids go along with whoever shows them anything of the slightest beauty, the poor things . . . Alfonso is devastated. I could never have kids, and ever since we got to know Marta, that boy has spent more time here than with his real grandmother . . .

The man brings up the little jug, full now, and begins to water the orchid, which shines its venomous color in the shadows. He asks himself why this thing with the boy had to happen now, this weekend, when all signs had pointed to calm.

We have to buy groceries, Alfonso. Groceries bought. And we need to get money to pay the light bill because what you gave me for household expenses has been spent. Lights paid. And please do me the damn favor of fixing the oven, because it's leaking oil. Oven fixed. And make sure that all your messy tools and parts are put away by the time I get back. Tools and parts picked up and put away. And go by Mirna's and return the blender, since I have to live my life borrowing blenders because it's never occurred to you to buy me a blender. Blender returned. And remember that Marta wants you to watch the boy this Saturday, that she's going out.

He turns the light on and closes the door to keep the voices out. Isolated phrases still come through. Seven years old, goddamn it, and no pity . . . Nude, smeared with blood and left in the mud, the little angel . . . The doctor on call at the clinic found out everything from the morgue. Yes, in the mud, in a ditch on the way to the river, behind the brickworks . . . It was the old man who gives massages who found him, he was looking for herbs for one of his teas . . . It had to be the ex-convict: Who else could it be but him? The only person who's sick in the head around here is that guy . . .

The man aims the flow from the little jug to water the fake branch to which the orchid is pinned. He knows that the water will soak into the organic matter in its thick layers, and that the orchid will suck it out later like a vampire. He sees the petals shining; they seem as alive as he is, but incapable of blossoming. He remembers Marta's boy touching the plump petals with his fingertips whenever he accompanied him on his ritual of watering the plants.

There was no need to water the boy's cheeks to see them shine. One time, in this very bathroom, Alfonso had emptied the little jug of warm water over the boy, and his color had not been venomous at all; on the contrary, it was the healthy color of a beautiful boy, with bright eyes and red lips, splashing water everywhere, never still like an orchid. His skin reflected all the colors of a rose, including a morbid mauve under his brow. They were the colors the man imagined on the flower to come, after watering that mute plant for so many years.

But now it is the same as always: The petals are dry and hard, like a fistful of indigenous, maybe obsidian blades. Not a single bud coming up anywhere. He sees himself, as he did so many times at sunset, sharing his secret hiding place between the trees by the river with the boy. They sit in an old abandoned truck covered with vines and flanked by piles of old bricks, and he listens to the boy's chatter while he gazes out at the trees that don't belong to him and imagines them covered with orchids.

He lifts the fake branch and waits for the water to drip off the stem and the petals, then scurry down the shower drain. Later, he holds it with one hand, keeping the other hand under it to catch the water that continues to leak through as he takes the plant out of the shower, with his flip-flops dragging, and back to its nail on the wall in the balcony. When he returns, he hears his wife's voice saying goodbye to the neighbor, tearing into him right away. There you go again with your hang-up with that orchid, instead of getting dressed to go help Marta, that poor woman, and then to the wake. I don't know how you can concern yourself with that idiotic thing with the boy's disgrace still so fresh, and knowing that it happened while he was walking over here . . .

The man doesn't say anything. He goes back to the bathroom and carefully closes the door so his wife doesn't hear him lock it. He puts the bucket and the little jug back where they belong; he uses the bathroom rug to wipe off the water that dripped on the floor, then stands before the mirror hanging above the bathroom sink. He looks at his faded eyes and hears the boy's voice pounding in his ears, telling him not to go to his house, that it's better to meet by the hideout near the river, the only really safe place. And he remembers his sudden rage, the childish eyes growing wider from shock, and that sensation of power once everything was finished. He pulls from his pocket the blade with the golden handle, a gift from his father, and checks the sharpness with the same spare discipline with which he performed the ritual of watering the plants.

Translation by Achy Obejas

WHAT FOR, THIS BURDEN

BY MICHEL ENCINOSA FÚ

Vibora

D aniela killed herself.

She fried her brains, that's what I mean.

They said it happened in the theater's restroom. During the blackout. She broke open an electrical outlet, pulled the wires out, and scraped them down with a nail cutter. Then she stabbed herself in the head with a pair of scissors, two times, and tied the wires to them. Right into her brain. They said that doesn't hurt, that you can't feel pain in your brain even if it gets bitten. Then she sat herself down on the toilet, they said. And when the electricity came back on, the volts and amps blew through her at will. They said you just had to see what was left after that. You could peer inside her skull through the holes. Can you believe it? And her panties were wet. But her makeup was intact. Daniela wasn't one of those lezzies who cries, they said.

Though apparently she was one of those who pees herself, they added.

Nobody actually saw anything, but that's what they said, that's what they're still talking about.

And I believe them.

I say thanks and take off down the shaded sidewalk because the red and blue riot of lights from the squad cars is driving me crazy.

It's a pretty day. There's a bit of sunshine, little clouds, an incredible clarity.

"Hey, is it true some crazy woman killed herself in there?" La Gloria asks, coming up to me with that perennial smell of garbage that's always about her. "Were you there? What happened? Hey, what the fuck are you laughing about?"

"It's a beautiful day," I tell her, avoiding the hand that's trying to grab my arm.

"That's because somebody wanted it to be that way and pushed some buttons in his office."

That's true.

It's horrible.

It's as if I had to be reminded that the contentment in my belly was owed to a calf that had been dismembered just a few days before.

Or worse: owed to the person who did the dismembering.

La Gloria insists: "What happened? Was it because of trouble with her lovers? Or did somebody tell her she had AIDS? C'mon, you fag, tell me."

"It's none of your business," I say. "Zip it, shove it up your ass."

She spits at my feet and walks back to the mountain of garbage covering the dumpsters.

I watch for a few seconds as she starts to dive, dig, salvage.

I'm tired of watching her. Every day, the same corners, the same dumpsters. This is La Gloria, from our neighborhood. The one who eats what you shit. The one who dresses in everybody else's clothes. The one who picks up cigarette butts at bars. The one who scours the whole city as if it were some free supermarket. You know, that one . . . barbaric, and so damn young.

Her Lycra's ripped at the butt. Her dark skin is cellulite-free. Thin and straight, her body. Curly and ash-colored, her hair. So young.

I turn my back on her and continue down 10 de Octubre Boulevard. It doesn't matter, up or down, but down's easier. Until the intersection with Vía Blanca. Then left, until the Lacret junction. Then down again to the boulevard. Triangles are always worse than circles. I walk along, contemplating my shadow, which moves ahead of me, until I realize I have no shadow at all to contemplate anymore. I don't know when but at some point the sky clouded over. I'm afraid I can be slow to notice things like that.

They always told me: "Don't go around breaking girls' hearts. Especially the young ones. The younger they are, the worse it is."

Ten years ago, Daniela was seven years old and I was seventeen. Ten years ago, we were both hungry. Like so many siblings in the tenements, we slept in the same bed; it was her fault I didn't find out for the longest time about nighttime masturbation, serene and alone. But I never held it against her. I never held anything against her. Not even the way she slapped and kicked at me when she had nightmares. Instead, I'd talk to her.

"Just imagine it, Dani, my little dove. A Harley Davidson. Do you know what a Harley Davidson is? It's a motorcycle like Uncle Patricio's. That big, like a couch. You and me on one, on the highway. Can you imagine it? A highway, like in the movies. You know: Kansas, Arizona, Omaha, Salt Lake City, sun, big sky, straight ahead, just straight ahead, right up to the clouded horizon. There's always lightning on that horizon, you know. Can you imagine it, my little dove? You see the light cut through the sky but the Harley's engine won't let you hear the thunder, so you go ahead and it never rains because the clouds run away when they see us, and there's almost no grass, and everything's quiet except the Harley's engine; you're laughing, and I just go faster and faster. Can you imagine it?"

"Yes," she'd answer. "We're gonna do that someday?"

"Just like I'm telling you, my little dove, someday, someday we're gonna do all that."

Yuri would come over and listen for a while, then leave. Yuri was a very boring older brother because he was never hungry. He'd dropped out of college to sell marijuana and PC components.

It was Yuri who pressured my mother to let me go on scholarship. "We're too crowded here," he said. "My clients come over, they see so many people and get nervous." Later, he found a lover for my mother so that she left the house too. Some guy from Miramar, high up, you know. "And don't worry; I'll take care of Dani. She's gonna be better fed and looked after with me than you anyway."

Mamá let herself be talked into it. I can't blame her.

I let myself be talked into it. Daniela never forgave me.

Seven years old. Daniela was just seven years old when I broke her heart.

She never sent it off for repairs. She learned to like the dripping of her fractured baby bottle. It lulled her at night; it gave her life a different beat.

When I came home from school, I'd lie down next to her, just like before, and I'd talk to her about festivals up at Dunlop Square, and about Mardi Gras and San Francisco.

"Stop talking shit," she'd say, and turn her back to me.

Yuri would sometimes come by and take a look at us, and it seemed like he felt sorry for us.

Yuri is sitting alone at the table. Standing next to the wall, the sergeant is smoking. But he doesn't count. Yuri builds a wall with dominoes. Then he knocks it down with his finger.

"I already know."

I sit down facing him, pick up a few of the dominoes, and build half a Stonehenge. Daniela was always intrigued by that sort of thing. Dolmens, menhirs, that stuff; neolithic drunken sprees, all that bullshit.

"We hafta keep going. Do you hear me, Omaha? We hafta let go, let go of old baggage," he says, raising his head to see beyond me. "What you got there?"

The man coming in is pushing a little boy in front of him.

"You can keep him overnight. But I need him back early tomorrow. You can pay me the usual."

"What's your hurry?" Yuri takes stock of the boy, who smiles at him.

"He's my sister-in-law's nephew. That's the hurry. Like I said, the usual."

The man leaves.

Yuri gets up. "Come here," he says to the boy.

I follow them.

In the back bedroom, Yuri sits the boy on the bed and offers him a cold ham-and-cheese snack and a TuKola from a little table. He watches for a while as the boy eats and drinks, then he gives him a Nintendo DS.

"I can't stand it when they bring them to me like that," he says. "They don't last the night."

I shrug and go back to the living room.

The sergeant's at the table, pawing a domino. He blinks like a kid who's been caught in the act, drops the domino, and returns his three hundred pounds of fat and muscle to their post.

I stick the first DVD I find into the player and throw myself on the couch.

Wesley Snipes with glasses and a sword. Just what I need. It starts to rain outside.

That night two weeks ago it was also raining out on Santa Catalina.

Héctor. Héctor and I shared a desk in primary school. He'd lend me his pencil. He'd let me play with the toy soldiers that he brought to school behind his mother's back. His hair was very blond, practically white, dry, curly.

He hadn't changed much.

"Omaha," Héctor said, "decide. We're not gonna be here all night."

Daniela looked scared. The other girl, her friend, did too.

When he was a kid, Héctor had been a loner. He only played with me. Now he'd switched playmates. And multiplied them—by a lot.

Those five guys looked very capable of waiting all night. But maybe they weren't.

They'd certainly seemed impatient when they stepped in our path and dragged us to that garage in Heredia.

I am not your rolling wheels, I am the highway, I am not your carpet ride, I am the sky . . . screamed Chris Cornell from the Panasonic on the Chevrolet's hood.

It seemed possible.

"Your brother's gone too far, Omaha," Héctor told me. "He's stepping on my territory. Gourmet meat is his thing, and that's fine, but selling weed is my business, and given how tight it's been, the last thing I'm looking for is competition. I hafta send him a message, okay? It's not that I wanna do you harm but I've got my buddies and the neighborhood watching me. That's all it is, so relax, nothing's gonna happen to you. Just decide already. Which of these two?"

Both girls stopped looking my way.

"C'mon, your sister or her little friend. You decide."

"All so that I turn around and let my brother know that you threatened us with a switchblade and—"

"What switchblade? Do you see a switchblade? Any kind of knife? Do you think we need that?"

I looked at them.

Héctor had really grown up. Quite a bit. The others too. I remembered them vaguely from primary school too. No. They didn't need any of that.

Daniela's little friend was still holding one of the sunflowers the actors had given out to the audience. The play had been fun. There were a lot of kids in the audience. There were a lot of laughs.

"Get my sister outta here," I finally told Héctor. "I don't want her to see anything."

The guy shakes his umbrella at the door and comes in.

"Got anything?" he asks.

Yuri nods. The guy takes out his wallet.

"And the other thing?"

Yuri nods.

"Thank God." The man puts two bills down in front of him, on the table. "I had a fight today with the union guys, because of last week's payroll. I told you about it . . . so I'm short. And when I get home my wife is going to want me to take her to the movies, and my daughter's fighting with her husband so she comes over now and then just to talk crap and . . ."

Yuri keeps nodding. He takes a couple of joints from his pocket and gives them to the man, who then heads to the back room.

"Gimme one," I tell Yuri.

"No," he responds. "No, unless you pay for it."

"Fuck, man, I'm your brother."

"Debt between brothers is the worst thing in the world."

Voices. The man's voice. I think I also hear the boy. I'm not sure.

They took Daniela out of my sight. Two of them grabbed the other girl. Héctor pumped up the volume.

I didn't look at her face as I unbuttoned her jeans. Or as I pulled them down. Or as I pulled down her panties. Her navel was pierced. It was a tiny Chinese lion's head, with a miniscule gemstone. Maybe it was just some piece of glass. Yeah, that's probably what it was.

I felt the tip of Héctor's boot on my butt.

"Not like that. Fuck her from behind. So she'll feel it. So you'll both feel it, you and her."

They turned her around. They bent her over the hood of the car.

I realized the best thing to do was get it over with as soon as possible, and I acted accordingly. She was good. She didn't scream.

"Okay," Héctor said as I zipped up my fly. "Tell your brother to keep his paws off my business. You were great, really. Just ask her."

I turned around, very slowly.

Daniela was behind me, at the garage door. Two of them were holding her; she had a handkerchief stuffed in her mouth. They'd held her there the whole time. Her jeans were at her knees. A third guy, at her back, moved away.

Daniela heaved as if she'd been holding her breath for hundreds of years.

The guy pulled up his zipper.

I don't know what was worse: that she saw me or that I saw her. Or knowing that she'd seen me, or knowing that she knew that I knew she'd seen me, or knowing that she knew I'd seen her.

Maybe I should have asked the other girl, her little friend, what was worse.

But I didn't. I never saw her again.

The woman leans against the doorframe, her hip pointing.

"Hey, Yuri, what about me? Are you gonna pay me or what? Look, I don't want any trouble with you but you can't disrespect me."

Yuri stretches in his chair.

"I've got your stuff, girl. But it's not time for me to give it to you yet. I'm about to make an investment, and I could need it at any moment. I've got a live one. Let it go for now, come back Thursday. Look, I'm not lying." He takes a wad of bills and fans them out. "Your stuff is right here, but listen to what I'm telling you . . . Of course, if you really need it, I'll gladly . . . I mean, you know that, right?"

"You know how it is, Yuri . . ." She comes in and stands by my side.

She smells divine.

"I don't think there's a problem waiting till Thursday."

And she heads for the back room.

Yuri puts the bills away and lights a joint. He blows the smoke in my face.

"Don't look at me like that. You just never had the balls for business."

That's true.

I'm just Omaha, you know.

Omaha, with the happy face.

The one who crosses the street without a lick of sunlight. The one who doesn't get wet at the beach when it rains. The one who knows how to talk to kids. The one who sells his only pair of shoes today and then tomorrow somebody gives him a motorcycle. The one who never pays but always invites. The one who leaves for church and comes back from the cabaret. The one everybody knows, and who everyone thinks tastes like honey. Or like really cold beer. Or smoked cheese. Or snapper. It's a matter of taste. The one who came to stay. The one who's always leaving. That one, yes, Omaha. The one you want to be.

It just won't stop raining outside.

But I have to go out.

Or I'm going to go crazy.

The rain masks La Gloria's stench so that it's bearable. She doesn't realize I'm behind her, staring at her ass while she's absorbed in her excavation, until a few minutes later. She turns to me with her arms full of empty bottles.

"Hey, c'mon, gimme a hand."

To her surprise, I say yes.

We put the bottles in a sack, already about half full with God knows what crap. We drag it one, two, three blocks in the rain, until she says, "We're here."

I follow her into the dark hallway. Stairs. She goes first. I miss a step and fall flat on the sack. It's a little softer than I'd imagined. We go on. Door, lock, key.

"Come in."

I manage to find a bench and sit down. La Gloria throws me something that feels like a towel and suggests I take off my shirt. I obey. She turns the light on and the first things I see are her tits.

Beautiful tits.

"You look like a wet cat," she says, throwing her sweater on the floor. "C'mon, you must have come for something."

She goes through a door and turns on another light.

The first room is a warehouse full of bags and trash. It didn't surprise me. But this one does. There are books to the ceiling, piles of them, lovingly stacked. In the corner there's a shiny hotplate. In the other, a naked mattress. In the other, a few things on hangers. That's all.

And La Gloria, nude.

I didn't see when she took off the Lycra and her tennis shoes. I'm still slow, very slow.

"We have to hurry," she says. "My man will be here soon."

Why not? All women have a right to get some, even the Glorias.

"What does your man do? Does he dumpster-dive too?"

"No way. My guy's big, he has his own thing. He's a businessman."

"Oh, c'mon. What businessman is gonna wanna be with a little pig like you?"

"Hey, I'm telling you. My man's the king of the neighborhood. His name is Héctor. Don't tell me you don't know him."

"Héctor, the blond guy who sells weed?"

"That's the one. You're surprised? There are a lot of men who like women like me, women who know how to move. He doesn't sleep with anybody else. I'm the one he likes. He's always bringing me gifts."

I approach her. She opens her arms to me.

I slap her twice, in rapid succession, across the face.

She collapses on the mattress, dripping blood from her nose.

"Son of a bitch! Cocksucker! What the fuck is the matter with you?"

"I don't like women like you."

"You're crazy, faggot."

"If Héctor asks, tell him it was Yuri."

"And who the fuck is Yuri?"

"I'm Yuri," I say, and leave her there, bleeding.

It was me who invited Daniela and her friend to the theater that night. Should I feel guilty about that? It was me who said, "Let's go down the street." Should I feel guilty?

Yuri's right at the door, brow furrowed.

I peer inside.

There are four guys playing dominoes. Two smoke and look out the window without speaking.

The sergeant is in the middle of the hallway that goes to the back, and he's making an effort with the Nintendo DS.

"I hate it when it gets like this," Yuri says to me. "Too many people hanging out. But since it's raining . . . If we only had two or three more . . . It's actually a good day to make money but I don't have many offers . . . Got any ideas?"

I shrug. What am I going to come up with?

A man walks out of the room in back and moves past the sergeant. Yuri signals another guy, who hurries to the back. The one who's just come out of the room talks to Yuri.

"You should clean him up." And he leaves in a hurry.

"Omaha, do me a favor, fire up the water heater," Yuri says. "And fill the bathtub. And grab a couple of clean sheets out of my closet too."

I obey.

Yuri's closet shares a wall with the other room, the one in the back.

Something can be heard.

Not much, but something.

In any case, I don't stick around.

I'm tired of hearing it.

Dani spent more than a week without speaking, without crying, without stepping outside. Practically without eating or sleeping. "I can't stand it, Omaha, I can't stand it. Why didn't you do anything?"

I told her to go to the doctor, to get drunk, to get some sleep. She ignored me.

"Are you going to be much longer?" Yuri peers in from the bathroom door. "Two more guys just got here, and one of them pays really well."

"I'm almost done," I respond.

He could care less, and he leaves.

I stick my hand in the water. It's still warm.

The boy looks up at me for the first time.

I return his gaze. It's easy. Too easy.

"Get in here . . . Sit down . . . Lean forward so I can wash your back . . . Stand up . . . Raise your leg . . . Now the other one . . . Sit back down . . . Now turn around . . . Close your eyes so you won't get shampoo . . ."

It's too easy.

And I like that.

I dry him, I dress him, I push him out, I leave him in the back room and go signal Yuri. Without missing a beat, he calls over to a man who could be our grandfather.

"He has a couple of bruises and some scratches," I tell Yuri. "So I turned off the overhead light and just left the lamp on. You know how some clients don't like that."

"You're learning," he says.

And it's true. I'm learning. Finally.

Not much, but something.

Enough.

At least, I hope.

Today, when Daniela told me she wanted to have some ice cream and then go to the movies, and then to the theater to see some friends rehearse, I felt so good.

Now I feel so stupid.

The sergeant throws the old man out of the back room, slapping him disdainfully, but not too hard. We all have bad days. We can all have a bad day followed by another bad day. We'll all have a worse day. Until the end of days. Until the end of us.

The old man leaves, crying.

The boy's on the bed facing the wall, and he's shaking.

Yuri brings him some pills. I look at him suspiciously, so he explains: "To get him up."

I nod. To get him up, whatever that means. Whatever those pills might be. Amphetamines. Tonics. Something for high-performance athletes. For desperate economists. Antidepressants. Hallucinogens. For housewives. For new wave santeros. Analgesics. For everyone. Maybe all at once. They're different kinds of pills. It's a lot of pills.

Or maybe just placebos.

Probably.

"There's fresh coffee in the kitchen," Yuri tells me. "Bring me a glass."

I go, serve the equivalent of one cup, and come back.

"I said a glass," Yuri says, raising his voice. "A whole glass. Filled to the brim."

I go, pour, come back.

Yuri makes the boy turn around and sit up at the edge of the bed while the sergeant crushes the pills with his fingers and sprinkles them in the coffee.

Maybe they're not placebos after all.

The boy just looks at the floor.

"Here, drink this." Yuri brings the glass to his face.

After a bit of a struggle and some splattering of the coffee on the sheets, the glass is empty. There's some sediment at the bottom. It's quite thick. Yuri hands the glass to the sergeant, who goes to the kitchen and then comes back stirring it, full again.

"C'mon, don't play dumb." Yuri starts the second round.

The boy surrenders even more. After he empties the glass, he coughs.

"Bring him a soda, carbonated," Yuri demands.

I go. While I'm at it, I grab a beer for myself. I down it in long swallows while the boy drinks avidly.

"How many left?" Yuri asks.

"Two," the sergeant answers.

Yuri nods and holds the boy by the shoulders.

"Okay, everything's all right. Act like a man and I'll give you a present later."

The boy doesn't say anything. Yuri takes his silence as a good sign and the three of us walk out, leaving him alone.

Hanging out by the window, I stare at my hands. For the first time, I notice that my little finger is slightly separated from the rest at the base, and it begins a little lower. I wonder if everybody else's hands are like this. Or maybe I'm deformed. Curious, I try to get a look at Yuri's hands. I can't manage it. He has them in his pockets. I try to see the sergeant's hands but he's always making fists.

I try to remember Daniela's hands.

It's useless.

The only thing I remember—I think—is that they were weak.

How much strength do you need to stab yourself in the head with a pair of scissors?

How long do I have to wait?

"Forget about it." Yuri appears at my side. "Forget about Dani. Have some balls and forget about it."

I think I detect sadness on his hard face. I start to feel an intense regret. Who knows, maybe things won't turn out so well. The sergeant is strong but I've never actually seen him work. I'm sure he can take two, even three, maybe even four, but who knows. Héctor is the king of the neighborhood. And there are so many people in the neighborhood. And Yuri . . . Yuri's my brother. He's as skinny as me. That's why he has the sergeant. My only sibling now. I should . . .

"In any case, she was a whore," Yuri says. "She was a whore, that Dani. A helluva whore. It's better this way."

I stare at him.

"I started fucking her back when you moved to Grandma's house. Dani liked it. She also loved it when I took pictures. I told the guys, I showed them the photos. Then one of them asked me if he could fuck her. I thought he was joking but he was serious. He said he'd pay, so that it wouldn't screw up our friendship. I said yes. Then came the other guys. Dani still liked it, not as much as before, but she still liked it. Later, some woman brought me a little girl. She was her husband's daughter, not hers, and she'd leave her with me on Wednesdays, when her husband had to do his turn at neighborhood watch. She said we could split the profits. I thought that was all right . . . That's how we started. One day, when Dani was older, she said she wanted to stop. I told her that was okay, that I didn't need her anymore. She asked me not to tell you, ever. I said okay to that too. But that's not important anymore . . . Can you imagine? She loved it when I called her *my little dove*, the way you do . . . It's so strange that after everything she took up each hole, that she cracked from being forced . . . Yes, I heard about it, though neither of you said anything to me. I also heard you were showing off . . . but it doesn't matter . . . Do you wanna see the photos of Dani from when she was a kid? I still have them."

I don't think I see anything on Yuri's face anymore. It's just a hardened face. That's all.

"Seriously, do you wanna see the photos?" he insists. "You can even keep them. For real. Consider them a gift. If you don't want them, I'll give them to the sergeant."

I tell him no. I tell him I don't need them. He can do with them whatever he wants. I look outside to the street, to the corner, and tell him I have to go to the bathroom.

While we were watching the rehearsal, I noticed that Dani had been quiet for a while, absorbed in something. I thought I knew what it was and put my arm around her.

"What you have to do is tell yourself that nothing happened. If you say it enough, it'll come true. Because it's the truth. Nothing happened. For me, you're still Daniela, my little dove. And if you want, when you feel better, I'll tell Yuri, and you'll see how that sergeant guy he has in the shadows shoves Morro Castle up Héctor's ass and then does the same to the others . . ." I was on my ingenious little speech, of which I was very proud, so I smiled when she said, also smiling, to wait for her a minute, that she was going to the bathroom.

I was still smiling when the lights went out.

I was smiling still when the lights came back on, when

somebody screamed in the bathroom, when everybody began running around.

How stupid.

I've lost sight of Héctor and his animals from my perch by the window; they're probably at the door. They're about six or seven, the animals. That's why I'm not so sure what's going to happen now. I'm not even sure what it is I *want* to happen.

Voices. Screams. La Gloria's name. Screams. Daniela's name. More screams. The thud of a fist on a table. Another thud. More screams. The volume drops. Then some more. Voices. Isolated words.

Silence.

I leave my post and move to the living room.

Yuri and Héctor are sitting at the table. There are a few bills between them. A bottle of rum. Glasses. Grave but serene faces. Men at the table. Business matters, men.

"When I catch whoever hit my baby's face, I'm gonna cut off his balls," Héctor says, and he seems to be repeating it for the fourth or fifth time. "Nobody hits one of my women like that . . . and much less while trying to fuck with a business associate . . ." He looks at Yuri. "The truth is, it's not your fault you had such an asshole for a sister."

Yuri nods: "You don't get to pick your family, as much as you may want to . . . About the other thing, business, let's meet tomorrow at the bar, and we'll talk about it then, with our heads cleared. You'll see that we come to terms."

"Damn right, damn right."

"Omaha." Yuri shakes his head in my direction. "Go up to the corner and get us a coupla bottles. My buddies here are soaked and we have to warm them up. Take that." And he points to the bills on the table.

The sergeant and the animals huddle around to look at photos the former is holding. They laugh. They click their tongues. In one of the photos, I see can Daniela's smile shining. A dumb-blonde smile, like Britney Spears, the kind she knew would make me laugh.

"The good stuff or the cheap stuff?" I ask Yuri as I pick up the bills.

"The good stuff, goddamnit, since everything's going so well."

We hear a man's voice and a boy's crying coming from the back room.

Yuri, Héctor, the sergeant, and the animals laugh.

And I laugh too, and go out under the pouring rain to get the bottles, because, truth be told, as often happens when there are men around who know what they're doing, everything's going so well.

Translation by Achy Obejas

THE RED BRIDGE

BY **Yoss**

Lawton

> *For Jorge, who knows the red bridge,*
> *both ends of it, and how it feels.*
> *For Angelito, for the story "La Puerca."*

From the moment Humbertico the Piranha staggered into the courtyard, Yako knew he'd come for him, cuz of Petra, and that he'd hafta decide once and for all whether to cross the red bridge. Yako glances at me sideways, as if looking for support, or a laugh, a nod, a joke, an *I told you so, for being such a trouser snake.* But I don't say anything, and that's worse. It's like saying, *Go on, this is your battle.*

Humbertico: mulatto, skinny, and sinewy, with a toothless smile that makes him look like a carnivorous fish, the scar on his shoulder carved by a machete boasting a crude tattoo, *But I Killed Him.* For that, he served six years in the tank and he just got out. He's still got a jailhouse wariness about him though, instinctively walking glued to the walls so as not to ever leave his back exposed, or give his ass away inadvertently. He's carrying a bottle in his right hand and a stream of curse words on his ragged tongue. He's looking for that *big ol' useless white s.o.b., so I can cut his balls off for being a dick.*

As soon as he walks in, the whole courtyard freezes, everybody well aware of the whole story with Yako and Petra, Humbertico's sister, cuz in Cuba everybody knows everything, and more so here: The domino pieces fall silent, just like the jokes about how Big-Assed Berta, Dagoberto's woman, is cheating on him with Yepo's son, Manolito the Tripod. Everybody folds and swallows dryly.

Nobody knows how Humbertico found out, if somebody snitched or what. That'll matter later . . . if it matters at all. The fact is, now he knows and he's come looking for answers. Blood'll wash this mulatto convict's honor clean, defiled when Yako broke his little whore sister's hymen. An eye for an eye . . .

When a man comes to force somebody across that red bridge or to drown him in shit, you can smell it in the air. It's a cold, salty tang, like dried sweat and old pee on dirty fabric. It's a smell that announces blood without being blood.

Yako and I thought differently about a lot of things. But we grew up together, like Don Quixote and Sancho Panza, or Batman and Robin, but without all that faggot crap, watching each others' backs, the way white boys hafta if they wanna survive in a neighborhood like El Patio. Especially if you're a scrawny white boy and not a huge mothafucka since you were a kid, like Yako. Yako's mother baptized him Jacobo but it's a name he's always hated cuz it sounds kitschy and stupid. *It sounds like shit on a stick,* he always said. Together we learned to be men, to fight without backing down, even with guys so big we never knew what was best, to just jump them or run, but in the end we always had to swallow our fears and fight, even if they killed us afterwards, cuz you've gotta be a man, and real men don't chicken out. Not in El Patio, or else you're a dead fish, a worthless whore, meat for bait, forced to put up with everything. We were so afraid of being afraid, we became men that way, and like it or not, that's gotta count for something.

Yako was always one step ahead of me, since we were kids. He played ball better than me, he had more luck with the babes; even playing Parcheesi it seemed like the dice smiled up at him while they stuck their tongue out at me. He was destined to win, the bastard. It looked like he was gonna be president of something, everything came so easily to him, effortlessly—while I was always runner-up. Later, I went to college and served my year of compulsory military service in advance, while Yako just did his military tour, tough and pure, and each of us found our path and matured. Or we just got old and started to rot, who knows. Everything was different then. His star dimmed, he stayed in El Patio. The elders say luck gets tired of not being taken advantage of.

Yako knew from the start that this one wasn't gonna be taken care of with a couple of slaps and yo-mama-you-fuckin-faggot-I-let-you-live-cuz-they-held-me-down, in the old El Patio tradition, playing at big man, being cool and pretending nothing's happened. This one had come thumbs up or down, blood and balls. He's probably remembering what we talked about three days before, how only imbeciles fight without being afraid, cuz the smart ones know just how much there is to lose in death and how painful pain really is, and they take care of themselves. But if you take too much care, no matter how smart you are, then you're a pussy, and there's nothing worse than that in El Patio. He may even have wondered if Humbertico the Piranha was carrying anything, cuz he was searching his back pocket, where those of us from El Patio carry a blade and our bad intentions.

He did it to be an asshole, to mindfuck, to distract and impress the Piranha. Cuz in fact he doesn't have shit. He's never carried a blade. A big guy who carries a blade is just asking to be hunted down, taken by surprise, so they can slice him with a machete, and then he can look like a fool in front of everybody. It's not a matter of playing clean; it's about risk, going naked, giving the other guy the blade's advantage if you've got him on size. El Patio's ethics.

My pal Yako is just over six feet, like a basketball player, pure muscle like tightened cords under milky skin, freckle-faced, blond naps, and sly blue eyes. I'm always telling him he needs to get it together to do weights, to drink less beer and homemade champagne, and to harden the muscles on all that height he won in the lottery of genetics, cuz with a little dedication he could be another Mr. Olympia, like Arnold in his better days. But he'd rather play hoops and spend the day hanging out on the curb talking shit, drinking bad rum, and trying to hit on any stick in a skirt that strolls through El Patio. He laughs and says he can't get into that whole queer thing with the muscles and the poses, that he doesn't need to sweat it out on weights or get all purple from taking hits learning karate—he doesn't need that shit cuz nobody fucks with the big guys, and then he shows me his hands, each one as thick as my two put together.

Those same hands are now tangled nervously behind his back; everybody in El Patio's looking at him, knowing he's gotta do something, better just to face the music before Humbertico sees him and there's no turning back. Maybe better to step up and not look like he's been corralled, like the orca and the whale in that movie they just showed, the little fish showing balls to the big one. Even if the orca and the whale are both mammals, it's the same thing: The fish with the biggest balls will eat the more cowardly one, no matter the size. That way, no one can say, *He chickened out*; or, *I can't believe it, who would have imagined Cachita's boy coming on so tough and then he turns out to be such a wimp . . .*

You do or don't cross the red bridge, but nobody does it cuz they wanna. Nobody thinks about it too much, you just fall into it and that's that. No matter how stupid you are, when you think you can kill you also hafta think you can die. But everybody wants to believe it's his own decision, and nobody can take away anybody else's right to play dumb. Yako likes that definition of free will: to pretend to choose what you know is inevitable, to try to think and reflect on what is actually imposed by your own instincts and the moment.

Yako did a pretty comfy military tour: He didn't go to Angola, he wasn't part of the Special Forces. We're a fortunate generation, after all, except for the Special Period. Cuz he's tall and handsome, Cachita's lucky son got his fate as palace guard handed to him from heaven. A total breeze, every night spent partying; sometimes during the evening's firing of the cannons, he'd be playing toy soldier next to Eusebio Leal and foreign girls in shorts who'd get their picture taken with him, pressing tight against him. Now that's the life. That's how he met Silvia, who went by La Cabaña with some Italians. Me, I had to wait a whole year before I could get into the CUJAE, with scarcities, hunger, marches, and guard duty even on holidays. And without a girlfriend other than Manita and her five little ones, guarding my ass like a fine rooster. Sometimes military units can be like prisons, but with different sentences.

Finally, Humbertico the Piranha spies his prey in the group and smashes a bottle against the wall. He advances and waves that glass flower like death's hand. But Yako and everybody else in El Patio know the real danger's in the other hand, which hangs practically down to his knee, as if it's not doing anything. Humbertico's a leftie, and no matter how drunk he may be, he knows the whole world knows that, though he tries to hide it to his advantage even if he knows it's not gonna do him any good. In the end he's gonna hafta use his left upfront to whack the fucking whitey who did his fourteen-year-old sister, even though he was trying to protect her like a dog with a bone.

To have females in the family is a trip in El Patio, where every male's all over anybody who slips. The worst part is that there's always something, then you've gotta sound off, have balls, and, if it comes down to it, kill. A man can't let anybody step all over his word, especially if he just got outta the tank, where if you lift your legs once, it's forever.

It was Yako who did Petra but it could have been anybody. What happened was gonna happen, and better sooner than later. A leopard never changes its spots and that half-breed girl was born with whoring in her hot blood, and with a body that even her mother Tomasa wished she'd had so she could have earned a few pennies with the guys instead of rotting her liver drinking bad rum. Maybe if she'd gotten outta El Patio, Petra could have been a model or a dancer at the Tropicana, who knows. But El Patio is a drain, a bloodsucker—whoever stays kicks out his or her future soaked in liters of ethyl; life is one long moment waiting for nothing, or everything, or Armageddon; no one knows or cares.

Ever since she was a kid, Petra liked to lean on her brother while he played dominoes, until she was a coupla feet off the floor and her ass started spilling from her shorts and her sweater started swelling from the push of her tits; by then she was already on a first-name basis with all the neighborhood thugs. So folks started taking bets that she'd wind up spending her nights hanging out in front of the Hotel Cohíba . . . It was a matter of time—and of getting her ass loose from her older brother and his menacing belt to discipline her with and his, *If I ever catch you in any hanky panky I'll kick your ass purple and kill the son of a bitch who's burrowing into it.* But somebody had to be first, and it only made sense that it be Yako, the pretty boy, the sexy white boy, the one who—to top it off—already had a superfuckingincredibly edible and hyperfuckable girl like Silvia. Women get into that shit too, so that before they get with hot guys, they actually prefer guys who get on with hot women. And that everybody know about it. Especially here in El Patio, where whoever's not keeping an eye on her old man is busy doing somebody else's lover.

Yako came outta military service drenched with an existential laziness: He didn't wanna do anything, not studying or working, not even close to being bad or thinking big, robbing banks or lending dollars at twenty percent interest, or selling weed like we dreamed of doing as boys, living it up in Yepo's little patch of dirt, smoking our first Populares and later our first joint, which is surely the most delightful ever. The boy came back defeated and philosophical: He just wanted to play basketball for hours and hours, to fuck Silvia and any other panties that passed by, and to talk about three things—the red bridge, Salieri, and the Theory of Shit. He didn't wanna hear about getting a job, even in jest. Construction or hunting crocodiles? No way. Not that he had anything else happening. Yako, the neighborhood philosopher, lowering his lids over his crossed eyes from behind a bottle of firewater, laying it down for whomever wanted to hear, the days getting lost in the dribble of the basketballs with their NBA logos penned by hand, the basket on the corner zigzagged by ocuje roots; watching porno pictures with Alfredo, the ex–merchant marine who was the last to be with Tomasa, Petra's old mama, and Silvia, though nobody got why she didn't kick him out given that she knew all about his infidelities.

Humbertico the Piranha says he shits ever so sweetly on the midwife who washed the pubes on Yako the faggot's motherfucking whore mother the day she was born, but knowing she's dead, that faggot sure as hell isn't gonna leap up to defend her. The stink of bad liquor adds fuel to his words. *He should step up if he's any kind of man, let's see if he's got the balls to take him—Humbertico—on, the way he had 'em taking advantage of an innocent girl.* His little sister is innocent the same way El Patio is a wealthy suburb, but for a moment it sounds like truth on his tongue, what Yako did seems abusive and indecent. Fourteen years of age is fourteen years of age, even if she uses a 38 bra. *Let's see, let's see how bad he is: Step up, let him try to take me, unless he's just a cherry-buster, an ass-fucker. I'm gonna gut him like a fish, so he learns not to mess around with real men.* Yako tries the thing with his back pocket again but the Piranha, fresh outta the tank, knows what's up, doesn't fall for it, sees the bluff, knows big guys never carry shit. He spits, his saliva thick with fear and shame spattering Yako's new Nikes, Silvia's most recent present. He's just waiting now. The silence is so deep Babas's gurgling sounds like a lion's purr.

Then the crowd parts, opening up some space for whatever's about to happen, cuz when things are fated and it's not your turn, all that's left is to watch. Yako—Caesar without too much desire to cross the Rubicon—bends and wipes the green phlegm from the tip of his shoe, but he's already on the red bridge and he knows it and I know it and what nobody knows is which way he's gonna go, if he's gonna cross or run.

Yako's Theory of Shit is very simple: If we come from shit, we are shit, and will return to shit, then it makes no sense to lift one shitty finger to get outta the great universal shit. Shit on Einstein and Newton and the whole fucking shitty world, and shit on the progress of mankind, and fighting for a cause and all that other shit. It may sound dumb, but after the shivers that come from the third shot of Tiger's Bone, which scalds your throat like a lash from the inside, everybody in El Patio stops thinking, *That's not so original,* or whatever, and then Yako's just right on, and even floating debris like Babas suddenly remembers thinking something like that at some point. Then it's, *Damn, white boy, you got it, you're the man,* and they pass around a fourth shot. Even before we knew each other . . . we drank together. Now that we know each other, we drink together. So to shit with it all, and let's drink until we can't recognize each other.

Humbertico the Piranha, a little rat since he was a kid, old-time hustler, jail meat, and brownnoser to every black section chief there ever was in La Cabaña, knows he has a chance when Yako bends over to wipe the spit off, but he seems afraid of the ballplayer's big hands, and he hesitates. He may not be too smart or have much to lose after getting outta the tank, but he has doubts, he has to be afraid and have his doubts. You don't dick around with death, and after all he's said to Yako, it's gotta be face to face, fuck or get fucked, no slapping, first blood, and they break them up, cuz in El Patio you can smell when it's *gotta* go to the very end, and not even God's gonna come between these two now. When there's a little sister's broken hymen on the table, honor demands death even more than blood. Now Humbertico the Piranha, drunk and all, realizes there's no going back, and he's probably cursing the moment he decided to deal with this . . . He may be gambling a shitty life, but it's his and it's the only one he has.

* * *

Sometimes Yako says, *My second surname is Salieri*. And then he goes off on this philosophical turn, very elegant, very erudite. For him, the great cosmic joke, the great fuck, is not being a genius, nor a fool, and knowing it or not knowing it, and living contentedly like Babas, with his idiocy, happily pushing his cart from one end of El Patio to the other all the live long day, no matter who's laughing at him. The chaos, the living end, the tragedy, is being in the middle: having the desire, knowing exactly what constitutes greatness, and not having any of it yourself. Salieri. Not the worst, just another good one. Not even among the best. Not the crackerjack, the number one, the top guy, the man, but maybe the guy who carries the main man's bag. And that can be the same whether you make it to the palace guard or not, or whether you have a career, or whether you ever play in the NBA with Michael Jordan, or even Team Cuba. Or whether you were born in El Patio, feral Lawton, half alley, half tenement, instead of Haiti or Switzerland. It's always being the midpoint, one more little mark among the statistics . . . and knowing it. Realizing it, that's the hard part. Some people get it, some don't, but everybody nods their heads and says, *This white boy speaks from the soul, with power in his words, brains, yes siree*. And then there's another drink, to forget what shit we all are, and just in case that Salieri . . .

Humbertico the Piranha doesn't have a piece, they're fifty bucks each and he doesn't have that kinda cash, he's just gotten out and he hasn't made his connections yet cuz Alfredo the ex-marine doesn't want ex-cons near his video thing. *Sorry bud, it's not like before, now you're branded*. What the Piranha has is a sharp, filed-down spoon, strapped to his hairless ankle with a rubber band. Ever since he was in that brawl with that fat black guy at La Tropical and he got out by the skin of his teeth, when he had to cut the guy and the razorblade broke in his hand, he hasn't had any confidence in switchblades. Or in any knife.

His hand knows by heart the sound of the filed-down spoon against the stone floor of the cell. Nobody knows how he got it out, maybe wrapped in brown paper stuffed up his big asshole, so used by the cellblock chief, or by dropping dimes on the guards, since that'll make anything happen. It's his treasure, and he doesn't like to show it around too much. The spoon is Chinese, you can still see the letters on the handle, dull from so much handling. Sometimes he has to squeeze it to fall asleep, and he cries then, in his slumber, just like back then. The wiseguys say his little rosy asshole misses a certain big horse cock, that he wants to go back to being its mare, like the loyal wreck fish he is. The truth is that having it close gives him courage, helps him feel complete, and to remember he's still a man and that he never *actually* gave his ass up to anyone in the tank, although the story goes that a coupla times he took advantage of Damián the Sewer from Cellblock 4. But that's not too terrible, cuz being without females is tough, and you've gotta get what you can.

If he bends to get the blade in front of Yako, those Nike 48s are gonna leave footprints all over his face. Maybe at that moment his liquored mind decides to shit on the shitty summer heat that makes it impossible to wear long sleeves and hide the steel, and he imagines a special strip of leather for his wrist so he can carry the blade like the gangsters in the Saturday night movies. Or he doesn't think at all, cuz in any case he's got the broken bottle. So it's fairly certain that the attack from top to bottom with the glass flower will come from a twist of the wrist, it will scratch but not kill, the product of alcohol and instinct and resentment, not from the former prisoner's guts or smarts.

Yako sees the glass coming for his eyes and he knows it's the red bridge's sentry. El Patio sees the bottle coming in slow-motion and the whole world explodes in screams, cuz the fight's real now, like those little whirls in the dust in the mid-day heat. It can end the same way, just like that, and it can all go back to being dust, even with a little bit of blood.

Yako says every life comes to a red bridge.

That's a joke I like, and him too, so he says it like ten times a day. Yako, the red bridge philosopher.

Maybe he read it in some Chinese book, though he doesn't read much. It sounds like the kind of philosophy that comes from people who dress in silk and drink tea, with a whole lotta time on their hands to watch the carps feasting on bread. Like at the Japanese Garden, where we went the last time—him, Silvia, and me—and I heard them arguing in the arbor and I pretended I was in my own little world but didn't miss a word. He to her: *Fuckin' whore.* She to him: *You knew it, and anyway, what right do you have to say anything to me, you lazy delinquent good for nothing?* This is a common exchange between Cuban couples these days, an inevitable refrain if the couple's from El Patio. It's another way of saying, *I love you, baby; I love you, too, Daddy.*

The red bridge is a blood decision, a bullfighter's choice, a gentlemen's agreement. You enter it cuz somebody's pushed you, and you exit only by crossing and killing, or chickening out and playing guitar, doing a faggot's twirl. Yako has given the matter a lotta thought, up in clouds of pure weed, which always give me a deadly cough: If you kill, everybody knows you crossed the red bridge, and you realize it's not so easy, but there's no going back. Cuz on the other side is the tank, and in there men aren't men anymore but beasts, and the lyrics from that song about Moncada is a lie—a crocodile will in fact eat its own. And if you chicken out, you may as well climb on a raft and leave the country, and maybe even that won't matter, cuz a man with a yellow stripe down his back can be sniffed out by his sweat, whether in El Patio or China. Once a coward, always a coward.

We argued about this a lot.

Yako and Silvia and me, by myself as always, we went to see *Lord Jim*, the Peter O'Toole movie, cuz I'd read the book. Yako liked it, though he said that no one comes back from a sea of coward's shit, that there's no redemption and no second chance. But later, Yako, who doesn't read, asked me for Conrad's book. Even for him, it must be nice to realize that somebody else has already laid down in black-and-white the ideas that have been making rounds in your head without quite landing. Must be nice to know you're not alone in your thinking, that's all.

The thing with the red bridge isn't too bad. It's like Moby Dick was for Ahab, or Hamlet pondering what to do with his whore mother and his bastard uncle after they killed his father. And, of course, Julius Caesar crossing the Rubicon. It's always the same shit.

Yako bends and rolls on the floor like a big, gangly, but still very agile spider. That's why the ragged end of the broken bottle only slices through his Benetton sweatshirt and barely draws blood from his shoulder before his legs collide with Humbertico the Piranha and they both get tangled up. Red's rushing now, El Patio shouts in a single voice, like at the cockfights, dogfights, or some adolescent brawl where they beat each other purple then turn up as buddies the next day, for the pure pleasure of throwing punches and then forgiving each other later. But everyone already knows this one won't have such a sweet ending. Although with all the screaming it does seem rather like a sport, like a game, and a couple of smart-asses even place bets. It's just that Tension, like a couple of springs in the air, doesn't actually scream, doesn't actually stand, but rather sits there next to Death, polishing her nails at the domino tables, cuz they know that something's gotta happen, and even what it is, but they're not saying.

Yako doesn't deserve Silvia, even if she turns tricks, and the three of us know it. But she's too much of a woman for Yako to leave her, and I'm too nice, too naïve, and too easily fooled for an ambitious street-smart girl from Bayamo like her, who's also determined to get some distance from her race, being a mulatta ashamed of her naps. I'm white too but dark-haired, short, with dark eyes. I'm no competition. That's the triangle in which I don't belong even when I'm present, in which I have no weight and won't have any even after I graduate as one more mechanical engineer, a grease monkey at some sugar mill, cleaning spark plugs, crucified for life unless I get on with some corporation, otherwise I won't have a chance to even sniff a bill from afar, no matter how many books I read, or how much weight I lift at the gym that Manolito the Tripod built under that same ackee tree from our childhood. It's not the same tree anymore either: During the storm of the century, it lost its smoking branch, which fell on Cachita's she-goat, out looking for who knows what, and killed her.

Maybe what Silvia seeks in Yako, or him in her, is just Salieri, to settle and that's it, just shit and a bridge that might be pink for women, pink or black lace with the smell of hotel air freshener, a fat Spaniard, Salsa Palace, Cayo Coco, and a passport to go abroad. Even I couldn't say what I'm looking for in my pal Yako's woman, cuz if he ever caught me I'd be dead meat, but truth is I always fall in her same trap even though there are so many little cheery student whores wandering around the CUJAE housing. Maybe it's cuz they're always giving me a hard time about my street style, no earrings or long hair, cuz in El Patio they don't put up with that fag crap . . . or maybe it's cuz we always like the challenge, the bridge, death escaping from the shithole even as we sink deeper.

Rolling around on the ground is Humbertico the Piranha's thing. He bites with the slightly bucked teeth that earned him his nickname, kicks, scratches, twists, he's got monkey arms and octopus tentacles. He's happy cuz so long as the big guy doesn't get up, he can always win, and he plays dirty too; with luck he'll get him in one of those strangle holds every one of El Patio's native sons learns practically before he learns to walk, and that way he doesn't hafta kill him. But size imposes itself. Yako turns in the dust, gives a couple of big thrusts with his shoulders, manages to kneel, and covers the Piranha's face with his giant hand, screaming like he's outta his mind. He grinds his neck on El Patio's dirt, like he's finishing off the memory of his having fucked Petra. And in that moment Humbertico remembers what he knew from the start but had hoped to forget: that he has to go for his sharpened spoon so the decision can finally be made, like that night in Cellblock 3 when he had to gamble his life with Saúl the Albino for the right to get any kind of scrap, and the big black chief just looked on to see who he'd get as a foot soldier and who he'd give up to get fucked by the others.

Even if he goes back to the tank, he has to do this, cuz whoever's survived there can't resist a fight, no matter what. Humbertico knows that every fight is about more than who wins and who loses, but also about what you're risking, what you win, and what you lose, which is why he finally twists his hand down for the spoon and tentatively searches for Yako's beer-filled guts, to cut him or rip him or win God knows what from him.

The red bridge is a fixed idea that hypnotizes. A path from which no one returns, a crossroads with no way out. A lot of people have known it, or know it, and they may call it some-thing else. It's the shady street in gangster movies. The door. The throne of blood in one Kurosawa film. For Conan Doyle it was the Brazilian cat, the night spent next to the beast, which turns your hair white and leaves you limping and changed forever, but alive. *The Driver*, that old Ryan O'Neal movie in which he's like a maniac behind the wheel, crashing cars to prove he was a tough guy. Or Matt Dillon in *Rumblefish*, looking for traces of his troublemaker brother and finally glad when the Motorcycle Boy dies and frees him. It's the bridge over the River Kwai. All that and nothing really, that's the red bridge. I've thought about this, but not as much as Yako. It's an obsession with him. To imagine what it must feel like to kill—realizing that you've violated a worldly law and that no one up high is gonna punish you for it, that Nietzsche was right, that God died outta sheer boredom, and that if other men don't take you up on an eye for an eye and a tooth for a tooth, there's no bolt of lightning that's gonna strike you down to purge the sin. So then to hell with morality: It's the law of the jungle that counts, fuck before you get fucked. The cops and the laws don't have any more right than their force and cunning, like everybody else.

God died by drowning in shit. Silvia and I fucked like crazy at the beach house, next to a drunken Yako, friend and lover, doing it just to do it, just cuz we shouldn't have, risking it all, doing it without love, practically without pleasure, knowing too well what would happen if he knew, imagining that in fact he already knew, all the while wanting him to know and to react, so that all the façades and the masks could go to shit.

Yako sees the spoon coming, wanting to scoop out a new navel for him, and he stops it by some miracle, his fingers all cut up now. I practically feel his pain, and I tense up wanting to help him, as if I were him, my heart beating open-mouthed.

It's at moments like this that all the Bruce Lee and Chuck Norris and Steven Seagal and Jackie Chan movies are revealed as indisputable lies. In real life, a blade is fear, cold, stinks of danger and death, adrenaline runs like a river, your muscles tense and you freeze cuz you're so scared, and there's no choreography for a ballet of kicks nor Jean-Claude Van Damme swiveling in the air. Or maybe you don't freeze, you can move but like in a dream: You wanna run but you can never run as much as you want, you wanna do a quick slip like in the movies but instead you cut your fingers, not even all the way, just about to the bone, so that they bleed and hurt. Slow and clumsy the slice, not like a samurai whose sword demands a clean swipe which sends a hand flying. You wanna come on with a chest-splitting suki chop but you just slap and fall back from the force of the rebound; this is a fight of handless morons and frail epileptics, and there's dirt and noise and you know you've gotta do something but you don't know what. There's a voice that tells you, *Yako's gotta come outta this no matter what*, and there's Humbertico the Piranha's rabid bite on his fingers.

But there is a God in heaven: You, Yako, your blood makes the blade slip from his fingers, now white from pressing so tight, and it bounces and clinks on the hard ground muddying with sweat, blood, and fear. And you grab him by the neck, walnut-brown mulatto shivering under your white forearm with black hairs, and squeeze and squeeze . . . and everybody's screaming, and I say, *Coño*, and run.

I run inside, to his house, searching for the key under the cactus pot, and when I go in I topple the chair and don't have the time or inclination to say anything to whoever's there, looking at me from behind the partition, still sort of taking a nap, maybe just waking up cuz of the scandal outside, maybe accustomed to it all from so many years of living in El Patio. I search under the mattress, find what I'm looking for, and rush back with my tongue hanging out, praying that what I left seconds ago hasn't ended badly . . .

On time. Cuz Humbertico the Piranha has gotten loose and is struggling to retrieve the spoon and its blade. And he's gonna get it, Yako can't stop him, he wiggles and wiggles . . .

Breathless, feeling like an s.o.b., I threw it at him: the horn-handled blade from Albacete province given to him by Gema, that Spanish girl he fucked last year. The one I wanted to fuck and didn't have the guts to face. The pitch turned out okay: There went that *Made in Spain*, already open and everything, spinning on the ground, right into his hand. There was no way he couldn't get it, and the rest was automatic.

We grew up together and he was cut and all the blood on the ground and on his clothes was his and all I'd wanted to do was help him . . .

That's what everybody said later, during the runaround and the ambulance and the squad car and the questions. That's what I told them. *Yes, I threw it at him, I wanted him to have a chance cuz he was my pal, but what happened wasn't all my fault,* I told the mustached lieutenant who was taking the report as the paramedics carried the body off, now a knot under the red-stained sheets. Tears started to fall. Without lament, with a tightness in my chest, the way men cry when they have no choice and there's an overwhelming impotence and there's nothing more that can be done. The way we cry in El Patio. The way Yako was crying when they took him away.

I cried until the mustached lieutenant, from Santiago like so many of these patrol car guys, but good people unlike most of them, took me aside and put his hand on my shoulder as if I were his son, cuz I was young enough to be his son, and said to me in a low voice that life is fucked and things just happen. He said he wished he had friends like me . . .

If things were looked at right, it wasn't Yako's fault either, since he was a big guy and wasn't used to fighting with a knife, and he used the spearpoint instead of the blade, the way you do when you think you might lose the weapon if it gets stuck in the wound, and he had such bad luck, or such good aim, that the blade shot right into Humbertico's eye and into his brain.

Simply put, it was the Piranha's day, that's all. Bad luck . . . If it's your turn, it's your turn. If you live by the sword, you die by the sword. Everybody knew it was going to end badly. You don't mess with knives, that's what the elders said. And his poor sister . . . now nothing can save her from whoring.

According to the lieutenant, they weren't gonna be very hard on Yako. He only had a few little things on his record, mostly peer pressure stuff like stealing jeans from laundry lines. Humbertico was already a jailbird, a bad egg, destined to return. And he'd attacked first, so it would be self-defense anyway, with a bunch of eyewitnesses to boot. It had happened in the heat of battle, Yako had been overtaken by passion . . .

That's what the lawyer said at the trial. So did Manolito the Tripod, and Alfredo who went in his marine uniform, and even Babas.

Petra didn't cry for her dead brother or make a scene during the trial. *He brought it on himself, the fool, for trying to come on so tough, for sticking his nose where it didn't belong, cuz I know how to take care of myself,* she was heard to say, and the women in El Patio wrote her off after that, cuz you can be a whore if you want, but blood is blood, even if it's the guy who took your virginity who spills it.

I also gave testimony, right after a test I had to take, and that also influenced things. As soon as the sentence was declared, Yako, with tears in his eyes, told me that I was his only friend and that he'd never forget it. That he'd get out, that in the end it was only one dead guy. But I knew he was lying, and he did too. There's a greater distance between zero and one than between one and infinity, and he was now on the other side.

In the last few months, I've dreamt now and then of Yako's face telling me, *Brothers forever.* And the blade, with its bent horn, zigzagging on the dirt, and later shining like a needle in the air. The cops kept it, of course, as evidence. It's too bad cuz it was a good knife, with a fine edge, firm and steady.

I still visit Yako now and then, but not as much as during the first few months. Those are the rules, everything's a waste, so they gave him four years; it's a lot . . . Silvia only went with me the first two times, and she never requested a conjugal visit with Yako.

I haven't seen her since. Well, there was that one time, from afar, in that little hotel at the CUJAE, she was with a French engineer who was attending a conference there. She pretended she didn't see me, of course, and I didn't even say hello. I'd fucked her a couple more times while Yako was awaiting his sentence, but she wasn't interested after that. The feeling's mutual. I'm not surprised, I knew it from the start. It was all cuz she was his woman and I was his pal. It may have been another way of getting even more of him, of entering his childhood, that little piece of his life which had never been revealed. Yako before he was Yako, before he thought about the red bridge that he feared and desired and ultimately crossed.

On a visit, the second one, he told me that someone had ordered him killed. Maybe it's not just paranoia. He thinks it was Petra, the Piranha's sister, and I didn't say anything one way or the other. Who can understand women anyway—one day lots of kisses, then the next they drive a stake through your heart. It's not true that they're all bad; some are worse.

Two guys attacked him in the bathroom: He had to be cool, he was hit by metal tubes, they broke his arm, but he got one of them in the eye, a fat, bald white guy sporting Santa Bárbara tattoos. Now nobody fucks with him, but they gave him two more years for blinding the guy. Between that and what he did to the Piranha, they've started to call him The Ophthalmologist. He laughs when he tells the story, then he puts his hand on my shoulder and tells me again how I'm really his pal. And what a blast we're gonna have, what a fucking blast, once he gets out. For now, he's pretty much okay: He has things to do, like surviving and watching his back, and climbing the cellblock's hierarchy. He's gotten it in his head that he wants to be a cellblock chief.

He's no longer afraid of losing his life. Maybe there's value in that: that absolutely nothing matters at all anymore. Now everything's easy, he doesn't hafta think much. He doesn't read anymore. Anvil or hammer. To hit or be hit, to kill or die. He knows the rules now, and he plays accordingly. Living on the other side of the red bridge is not so hard. He told me maybe he'll get a tattoo, old-school prison style, by hand, with a sewing needle and ink made from burnt shampoo. Maybe he'll get a Santería emblem, or a kimyankela, a one-eyed spirit with one leg, one arm, to impress the black hordes in the tank. He's using five necklaces now, never mind that he didn't believe in any of it.

In his own way, Yako's happy. I go along with him and tell him how things are on the streets, and we make plans together, even though we both know it won't be the same. Never again. Maybe that's real freedom, knowing the limits. The red bridge isn't so bad. What's worse is being in the middle, or on the other side, knowing you still hafta cross it, but not knowing when . . .

At first, in spite of everything, I envied him a little. Not now. I've crossed the bridge too . . . my own bridge, more green than red. After I threw that blade his way that afternoon, everything's been easier, as if I'd always laid low, in the shade of the hill it took so much to climb. You could say that El Patio's fate has finally caught up with me, but I live ten times better than before: I bought a color TV for my old girl, and I have as many women as I want—me, the shy one.

It wasn't even my idea but now the trap is well-greased: port-transportation-domestic economy. Petra lures them from in front of the hotel or when they're trying to hitch a ride, and she brings them to my house, where I offer them PPG, cigars, rum, as if it were all mine to give. Alfredo the ex-marine has his contacts and procures the product. There's always something for me, for being the face of the operation. Everything cuz I gained the guy's trust by throwing the knife to Yako when he needed it.

Manolito the Tripod and Alfredo fuck Petra now and again . . . I don't get it: She looks good but she's cold as the wind. I gave her a couple of turns but I got bored. Her clitoris is about the size of a plantain seed . . . except they don't really have seeds. All that flaunting, all that heating up, and then she has to fake it. Pity all those foreigners who believe it . . .

A few days ago, she asked me if she could go see Yako, if she could get a conjugal visit with him. Life is full of surprises . . . true love, or maybe she just really wants to fuck him and pay him back for the Piranha? I hafta think about what I'm gonna say to her.

I imagine Yako never cared whether Petra could come fucked up the ass or whether she was frigid. It was all about appearances, about not letting panties walk by without getting in them, and about daring the Piranha, with the invisible sign on his head advertising him as a tough guy just outta the tank. The challenge. Yako the mothafucka, the hard one, the guy from the red bridge.

Who cares. Life is shit, from shit we come and to shit we shall return, and between shit and more shit, there are a few shitty dollars from the black market which we'll spend buying more shit or horrible liquor for fighting, until one day it's all over, with blood and dirt or with sheets and intensive therapy. Then somebody, like so many others, will say, *Alive*.

For the time being, I've dropped outta school. I asked for a leave and they gave it to me without questions. It was my third year, but to hell with it. I don't plan on going back. What's a white boy from El Patio doing wasting his time at the CUJAE anyway, studying for an engineering degree which isn't gonna do shit for him? With so much business and so many whores and so much life waiting out here—in El Patio or beyond—it's all the same.

Even so, I can't forget that afternoon, the fight, the dash to get the knife, my pitch, and the horn-handle on the ground, the hit and the burst of blood from the Piranha's eye. I've lived it a thousand times in my memory. And each time I'm more sure of why I did it . . . but a lot less sure of *how* I did it. If I did it on purpose, or if I made that up later.

Yako on the red bridge. I saw him fighting but didn't feel his fear. He was gonna win—he was big and he was winning, he would have won cleanly anyway. He was blond and had light eyes and played basketball pretty well, he fucked Silvia without having to hide and she had more fun with him and his drunkenness than she ever did with my desire. He had eight inches on me, and he'd always been better at everything. That I was studying toward a degree and read a lot and knew that someday I could suddenly leave El Patio if I wanted to didn't matter. It wasn't books about exotic places or incredible cold-blooded adventurers in monstrous heat that mattered at the moment of truth. It was him and not me. That was real life, sweat and blood and guts and brawls, and he lived them and I didn't. And he was on the red bridge, on the ground in a fight in which only one would come out alive, even if neither actually died. Dying? Everything ran smoothly until . . . it was like a nuclear explosion, like when Uranium 238 boils until it hits critical mass.

My decision—if it was a decision—was spontaneous, without premeditation, not the way I once insinuated to Silvia during a fuck, in fact the last time we fucked. You can take a lot of shit when you have a half bottle of bad rum inside you.

It was a lie—I didn't contemplate it for weeks beforehand, eating my liver while fueled by old envy and resentment; I didn't plan it all ahead of time; I didn't talk Yako into fucking Petra; nor did I pay her all my savings to open her legs to him, knowing full well what Humbertico the Piranha would do. It wasn't me who told him, and I didn't throw the knife knowing that Yako always talked about a Florentine-style stabbing: eye-brain-death. It simply happened that way, and I took advantage of the timing, the situation, the sinister series of linked coincidences, the circumstances. I'm not that much of a sonovabitch or that Machiavellian.

Or maybe I am . . . ?

The fucked-up part is that I can't be sure. Maybe God exists, and if he exists . . . I'm afraid that just thinking about it is enough.

In El Patio they say I'm an educated guy cuz I read and I went to school. Everybody says there are answers to everything in the Bible. I went leafing through it for the first time a coupla days ago. There was once a Jacob who saw a ladder to heaven and fought with an angel. But it doesn't say anything about a red bridge. Nor about a horn-handled knife, of course.

Translation by Achy Obejas

LA COCA-COLA DEL OLVIDO

BY LEA ASCHKENAS

Centro Habana

She was a fifty-four-year-old light-skinned black woman, a technical engineer at the H. Upmann Tobacco Factory by day, and under the cover of darkness, a black market beautician prowling the poorly lit alleys of Centro Habana, trimming beards and plucking eyebrows for those too elderly to do so for themselves, giving pedicures and cleaning pores for those too young and too vain to see past their own noses.

She hadn't always been this snide. Once, she too had believed in beauty, revered it even. As a child, she had chosen her career because of it. This was back in the days of Batista, when she had noticed that all the beautiful people in La Poma, that bottleneck of chaos and corruption and color that has forever been Havana, were professionals—doctors, architects, lawyers, engineers.

When the Revolution triumphed on the eve of her tenth birthday, she had been immediately caught up in its spell of social justice, its promise of education (the path to professionalism) for everyone. When the Literacy Campaign came in 1961 and she was only twelve, too young to go into the countryside to teach the guajiros how to read, she volunteered to tutor illiterate workers at a factory in Havana. At eighteen, she accepted a scholarship to study in Moscow, emerging eight years later with her PhD in engineering. She returned home in 1975 and in less than a year secured a job at the tobacco factory, met Manrique, a flautist with the National Symphony Orchestra, and got married. When Marisol was born two years later, everyone declared her to be the most beautiful baby they'd ever seen. *Una hija de Ochún*, they said as she grew into a striking adolescent, her skin a milky brown, her hair a long curled black with sun-streaked highlights of red-gold. She was an artistic youth whose vibrant, wildly distorted paintings of the neighbors entertained everyone. *She will be successful, just like her parents*, people said. *Qué familia más talentosa*, they said. When the babalao next door prophesied, at Marisol's tenth birthday party, that the three of them would live a happy and fruitful life, everyone had nodded their heads in envious agreement.

Sixteen years after that flawed prediction, Beatriz lived alone in a crumbling five-story apartment in Centro Habana. Several years before, the buzzer system had broken. Now when her friends came to visit, they knew to call out her name from the street. They stood just far enough away from the balcony so she could see them, but still close enough so they could catch the key when she tossed it down from the third floor.

Unfortunately, Beatriz had yet to encounter such a simple solution to the many other malfunctions of her apartment. The bathtub faucets worked only infrequently. The refrigerator froze up and then defrosted at will, leaving soupy puddles around the icy mangoes and spilling a sweet, sticky syrup onto the floor whenever she opened its door.

Her TV was color when Manrique bought it ten years ago, but now it produced only a grainy black-and-white image on each of Cuba's two stations, both government-run. If Beatriz smacked the shelf beneath the television really hard, sometimes a streak of magenta would flash across the screen, but it always faded. To hear the sound, she had to connect it to the stereo she'd given Marisol for her quinces.

Beatriz still remembered how everyone had danced that night, more than twenty tightly packed bodies swirling around her, sweat streaming down their foreheads, the living room gallery of Marisol's paintings blurring before their eyes. They had kept dancing even after the lights went out and the stereo stopped (Manrique tapped out the rhythm with a spoon and a frying pan), signaling the start of the daily apagones at the height of the Special Period, those spare years of sugar-water tea and salt-water baths immediately following the collapse of the Soviet Union. Looking back now, Beatriz felt an unexpected tenderness toward that time when, despite the difficulties, they had managed to pull through. Together. As a family.

It was only 7 in the evening, but already a dreary, drizzly darkness enveloped Centro Habana as Beatriz stepped out into the grime of Industria Street, turning left at the corner of Virtudes. Lately this intersection, where she had lived for forty-six years and never given much thought to the meaning of the street names, had begun to seem rife with metaphor, with irony. She had always been industrious, but in the last two weeks, virtue had felt further from her reach than ever before.

Fearing that her refrigerator would completely conk out any day now and feeling desperate for money to buy a new one, Beatriz had begun rubber-banding so many cigars around her thighs and calves at work that she had to wobble her way out of the factory at the end of each day. Each evening, she stashed her loot at the house of her friend Clara, a school-teacher who no one would suspect of having access to stolen cigars. In three weeks, once she'd acquired (the word Beatriz preferred to describe her actions) enough cigars to fill seven boxes, she would pay Clara ten dollars for her help, and then, for thirty-five more dollars, she would hire her friend Orestes, a wood-worker extraordinaire, to make the cedar boxes. Orestes had once produced the drums for Havana's most popular percussion band, Los Sobrevivantes. But then the members had gone to New Orleans for a performance and never returned. Orestes's wife, the lead drummer, had promised to file the paperwork for him to join her, but soon she'd stopped responding to his letters. Now, whenever Beatriz asked Orestes if he'd heard from her, he'd invoke that old Cuban aphorism of abandonment, blaming his wife's silence on the lure of her new capitalist life in La Yuma. He'd shake his head and say, *La Coca-Cola del olvido*—the Coca-Cola of oblivion.

As far as profitability went, Beatriz's cigar-selling business was a good negocio, bringing in eighty dollars for each pungent package she hawked to the tourists hanging out along the Malecón. But the risk of getting caught—and the shame of losing her job—had convinced Beatriz that this would be a one-time deal. She felt much safer with negocios unrelated to her official work, even if they didn't bring in such big profits. She felt safer outside of the factory, and in the streets.

At the intersection of Virtudes and Consulado, Beatriz stepped over a puddle of doggie diarrhea and narrowly missed being splashed by a stream of wastewater dripping down from an overhead balcony. In the street, a game of pelota was in progress. The players had created baseball diamonds from the negative space, and ran to invisible bases between the bici-taxis and the stationary, not-abandoned yet not-functioning automobiles that pushed up against the deteriorating sidewalk.

Beatriz's first stop tonight was the ciudadela where Marilys lived. A one-family mansion in pre-Revolution times, it now housed five families, each of which lived in what had formerly been one large room. In an attempt to make it feel like a house, the inhabitants had built in bathrooms and kitchens and barbacoas, makeshift lofts that doubled as bedrooms, jutting out in the middle of living rooms and cutting the head space in half.

Outside of Marilys's ciudadela, a group of teenage girls in spandex body suits stood surveying the street scene.

Inside, Marilys was where she always was (in front of the TV, watching that interminable Brazilian telenovela, *El Rey del Ganado*), wearing what she always wore (a gauzy yellow mumu), sitting as she always sat (in her rocking chair). Her wrinkled face glowed in the blue light of the television, and Beatriz invited herself in.

Marilys smiled, pleasantly surprised by the company, and asked, "What brings you here?"

"It's time for your eyebrow pluck," Beatriz replied. "Remember, you asked me to come by sometime tonight?"

Marilys looked suddenly worried. She raised a veiny hand to her nose, her fingers between her eyes. "Oh my, I'd forgotten," she said. "I'm actually okay now. Do you think you can come back in another week?"

Beatriz nodded. Sometimes it went this way with los viejos, their memory not what it used to be.

As Beatriz turned toward the door, Marilys called out, "Since you're here, would you like to join me for the telenovela?"

"Ay, mi vida, no," Beatriz said, softening her voice so as not to appear irritated. "I have a lot of work to do tonight."

* * *

The word on the street was that things were supposed to have gotten better after the worst of the Special Period ended in 1994. But for Beatriz, this was when the built-up stresses really began to take their toll. Within a year, her husband left her, claiming incompatibility, and her parents, who had shared their two-bedroom apartment with them and whose constant bickering over finances had certainly not helped the situation, died within days of each other. Although Marisol, age seventeen and at the height of her teenage angst, had frequently argued with all of them, she nonetheless cried for a week straight. Her paintings went from colorful cubist portraits to dark post-modern smears of varying shades of gray, and then over time, she just stopped painting altogether.

Two years after her grandparents died, and against her mother's objections, Marisol accompanied Beatriz to the Colón Cemetery. It was their pre-assigned time to retrieve the bones, making space for the bodies of the newly deceased. When the caskets were opened, the half-decayed corpses Marisol saw—rotting flesh still clinging to their bones as an other-worldly stench swirled around them—made her want to run away. She told Beatriz she wanted to flee not just the cemetery but also the island itself, where everything—from buying milk after the age of seven (when it was no longer available through rationing) to purchasing paper and paints for artwork—was a struggle, and rest, even after death, remained elusive.

Unlike Marisol, who had not lived through the Revolution, Beatriz knew that it was important to stay put, to be patient and prepared for the inevitable sea change that, however slowly, was on its way, for the day when professionals would once again be paid their worth (instead of the measly twelve dollars per month she earned as an engineer) and the world of negocios would be a thing of the past. Beatriz tried to share this wisdom with Marisol. She encouraged her to return to her painting, to pursue it professionally by applying to El Instituto Superior de Artes, but Marisol would have none of it.

"I'm young, mimi," she protested. "I don't want to spend my life sitting around, waiting for change."

Instead of El ISA, Marisol applied for el bombo, the Cuban lottery that gave one hundred and twenty thousand Cubans permission to move ninety miles north to La Yuma each year. And then Marisol waited, biding her time by befriending visiting foreign boys who, blinded by her beauty, did whatever she asked of them. To their surprise, it never involved a ring.

Marisol wanted out, she was quick to tell people, but she wanted it on her own terms, not on the arm of a man she didn't like much to begin with. The foreign boys were good for their fula, however, and Marisol didn't turn down any of their offers to take her out for fancy meals or buy her presents, all of which she handed over to her mother. Since the departure and deaths of the rest of her family and the passage of her moody seventeenth year, Marisol had transformed into a dutiful daughter. Like a cat with its proud catch of a mangled bird, Marisol brought her greasy-haired Italians and beer-bellied German men back to the house to bestow Beatriz with groceries like cheese and eggs and fresh fatty cuts of pork that she never could have afforded on her engineer's salary. And then, with an airy goodbye kiss, Marisol would shoo her surprised suitors out the door.

Five years after she'd applied for el bombo, Marisol's number had finally come up. Now it had been three years since she'd moved to Miami, and six weeks since Beatriz had last heard from her, the longest they had ever gone without communicating. Usually, Marisol called for a fifteen-minute check-in on the first Sunday of each month, and also, at some point each month, Beatriz received a letter with twenty-five or fifty dollars sent via a visitor Marisol had met in Miami. But this month there had been no phone call, and without Internet or even a way to dial the U.S. directly, Beatriz had been unable to contact Marisol on her own. She'd tried calling collect a few times, but Marisol was never there—she worked odd hours, a different schedule each week at an all-night restaurant whose name Beatriz couldn't remember.

People tried to reassure her that everything was all right. It was just the distractions of Marisol's new life, they would say. It was just la Coca-Cola del olvido.

Beatriz had suffered through so many secondhand stories of good-kid-turned-selfish-capitalist-pig that she'd wanted to scream. Each time, she'd shaken her head and recounted how, through all Marisol's travails of the past three years, she had always managed to call, to send some small amount of money home to help out.

But this is how it is with la Coca-Cola del olvido, Beatriz's friends had told her, as though this were not just an expression but the name of some unpredictable, incurable disease. It happens without warning, they said.

To occupy her mind and time, and to make up for her absent allowance this month, Beatriz had taken the remaining twenty-five dollars of Marisol's last remittance and, through an extensive network of friends who could acquire the objects at their workplaces, had invested in some sharp scissors, a small plastic squirter, bottles of rubbing alcohol and hydrogen peroxide, some shaving cream and aftershave, a pair of shiny metal tweezers, a nail clipper, three bottles of nail polish (red, purple, and pink) and some nail polish remover, a file, a fine-toothed comb, and a pack of six razors. She'd practiced on a friend next door, and then she'd begun her black market beautician tour where, by shaving one face each night and performing one eyebrow pluck for just eight pesos each, she could earn twice as much as she made each month at her engineering job, which she felt obliged to keep so as to not provoke suspicion. And, of course, to maintain her professional status for when the next revolution came, after which, she was certain, Marisol would return.

Beatriz's second stop tonight was at a solar, a step down from a ciudadela. Here, most of the one-room houses did not have bathrooms, and several were without kitchens. Through a narrow doorway with no door, Beatriz stepped into the courtyard of the former mansion, now a cement floor covered with little puddles of water. The only light inside the solar came in the form of a thin orange glow from beneath the individual families' doors. The courtyard walls were cracked, and Beatriz could hear cockroaches scurrying in the shadows near where a shirtless man stood stirring some pot over a communal stove. A corner shack served as a bathroom, minus the toilet paper and lightbulb, which each occupant supplied for herself.

This stop was not actually prearranged, but Beatriz felt the need to find an extra customer to make up for Marilys asking her to come back next week. Her postponement of the eyebrow pluck was unusual. Habaneros were a proud people; they might be suffering through their third night of pollo al bloqueo (chicken meat the first night, rice and fried chicken skin the second, chicken-bone soup the third), but look askew at an Habanera's fingernails and she would find the money for a manicure.

If she must, Beatriz decided, she would use this tactic to convince Rita, whose gray hair she had bleached a platinum-blond ten days ago, that she needed a haircut.

Rita lived on the second floor of the solar, and as Beatriz used the banister to feel her way up the unlit staircase, she stumbled on a chipped step and felt her knee slam into the cold, hard marble. Her beautician bag slipped from her shoulder and tumbled back down the steps. By the time she regained her balance and retrieved her goods, her hands were trembling and her knee throbbing. She arrived at Rita's door out of breath and with her heart beating so loudly she was sure it could suffice for a knock.

Rita opened the door a crack and then, once she recognized Beatriz, a crack more, flooding the corridor with light. In her long white nightgown, she looked like an aging angel.

"I almost killed myself on your steps just now," Beatriz said, going for the sympathy sale. "I came up to ask if you'd like a haircut tonight."

"Oh my!" Rita said. "You didn't bring your flashlight?"

"Battery's dead," Beatriz replied.

"Mine too," Rita said, nodding. Timidly, she patted at her short and, in this light, neon-blond hair. "Well, I guess I could use a trim tonight. I'd invite you in," she added, hesitating, "but my husband's in his underwear. We've just finished watching the telenovela."

"He can sit in the bedroom. It shouldn't take me that long," Beatriz said, surprising herself with her assertiveness.

"Oh, all right," Rita conceded. "You hear that, Ernesto?" She stepped back as a fleshy white figure with droopy boxers darted into the bedroom, separated from the main room by a thin sheet suspended from the ceiling.

In the living room, Rita settled into a rocking chair, and Beatriz used two clothespins to attach a worn white pillowcase to her upper back. She squirted water in Rita's hair and handed her a tiny broken slab of mirror to inspect the process.

"Still no word from Marisol?" Rita asked as her friend began cutting.

Beatriz shook her head into the mirror, her reflection smudged and distorted. "And your son, how is he?" she asked. Rita's son, a musician who had requested political asylum while touring in Mexico two years ago, now lived in New Jersey.

"He's well, I think," Rita said. "Although I haven't heard from him for a while either. Bueno, ya tú sabes."

Beatriz nodded, grateful to Rita for not starting in with la Coca-Cola del olvido. Rita told her about a woman she knew who had been changing jobs a lot lately, provoking suspicions in the neighborhood. Rita became animated as she told the story, waving her arms and the mirror.

"Rita, stay still," said Beatriz, clipping close to her ear.

A small white dog walked in from the balcony and started sniffing under Rita's nightgown.

"Ay, Yochi, vete!" Rita kicked her legs at the dog.

Beatriz sighed and put her hands firmly on Rita's head. She had a sudden, stinging flash of déjà vu, recalling how she used to take the same stance with Marisol when she was little and refused to sit still for her haircuts.

"Don't cut too much," Rita said as Beatriz trimmed a piece she had missed in the back.

"Don't worry. It looks good," Beatriz said, placing her hand gently on Rita's neck. "And actually, if you're satisfied, I think I'm done."

Rita studied herself once more in the jagged mirror, smiling at what she saw. She handed Beatriz her pay at the door and then stood with it open, shedding light on her friend's descent.

* * *

In Marisol's last letter, she'd written that she had enrolled in English classes.

I'm getting tired of the politics in Miami, all the anger and constant rehashing of the past, she'd written. *And I've decided that I want to leave, and that the first step to doing so is to improve my English.*

Marisol went on to write that she had come up with a plan for her future. She wanted to move to New York and enroll in art school. She had recently started painting again, and she was going to submit some of her slides for a few scholarships for Latino students.

When I receive one, she'd written, *I'm hoping that with some money I've been saving I can come home for a visit.*

As much as Beatriz had wanted to tell someone, to tell everyone that her daughter would be back to see her, she had refrained, not wanting to jinx this good news by discussing it prematurely. She had decided to hold off on saying anything until a ticket had been purchased. She had decided to wait patiently until she received word from Marisol, not knowing at the time of the even greater patience that would soon be demanded of her.

As Beatriz made her way down Zulueta Street to what she hoped would be her final house of the night, the drizzle turned into a full-on downpour. The few unfortunate souls still in the street ran as if on fire, intent on getting home before the dilapidated balconies above them began falling, as they were known to do during hurricane season. A lone cyclist futilely spun the pedals of his clunky Chinese bike, his fenderless wheels spitting street slime all over his bare legs.

The sky echoed with the crash of thunder, and the eerie,

almost human cry of cats mating emanated from behind an open dumpster.

Outside the house of her friend Fefé, who had requested a haircut tonight, Beatriz heard what sounded like foreign voices. Before she could get close enough to listen more carefully, a gust of wind blew open the front door, revealing a party gathered around a small color TV. There were grandmothers and babies, middle-aged men and children of all ages watching a cartoon family sit down for dinner. The curvaceously drawn mother whose hair was styled in a beehive was pointing her finger angrily and yelling in English at a beer-bellied man at the head of the table, while a baby sat in a high chair, sucking a pacifier.

Beatriz's first thought was that Fefé's sister, who lived in La Yuma, must have sent back this video of American TV. Her second, more wishful thought was that maybe there had been money padding the video package and, maybe, if Fefé was feeling generous tonight, she would offer her guests a round of haircuts on the house. Beatriz spotted a woman who could use a new bleach job, and there was a teenage girl who could certainly benefit from her pore-purifying treatment.

But at the moment, everyone was too mesmerized by the muñequitos to even notice Beatriz standing tentatively in the doorway. She cleared her throat, and said, "Oye! Y aquí, qué bolá?"

"Oh, Beatriz!" Fefé said when she turned around along with the rest of the party. "With all the excitement, I completely forgot about my haircut."

Fefé motioned for Beatriz to come in, and the crowd parted to make space for her. To the side of the TV was a white, plate-shaped structure that Fefé pointed to proudly.

"It's an antenna," she told Beatriz. "My son in Spain sent

me some money last week, and I bought it from this man on Concordia who sells them as his negocio. Now we can get every station they get in La Yuma. It's amazing the variety, and the crazy things they watch there."

"Like what?" Beatriz asked, glancing at the screen again. She couldn't understand a word of what was being said. "Does anyone here speak English?"

Fefé looked around, perplexed, as if the thought had never occurred to her. They all shook their heads.

"There are a lot of programs in Spanish," Fefé said. "I'll give you a taste of the stations while you give me my haircut."

Beatriz positioned herself behind Fefé, took out her pillowcase, and, as discretely as possible, wiped off Rita's stray hairs. "How much?" she asked as she pulled back a ponytail of Fefé's thick brown, shoulder-length hair.

Fefé put a hand on her neck, just an inch below her ears. "I saw a woman on one of these channels with her hair this length, and layered—make mine layered—and it looked very nice."

While Beatriz pinned her hair, Fefé flipped through the stations. It was true what she'd said about what those Americanos watched. There was every type of program imaginable—telenovelas and comedies and scientific shows. There were, Fefé said, stations that ran movies all night, and ones that showed twenty-four-hour sports, the likes of which Beatriz had never seen before—people scaling sheer rock walls, suspended by a series of thin ropes and supported, it seemed, by nothing; people trying to balance on oval-shaped boards in the ocean as the waves beat them down; and people standing on still smaller boards with wheels and riding up and down treacherously sloped platforms. Why would anyone willingly put himself through this? Beatriz wondered.

On a Spanish-language station, there was a show without any actors, just real people, a panel of three women accusing their partners of having slept with the other women's daughters or mothers. Things like this went on in Cuba, Beatriz knew, but why were all these people on TV, airing their dirty laundry for the world to see? And then, also in Spanish, there was a courtroom show where, in the two-minute clip Beatriz saw, two former friends were yelling at each other about a slippery spot on one's driveway that had caused the other to fall and break her leg when she had stopped by for a visit.

Beatriz made a mental note to ask Marisol if she knew about this case, to remind her to clear all slippery things from her driveway. She felt strange thinking about this side of American life she had never known about before, and she felt disturbed by her inability to picture Marisol in this world.

In their first few conversations after Marisol had left, she had tried to tell Beatriz about all the differences in La Yuma, but it had been too much for Beatriz to comprehend, and soon their conversations had reverted to simpler and more universal topics, like the weather and the salaries at different jobs. They had talked a lot about money and, Beatriz now realized, most often their conversations had focused on the problems in Cuba. At some point, Marisol had stopped trying to explain her life in La Yuma.

"Very early in the morning there is even pornografía," Fefé announced as she flipped the station once more, pulling Beatriz out of her thoughts. "Men with pingas the size of elephants'!"

There was a hearty round of laughter, and then someone called out, "Las noticias!"

"Oh, right," Fefé said. "There's Spanish-language news right now on Univisión."

Unlike Cuban news, which was essentially a recapping of all that was going well on the island, Univisión seemed to recount only the disastrous. It was a litany of loss—a baby stolen from a shopping cart as the mother turned her back for a split second to pick out a green pepper, a man who returned to his hometown twenty years after he graduated from high school and murdered the teacher who had failed him in geometry.

"Escucha eso!" Fefé announced. "Their news is more sensational than our telenovelas." Everyone nodded their heads in shocked silence.

When a photo of George Bush came on the screen, a loud hiss reverberated through Fefé's living room, making it impossible for Beatriz to hear what the newscaster was saying.

By the time the local Miami news came on, Beatriz had cut a good four inches off of Fefé's hair, and she was beginning to feel a little worried about how Fefé would react to the end result. Personally, Beatriz didn't think that she had the type of face for short hair. It wasn't angular enough, and would now look even rounder.

Beatriz was about to hand Fefé the bit of broken mirror when she heard the newscaster mention something about Havana.

"... *After nearly two weeks of investigations into the bombing of the gallery, located on a side street in Little Havana* ..." the newscaster was saying, and Beatriz realized she'd misheard him.

Fefé was so caught up in the news that Beatriz decided to wait for a commercial break. Even after just two weeks of cutting hair, Beatriz had learned her lesson about asking people to approve further cutting when they were distracted, only to have them angrily retract their consent after the fact.

Beatriz set down her scissors and held the mirror in her hand, turning her attention back to the TV.

"Police have reported that the explosion was set off by a group of Cuban exiles who refer to themselves as 'Los Rectificantes,'" the newscaster continued. And once more, a loud hiss filled the living room. "They claim to have been protesting the five painters whose works were exhibited, all of whom still reside in Cuba and have been labeled as Castro-supporters by the bombers."

"Son terroristas todos!" a man next to Fefé declared angrily.

"Although the bombing took place when the gallery was closed, police have confirmed that there was one casualty, a young woman who had been peering through the window at the moment the bomb went off."

As the photo of a smiling mulatta flashed onto the screen, her face framed by long black ringlets sun-streaked with red-gold, the newscaster's voice was once again drowned out, not by hisses this time, but by a lone, shrill wail, and the sound of shattering glass.

PART IV

DROWNING IN SILENCE

ZENZIZENZIC

BY ACHY OBEJAS

Chinatown

There it was, framed by the oval of my airplane window: a shout of palms and prickly grass, low concrete buildings with exposed stones in hopeless need of paint and repair. As we descended, plumes of smoke, both black and white, spiraled up to meet us. I'm told exiles returning to Cuba sob as soon as the plane door pops open and the blinding Caribbean sky spills before them. But not me.

When I stepped onto the tarmac, the wet tropical air pawed at me reeking of mildew. The skies were a sweet pastel but I could barely see. I held my breath for the first few steps thinking the smell was just a bad patch—one of those sulphurous smoke trails having descended back to earth perhaps—but all was lost the minute I had to respond to the military guy with the official passenger list flapping wildly on his clipboard. His finger pointed at something and sweat ran from behind my ears.

"Yep, that's me, Malía Mercado," I muttered. It'd be rude to hold my nose or cover my mouth, so I was praying for my senses to acclimate quickly, very quickly. How could anybody stand this for long?

"María Mercado, sí," he said, and went to correct the spelling on his neatly typed list.

"No, no—Malía, not María—Malía's right," I said in my best Spanish.

"Malía?" he asked, a hint of a smile disturbing his officially somber face.

"Yes, it's Hawaiian," I said, the Spanish accent my parents had added notwithstanding.

The military guy nodded. "Ah, well, it sounds Chinese," he said.

I'd been warned by my parents and my sister Rocky, whom I was visiting, that most Cubans don't feel the least bit uncomfortable making racial comments. And when it came to Asians—who were all Chinese to the Cubans—it was a long-standing pastime to base double-entendres on their supposed inability to pronounce the ferocious Cuban *R*, which the Chinese were said to render as *L*s. Thus, in this guy's mind, my Malía couldn't be anything but a mangled Chinese María.

I nodded at him, not exactly hiding my annoyance, which seemed to amuse him. But behind me the line was lengthening—I could sense the next passenger within inches of me, like a restless shadow—so the guard motioned me toward the blurry building in the distance. My bags were promised inside but mostly I was praying for shade. My heart was fluttering in the sticky strait jacket the humidity had wrapped around my chest.

"Buenas tardes, compañera," I heard a voice say just behind me. It drew my immediate attention because it was so cheery, and because the Spanish was so masticated and rough.

I'd noticed him before, on the hop over from Kingston: a forty-something American with a weedy mustache and long strands of thinning hair. He was slender but I could tell, even with the scorching wind making his Che Guevara T-shirt billow into a small, curvy balloon, that he was probably really fit. He had the sunbaked look of a cyclist, lean and disciplined.

"First time back?" he asked me with a wink. He'd come up behind me so we were walking side by side, unexpectedly in step.

"Uh . . . yeah," I said. "How'd you know?"

He shrugged. "I've been coming for so long, I can just tell."

We pushed back the doors to the terminal. Not that the air-conditioning inside was much relief. I imagined a small unit hidden somewhere huffing and puffing as I scanned the waiting area, men and women in uniform milling among the passengers. Neither their rank nor purpose was clear to me.

"They won't bite," the man said, his head nodding in the direction of the customs officials. "They've forgiven you."

"Forgiven me?" I asked.

"You're an exile, right?"

I nodded involuntarily. Being Cuban without being born in Cuba is a tricky proposition; the notion of exile even more complicated. But I'd just met this guy and I certainly wasn't going to go into any kind of philosophical discourse while I was melting away in the tropical heat. Exile residue required more time to explain than I had right then.

"Forgiven . . . ? I guess I don't—"

"Yeah, forgiven you," he said.

"For what?"

"For abandonment," he said, grinning now, "maybe even treason."

"Wha . . . ?"

He grinned from ear to ear, immensely pleased with himself.

"Fuck you," I said, and stormed away. This was my first time in Cuba (I was taking a semester off from my studies at the University of Hawai'i and was to stay in Cuba one month)—maybe my last too—and I sure as hell wasn't going to cause a commotion at customs.

I grabbed my bags but kept a wary eye on the jerk. A baggage handler stacked box after box next to him. They were perfectly square, identical, and the handler treated them with loving care. The jerk, for his part, ignored the returning exiles, not even trying to hide his contempt as he looked over and through them with their anxious faces and excess baggage. While the mostly elderly in the crowd struggled with their overstuffed suitcases, he reached around them for his own bags, holding his arms out as if to avoid touching them. I couldn't help but notice that his lips didn't move, keeping any sort of courtesy from slipping out. In turn, the exiles eyed the jerk's Che T-shirt with pained expressions. In Havana, even in customs, it certainly seemed redundant.

This guy, however, appeared to know everybody in any kind of official capacity: the customs inspectors, the nurse, the woman who checked the luggage tags. He shook each of their hands, even hugged some of them. In a few strategic cases, he gave out little presents—bribes? I wondered. It all seemed very acceptable. I wondered if I'd have to come up with something at any point. As per my sister's instructions, I had brought plenty of generic ibuprofen, Band-Aids, deodorants. I'd also brought wasabi and packages of seaweed, macadamias, Kona coffee, and spices. Would any of these count as gifts here? And if so, would I know when to make an offer?

I lost sight of the guy when we stepped out to the searing sun. It took me a minute to adjust to the maddeningly white light (for a second I thought I was hallucinating, or fainting) but then I spotted Rocky—she was jumping up and down, just like the Cubans around her. Her dark frizzy hair was pulled back carelessly, an orchid with fat watery petals behind her ear. She seemed as eager to hug me as they were to hug their relatives, all apparently recovering from long separations. Except that Rocky—it was my childhood pronunciation of Raquel, which I'd soon learn had become *Roh-keee* in Havana—had just seen me briefly three weeks before, back on the family homestead on the other side of the world, in Honolulu.

Rocky's unexpected return to our barely acknowledged Cuban homeland was, in fact, precisely why I had followed her back to Havana. Maybe because she was born in Cuba and uprooted early, she had always been emotionally tethered to it, considerably more so than my parents, certainly way more than me. When our parents won the visa lottery to enter the U.S., they were almost relieved to wind up in Hawai'i, so far away from all known Cubanness that most of the time, when we were confused for Puerto Ricans or Portuguese ("Potagee," as the locals not so kindly said: "How do you get da one-arm potagee out da tree? Wave at um")—the islands' few Latinos—they never bothered to correct anybody.

It's not that they weren't proud of their Cubanness, but rather that folks in Hawai'i were completely indifferent to it. As a kid, Rocky used to walk around with T-shirts emblazoned with legends such as, *Not only am I perfect, I'm Cuban too!*, drawing stares from the Hawaiians, Samoans, Filipinos, and other Pacific islanders who looked at her sorrel skin and probably assumed she was one of them. (Though Honolulu-born, I elicited nothing but haole wariness with my freckles and blondish hair.)

All my life, I'd listened intently to Eddie Kamae and Keali'i Reichel; Rocky swooned to Charanga Habanera and homemade tapes of the band Porno Para Ricardo. I ate poi stirred with milk and sugar; she flatly refused it in any form, preferring when my mother sliced the taro—which they called malanga—and fried it in olive oil. I took hula lessons after school while Rocky had my dad teach her how to dance timba, and later, when she deemed he'd taken her as far as he could, she began buying videos that showed her how to shiver and thrust. My dad teased her about being so Cuban, and I said once that she was Cuban squared, which in the family vernacular became simply "Cubed."

"Zenzizenzic," suggested my mother, the scientist, upping the stakes, "to the fourth power."

When my parents first arrived in Hawai'i—when Rocky was six and before I was even born—they each found fantastic, ridiculously well-suited jobs. My mother's a marine biologist and got plugged in to a government-funded program that operated for a while off Ni'ihau, a feudal island community, normally off-limits to all but its residents. I think she was the first Cuban to ever set foot there. She spent days diving, coming back to our house with bizarre creatures and assorted ocean debris. For a while, her prized possession was an organism called a xenophyophore, which was about the size of a golf ball and looked like a moon rock. I could never tell if it was dead or alive but when it finally, officially expired, my mom moped around for weeks.

My dad also landed on his feet. In Havana, he'd studied Chinese. In Honolulu, that skill became a bonanza. Moreover, his experience coming from a Communist country gave him an aura of expertise well beyond language, even if the Cuban and Chinese models really had very little in common. As a result, he was able to pick and choose consulting clients, and our lifestyle slowly became more and more comfortable—a fact that seemed to shock my parents, who'd dreamed but never expected much in Cuba.

Whenever something wonderful happened—and in their minds, a working car and a full fridge fit the bill—my parents were dazed by their good luck. Delighted by how sunny their lives were in Hawai'i, they added a fist-sized volcanic rock—representing Pele, one of the Hawaiians' main deities—to the tropical tableau of Oshún and Yemayá on their altar.

We weren't Hawaiian but we identified with the natives in unexpected ways. Perhaps after all of those years hearing about America's imperialism from the Cuban government (and because Hawai'i really didn't seem American to us), my family drifted seamlessly into Hawaiian sovereignty activities and frequently found ourselves at rallies and other independence-related events. For me, it was what we did in Hawai'i—it never dawned on me that these issues didn't matter to the rest of the world until I began to travel.

Rocky, however, was completely indifferent to Hawai'i. Rocky's return to Cuba, initially just a visit under the auspices of a Japanese travel group, had been a total shock to my parents—but not to me. Rocky had always aimed her brown Cuban irises at the horizon, convinced that Hawai'i, for her, was a geographical accident. In fact, if I speak any Spanish at all—and I confess that mine is tentative—it's because Rocky, even as a kid, insisted on talking in Spanish at home, long after we were all functioning mostly in English and I was deeply immersed in Hawaiian language classes.

"We'll have to know Spanish when we go back," she'd say, while my mom, dad, and I just kind of looked away, out to the Pacific. It all seemed so foolish then.

"Aloha, Malía! Que bolá!" Rocky exclaimed at the airport, all feisty and mostly Cubed. She unraveled her warm arms from around my neck and led me by the hand toward a shiny Fiat, where she flung my bags into the sliver of a backseat.

"Spiffy car!" I said, admiring the unexpected little sportster. It really stuck out next to the sad tangle of the patched Eastern European models with no names that populated the parking lot.

"We're going to be tight," she said, grinning.

"Tight? We can fit in there, no prob!" I said.

Rocky shook her head. "No, there's one more person, a friend of Dionisio's," she said.

Dionisio was Rocky's fiancé, her reason for staying in Cuba, and the real source of my parents' concern. We'd seen him in photos: a winsome young man in his late-twenties, just about her height when she wore flats, pale and soft featured. She'd fallen for him on that first trip three years ago and she'd never looked back. But for an annual trip to Honolulu to see us, she'd stayed in Cuba, translating and teaching English to foreigners and Cubans with dollar connections.

Technically, I was in Havana to visit Rocky—a trip organized during her brief sojourn in Honolulu weeks before—but, frankly, more than anything I was to serve as a kind of scouting party for my parents: They needed time to acclimate to the idea of returning to Cuba, and even more so to the idea of their eldest daughter's wedding (though no date had been set, we all understood it would happen). Because Dionisio was a doctor, his chances of leaving Cuba were virtually nil. Marrying Rocky meant little to the Cuban authorities, who expected him to stick around and perform medical duties until he'd given back enough to justify his free education.

"That's our guy," Rocky said, pointing with her chin in a way Hawaiian locals think particular and which the Cubans, as Rocky explained later, claim as uniquely theirs.

I turned my head to see, then snapped back to Rocky. "Are you kidding me?" There, striding toward us in all his smug glory, was the jerk. He was alternately waving hello to us and goodbye to a guy who was carting away the boxes. "He's . . ."

"He's a friend of the family," Rocky said before I had a chance to finish. "A really good friend." Her look was cautionary.

"La Hawayana! Raquelin," he oozed, taking my sister in his arms. As his chin rested for a second on her shoulder, he winked at me from behind her back. She hugged him too, but quickly, not letting it go beyond courtesy. "And this is the baby sister?" he said, laughing as he pointed at me.

"I'm nineteen, I'm not a baby," I protested, realizing immediately how childish I sounded. "And we've met," I said, my embarrassed words aimed at Rocky.

"Oh yes, we've met," he said, extending his hand to me but pulling it just as I approached, bringing me in to him for an unexpected—and unwanted—embrace. I decided to play like Rocky, feigning courtesy. "I'm Tom Mahler," he continued, "practically Dionisio's brother. Which means I'm practically your brother-in-law—that's what we'd be, no? In any case, family!"

Dionisio's family lived in an early–twentieth century house on San Nicolás Street, perched on a busy and narrow corner in Havana's Chinatown, where I immediately noticed that the vast majority of the workers—vendors, shop clerks, incredibly aggressive maître d's and hostesses in front of the restaurants—were not Chinese, in fact not Asian at all. They wore Mandarin blouses or jackets, and rayon pants imitating Heung Wun silk, but with a looseness that made them seem like careless costumes.

Very few people in this Chinatown, Rocky explained, actually spoke Chinese, even the few Chinese who were left.

"This is largest two-column Chinese gate outside of China," Mahler piped in as we passed under the Dragon gate into the neighborhood, "measuring almost sixty-three feet by forty-three feet." I made a face behind his back but Rocky didn't see me.

Mercifully, the family's home wasn't buried in the neighborhood labyrinth but just off the main streets of Zanja and Dragones, where pedestrian and bicitaxi traffic clogged the arteries. I noticed right away that noise was constant: in the predawn hours, the local agro-market opened (the only one in the city with eggplant and bean sprouts), restaurants began pounding meat, and, later, kids trotted off to school yelling and fighting. At night, crowds lingered, with laughter and music everywhere. It never let up. (Curiously, once off the little official Chinese food mall, most of the eateries—and there were dozens of them, usually just carry-out through somebody's living room or kitchen window—served up regular Cuban menu items like ham-and-cheese sandwiches, roasted pork, and black bean and rice concoctions—nothing Chinese at all.) Just when a lull was conceivable, a group of tourists would stampede through, fascinated by Cuba's Chinese-less Chinatown, seeing Chinese eyes on mulattos and blacks and, after a few days into my visit, even me.

"We grow Chinese after a while," Dionisio said, pointing to his own eyes, which he swore had an Asian slant neither Rocky nor I could discern. He spoke to me in a mix of Spanish and elementary English. "Didn't you become a little Hawaiian after a while in Hawai'i?"

"Yeah, but there are real Hawaiians in Hawai'i," I said,

trying first in Spanish, then surrendering to English. "And, you know, we wouldn't presume to be Hawaiian."

"But you were born in Hawai'i!" he replied incredulously.

"C'mon, Dionisio, I've explained this to you," Rocky said, tugging at his arm.

"We don't have too many Chinese left, see, so sometimes we have to step in for them."

I had noticed, though, that the occasional high-level Chinese diplomatic tour groups were frequently led by an elegant elderly man who looked really Chinese, even as he moved with the ease and flair of the Cubans.

"That's Moisés Sio Wong," Tom Mahler said when I asked the family about him. "He's one of the original revolutionaries; he's been with Fidel from the very, very start. One of three Chinese Cuban generals in the Revolution. Now, that is a hero!"

To my surprise, the family appeared expressionless—certainly only silence followed Mahler's declaration—but then I thought I saw Dionisio roll his eyes. And Rocky smiled conspiratorially, apparently unaware I had noticed.

According to Dionisio's family, they had all been very happy when he unexpectedly fell in love with Rocky, La Hawayana, as they affectionately referred to her. They could never have imagined my own amusement at my sister cast in any way associated with Hawai'i. But in Cuba, where she'd always wanted to be, Rocky reflected her Hawaiian upbringing more than ever. Around Chinatown, she wore flowers in her hair in a typical Polynesian style (which seemed to me should not have been so exotic to the Cubans). She'd found a connection through a Japanese diplomat for fresh fish for sashimi and had us shipping wasabi and seaweed regularly. In her room, I found Eddie Kamae

294 // HAVANA NOIR

CDs, and both Dionisio and his mother confided that Rocky frequently cried when she heard a particular Hawaiian song. I was flabbergasted—not at her emotions, because my sister has a tender heart, but at the source of such displays.

"What song?" I asked them.

The two hummed a few bars of something completely unrecognizable, frequently interrupting to correct one another.

"Do you know what the song's about?" I asked.

"Oh, it's about Hawai'i," said Dionisio's mom.

"Yes, about missing Hawai'i," added Dionisio, quite seriously.

"Rocky misses Hawai'i?" I asked.

"Oh yes, she misses Hawai'i very much," he responded, "sometimes I think so much that she'll leave."

I could tell he meant it—his voice actually cracked a bit, then withered. And his mother quietly stroked his back, already comforting him for his future loss—something she was familiar with, I was told, since her husband had died only a few years before.

"It was an embolia," she explained to me in Spanish.

"What's that?" I asked. The noise from the street was filtering in and I wasn't sure I'd heard her right.

"An attack," she said.

"What kind of attack?" I asked.

"A special attack," she said, shaking her head with just enough annoyance that I was sure she thought I was an idiot.

Dionisio had met Tom Mahler years back, during one of his medical tours in Haiti. Mahler had swooped in with computers and medical software that dazzled the Cubans and Haitian authorities. All of it was top of the line, and all of it was donated. Mahler wasn't a doctor or a salesman, just a guy who'd done incredibly well during the boom years of the computer age and had committed himself now to charity work. When Dionisio invited him to Cuba, Mahler immediately set about to modernize the island's medical networks, a haphazard system that cribbed parts from ancient Soviet, Chinese, and Korean computers with the same spirit that Cuban mechanics rescued classic American cars.

From the beginning, Mahler had stayed with Dionisio's family rather than at a hotel. He'd come four or five times a year, visits that could last a few days or as long as a month. His presence became so constant that Dionisio's family had formally surrendered a room to him off the courtyard. During my visit, I was in Rocky and Dionisio's room, which put Dionisio with his policeman cousin Raúl in another room.

"He is a wonderful person," Dionisio's mother told me about Mahler, "and a very good cook."

During each visit, Mahler would fill the fridge and cabinets with foods normally out of the family's reach: beef and seafood, dry cereals, fresh milk and cheese, canned veggies, and condiments such as mayonnaise and mustard. Each morning before taking off for work, he'd take over the kitchen and produce the kind of hearty breakfast the Cubans went wild over: steak and eggs or pancakes, skillets brimming with sausage and bacon or, once, biscuits and gravy.

His revolutionary fervor was well-known, yet after unsuccessfully trying to enlist the family in marches and volunteer projects, he had mostly gone about his business, talking things up but not pushing. It was no secret, though, that Mahler had been deeply disappointed when Dionisio took up with Rocky. But because Rocky had chosen to stay in Cuba, his feelings of "betrayal"—if I'm to guess from his words to me at the airport—had been somewhat assuaged.

Mahler didn't see their relationship as a triumph of love over politics. Instead, he considered Rocky the cause of potential revolutionary slippage. Rocky, according to Tom Mahler, was a temptation—not necessarily erotic (it was actually appalling how he seemed to see my sister as a cut-out figure instead of a real girl) but economic and political. He would joke about how Rocky had almost brainwashed Dionisio into leaving Cuba but not quite.

"Was he falling into temptation, is that it? Are you the reinforcements?" he harangued me one day while we were cleaning rice in the kitchen, his face all smiles but the meanness in his tone evident. "He's not gonna follow you guys back to your capitalistic island paradise when he has a revolutionary one right here, okay?"

"Tom, por favor, ya," Dionisio said, irritated. That was probably the first time I'd heard Dionisio actually confront Mahler; usually he was like everybody else, smiling and shuffling.

But no sooner had Dionisio left the room than Mahler started in again. "Are you here to try to get me to fall in line too?" he said, again screwing up his face so that his eyebrows danced in a clownish manner. "You know, there's nothing you can show me. I've not only lived in the belly of the beast, I was born there . . . I know it better than anyone here, including you two Hawaiians."

"We're not Hawaiians," I corrected him, exasperated.

"Right—sorry!" He smiled, his face now feigning concern. "I have to get that. Of course you're not Hawaiian. I guess I want to equate it with, like, New Yorkers or Hoosiers. I don't know why I keep tripping on that, although it is a mouthful: not Hawaiian, but from Hawai'i. What do you call that? Not Hawaiian, not mainlander? Haole? But you're no haole, though you certainly look like one!"

* * *

At Dionisio's family home, the doorbell—a merciless and ear-splitting metallic buzzing—rang constantly. There was the man selling illegal crabs ("How many can I buy?" I heard his mother cautiously ask); the man selling a fluorescent tube, maybe several feet in length, frosty and miraculously intact ("No, thank you," said Dionisio himself, then quickly added, "but Mrs. Wu down the street, Estrellita's mother—yes, the widow with the balcony full of flowers—I bet she could use this"); the woman selling illegal bags of cement who appeared with backbreaking knapsacks as local kids with features I too had begun to see as increasingly Asian paraded through the family courtyard, stacking the cement under an awning and covering it up with sheets of paint-splattered plastic. The cement was meant for an illegal addition the family was planning on the roof—in fact, a kind of studio apartment for Dionisio and Rocky.

I was told—by both Rocky and Dionisio and later, again, by his mother and Raúl, the policeman cousin who'd come in from Banes, the family's provincial home, to live with them in the capital—that I was not to let Tom Mahler know about these purchases, that in fact Tom was not to know about the cement at all.

"He wouldn't approve," Rocky said.

"But won't he like seeing that there's more permanence to your stay?" I asked.

Rocky shook her head.

Still, I thought it peculiar at best to try withholding the information since the plastic sheets were obviously changing shape, growing both taller and fatter by the day as more cement bags were delivered, but Rocky assured me this was the agreed on strategy.

"Don't you think he'll be able to tell?" I asked.

She shook her head. "In Cuba—it's strange—people are remarkably good at not seeing anything they don't want to see."

"But he's not Cuban," I pointed out.

"He thinks he is," she said by way of explanation. "He's zenzizenzic, actually."

I laughed. "But he's American!"

"Gringo Z!" Rocky exclaimed. "Mami would be so proud that we've discovered a new species!"

Indeed, I already had so much to tell her and my dad.

The first couple of weeks in Cuba, I really struggled to make myself understood (and heard above the barking and horn blowing and general human effusiveness that leaked into every corner of the house). Cubans swallowed letters, syllables, whole words sometimes. And they spoke at rocket speed, punctuating everything with a physicality that was equally quirky and anxious. They slapped their hands, punched their fists in their palms, snapped their fingers in the air (all at once!), thumped their chests, rubbed their tummies, and danced their digits on any and all surfaces. Plus, the heat didn't seem to bother them at all, while I felt like there was a giant iron on my head all the time.

"But Malía, isn't Hawai'i tropical too?" Dionisio's mother asked me as she cut up a large avocado in the family kitchen. She lifted the knife into the air, whirling it around to suggest something akin to a vortex but which I understood to be shorthand for climate.

"Yes," I explained, "but there are trade winds, and the islands are smaller, and we have mountains."

"We have mountains too," said Raúl, leaning against the counter while waiting for water to boil so he could bathe. He raised his right arm, his palm capping off what would be a mountain top, then brought it down and scratched his chest. The pot next to him—caked white on the inside and used exclusively to heat bathwater—hummed on the flame.

"Yes, but . . ." How to explain the difference between Cuban mountains—thick, green, and sloping—and Hawaiian mountains that go straight up, like sheets of rock, and dominate every landscape? How to explain that a tropical island can have snowcapped peaks?

"And you have volcanoes, right? Rocky is always showing us pictures and videos of the volcanoes," said Dionisio's mother. This time, the knife indicated an incline. "She loves the volcanoes; I guess that's very Hawaiian."

I nodded, amused. "Yes . . ." Rocky had warned me not to bother to correct the Cubans: They would insist we were Hawaiian, no matter what we said. And, in fact, it was almost dizzying. Everywhere we went, to whomever I was introduced, we were Las Hawayanas, over and over.

"So it's actually hotter then, hotter than here, because a volcano would be spitting out fire, right?" the policeman cousin asked, smiling courteously as he puckered then extended his fingers outward. He turned off the fire and lifted the pot to take to the bathroom. He stood there, perspiring, waiting for my response as the steam rose. His face was so kind, it was nearly impossible to imagine him as a cop.

"Yeah, but it doesn't work that way," I tried again with my limited Spanish.

They nodded at me politely.

"We are on the same latitude, no?" Dionisio's mother asked. The knife crisscrossed the air horizontally now.

"Yes, but it's different," I said, realizing even as I insisted that I would never convince them.

"Of course it's different!" exclaimed a buoyant Tom Mahler, bounding into the kitchen for a glass of water for Mrs. Wu, whom he was entertaining in the living room. He'd obviously heard the tail end of our chat. "Hawai'i is an American colony, ripped of all its freedom and tradition. Cuba is a free and sovereign nation!"

"Look, Tom, you don't know—" I started to say, but then Raúl excused himself and trotted off to bathe, bumping right smack into me.

"I am so sorry!" he said, the hot water having splashed him, not me. "Are you all right?"

I nodded as Raúl and Dionisio's mother shrugged, both slightly chagrined.

In the meantime, Tom laughed, practically skipping back to Mrs. Wu with a cold glass of water.

I confess I was amazed in Cuba—not at Socialism's wonders, even as Tom rattled off literacy rates ("The highest in the Western Hemisphere—even higher than the United States!" he exuded) and infant mortality rates ("The lowest in the Western Hemisphere—even lower than the United States!"). More precisely, I was astounded by how my sense of being an islander was constantly challenged. Nearly every Cuban I met happily confessed he or she couldn't swim. This, of course, was nearly unheard of in Hawai'i, where learning to swim is no more of an option than learning to breathe. The Cubans sat on their weathered Malecón with their backs to the sea, unaware and undisturbed, chatting and drinking and sometimes even fishing, their lines dangling behind them as they continued their social dalliances. Just looking at them facing away from the water like that gave me the willies.

They wore shoes—flats and loafers but often heavy-soled shoes, more suitable for mountain climbing than anything else, and even better if the shoes were some brand they recognized: Mephisto, Doc Martens, and Prada of course. And they kept those shoes on all the time, even in their own homes, constantly wary of germs and viruses that, according to them, were both ubiquitous and lethal if they attached themselves to a naked foot.

"You don't die from the virus," Raúl explained, trying to reassure me, "but from the symptoms."

These were said to be utterly extravagant. There was the patatú, an attack of undetermined origin completely undetectable by medical science, the sirimba (a milder form), and a whole series of weird medical conditions with no translations that even Rocky openly laughed about. What was crazy was that Dionisio—a medical doctor!—actually seemed to sign on to these diagnoses.

"You're telling me that you really believe empachos can only be caused by eating too much Cuban food?" I asked.

Dionisio nodded serenely. He was less handsome than charming, with a gentility in his eyes that made my sister's attraction to him completely understandable.

"But isn't that just indigestion?" I asked, irritated. "Couldn't you just get it from overeating anything?"

He shook his head. "No, no—this is particular. Malía, it doesn't happen to people who don't have a regular diet of Cuban food."

Was he kidding me? I couldn't tell. I was going to ask him about embolias, which I suspected, having killed his father, might take us down a more serious path, but then he started talking about serenos, a condition said to occur when you step outside and are enveloped in the night air.

302 // Havana Noir

"The night air? For real?" I asked, looking for cracks in his façade.

Dionisio shrugged. "And only old people can tell if you really have it."

"That's so mental! C'mon!"

Rocky laughed and laughed. "She's not very Cuban, see?"

"Of course she is," he said sympathetically, then reached out to touch the back of my head. His fingers dug through my hair to my scalp. "Absolutely she is."

"What are you doing?" I snapped, pulling away from him. Rocky was holding her sides now, she was laughing so hard.

"Well, it's as I suspected, somebody probably touched your mollera when you were born," he said after his cursory examination of the spot at the very top of my skull.

"My what?"

"Your mollera."

I looked at Rocky for clarification but she was bright red, tears streaming down her face. "Your . . ." She pointed at the back of her head between gulps and hysterics.

"It's a soft cranial spot, very sensitive, much more sensitive on Cuban babies than on any other babies," Dionisio said, still straight-faced. "You know, if it gets touched when you're little—if it gets touched the wrong way—you can suffer irreparable harm, like losing your Cubanness. But yours—"

"Por dios!" I said in Spanish, naturally Cubed for once. "You're just playing with me!"

And they both fell back on the couch, Rocky bubbling like lava and Dionisio finally erupting, slapping his thighs and his chest in the national fashion.

It wasn't until later, alone in my noisy room writing in the travel journal I'd decided to keep for my parents, that I realized I'd never gotten a chance to ask about embolias.

As a result of the Cubans' collective hypochondria, we had to watch for germs and viruses that could cause these things, and wear shoes—real shoes—all the time. To me, it was a real hardship not to go barefoot in the house. But my slippahs, which were the only things that really made sense to me day to day in the tropics, were a source of such embarrassment that one night, Dionisio's mother asked Rocky to please suggest I not wear them as we headed out to a nearby casual restaurant.

"Just wear sandals," my sister said, amused.

But it was all I could do to keep from laughing when Tom Mahler showed up that night with his feet encased in the dirtiest, most disgusting rope sandals I'd ever seen. Halfway to the restaurant, the left one came apart and he just chucked it to the side of the street (trash cans were virtually nonexistent, even in touristy areas like Chinatown, so that Rocky and I, our American habits ingrained, tended to walk around with handfuls of trash at any given moment) and kept going with only one sole protected.

"Oh, Tom, you can't do that, it's littering!" Rocky said, picking up the sandal remains between her thumb and index finger.

The entire family looked on in horror at each step Mahler took, warning him about upcoming dog feces, unidentified animal remains, vomit, and other revolting obstacles.

"You're such gringas!" he exclaimed, motioning to the rest of the family for support with a flail of his arms. In response, they just nodded again.

"Tom—" I started to say, but Rocky elbowed me so hard, I almost lost my balance.

"That's not ordinary trash—it's hemp, it's organic, it'll de-compose," he explained.

"Not for a long time, Tom, not for a long time," Rocky said.

She carried that thing all the way to the restaurant, dumped it in the kitchen trash, and, because she was carrying her own bar of soap in her purse, was able to scrub her hands before settling down to eat. The entire family maneuvered to avoid Tom Mahler, so he sat next to me, his left leg across his right knee, the germ-infested bottom of his foot bumping into me and leaving viral traces on my skirt throughout the meal.

"Careful or you'll have an empacho," Dionisio said, his chin pointing at the huge chicken and rice dinner before me.

In all honesty, I could hardly eat. Rocky's jab had had its effect. "I thought you needed a regular diet of Cuban food to be vulnerable to those," I shot back, trying to be jovial.

"Well, you're on your way," Mahler said, grinning malevo-lently, "don't you think? Soon you'll be like your sister, Cuban again, wanting to stay. Then you'll have a fully rounded Cu-ban diet all the time."

Infuriatingly, the family—Dionisio and Rocky included—again just smiled, their lips zipped.

It was just a few days before my scheduled departure (a long, roundabout trip from Havana to Kingston to Miami to Hous-ton to San Francisco to, finally, Honolulu) when Dionisio and Rocky announced a party.

"But not just any party—a luau!" said Rocky.

"A luau?" I asked. Was she kidding?

"Turns out," she said, all excited, "that Eddie Kamae is in Havana for a world music festival. Dionisio found out and invited him to dinner."

"So maybe he'd like a typical Cuban fiesta or something instead of another luau, don't you think?"

Rocky waved me off. "Don't you see? It's such a great opportunity to show the family a little bit of Hawaiian culture. Eddie's probably getting plenty of Cuban everything from his festival hosts."

When we told Tom Mahler, he immediately filed his protest: He thought it inappropriate that Rocky and I—non-Hawaiians—should be leading anyone through a Hawaiian experience. "You yourselves have gone out of your way to tell me you're not Hawaiian, and now you're pretending to be our cultural tour guides?"

"Don't worry, Tom," Rocky said with a wink, "it won't be authentic, but diluted and commercialized—as much as we can do that here."

To my surprise, the family laughed openly and Mahler, stuck somewhere between pride and embarrassment, shrunk a little.

To prepare, we put together the Hawaiian supplies I'd brought and went out searching for a few other necessary items, like flowers and pork. Raúl was negotiating for a lively little piglet raised on a neighbor's balcony when, unable to keep silent anymore—it'd been almost a month of putting up with Tom Mahler and following everybody else's passive example—I confronted Dionisio and Rocky.

"What's the deal with Mahler? I mean, why do you guys even put up with him?"

Dionisio grinned. "Malía, you don't believe he's part of the family?"

"No, I don't think you guys can stand him—which is why I don't get why you let him think that he is."

Rocky cleared her throat. "It's another one of those Cubed things," she said.

306 // H<small>AVANA</small> N<small>OIR</small>

"What did you call him when I first explained it to you?" Dionisio asked her.

"Pet foreigner," Rocky said in English.

"That's right, he's our pet foreigner," Dionisio repeated.

"Your what?"

"Our pet foreigner," he repeated, relishing the English through his laughter. "It's every Cuban family's aspiration to have one. See, we need someone who can travel back and forth, bring us things, bring us dollars, and remind us that there is another world."

"One of the pet foreigner's obligations," Rocky chimed in, "is also to give hope."

"And you don't count?" I asked pointedly.

"Sometimes, yes," she said.

"But sometimes not," said Dionisio, now screwing up his face with mock concern. "Because, frankly, these days she doesn't bring in much more in real dollars than a well-connected Cuban. Yes, we get wasabi and ukulele music, but no hulas—did I tell you?—she won't grace us with a hula—"

"That's *her* job," Rocky said, her chin aiming at me.

"I'm not dancing hula here," I said. "But—wait—you're going off subject."

"Ah, yes, the pet foreigner. How is my English, eh?"

"Diiiiiiiiiiiiioooooooooonisio!"

"Yeah," he said as he and Rocky laughed it up, slapping their chests and snapping their hands in the air. "Okay, so what can we do? He attached himself to us and we realized, here's one lonely little leftist. So we took him in. Don't get me wrong—there's real affection there. And he is well-intentioned. You see, he really believes. He believes so much that he just can't see *why* we need him."

"Or that you might be using him."

"Malía!" Rocky said, aghast.

"Well, that's it, isn't it?"

"Don't you see that it's mutual?" Rocky argued. "Don't you see how Dionisio's family authenticates his experience?"

"Sure, but—"

"Wait a minute, wait a minute!" Dionisio literally put himself between us. He turned to Rocky. "Why pretend? Of course we're using him." Then he turned to me. "His services are invaluable, what he does for our hospitals and clinics. Do you realize every clinic in Chinatown has a computer now? And us—well, before Rocky, how else would we get medicine? Who would negotiate for us, even with other Cubans? Here people do for foreigners—for strangers—what they would not do for their own mothers."

Just then, Raúl stepped up, the squirming pink piglet in his arms, its unsuspecting mouth turned up. "Beautiful, no?" he asked as we left, bopping his head cheerfully.

There is a terrible joke in Cuba which people perversely insisted on telling me over and over while I was visiting: A global conference is being held on the future for young people. The CNN reporter—all foreign TV reporters in Cuba seem to have morphed into CNN—asks a young Belgian, "What do you want to be when you grow up?" The girl says, "A chemist!" The CNN reporter poses the question to a Chinese kid, who says, "An investment banker." Finally, the CNN reporter asks the Cuban delegate. "Me?" says the boy, inevitably named Pepito. "I want to be a foreigner!"

The joke's tragedy is not just that it underscores Cuba's obsequious deference to outsiders in order to survive, but also that it betrays history: Cubans—and my sister's the proof— have never wanted to be anything but Cuban. Scattered to

New York and Madrid, Tampa and Luanda, Miami, Moscow, and Honolulu, they hold onto their Cubanness with audacious caprice.

But bizarrely, in Cuba, I told Rocky, it seemed Cubanness was diminished.

"No, no, no," she said, annoyed.

"C'mon, it seems like Tom Mahler's more interested in Cuba, more Cubed than most people here!"

She sighed. "He's a necessary evil, in spite of his good intentions. And that's just for now. You're missing the point. The idea, Malía, is that Cuba not turn into Hawai'i."

"Hawai'i? Please . . . there are worse fates." I was appalled.

And now it was Rocky's turn to be amused. "Really? Because back in *Hawai'i nee*, hearing you and Mami and Papi, but especially you—with your Hawaiian language classes and your sovereignty speeches and your Pele—Hawai'i isn't exactly paradise."

"By comparison? Are you out of your mind?"

"Aren't you the one who's always worried that native Hawaiians will be wiped out by development and 'immigration' from the mainland? I mean, isn't that part of the tragedy, that native Hawaiians are already outnumbered in their own land?"

"But Rocky, there are no native Cubans!"

"There are no indigenous, Malía, but what the hell do you think we are? What the hell do you think *I* am?"

As it turned out, the luau came off fairly well. I'd brought spices for the pork, and between Dionisio and Rocky they'd found taro leaves and something they said was a butterfish (it didn't look quite right to me but Rock swore by it). The

Cubans were skeptical, made faces about it, but polished off every last shred of meat nonetheless. We also made lomi lomi salmon and cold mac salad, which didn't seem to do much for them, but they were knocked out by our fried rice—not Hawaiian or Chinese but a Mercado family recipe that included all of those crazy influences (like huli huli sauce and chorizo). Tom Mahler ate with enthusiasm.

"So long as he keeps eating, nothing to worry about," Raúl whispered to me as his chin aimed at the family's pet foreigner. The guests lounged about the courtyard, oblivious to the plastic-covered cement bags lining the walls.

Most importantly, everybody loved Eddie and Myrna Kamae, both of them impish and kind: Eddie's twinkly eyes nodded approvingly while sipping from his iced red wine, Myrna bravely trying on new Spanish phrases and laughing heartily. With them was Eddie's accompanist, a boyishly handsome Hawaiian named Ocean, who the Cubans adored for his playfulness. After much eating and drinking, Eddie slipped his ukulele into his arms and—the Cubans again unabashedly skeptical—graced his fingers across its strings. As he played, the Cubans' astonishment was obvious: Their mouths eased open as Eddie pulled sounds from that little box that not one of them had ever imagined. Clearly loving the way Eddie had upended expectations, Ocean grinned and followed on guitar. All the while, Mahler's eyes glistened without his usual malice.

"He plays the cuatro so well!" exclaimed Raúl, reappropriating the ukulele, if not for Cuba then for the generalized Caribbean.

I don't know how long Eddie and Ocean played. I know that I was flush with satisfaction, the closest to happiness I'd been since arriving in Havana. I looked up, past the enthralled group, leaned on Myrna's shoulder, and found the sky. Like

Honolulu, Havana glowed right back at the stars, a duel of lights canceling each other out in a shimmer. The air smelled of a dark sweetness, like molasses. And the faces, familiar to me now—even Mahler—were, I knew even then, the touchstones of future memories.

"Ake a e kamanao e ike maka," sang Eddie and Ocean. I closed my eyes and joined them: "Ia Waipi'o e kaulana nei." *The mind yearns to see / Waipi'o so famous.*

"What's the song about?" Dionisio asked, leaning across Myrna to me. I looked around: Rocky was nowhere to be seen. He smiled, unconcerned.

In English, I explained Waipi'o: its fecundity, its five deafening waterfalls, the tension between the water's beauty and our volcano, how Pakaalana—the ancient place of refuge nestled in the valley that protected innocents during wars—is now nothing but a rumor. I didn't tell him about all the weekend camping trips my family took to the Big Island and Waipi'o, trespassing onto what is now private land to look for Pakaalana and other signs of Hawai'i's glorious past. We'd pick opihi—those stubborn little limpets that attached themselves to rocks—by prying them off with knives. I loved them grilled over an open fire but Papi would just salt them, like the few natives left on the islands, and pop them into his mouth whole and fresh.

"Huli aku nana i ke kai uli," I whisper/sang, my eyes closed—*Turn and gaze at the dark sea.* "Ua nalo ka nani o Pakaalana . . ." *The beauty of Pakaalana has vanished.*

When I lifted my lids, I couldn't believe what I was seeing: Rocky was dancing hula, dipping and swaying, her torso liquid, fingers fluttering. Eddie, Myrna, and Ocean beamed but she was somewhere else: back in Hawai'i, back in misty Waipi'o perhaps.

"Haina ia mai ana ka puana / Ua ike kumaka ia Waipi'o," we sang as she turned her back, its slope a wave. *Let the refrain be told / The mind has seen Waipi'o.*

The Cubans went nuts. They clapped and shouted. Rocky laughed. Then the policeman cousin started tapping out a rhythm on his chair. It had the same wooden tone as Hawaiian meles but I realized immediately he was building a rumba, the beat hiccupping, sparkling. Dionisio palmed his thighs. Mahler, who was squatting during Rocky's hula, stood up and raised his arms in jubilation, as if the Cubans had won some kind of competition.

I thought Rocky would stop then. But instead, she stamped her feet, twisted her heels like they do on Moloka'i. "A la 'a ko ko i ke a u!" she shouted in Tom Mahler's direction, and he grinned, not realizing she was taunting him.

"That means a swordfish is jabbing you," Myrna explained, and Dionisio nodded but I wasn't sure he got it.

Rocky bent her knees, thrust her pelvis, and aimed her ass at him. While I sat agape, she mercilessly slid from hula ku'i to guaguancó.

"Eh mamá / eh mamá," the Cubans chanted.

Now it was Eddie, Ocean, and Myrna who stared wide-eyed.

Suddenly, everybody was up—Raúl had acquired actual bongos, Dionisio's mother was scratching at a gourd with a thin stick, and a crowd of friends and neighbors I'd barely noticed before were singing. I couldn't understand any of it. It was as if they'd excised every consonant from the words. Out on the floor, Dionisio and Rocky mesmerized us with their turns and twirls, their busy feet. When Raúl finally slapped the bongos to conclude the dance, his hands like starfish across the skins, there was explosive applause.

Dionisio leaned on my sister and put his moist cheek on her shoulder for an instant, then made a motion for us to calm down. "We have . . . we have an announcement," he declared in English between labored breaths. Rocky leaned down and giggled something into his ear. I noticed Mahler, his arms across his chest.

"You know, when Raquel and I met, well, it was like east and west, the four cardinal points coming together, all the distances reduced to nothing," Dionisio said.

I translated his Spanish/English mishmash as best I could for our guests from Hawai'i.

"We promised to be together and, you know, she threw her lot in with us, she stayed here . . . in Havana!"

"That's love!" interjected a sarcastic neighbor, and everyone laughed.

"Yeah, yeah," Dionisio continued, so giddy he seemed a little drunk. "That *is* love . . . Hey, she has bathed with just *one* cup of water!"

Rocky nodded, bending at the waist to acknowledge the Cubans' spontaneous applause.

"And stood in line with us for eggs!"

The Cubans continued with their merriment but Mahler was shaking his head now, scowling.

"What's wrong, huh?" I asked him.

"What's special about any of that? Cubans do that every day, it's ridiculous that they're making such a big deal out of her doing what they do every single day here as part of the revolutionary project."

"God, Tom, do you ever get off your soapbox?"

"This is wrong," he said.

"Relax," I told him. But when I went to uncross his arms, he shook me off. "Oooookay," I said, and backed away.

"So now . . . after three years, it is *my* turn," Dionisio continued.

"Yes!" Rocky said in English, pumping her fist in as American a gesture as I'd ever seen on her.

"My Cuban sister . . . disappeared!" I joked with Myrna. "Who *is* this woman?"

"That's right, that's right—my turn," Dionisio repeated. "We're delirious because we can't believe it—I got a fiancé visa to La Yuma—and the Cuban government is letting me go!"

Dionisio's mother bit her trembling lip and held her hands to her heart. I could feel her prayer of gratitude even in the wild screaming and hugging that was now taking place.

"How is it possible? You're a doctor! The government doesn't let doctors go to the U.S.!" Raúl exulted.

"It was some weird mistake," Rocky said, her own limbs now echoing Dionisio's mother, her hands folded over each other right at her chest, reaching to her throat. "The papers somehow—we don't know, we don't care—they left off Dionisio's occupation."

Raúl shushed her, his fingertip to his lips. "There are Moors on the coasts," he said, indicating the guests.

"And ideologically correct pet foreigners," I muttered under my breath.

"We're just going to try it, that's all—see how we feel in La Yuma," Dionisio said, clearly backpedaling. "It's an—"

But he didn't finish. Tom Mahler had stepped up, his red face within inches of Rocky. "Try it, my ass," he fumed. "You're trying to take him, you're trying to take him from his country, from his family—from all the people who need him. Are you happy now? Are you? Because I, for one, am not just going to stand by and let you get away with this! First thing tomorrow morning, you'll see!"

Before anybody could figure out what had actually trans-pired, Mahler rocketed out of the courtyard to his room. The force of the door closing slammed into us like a storm surge.

Dionisio took a step after him but Raúl, for the first time showing the iciness needed to do his policeman's job, put a hand on his chest and effortlessly held him back. "Forget him," he hissed. "You're going to La Yuma. We can take care of this; we don't need him anymore."

Eddie, Myrna, and Ocean left sometime after that, and though I offered to help clean up, everyone told me to go on to bed, since the next day would be my last in Cuba and I still had much souvenir shopping to do. I decided I was tired enough to accept. Sometime near dawn, when I made a somnambulistic trip to the bathroom, I heard voices and what seemed like a scuffle, but I couldn't tell where it was coming from. The noisy spillage into the courtyard made everything fuzzy, and at that moment I was instantly nostalgic for the breezy peace of Honolulu. It was definitely time to head home.

The next morning, Tom Mahler did not emerge to make breakfast. Without need of notice, everyone of their own accord made coffee and made do with the bread rolls from the ration book. When I emerged from my room, I heard Dionisio muttering as he and Raúl left for the day. I confess I was thrown off—I'd gotten used to Mahler's breakfasts, which were just scrumptious.

"Where's Tom?" I asked Rocky, who was making coffee when I stumbled into the kitchen. She shrugged and looked away.

"That was pretty crazy last night."

She nodded and poured us each a demitasse of espresso. She was still in her bathrobe, her hair a mess.

"Have you seen him yet? Has he said anything?"

She shook her head.

"My God, are you mute now?"

Rocky shook her head again. "No, I'm just . . . tired," she said, and I saw through her morning hair that her eyes were red-rimmed.

"Hey, what's going on? Everything all right?" I settled an arm around my sister's shoulder.

She finally turned her sad face toward me. "Rough night, that's all."

"Yeah, I'll say . . . What an asshole Mahler was." I didn't mention Raúl; I still didn't know what to make of that. But I'd written quite the journal entry about the whole episode.

Rocky moved away from me, her free hand massaging her temple.

"I mean, there was just no excuse for that, none at all."

"Malía, please . . ." Rocky said softly.

"What? C'mon, that was not appropriate pet foreigner behavior."

"I'm begging you . . ." She scrunched up her face, as if my words were lacerating her brain.

"Okay, okay, " I said, gulping my espresso and going off to shower and pack. "But honestly . . ."

Tom Mahler did not show up for the rest of the day. I hung out until about 2 in the afternoon without any sign of him. When I returned many hours later from souvenir shopping (books, CDs, T-shirts, and tchotkes for my parents and friends) out in the scorching heat, I found Dionisio and Rocky in a morbid silence at the kitchen table.

"Who died?" I asked in English.

"Qué . . . ?" Dionisio replied, his face losing all color.

"Malía!" Rocky exclaimed, shooting up from her chair. "It's just an expression," she said in Spanish to Dionisio, who seemed on the verge of an anxiety attack.

"What?" I asked.

"Just, please . . ." But she couldn't quite finish it. Then she spied my shopping bags. "What'd you get?"

"I'll show you," I said, hoping things might lighten up. "Let me change first." I stuck my foot out and shook it a bit, showing off a shoe I'd borrowed from Rocky. It was flat and relatively comfortable but it still felt alien on my foot. Dionisio smiled weakly.

I dropped the shopping bags on the table and ambled back to my room, past Mahler's, which remained shut. I thought I smelled a bad patch right at his door—something thick, sulphurous like that breeze that had caught me at the airport the day I arrived. I continued to my room, undid Rocky's shoes, and put on my slippahs, then grabbed a scrunchy and pulled up my hair. The back of my neck was sticky with sweat. I decided to wash my face and neck and noticed, at a different angle as I passed Mahler's en route to the bathroom, that his door was slightly open. On the way back to the kitchen, my neck cooled, there was a sliver of view into Mahler's. Had Tom, who always made himself heard, come back in that split second? I hadn't heard any voices greeting him. Was it possible Mahler could be tiptoeing about in shame?

I touched my finger to Mahler's door and gently pushed. The hinges whined. I pulled away, but not before I caught a glimpse of a fully dressed Mahler on the bed, his eyes and mouth open.

"Tom . . ."

"Malía!" It was a frightened Rocky, with Dionisio right behind her.

"What are you doing?" he asked, grabbing me and pushing us out of the room. I felt his fingers hot on my flesh. His Spanish was so furious I barely understood.

"What . . . ?" Mahler hadn't stirred. "Hey, I think there's something wrong."

"He's a very sound sleeper," Dionisio insisted, closing the door to Tom's room behind us.

I looked to Rocky but she avoided my gaze. "Dionisio, his eyes are open." I couldn't conjure anything in Spanish.

"You will wake him," Dionisio said in English, his voice steely and cold like Raúl's the night before.

"Malía, let it go, let it go," Rocky whispered, pulling on my arm, trying to drag me back to the kitchen.

"What the hell is going on?" I asked, angrily yanking myself free from them. "Mahler's in there, and something's not right."

"Malía, calm down," Rocky said, but she was unsteady, glancing over at Dionisio for reassurance.

I suddenly remembered the noises from the night before, the scuffle. "Tom!" I yelled toward Mahler's room. "Tom, can you—"

Dionisio grabbed me, his hand over my mouth as we struggled, all the while whispering fiercely in Spanish at Rocky, who didn't seem to know whether to help him or me.

"Qué pasa aquí?" a voice rumbled behind us. Raúl pulled Dionisio off me. "What are you doing?" he demanded. He was wearing his uniform, his hand on the service revolver tucked into his holster.

"She went inside," Dionisio said defensively, and in Spanish, all the while pointing at me. "She was disturbing Tom."

I started to say something but Raúl put up his official policeman's hand. "Enough," he commanded. He turned to me.

318 // Havana Noir

"Tom is a deep sleeper, and a monster when he's awakened by noise."

"But—" In a month, I'd seen and heard many things about Mahler but this was not one of them.

"Malía, shut up!" Rocky interrupted. She'd made fists and was holding them out in front of her now, her eyes shut hard, no longer able to keep back tears.

"For God's sake—something is wrong in there," I insisted. "Don't you think it's weird he hasn't reacted to all this noise? And his eyes were wide open!"

"I will take care of this," the policeman cousin said, pushing me aside.

He strode purposefully toward Mahler's door, then stepped inside. We heard him make his way to the bed and back but I noted that he did not call out to Tom or make any kind of attempt to wake him. He emerged from the room in seconds, closing the door behind him.

"He is dead," he said conclusively.

I gasped. "How do you know?" All three of them were staring at me, their reactions seemingly dependent on mine. I swallowed. "I mean, try waking him," I persisted. "I thought I heard something last night . . ."

Raúl, who hadn't understood a word I said, dismissed me with a wave of his hand. "Dionisio, as a doctor"—he underscored the word *doctor*—"I need you to determine the preliminary cause of death," he instructed. "I will call the station to file a report and the coroner. You two"—he meant us, Rocky and me—"you will stay out of the way. Do you understand me?"

Rocky nodded but I must have made some other movement because Raúl turned on me with a barely contained rage. "Do *you* understand?"

* * *

Soon the house was filled with cops, paramedics, and grave-looking men and women who talked almost exclusively to Dionisio and Raúl. They glanced now and again at me and Rocky, who paced in the kitchen, her eyes watery (but not crying). Dionisio's mother wrung her hands, worried about bearing the curse of an American dying under her roof.

"Every foreign journalist in Havana is going to be at the door wanting to know what happened," she complained, then looked pointedly at me. "Malía, you must remember, if someone—if anyone—asks, *nothing happened.*"

I nodded, not because I intended to keep that promise (I honestly had no idea what I'd do if anyone asked), but because it was clear that's what was expected of me. Rocky looked at me approvingly but I wondered, with dread flooding me, how I fit into all this, how I was supposed to deal with it all.

"Do you know what happened?" Dionisio's mother asked when he came back to the kitchen.

He shook his head. "Probably an embolia," he said solemnly.

"How old was Tom?" I asked, regaining some of my Spanish.

"I don't know, in his forties," Dionisio said. "He was young."

I stood up from the kitchen table, pushing my feet into my slippahs, and made my way to the courtyard.

I saw the panicked look on Dionisio's face. "Where are you going?" Rocky asked in English, articulating his fears.

"To get some air," I said. "I'm not leaving, I'll be right here."

Outside, the yellow streetlights poured into the courtyard and obscured the night sky again. I ambled until I found a dark patch, somewhere to stand where I could merge into the shadows and disappear. I leaned against the wall and let my body drop into a squat. All I could think was how very zenzizenzic, how ironic this was: Tom had had a Cuban death, except that his last meal had been our Hawaiian extravaganza. The neighborhood soundtrack of yelling, music, and cars continued unabated. I could see Rocky fidgeting through the kitchen window. I really wasn't sure I could ever tell my parents about this.

In a moment, there were sounds coming from Mahler's room. A man and a woman emerged with Tom's body on a stretcher, wrapped from head to toe in a white sheet that made him look like a cocoon. Dionisio followed with a police officer I hadn't seen before, while his mother peered from the door to the courtyard, tracing their route.

I waited a bit, just watching the goings-on in the kitchen as if the window were a TV screen. Everyone seemed appropriately sad and worried except Raúl, who I could see was relaxed enough for an occasional laugh. I finally surrendered to the inevitability of going back inside for my last night in Cuba, rappelled up the wall like a crab, and strolled over, the direct light making my vision fuzzy for an instant.

"Malía, there you are," Dionisio's mother said.

"Sit down," suggested Dionisio, leading me to the table.

As my eyes began to clear, I looked for Rocky but saw only Raúl, his cheeks moving as he chewed on something, his arms outstretched in my direction. I redirected my vision to his offering: a plate brimming with garlicky pork chops, shimmering black beans poured over rice, and toasty plantain coasters.

"Eat, Malía," he ordered.

I nodded but slowly stepped back and away.

VIRGINS OF REGLA

BY MABEL CUESTA

Regla

for Yemayá
for Raquel Pollo

T he emptiness by the wall. Her and her shadow, both escapees, in a panic. Lost now in a place unknown, far from their home in the provinces.

They always knew that Regla, ultramarine, was a place for fishermen and stevedores. Whenever they went there to see the Virgin, they were surprised by the black men who walked past them on their way from the docks, stinking from the dirty sacks.

That dawn, after running from the bitter scene (that's how she'd remember it for years to come), she feared one of those men from the docks would show up to continue the violation. Afraid they'd confuse her for one of the sacks they hauled, possessed, dragged from the ships to the docks, trucks, roads, or warehouses anywhere on the island. She feared being mistaken for one of those inanimate sacks, prime for theft, expropriation, sale, or scrap.

She had no way of getting home at that hour. She was broke. She had no map with which to orient herself, and worse, she had no idea where exactly she was in the neighborhood. All she wanted to do was go home.

To leave Regla there were always the ferries, with their eternal and tired run all day long and a good part of the night across Havana's oily, filthy bay. But not at dawn. Dawn in Regla was all silence and fear.

She and her shadow rested against the wall. They became one to try and figure out a way through the terror—the terror provoked by her trembling legs, smeared with a substance that she could not identify. She remembered what she read somewhere—probably Margarite Yourcenar: *love's white blood* . . . could that be it? The viscous substance that drenched her underpants—could that be the blood that Yourcenar talked about in one of her novels? Impossible. The writer had placed the word *love* next to the image of the *white blood*. Neither she nor her shadow would confuse the two concepts; they were both excellent readers.

Her shadow could, in fact, tell jokes, recall, for example, the famous Arab telenovela in which, during an unusual dialogue between the barbarous and the civilized worlds, the Muslim man asked the beautiful, kidnapped North American lady in a subordinate tone, *And who has asked you for love, Diana Mayo?*

She and her shadow relished that scene from the telenovela, which made them and their friends laugh so much because of its kitschy language and its singularly disturbing and maladjusted hero . . . but this was no time for jokes. Now they needed to understand if that stuff that made her feel wet and broken was in fact the *white blood of love*. Leaning against the wall, they wanted to determine how the unknown substance had been deposited inside her. They wanted to determine who had extradited her from her peaceful world in the provinces to bring her to this place, and especially to this corner where it was impossible to see the small turret of the chapel in which resided the city's most loved virgin—her patron.

If we could at least see the steeple, she thought, *we'd know which way to walk*. If, at the very least, they could reach a small fragment, a miniscule piece of the compound around the Virgin, they'd be saved. The Virgin would protect her shadow and would bring back all that had been taken.

But here at the wall the only things in sight were her and her shadow. They looked at each other with shame because of the twisted projections on the wall, still in the thrall of recent events.

She let herself fall. With her back against the wall, she eased her way down it, and once on the ground, she opened her legs. The substance was still there, lingering. The substance took her back to the memory of a drunk Horacio, his tongue in her ear, saying, *Let me suck your tits* . . . Horacio squeezing her against the bed while Michelle brushed her teeth at the bathroom sink. Horacio saying over and over how he wanted to tangle them both with his body, to join them in an infinite night. She was going to say *in an infinite night of love*, but the words got stuck in her throat and she left it at that.

Michelle, an innocent, would talk to him from the bathroom: *My love, let the girl rest* . . . *Get her ready for bed and come to our room, I'm waiting.*

The girl kicked. The girl had no shadow to defend her then because the house was full of light. The girl cried and hit Horacio so that he'd leave her in peace, so that he'd get off her, so that he would not stick his hard flesh into her flesh . . . and Horacio just laughed . . . Horacio never answered Michelle but rather bit the girl's mouth. A girl almost as small as Michelle, but more lost, more alone in the storybook wilderness of his mouth and then the neighborhood to which Horacio had brought them.

That's when she stopped fighting and just let things happen . . . She decided to pray, but she didn't know any prayer in its entirety, didn't know any potent psalms, but she prayed nonetheless—so that Michelle wouldn't step out of the bathroom and surprise them, so that she wouldn't have to offer explanations, so that she wouldn't have to ask forgiveness, that's what she prayed for.

The only thing left was Horacio whimpering, his continued delirium: *Gimme your tits, gimme the milk from your tits, lemme drink it, lemme . . .* and then silence. Silence and an acute pain in her vagina. A sharp pain that hours later was still present. A pain that made her shadow bend over while the two of them ran through the blackness of the night in Regla, looking for the Virgin. A lacerating pain, acidic and nauseous. A pain that made her breathing short, a pain that made it impossible to shake off her worsening, perpetual tremors.

Michelle didn't come out of the bathroom. Michelle never knew what Horacio did to her. Michelle found him on the floor, without his pants but with his underwear undeniably on. Michelle was so determined that he be a part of things that she refused to look at the condition of the girl's bed. Michelle did not see the disoriented eyes of her friend, nor did she feel her tremors or the sharpness in her lower abdomen. She only had eyes for him: *Sweetness, you're so drunk.*

Nor did Michelle ever understand why the girl used the pretext of getting some fresh air to go out the door and never come back. Years later, they would talk about these things. Years later, the girl would say she had a panic attack and decided that the best time to visit the Virgin on the shores of the bay would always be right then, at dawn. Years later, Michelle would feign belief in this excuse, as if she was actually convinced, then change the subject.

But in those wee hours, she and her shadow were not thinking about Michelle. They imagined as they wailed against the wall that Michelle had been devoured by Horacio, swallowed by his dark mouth. His mouth and the streets were part of the same image. Horacio's mouth extended the length of the neighborhood, through all of Regla. He couldn't live anywhere else in Havana. He and Regla belonged to each other. His mouth and this ultramarine district, black lines on the same color strip. Black like the sea and the Virgin; the only black woman adored on this island.

They adored her too. Ever since Emilio, right smack in the middle of a trance, had told them that the Virgin was their mother too, she and the shadow had made intermittent pilgrimages to the chapel just to leave white flowers at her altar. Trips made on the mythic ferry, each one to view the appearance of the black mother in the midst of the stench, in that bay saturated by oil; so many journeys to Horacio's neighborhood without ever going as far as his house out of sheer terror that that night could be repeated; so many restrictions; so many pleas to the mother-virgin-black-woman-Yemayá-patron-of-Havana-guardian-of-fishermen-docks-stevedores-seas-pregnancies-fury-storms-peace-and-pools-of-water. So much begging: *Please don't abandon me, please don't leave me, don't leave me, oh Virgin, men's anger is aimed at my sex; liberate me from heartlessness and wildness; liberate me from lack of affection; be my mother; make me virginal always, before and after each birth, so that each one leaves my womb untouched.*

There was so much supplication to the small black woman dressed in that intense blue, to the talismanic stone that Emilio had given them the day of the baptism—deadline day to name guardian angels—only to falter in the end, to let Horacio drag her along with Michelle; to leave a celebration that could not be postponed, and the long list of acquaintances who kept leaving, finally abandoning her in the vestibule full of fear, knowing that once Michelle went off to the bathroom there was no going back, that the only relief would be exposure to that darkened place, chock full of thieves from the docks, workers, traffickers in whatever merchandise filled their hands or their bellies; all that praying, for this. It wasn't fair.

Emilio said the black mother was obsessed with justice. Emilio, godfather-father-big-brother-blood-of-her-blood poisoned against other men, said their mother would never abandon them, especially if they were in Regla, her home, the ultramarine. But on this airless night, as dawn neared, the only thing she and her shadow had to hold onto was a wall that left them exposed. It was so high they couldn't possibly climb it and try to guess the way to the chapel.

If only we could hear a siren, they thought, any kind of sound from the boats, a sign from their mother that would allow them to slow the infinite tremors in their legs, in their belly, in the head that could barely sustain itself. Her body continued to lean against the white wall, the screen on which her disharmony was amply projected. Her shell of a girl, broken, deflowered, stained . . . This wall that took in her shadow just to show her how naked she was under the only streetlight in the area. *If only we could hear a siren,* they thought again.

But the silence insisted on swallowing all hope. Silence crowned her, covered her, enclosed her, surrounded and embraced her; the silence whispered to her: *I am as divine as you'll ever get, only to me should you direct your prayers; only I will be your guide in this city that has never wanted you, little provincial girl, simple, simple country girl, backwards girl, so backwards, adorer of false gods, lover of women who will not save you. I am Almighty Silence, I'm the man you cannot hurt, now you see me, now you don't, but I'm always here . . . Let me caress you and your terror will be different . . .*

Silence overwhelmed them. Silence like a million voices circled them. Silence through their viscera; silence through their body in a long loop. Long and sonorous, like the siren they so wanted to hear. More and more voices accumulating.

The voices took them to the very edge of consciousness, a total disconnection between flesh and the senses. The silence screamed its insults and they closed their eyes. They allowed themselves to be dragged under by the perpetual noise of the absolute silence coming from the place where they'd lost track of the Virgin. They were going to drop to the sidewalk forever, remain stuck to the asphalt; they wanted a small death, definitive; their own screams stuck in their throat; they wanted to ask the silence to stop, wanted a blue cape to rescue them, to lift them above the houses with red-tiled roofs, the ruined edifices; a blue maternal cape, a refuge that enveloped them together, that transformed them in mid-flight, so that when she finally opened her eyes, she would find herself at the edge of the docks, ready to traverse the bay on the morning's very first ferry.

Translation by Achy Obejas

OLÚO[1]

BY ARNALDO CORREA

Casablanca

Eulogio Gaytán realized that after he lost his hearing, he could penetrate more deeply into the folds of his clients' and godchildren's[2] thoughts and sexual desires. He realized that because words can be deceiving, they can take you down the wrong paths, they can hide the truth in a warp of sound. That's when he grasped that he'd reached the highest level in his ministry as a babalao. From that moment on, his deafness was no longer a punishment come late in life, a life dedicated to pursuing happiness, health, and the well-being of society's most humble and least appreciated folks. All of a sudden, he understood it was a gift from Orula at the end of an existence that had been plagued with the same misery and deprivations as those of his flock. The absolute silence now allowed him a greater balance, a greater closeness with the Eternal Father, who had given him the gift of divination, and the cosmic energy that put such astonishing words in his mouth.

He was well aware of his goddaughter Elodia's movements as he tried to determine if this was another of her long pauses

---

[1]An olúo is the highest level that can be achieved by a babalao, or babalawo (both forms are acceptable). The only hierarchy that exists in the Rule of Osha (also spelled Ocha) is the Order of Babalaos, who are children of Orula (also known as Ifá), god of divination.

[2]In Santería, godchildren are those sponsored in the rituals by particular santeros or babalaos—godfathers or godmothers.

filled with thoughts, tranquility, and suggestions from eyes of singular beauty, or if she was finished telling her story. At the beginning of his deafness he'd tried to lip read, but the effort of following each word actually distanced him from the conversation's real meaning, so he'd stopped trying and began to concentrate on the language used by other parts of the body: the infinite facial expressions; the revealing light, intensity, and expression of the eyes; the hands' flights and the movements of the feet and legs, which said so much about a person's mood; the tension in the muscles and the breath's rhythm, which betrayed the most intimate feelings . . . All of those things came together in his mind, along with conscious and unconscious memories of the river of people who'd consulted him during a life dedicated to solving other people's problems; all those things said so much more than words.

Now, one of his most devoted goddaughters was in anguish over something no doubt terrible, since she was a strong person who only came to see him about important things. She had grown up in the home of a refined and prosperous family where her mother had been a domestic worker. The owners of the house had raised her as the daughter they'd never had. She'd learned good manners from childhood; she'd studied at select schools until she'd fallen into this grave crisis.

She had been brought to Gaytán years before by a godson who was already famous as an oriaté, a diviner, and who was considered deeply knowledgeable about the science of seeing the future. Gaytán's disciple had been trying to untangle the girl's problems without success. He told Gaytán that all of the girl's difficulties had begun after the owner of the house where she lived, Dr. Casals, a well-known lawyer, had died abruptly during a party in his home. The forensic pathologist had diagnosed a myocardial infarction, but back then all sudden deaths had been diagnosed that way. The oriaté confessed that he'd gone to investigate and the widow had told him she was certain her husband had been poisoned. According to her, there had been too many important people at the party for the police to open an investigation into each and every one of them. "Yes, of course Casals had enemies—what famous lawyer doesn't have lots of enemies?"

Since that time, the girl had suffered from terrible nightmares. She opted to stay awake all the time by taking pills, ruining her health in the process. The oriaté was convinced the dead man was one of the clues to the case, since his Diloggún shell-throwing ritual had turned up four and five, Eyiolosun-oché by way of Osobbo: The dead man was looking for someone to take with him. Moreover, whenever the oriaté consulted the oracle through the coconut shells, the letter Oyékun kept coming up in the girl's readings, four shell pieces facing down, definitively signaling that one of the dead wanted to talk, but all efforts to establish communication had been unsuccessful. It seemed he was a very backwards spirit, unaware of his own situation, something that happened often with the souls of those who died unexpectedly.

In the first reading that Gaytán did for Elodia, he was left astonished and perplexed by the ípkuele's[3] revelations. For the first time in many days, the girl slept, falling gently facedown on Gaytán's chest immediately after the reading. He cancelled the rest of his appointments for the day and remained there, without moving, watching over the girl's dreams until the following morning. When she awoke, he saw the smile on her face, those bright eyes that he'd later see furious, in love, and hateful.

---

[3] A tablet and necklace used for divination.

Elodia's physical and psychic states were horrible. It was imperative to act immediately; Gaytán recommended she be given to Olokun[4] immediately so she could get her strength back and ease her ailments. But her troubles dictated only one possible solution: The young woman would have to undergo the Kari Osha and live by the strict mandates set for her by the orisha who ruled her destiny.

Making good use of the fact that he'd already scheduled a spiritual possession by Orula, Gaytán and three other ba-balaos decided the girl was a daughter of Oyá Yansa, the ori-sha queen who reigned over cemeteries, lightning, winds, and storms; she was also Changó's lover. Gaytán gave Elodia to Margarita, a very experienced and smart santera of the highest order, so that she could be her godmother for the Kari Osha, the ceremony in which the saint is given to her, or "made," as it's commonly called.

Elodia then began to prepare for this great event, in which the initiate is born again and the orisha receives her in the appropriate ceremonial way, promising to protect her in this new life. But whoever is reborn must commit to the rules of their celestial father or mother, and those determinations are made in the Book of Itá, on the "middle day" of the Kari Osha.

After receiving the Olokun, the young woman had faltered at first, dazed, as if absent from the natural world, tormented by visions she didn't dare describe. During that time, Gaytán was at his family home in the Escambray mountains, where his centenarian grandmother had just passed away, and so he was unable to help with the new crisis. After two weeks of intense work with the sick young woman, however, Mar-

---

[4]Olokun is a very mysterious deity who reigns over the bottom of the sea. "Giving to Olokun" is usually recommended by babalaos, not santeros or diviners, and only when a person is on the brink of death.

garita managed to reanimate her spirit and make the proper connection with her sponsoring orisha.

For long afterward, everyone in Margarita's house remembered "the middle day" of that initiation, when the babalaos consulted the Book of Ífa. Without any sign of her prior illness, a finely dressed Elodia, on her queenly throne, received her friends, godchildren, and non-initiated friends who came by the house. These were left dumbfounded by the beauty and majesty she projected even before turning thirteen years of age. They all left deeply moved, awed by the bright vision, as if a real goddess had sat on that make-believe throne.

It wasn't until many years later that Gaytán realized that Margarita had actually given Elodia to a different goddess of the dead, Yewá, instead of the one he had thought was appropriate, Oyá. He considered this a terrible mistake, which doomed Elodia to a life without sex or children; the daughters of Yewá cannot have sexual relations without risking death or dementia. Margarita's action had been a grave transgression, because he had been precise when he told her about the infallible dictates during the spiritual possession by Orula.

Gaytán immediately sent for the santera, who refused to explain her actions and bid farewell after a bitter argument.

"You babalaos think you know everything, but it's only us, the santeros, who can perform the ceremony to connect with the right orisha, that's our responsibility," she said. "I gave her to Yewá for a very powerful reason that you, you silly old man, couldn't divine. There is no mistake. I know what I'm doing."

As time passed, Margarita appeared to have been right. The girl's previously fierce, rebellious character seemed to get sweeter. Her health improved to the point where she was leading a normal life, and she seemed happy, though she was destined to live alone. Yet Gaytán was never convinced; there was too much fire in her to be Yewá's daughter. And although she was calm, she had not found spiritual peace or the deeper happiness she should have attained. He believed that behind her apparent humility and the simplicity appropriate to Yewá's devotees, there lurked the fury, appetites, and passions typical of the daughters of Oyá. Why did Margarita accuse him of not understanding why she'd done what she'd done?

Now Elodia was before him again, explaining why she'd come back. Through her fingers folding and unfolding one by one as she spoke, the pauses in the rhythm of her breath, the intensity of her facial expression, and the excitement betrayed by her nipples at certain moments, he'd come to understand that there were three important problems, all springing from the same cause: His goddaughter was in love, she craved sex, she was burning with need. Her desire stole her sleep and was disrupting her health. She had come to him as a last resort.

Gaytán got up with the aid of his caguairán wood walking stick. He took two steps toward the window in the little room where he received his godchildren and clients. He surveyed the blackened tile rooftops of the neighborhood down below, and focused on a ship unloading coal at the dock. He took notice of the passengers getting off the ferry that had just docked. He watched the bay for a long while and finally gazed up at the horizon, at the immensity of the sea where Yemayá reigned . . . As always, he thanked his father Orula for conserving his sight, augmented now by the memory of the clear and vibrant siren sound from the ships coming and going from the bay; the noise of the people getting off and on the ferry that came and went from Casablanca to Old Havana; the crashing of the waves against the Malecón . . .

Two neighboring women, employees of the Observatorio Nacional on their way up the concrete stairway to their jobs at the top of the hill, stopped to catch their breath and waved hello to him. Gaytán came out of his daze and waved back. Now that he could no longer go up and down that stairway, the only way to get to his house, his life had been reduced to the living room where he spent his mornings, the room in which he slept, the good-sized kitchen, and the terrace, which was the real heart of this place he loved so much. It was there that his clients and godchildren patiently waited for their appointments with him, sitting on the rocks with flowers sprouting here and there, in the shade of the great ceiba tree, or in the chairs that lined the hallway, much wider because it led to the back.

Gaytán quickly turned his head and saw that Elodia was waiting for him. Then, as he often did, he began to speak when things came to him. Sometimes even he didn't understand the relationship between what he was saying and the problem he was treating. But those were the words Orula put in his mouth and his job was to transmit them to his clients and godchildren, because Orula never said anything without a reason.

"I'm old. My memory plays games with me, forgets what happened just an instant ago but remembers details from my childhood. I think I see my father walking down a dusty road in the Escambray hills, to San Juan, where we went every year during the summer to visit family. *So you want to know what life's about, son?* he said as he looked at me and smiled. *Come, we're going to follow that little stream of water and you'll see* . . . He lifted the bag with our provisions onto his shoulders, took my hand, and we began to walk, following the stream which flowed eagerly around the rocks and down the hill. At sunset the little stream was now a creek. In a quiet area, we fished for langostinos and cooked them in an old can of Spanish sausages that my father had brought in his bag. We ate them with salt and lemon from a tree that grew nearby. Dessert was guava paste with homemade white cheese. Life can be so marvelous! I can still taste those things . . . We slept at the foot of a waterfall, with the sound of the crashing all through the night. We woke at sunrise. That day we walked a great deal, always following the rush of water as it became stronger, until we reached a little town in the middle of the Escambray mountains. The stream had become the powerful Agabama River, which was churning everywhere we looked, dragging rocks from the shore, or from very far away, bringing down tree branches, animals caught by surprise . . . We camped below a cliff, by the water, beneath a very high bridge that connected the town and the sugar plantation. It was incredible to see the audacity and force of the waters as they hurled themselves off the cliff, and how they roared. I was awed and frightened. I'd never seen a waterfall of such magnitude nor heard such a terrible sound."

Gaytán sat down again, looked for a moment at Elodia, and then continued with his story.

"From that point, we followed the train tracks that bordered the gorge the Agabama had carved into the mountains over thousands, perhaps millions, of years. We continued walking for a long time, gazing at the way the deep waters shone as they cut through. My father leapt from one tie to the next, while I tried to balance myself on the tracks, until we finally reached the giant valley in Trinidad. There the river widened, started to slow down, flowed about the sugarcane fields as if it had lost its way, only to surrender its currents to the immensity of the sea. *That's life, my son,* my father said, now sitting at the start of another dusty trail. It was the first time I'd seen the ocean and I was mortified."

Gaytán went quiet; he couldn't get that blue immensity out of his mind; it kept calling to him, as if the river of his life had finally reached the sea. He was drenched with sweat.

He noticed that Elodia was looking at him with a great deal of worry, still struggling with finding something in his story that addressed her problem. He was convinced his goddaughter would destroy herself if she could not satisfy the passion that was obsessing her. That's how the gods had made her. Love for his goddaughter was a devastating fire, a four-alarm blaze. She was Oyá's daughter forced to live with great restraint, contrary to her true nature, subject to the strict rules of the daughters of Yewá. No sir, Orula had not been wrong!

But neither could the santera Margarita be underestimated; he could still feel her screams in his deaf ears: "I gave her to Yewá for a very powerful reason! There is no mistake!"

But to what powerful reason could Margarita be referring? Was she simply trying to avoid explaining? Then Gaytán remembered how disconcerted the oriaté who'd brought Elodia had been over the readings he'd done for her and the dead soul who'd kept coming up. And suddenly everything became clear to Gaytán. How could he have missed it before? What had he been thinking? Why, he really did deserve to have Margarita call him a fool!

"Elodia, my dear, give me your hand, I want to feel the beating of your heart when you answer this next question for me."

She extended her hand and the old babalao took it between his.

"Now, tell me, why did you poison Dr. Casals?"

Elodia's face froze for an instant, then hardened. She was quiet for a bit, as if she was asking herself the question for the first time and was searching out her brain for an answer. Then she began to speak, very slowly, so that Gaytán could follow what she said by watching her lips move.

"I had to do it, Godfather! He was going to leave me. He told me to stop going to his room. Do you understand what I mean? Ever since I was a little girl, I'd been getting in his bed with him as soon as his wife left for work. He showed me everything I had to do . . . Now he wanted the cook's daughter, who was younger than me . . . I consulted a santera who threw the coconut shells for me and it came out Eyife, and she said that the orishas told her that we shouldn't ask about what we already know—that I knew very well what I had to do!"

In other circumstances, Gaytán might have consulted his ípkuele. But he was too old, he'd lost the faith to blindly follow the oracle's dictates. He felt that his Eternal Father had been filling his heart with doubt even as his mind got wiser—though in the end, mankind can never be God.

He stayed like that a long while, just staring at the four coconut pieces he'd been shaping to use in divination as Elodia told him her troubles. It was from that prodigious fruit that the most effective way to talk to the gods had developed, the best way to ask concrete questions and receive blunt answers. Now he had to ask what to do with Elodia, and he was well aware that this time he could not fail.

He took the four pieces in his hands. He said a brief and silent prayer, and threw the pieces of coconut on the yarey mat in front of him. Two faced down and two faced up. Eyife! The clearest of all the coconut oracle's letters. An unquestionable yes: You do not ask about what you already know.

"Listen to this, my dear. Oyá, your real mother, says she left you years ago in care of Yewá because it had to be that way," Gaytán explained. "You have been very good and as a result she will take care of you from now on. But she asks that you not consult her about what to do with this new life she offers you. You need to decide for yourself, and to answer before mankind for whatever it is you do."

Translation by Achy Obejas

SETTLING OF SCORES

BY OSCAR F. ORTÍZ

Cojímar

The rodents are relentless; they've been feasting on me for days. Everything hurts inside; I feel close to death, which is good news now. I'm sick of living. I could have had a happy childhood, like anyone else, but it's not easy to carry the burden of dishonor. My soul weighs on me because I've been left alone. Papá and Mamá are not here anymore; they've gone on to a better place. I'm in agony but . . . I laugh.

They think I'm going to give them the satisfaction of pleading for a quick death instead of wasting away from the infected bites from the giant rats that share this stinking cell with me. Oh, how wrong they are! If I cling to this damn existence it's to pass on the story of my life (even if it's only to these walls) and how I turned into a killer. Nothing could have been further from my mind, but even killing can seem necessary when life deals us a bad hand. For sure, no one I killed was innocent. Whoever has died by my hand was paying for their sins. Everyone I got rid of had murdered, stolen, snitched, hurt, betrayed, and persecuted. This should be clear.

For what it's worth, here's my story . . .

Cojímar is a tiny town just north of Guanabacoa, which borders Havana to the east. It's more a neighborhood than a town, although at the time of this story it was home to about

8,000 residents. Cojímar has a beautiful beach and a tiny port which bears the same name. Before the Revolution, it had an active trade in all sorts of supplies—liquor, hardware, and other miscellaneous items. There were clothing stores, shoe stores, and places to buy perfume, jewelry, etc. We had drugstores where we could get any kind of medicine and a druggist who thought he was as qualified as a doctor when it came to filling prescriptions; he'd write the script himself without ever worrying about being wrong.

There is a church, Nuestra Señora del Carmen, named after the town's patron saint. Her feast is held in July, in splendid weather. The Cojímar River, as beautiful as it is tranquil, empties out to the bay. Right off the port, there's a fort called El Torreón. It was built in the seventeenth century, then destroyed by the British almost a hundred years later, then restored. It's the only thing at the port, a huge block of stone looking out at the waters.

The story goes that the town arose from the workers who came to build it, and that before that, there were only indigenous here. I have fond memories of the place because my father would often take me strolling to the port and we'd pause in front of it. Pointing with his index finger, he'd whisper: "Freedom."

Freedom, for those in the Cuban-Chinese community, is a sacred word.

When the Revolution triumphed, Papá was a prosperous merchant. Soon thereafter, private businesses were integrated by the government and folks who resisted indoctrination, and those who chose not to join the vulgar crowds, were persecuted. One night when I couldn't get to sleep, I heard a heated argument between my parents, although back then I couldn't understand what they were talking about. It wasn't the first time, the argument actually repeated itself frequently, and none of the three of us could get any rest, although they never knew I was eavesdropping on them. My father and various other Chinese businessmen were preparing to escape by boat behind the backs of the government dupes. The idea was to flee to the United States with whatever they could get off the island. Of course, the treasure was considerable; we Chinese are a hardworking people and know how to manage things. We've shown that everywhere we've ever emigrated.

Since it was a fairly dangerous proposition, not exempt from tragedy, all the conspirators had decided to talk to their spouses and explain that they needed to stay on the island with their children until the men could get to the United States and file legal claims to bring them over. As my mother later told me, she was anguished because she didn't want to break up the family, even if just temporarily. But Papá convinced her in the end. Well, Papá and the circumstances.

Things got tighter every day, and life got tougher for those who didn't accept the commander-in-chief's wild whims. That's why my mother finally gave in.

But the escape didn't work out. The coast guard surprised them and they were machine-gunned without mercy when the government's henchmen ordered them to stop and they refused. My father's death was a hard knock, though the actual killings weren't enough for the Communists. They brought the bodies back and laid them at the foot of the imposing Torreón, which my father had so loved. They left them strewn there for twenty-four hours, so that all of Cojímar would learn the lesson. I saw it all; so did my mother.

From that day on, at eleven years of age, I began planning my revenge.

The first thing I did was start to act abnormally. Some

people lose their minds after a devastating emotional shock, so no one was really surprised when the Wongs' only son started behaving oddly. The neighbors would see me in all my foolishness. Some called me an idiot, others a silly little Chinese boy; most of the time, they'd try to reason with me, but I would fake them out with a blank look and a dazed smile. The crueler among them would engage me in mischief and then turn me in; it was never anything serious, just kid stuff.

Once all of Cojímar had me tagged as the neighborhood's official cretin, I started to cultivate effeminate mannerisms and pretend to be disabled. When puberty arrived, I stopped being the silly Chinese boy and became the little Chinese faggot. All this was fine by me because I wanted to be seen as a completely defenseless creature.

The next step was to locate and study each and every person who had taken part in the massacre. The most dangerous of those responsible was Captain Correa, who everyone called *Pirigua* (I'll never know why). Pirigua was a forty-something man, short but sinewy. He drank too much, especially rum, and smoked cigars, helping to project his stereotypical rebel image. He always wore the olive-green uniform of the hated Territorial Militia, wrinkled and marked by sweat stains under his arms, his chest, and knees. Just like every other militia guy I knew, he had a beard and a mustache. Pirigua's men were cut from the same mold, and they all tried to copy him; Correa, for his party, tried desperately to be the Maximum Leader's clone.

After the murders, Pirigua became the town's master. He didn't hesitate before harassing the widows of those he'd killed, especially those he found most attractive. Unfortunately, my mother was one of these and he was soon installed in my house. My resentment grew by the day . . . If he'd only known how many times I fantasized about cutting his throat as he snored and slept soundly in my parents' bed, he would have died from fright. But I knew that if I did it, that's as far as I would get. The others would outlive my revenge. So I stoically tolerated everything he did to my mother. She hated him as much, or even more, than I did, but played along because of me, because Pirigua never tired of threatening with all he'd do to me if my mother didn't accept his passions (even if it was reluctantly). So that was our situation.

As time went by, my plans for revenge began to take shape, and once I had it clear in my own head, I started preparing to act on it. The hardest part was getting everybody accustomed to seeing me shovel dirt in a wagon and then run from one end of town to the other with it, making like I was playing at being a construction worker. Initially, I got stopped a few times and they took me down to the town jail, because they were sure I was up to some mischief, but my mother always intervened with Captain Correa and he finally ordered everybody to leave me alone. After all, I was not normal, there was no malice in anything I might do, and my atrophied brain really wasn't up for delinquent activities. Pirigua's men left me in peace and I spent the livelong day pushing that wagon full of dirt from one place to another. I always did it around the port, in a fairly orderly fashion that didn't cause anyone any inconveniences.

What seemed like sheer idiocy to everyone in town was actually quite useful to me. For starters, it made me stronger. I began to develop muscles that, quite frankly, were rather rare for a boy my age. But it also made the militia completely indifferent to my presence, so that eventually none of Captain Correa's men even looked at me as I went from one place to another with my wagon full of dirt. Whenever anybody stopped to make fun of me, I'd just look at them stupidly and say, "I'm a little Chinese construction worker!" They'd laugh and then let me be. After all, the little foolish Chinese boy was harmless.

Pirigua continued his visits, and when his drunkenness would render him unconscious on the bed, and my mother would run to the bathroom to wash her body and spirit of that jerk's residue, I'd sit by the bed and contemplate Captain Correa, thinking about all the things I'd do to him when the moment came. Although it may seem unbelievable, this gave me strength to continue with my plans for revenge, because I knew I could keep control of the situation. There was the pig, snoring effortlessly and without an ounce of strength to put up a fight if I picked up a kitchen knife and decided to dismember him alive.

Assimilating that power was addictive, and stimulating. Besides, one thing I'd learned from my father, before the tragedy, was that to put a plan in play, it was best to "see" it first through the prism of the imagination. So, as I sat at the captain's side while he snored, I'd "see" exactly how I was going to cut him up into little pieces, and how he could do nothing to stop me, just as helpless as my father and his friends had been to stop the militia from gunning them down.

When I killed the first guy and buried him at night, near the port, no one found out. They had no idea that I'd strolled with the dismembered body buried in the mound of dirt in my wagon right under their noses. Who was going to suspect a foolish Chinese faggot? That's how rumors began to spread that there was a curse on Cojímar. Most people in the know, those who weren't all that superstitious (like Captain Correa and his remaining henchmen), knew, or believed they knew, that the curse was pure myth . . . Those "disappeared" militia, the henchmen said, had fled for Miami. The misery they were enduring under the Communist system was pushing them to leave the country and turn their backs on the dictatorship. But neither Correa nor any of the others ever said this publicly; I only knew about it because of some confidences he shared with my mother.

My mother was nobody's fool, and I'm sure she soon suspected the truth, though she never said a word. I would surprise her sometimes while she was gazing at me; when I'd turn to her and smile with that beatific expression I'd developed as an organic mask, she'd smile too, and something would filter between us without a need to speak directly. That ethereal thread of silent complicity brought us closer together and gave us strength. Mamá understood then that keeping Correa happy was a fundamental part of the game, because it gave her a certain power over him (the most feared man in Cojímar) that we would not otherwise have. And she also understood that this power she had, if used astutely and subtly, could save our lives. That's why it was such an important part of my plan to keep Pirigua alive until the very end; although that was a hard bargain with myself, for sure. To cope with the situation, I'd imagine Captain Correa like that pig you fatten all year in order to slaughter it at Christmas.

One evening, I noticed my mother was acting different, irritated. Pirigua had taken a trip outside Cojímar for reasons I didn't know and so we had more space to ourselves. I sat down in the corner of the living room and watched her pace from one end to the other, wringing her hands. I didn't ask what was going on, but I did smile at her, the same as always, and my eyes invited her to share her torments with me.

She finally decided to let me in on her thoughts, but in keeping with the style we'd established of communicating without talking directly. Mamá approached me and held my hand.

"Come with me, son. Let's take a little stroll, like when you were younger and your father would take you down to the port."

She didn't need to say anything more. Her restlessness had everything to do with our tragedy and revenge. Papá, the port, the walks that always ended up at El Torreón, where my father would pause and point and whisper (with an intense light in his eyes) the word *freedom*.

I let myself follow her. Mamá took note of the calluses on my hands, the result of the constant back and forth with the weighty wagon, and she caressed me very tenderly, as if with that gesture she could make me understand that she was giving silent assent to my activities. Real Street was deserted, weirdly deserted, as if everybody was hiding from some terrible monster let loose in the neighborhood, looking for someone to devour. Fear floated in the air. In those days, the government wouldn't stop yakking about a fictitious yanqui invasion which never materialized but which kept everybody on their toes and distracted from the country's real problems—things like the lack of food, censorship, the total denial of human rights . . . Actually, why go on? It was always better to blame yanqui imperialism. And the yanquis were coming soon (or so they said) . . . Fatherland or death and all that.

We arrived at the Port of Cojímar without being bothered, since the days when people made fun of me were now in the past; I had become something of an invisible person, no longer a novelty. We walked holding hands without making any stops until we had circled the port, then went back to Real Street. The afternoon became night. My mother guided me toward El Torreón and I knew in an instant that I needed to sharpen my senses and pay close attention to whatever she said or did, whatever she revealed that was roiling inside her.

"Remember how much your father loved this place?" she asked without waiting for a reply. "Do you know why? In a boat not far from here, the first Chinese arrived in Cuba. They left from a port called Amoy, in the south of China, in the 1840s. The ship was called the *Oquendo*, it was a Spanish brigantine. The English ruled our land then, and they'd taken it upon themselves to repress our collective spirit, and to addict Chinese youth to opium. Those first exiles that came to Cuba did so under horrendous labor contracts, practically slaves, just like black people."

She continued: "The hours of forced labor were abusive. Everyone worked in agriculture or as domestics, with a miserable salary of five pesos a month, two sets of tops and pants, a blanket, and two pairs of rope and rubber sandals. The diet consisted of rice, cornmeal, dried beef, codfish, and a few tubers. Those who worked in the countryside lived in barracks where they slept in hammocks made of rope and hemp. It seems crazy, but it feels like we're going back to those times. In the days of our pilgrim ancestors, the labor contracts were for ten years and then you could go back to your birthplace, if that's what you wanted, so long as you could pay the passage. But our compatriots didn't leave. They chose to stay on in Cuban land and make this our home. Sometimes I ask myself how it's possible, after nearly two centuries of such hard work and sacrifice, that new slave masters could arise like this to displace us again."

She went on: "The ancestors who came from Amoy, Canton, Shanghai, and Manila created strong communities, well-organized, which preserved our symbols and our religion, always obeying and respecting Cuban laws and customs. They also enthusiastically set about to learn all manner of trade and honorable work, and in due time they greatly improved their economic fortunes. By the end of the 1850s, there were Chinese-owned businesses in Havana: restaurants, laundromats, grocery stores, fruit and vegetable stands, ice cream shops, and small lots for cultivation by the riverside.

"Everything was achieved with long hours of sacrifice. The Chinese work day isn't like that of Westerners. To this you add a tenacious management style that has always allowed us to save for the future. Another thing that has always characterized us," she explained, and Mamá paused and looked me directly in the eyes, "is our loyalty and respect for others. In the long struggle for Cuban independence, we Chinese threw ourselves into the fight with vigor and valor alongside the liberation army. General Máximo Gómez, talking about our people, once said, 'There's never been a Chinese traitor, or deserter, in the Cuban army.' And as a sign of appreciation of our courage and fidelity, a park was built in the capital to honor Chinese veterans."

At this point, Mamá paused again and pointed to the fort-like Torreón, its impenetrable stone walls.

"Loyalty, my son, is very important. Unfortunately, your father's expedition was betrayed."

So there it was . . . finally. It had taken a lot for her to tell me, and she'd certainly danced around it for a long time, but the moment had come to reveal the truth: There was a traitor among our people.

"In every ethnicity, although it's not common among ours, there are greedy and unscrupulous people who envy other people's achievements and riches, and this causes them to commit terrible acts. Your father was a prosperous merchant and I, so it seems, an attractive woman. There was no lack of envy in our community. Do you understand me?"

She looked at me and I smiled.

Then she caressed my shoulders with her hand and we walked back to the house. We moved without hurry, enjoying the evening, the views, the strange and black emptiness of the neighborhood, the moon. Mamá was quiet until we reached the front door of one of our neighbors.

"Isn't this Mr. Lin's house?"

That's all she said, and that's all I needed. She gave me a knowing look and I answered by nodding and smiling again.

Captain Correa returned to Cojímar the next day. Since he'd practically moved in with us (Mamá made sure he was comfortable), he now told my mother his problems. The trip to Havana had been disciplinary. They'd asked for him so they could reprimand him because of the disappearance of some of his men. What was going on in Cojímar? How was it possible that a guy like Captain Correa—revolutionary hero and all that—was letting this happen with his troops? Poor guy, he was so disconcerted about the scolding, I felt bad for him . . . But there were also some things my mother had put in my head that I wanted to confirm. Papá had been a jeweler. When the Communists impounded his business, he managed to hide two bags full of diamonds and other gems. Mr. Lin, like all the others trying to escape, knew these details and was the only one who, on the agreed upon day, did not show up at the port at the appointed time.

"Your father was a prosperous merchant," my mother had said, "and I, so it seems, an attractive woman. There was no lack of envy in our community . . ."

Two days later, they found Mr. Lin's head at the foot of El Torreón, his tongue cut out. All of Cojímar headed to the port to see it. I went with my mother, and while everyone else whis-

pered and gossiped, I studied my mother's face and the movement of the militia men with feigned indifference. Standing
there, checking out everything, I had the feeling the circle was
finally closing. If I wanted to take the final revenge for what had
been done to my father, I needed to up the ante. Captain Correa would begin to put the pieces together soon . . .

That night, he came to our house but he didn't get drunk,
although he did have his usual tumble with my mother. After
she pretended to fall asleep, Pirigua got up, and thinking I
was in my room, he moved toward the patio, which was quite
large and had guava, mango, and anon trees that my father
had planted. I tiptoed after him. The door to the patio was
in the kitchen, and to get there we had to cross an open-air
vestibule; the moonlight fell on his wide back and his tangled
black hair. He was actually quite a strong man—at another
time he might have intimidated me. But so much time shov-
eling dirt and carrying that wagon from one place to another
had hardened my extremities to such an extent that when I
flexed, you could see my muscles moving. I knew I could beat
him if I had to because, more than brute strength, I had ac-
cumulated so much rage that Captain Correa, or even ten of
him, could not possibly stop me.

Pirigua crossed the vestibule, passed by the dining room,
and arrived at the kitchen. Ours was colonial, much longer
than it was wide, and from where I was I could see him struggling with the back door. He opened the lock then went out to
the patio. When I got to the kitchen, I stopped to grab a long
butcher's knife. With weapon in hand, I looked out the window and saw Captain Correa heading down the stone steps,
past the outhouse and sink, and straight for the guava tree.
He knelt and started to dig at the earth with his hands. So my
suspicions were dead on: Papá's jewels had been returned.

I came up to him without him hearing me. He was breathing heavily and had dug quite a bit already. He had powerful hands and he moved them well, excavating large chunks of dirt. When I thought it right, I let him know I was there. He was so terrified that he gasped and stood up in one single movement.

"What the . . . ?"

"Just a little foolish Chinese boy," I said, then plunged the knife deep into his belly.

"Aaaaggghhh!"

I grabbed the handle with both hands and pulled up with all my might. I practically lifted him off the ground.

"Just a little Chinese faggot," I said, and I helped him down, feeling his blood and viscera ooze through my hands.

After he died, I cut him in pieces and went to get the shovel and wagon. From the very same hole Pirigua had been digging, I shoveled the dirt onto the bloody load that Captain Correa—great revolutionary hero and my father's killer, jewel thief and oppressor of women, dirty Communist s.o.b.—had become. I mixed the flesh and the dirt and pushed the loaded wagon out the back door of the patio.

Armed with an icy calm, I went down Real Street until I got to the foot of El Torreón. If anybody saw me, they did nothing to stop me; as I've said, everyone in Cojímar was already used to my comings and goings at all hours with the wagon full of dirt, and no one paid any attention anymore to the Wong boy, that effeminate fool who just smiled stupidly whenever anyone insulted him or laughed at him.

I went to my private cemetery near the port. One by one, I unearthed the heads of all those among Captain Correa's men who'd disappeared. I buried Pirigua's remains with the others, and with the seven heads in my possession, I headed back to El Torreón. I was exhausted but satisfied.

Oh, revenge can be so sweet!

I set the heads out like they'd done with my father and his friends. I sat down in the center of the circle of rotting heads and waited until dawn. At first light, they found me. Someone sounded the alarm, and when the first militiamen showed up, I stood up and put the knife to my own throat.

"For my father!" I screamed as loudly as I could before the stupefied crowd so that they would know exactly what was going on.

But they didn't let me kill myself. They shot me three times: once in each knee, another in my chest. They fell on me like a herd of rabid dogs, but I fainted.

Now I'm being held in this windowless cell where the rats are eating me alive; but I don't mind. There's not much time left. My mother didn't survive my imprisonment; she poisoned herself as soon as she heard the news of my capture and realized our settling of scores was complete.

Translation by Achy Obejas

ABIKÚ[1]

BY YOHAMNA DEPESTRE

Alamar

I'm the assassin. I did it for a bit more space on the floor tiles, 845.1 centimeters to be exact, not just the lousy seven tiles where my bed stood. Yeah, even though seven's supposed to be a lucky number.

Everybody else had a bigger slice, although not equal in size. My miserable little seven tiles didn't provoke anything; no one even had an opinion about them.

My mother was the number one accumulator of space. Her territory extended from the biggest bedroom to the bathroom, kitchen, balcony, and then stopped there, at the very foot of my bed. All that measured exactly 372.5 centimeters of tile space. And 372.5 centimeters of tiles entitled her to:

1. Walk by with the excuse of needing to go to the bathroom whenever the owner of the seven tiles was making love with her husband so she could peek at his thing.
2. Say: *Wrap it up or you're screwed.*
3. Stick her nose in every single discussion because she believes the owner of the seven tiles is useless.
4. Ask where everybody's at all the time.

[1]In Santería, a restless spirit, a child who's born to die and be born again.

I killed her, she didn't let me think.

The second one was my brother-in-law. His territory extended from the smallest bedroom all the way to the couch, which he usurped during the heatwaves, because as a paying tenant he thought he was first in line. All that measured exactly 225.6 centimeters of tile space. And 225.6 centimeters entitled him to:

1. Stare suggestively at the owner of the seven tiles.
2. Bring undesirable friends over and act like a clown.
3. Shout to the world that he has more buying power than the owner of the seven tiles.
4. Listen in whenever seven tiles made love.

I killed him, he didn't let me think.

The third one, my sister. Her territory was in the same room, but as a wife and homemaker her territory extended 191.0 centimeters, which was enough. And 191.0 centimeters entitled her to:

1. Have complete authority over the TV, the radio, and to scream at everyone about everything.
2. Hang clothes out to dry in the best spot on the balcony.
3. Demand that the owner of the seven tiles' bed be made by 5 in the morning, because the brother-in-law has company and the bed can be seen from the living room.
4. Play Parcheesi until 1 in the morning.

I killed her and ripped out her daughter's tongue, because she screamed too much at bath time. Who could think with all the racket?

I could stack up my humble seven-tiles entitlement in one tiny little corner. And seven tiles entitled me to:

1. Sleep (whenever possible) and shut up.
2. Shut up and eat.
3. Scream at my husband, since he had only 0.0 centimeters of tiles.

And 0.0 centimeters of tiles entitled him to:

1. Put up with everything and anything.
2. Snitch.
3. Keep 845.1 centimeters of tile, plus my seven, of course.

I have my territory marked out like a sacred animal. My pee and shit ooze out from my seven tiles and beyond my cell, past the bars. The guard tells me it stinks in here, that it's impossible to eat. I keep an eye on him. His foot falls on a mark I made with my own hands.

Translation by Achy Obejas

ABOUT THE CONTRIBUTORS

ALEX ABELLA is an EMMY-nominated TV reporter and screenwriter. His experiences in the world of law and law enforcement inspired him to write a legal thriller, *The Killing of the Saints*, a *New York Times* Notable Book. Abella's latest work, *Shadow Enemies*, is a nonfiction account of the plot by Adolf Hitler to unleash a wave of terror in the United States. He was born in Havana and now lives with his wife and children in the suburbs of Los Angeles.

Ron Taft

ARTURO ARANGO is a novelist, essayist, and screenwriter. He is the author of two short story collections and his novels include *Una Lección de Anatomía, El Libro de la Realidad,* and *Muerte de Nadie.* Since 1996 he has been managing editor of *La Gaceta de Cuba,* arguably the island's most influential cultural magazine. He is also a screenwriting professor at the International Film School in San Antonio de los Baños, Cuba. He resides in Cojímar, a suburb of Havana.

Alejandro Arango

LEA ASCHKENAS is the author of *Es Cuba: Life and Love on an Illegal Island.* She has written about travel, literature, and life at large for the *Washington Post, San Francisco Chronicle, Los Angeles Times,* and Salon.com. She is also included in the books *The Best Women's Travel Writing 2006, Travelers' Tales Central America, Travelers' Tales Cuba, The Unsavvy Traveler, Two in the Wild,* and *Beside the Sleeping Maiden: Poets of Marin.* In 2000, she lived in Havana for more than ten months.

Alfredo Sánchez

MOISÉS ASÍS is the author of fourteen books, including *Cuban Miami,* coauthored with Robert M. Levine, and many articles on scientific and social subjects, including Judaism. He won several national prizes in literature and science in Cuba, and he is a graduate from the University of Havana, the Open International University for Complementary Medicines, and Florida International University. He was born in Havana and lives in Miami.

Dina Lilit Asis

ARNALDO CORREA is one of the founding fathers of Cuban noir. A mining engineer by training, he is the author of two highly praised novels published in English by Akashic Books, *Spy's Fate* and *Cold Havana Ground.* He lives in Havana.

Aramis Correa

MABEL CUESTA is the author of the books *Confesiones On Line* and *Cuaderno de la Fiancée,* both published in Cuba. Her stories and essays have appeared in magazines in Cuba, Spain, Brazil, Mexico, Honduras, and the United States. She lives in New York.

Maya Islas

YOHAMNA DEPESTRE is the author of the prose collection *D-21,* and her writing is included in a number of anthologies published in Cuba and Puerto Rico. She is also the principal storyteller for Ommi-Zona Franca, a hip-hop performance group. She lives in Alamar, Cuba.

Luis Eligio

MICHEL ENCINOSA FÚ received a degree in English Language and Literature from the University of Havana; he is a member of the Saíz Brothers Association and the Union of Writers and Artists of Cuba. His books include *Sol Negro, Niños de Neón, Veredas,* and *Dioses de Neon.* His work is included in anthologies published in Argentina, Spain, Mexico, Brazil, the United States, and Cuba. He has been honored for his writing in Cuba and abroad. He lives in Havana.

MYLENE FERNÁNDEZ PINTADO has a law degree from the University of Havana and has worked as a legal consultant and editorial coordinator at the Instituto Cubano del Arte e Industria Cinematográficos. Her first book of stories, *Anhedonia,* won the 1986 David Prize in Cuba. Her first novel, *Otras Plegarias Atendidas,* received the Calvino Prize in 2002 and the Cuban Critics' Award in 2003. She lives in Havana and Ticino, Switzerland.

Paolo Gebhard

CAROLINA GARCÍA-AGUILERA is the author of eight books, the first six of which are a series featuring Lupe Solano, a Cuban-American private investigator who lives and works in Miami. García-Aguilera, a private investigator herself, has been the recipient of many literary awards, including the Shamus and the Flamingo. She was born in Havana and lives in Miami.

Ali

Stephen Spera

PABLO MEDINA is the author of ten books of poetry and prose. His works include the new novel *The Cigar Roller* and the essay collection *Exiled Memories: A Cuban Childhood*. He is collaborating with Mark Statman on a new English version of García Lorca's *Poet in New York*. Medina is on the core writing faculty of Eugene Lang College at The New School in New York City. He is currently a Visiting Professor of English at the University of Nevada, Las Vegas. He was born in Havana.

MIGUEL MEJIDES is one of Cuba's most internationally published authors. He penned the story collections *Tiempo de Hombres* (winner of the David Prize), *El Jardín de las Flores Silvestres, Mi Prima Amada,* and *Rumba Palace,* as well as the novel *La Habitación Terrestre*. His work has been translated into English, French, German, and Italian. He lives in Havana.

ACHY OBEJAS is the award-winning author of *Days of Awe, Memory Mambo,* and *We Came all the Way from Cuba So You Could Dress Like This?* Her poems, stories, and essays have appeared in dozens of anthologies. A long-time contributor to the *Chicago Tribune,* she was part of the 2001 investigative team that earned a Pulitzer Prize for the series "Gateway to Gridlock." Currently, she is the Sor Juana Writer in Residence at DePaul University in Chicago. She was born in Havana.

Angel Rivera

OSCAR F. ORTÍZ went into exile at the age of eleven and has lived in South Florida ever since. His work includes the acclaimed *Archivo Delta,* a collection of novellas and novelettes, as well as *El Elegido, El Negocio del Siglo,* and *El Santo Culto.* He is currently working on a story collection featuring a Miami detective. He was born in Matanzas, Cuba, and now lives in Hialeah, Florida.

Cedric Vignareut

LEONARDO PADURA is one of Cuba's best known crime fiction writers. He is a graduate of the University of Havana and has won literary awards in Cuba, France, Spain, and throughout Latin America. He has been the recipient of three Dashiell Hammett Awards from the International Association of Crime Writers. His books, which have been translated into more than a dozen languages, include *Havana Blue, Havana Yellow, Havana Red,* and *Havana Black.* He lives in Havana.

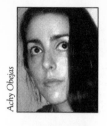

Achy Obejas

ENA LUCÍA PORTELA is the author of various novels, including *Cien Botellas en una Pared*, which won the 2002 Jaén Novel Prize in Spain and the Dos Océanos–Grinzane Cavour Critics Prize in France. Her work has been translated into more than seven languages. She was recently named to the Bogota 39, the Colombia International Book Fair's list of the thirty-nine most important Latin American authors under the age of thirty-nine. She lives in Havana.

Ramón Legón Pino

MARIELA VARONA ROQUE is an engineer at the Empresa de Construcción de la Industria Eléctrica in Holguín, Cuba. A David Prize winner, she is the author of two books of short stories, *El Verano del Diablo* and *Cable a Tierra*. Her work has been published in Cuba, Brazil, Spain, and Puerto Rico.

Elena Couret

YOSS (José Miguel Sánchez Gómez) has a degree in biology from the University of Havana. He is the award-winning author of the story collections *Timshel, W,* and *Precio Justo;* and the novels *Polvo Rojo* and *Morfeo Verdugo*. His fiction has appeared in numerous publications, including the journals *Eleftherothypia* in Greece, *Galaxie* and *Les Auteurs* in France, and *MAX* in Italy. He lives in Havana.

Also available from the Akashic Books Noir Series

CHICAGO NOIR
edited by Neal Pollack
252 pages, trade paperback original, $14.95

Brand new stories by: Achy Obejas, Adam Langer, M.K. Meyers, Bayo Ojikutu, Kevin Guilfoile, Joe Meno, Claire Zulkey, Daniel Buckman, Amy Sayre-Roberts, Peter Orner, Neal Pollack, and others.

"*Chicago Noir* is a legitimate heir to the noble literary tradition of the greatest city in America. Nelson Algren and James Farrell would be proud."
—Stephen Elliott, author of *Happy Baby*

BROOKLYN NOIR
edited by Tim McLoughlin
350 pages, trade paperback original, $15.95
*Winner of SHAMUS AWARD, ANTHONY AWARD, ROBERT L. FISH MEMORIAL AWARD; finalist for EDGAR AWARD, PUSHCART PRIZE

Brand new stories by: Pete Hamill, Arthur Nersesian, Maggie Estep, Nelson George, Neal Pollack, Sidney Offit, Ken Bruen, and others.

"*Brooklyn Noir* is such a stunningly perfect combination that you can't believe you haven't read an anthology like this before. But trust me—you haven't. Story after story is a revelation, filled with the requisite sense of place, but also the perfect twists that crime stories demand. The writing is flat-out superb, filled with lines that will sing in your head for a long time to come."
—Laura Lippman, winner of the Edgar, Agatha, and Shamus awards

MIAMI NOIR
edited by Les Standiford
356 pages, trade paperback original, $15.95

Brand new stories by: Carolina García-Aguilera, James W. Hall, Barbara Parker, John Dufresne, Tom Corcoran, Paul Levine, Preston Allen, Christine Kling, Lynne Barrett, Vicki Hendricks, and others.

"Variety, familiarity, mood and tone, and the occasional gem of a story make *Miami Noir* a collection to savor."
—*Miami Herald*

LOS ANGELES NOIR
edited by Denise Hamilton
360 pages, trade paperback original, $15.95
*A *Los Angeles Times* Best-seller

Brand new stories by: Michael Connelly, Janet Fitch, Susan Straight, Héctor Tobar, Patt Morrison, Robert Ferrigno, Neal Pollack, Gary Phillips, Christopher Rice, Naomi Hirahara, Jim Pascoe, and others.

"Akashic is making an argument about the universality of noir; it's sort of flattering, really, and *Los Angeles Noir,* arriving at last, is a kaleidoscopic collection filled with the ethos of noir pioneers Raymond Chandler and James M. Cain."
—*Los Angeles Times Book Review*

NEW ORLEANS NOIR
edited by Julie Smith
298 pages, trade paperback original, $14.95

Brand new stories by: Ace Atkins, Laura Lippman, Patty Friedmann, Barbara Hambly, Tim McLoughlin, Olympia Vernon, Kalamu ya Salaam, Thomas Adcock, Christine Wiltz, Greg Herren, and others.

"The excellent twelfth entry in Akashic's noir series illustrates the diversity of the chosen locale with eighteen previously unpublished short stories from authors both well known and emerging."
—*Publishers Weekly*

BALTIMORE NOIR
edited by Laura Lippman
294 pages, trade paperback original, $14.95

Brand new stories by: David Simon, Laura Lippman, Tim Cockey, Rob Hiaasen, Robert Ward, Sujata Massey, Jack Bludis, Dan Fesperman, Marcia Talley, Ben Neihart, Jim Fusilli, Rafael Alvarez, and others.

"Baltimore is a diverse city, and the stories reflect everything from its old row houses and suburban mansions to its beloved Orioles and harbor areas...Mystery fans should relish this taste of Baltimore's seamier side."
—*Publishers Weekly*